Buncololi

Illustration by **Kantoku**

1

Sasaki and Peeps

That Time I Got Dragged into
a Psychic Battle in Modern Times
While Trying to Enjoy a Relaxing Life
in Another World
~Looks Like Magical Girls Are on Deck~

とり いちばん

小鳥

"Peeps, what about this?"
"How is it different from a normal pot?"
"It's incredibly hard to burn."
"This is good."
"I'll just throw it in, too, then."

《 Peeps 》
Java sparrow.
A great sage.

"My name is Piercarlo the Starsage, inhabitant of another world."

"......"

It just talked.
The sparrow
spoke to me.

《 Sasaki 》
Average corporate drone.

"So this is Kobe beef chateaubriand?"

"How is it? I know Mr. Yamada at the pet shop was raving about it."

*"It is good.
Oh my, this is good."*

"Glad to hear it."

It was cute watching Peeps peck away at the chateaubriand, which I'd cut into slivers and set up on the round dining table. One after another, the pieces of meat piled on the plate disappeared into his mouth. He was like a one of the pigeons at the park eating scraps of sweet treats some kid dropped. He was so cute—although, I was a little anxious as I watched him.

"I could eat this every day and never grow tired of it."

"This is quite good. I have never experienced this flavor before."

"Could be because there's so few spices in this world."

We were eating soup curry. In general, the curried rice popular in Japan didn't look all that good on the outside. It was possible nobody would eat it if they added it to the menu. Predicting that, I had instead proposed soup curry— and it was surprisingly popular now.

However, most of the spices came from the Japanese supermarket where I bought sugar and chocolate. They were limited and could only be used for ten meals in one day, apparently. In the future, I wanted to try re-creating it with local ingredients.

〈Miss Hoshizaki〉

"What...?!"

A shriek escaped Miss Hoshizaki's lips once she saw the girl. An unusual response from the bellicose woman.

"My, this is more exciting than I'd thought."

But my mistake was worrying about everything too much. A new figure suddenly emerged from the corner of the space.

She appeared in the main area with the bowling lanes, on a path leading back to the restrooms. She was dressed in traditional clothing and, at first glance, looked like an elementary schooler. Her black hair reached down below her waist, and her skin was as pale as snow—both striking features. Was she the cause of this chain of hurricanes?

08/05/20xx
Sasa Tree @wiQ2fK9p2xHgi4J

Coworker adopted a cat.
He showed me a ton of pictures.
It was a baby kitten and really cute.

08/08/20xx
Sasa Tree @wiQ2fK9p2xHgi4J

Went to the zoo.
Really got rid of my frustration.
Bought a yearly pass since it was cheap.

💬 3

Ranran @natori980102
Replying to @wiQ2fK9p2xHgi4J
Wait, did you get a girlfriend?

Sasa Tree @wiQ2fK9p2xHgi4J
Replying to @wiQ2fK9p2xHgi4J
I'm embarrassed to say,
but I went on my own…

Ranran @natori980102
Replying to @wiQ2fK9p2xHgi4J
Oh. Sorry, I guess.

08/15/20xx
Sasa Tree @wiQ2fK9p2xHgi4J

Went to the zoo again.
Are zoos not the greatest things ever?
If I had my way, I'd be playing in the
petting zoo.

08/22/20xx
Sasa Tree @wiQ2fK9p2xHgi4J

I have decided to adopt a pet.

Sasaki and Peeps

That Time I Got Dragged into a Psychic Battle in Modern Times

While Trying to Enjoy a Relaxing Life in Another World

~Looks Like Magical Girls Are on Deck~

1

Buncololi

Illustration by **Kantoku**

YEN ON

New York

Sasaki and Peeps

1

Buncololi

Illustration by **Kantoku**

Translation by Alice Prowse
Cover art by Kantoku

This book is a work of fiction. Names, characters, places, and incidents are the product of the author's imagination or are used fictitiously. Any resemblance to actual events, locales, or persons, living or dead, is coincidental.

SASAKITOPICHAN Vol.1 ISEKAI DE SLOW LIFE O TANOSHIMOTOSHITARA, GENDAI DE INO BATTLE NI MAKIKOMARETAKEN ~MAHOSHOJO GA UP O HAJIMETAYODESU~
©Buncololi 2021
First published in Japan in 2021 by KADOKAWA CORPORATION, Tokyo.
English translation rights arranged with KADOKAWA CORPORATION, Tokyo through TUTTLE-MORI AGENCY, INC., Tokyo.

English translation © 2022 by Yen Press, LLC

Yen On
150 West 30th Street,
19th Floor
New York, NY 10001

Visit us at yenpress.com
facebook.com/yenpress
twitter.com/yenpress
yenpress.tumblr.com
instagram.com/yenpress

First Yen On Edition: August 2022
Edited by Yen On Editorial: Emma McClain, Kurt Hassler
Designed by Yen Press
Design: Andy Swist

Yen On is an imprint of Yen Press, LLC.

The Yen On name and logo are trademarks of Yen Press, LLC.

The publisher is not responsible for websites (or their content) that are not owned by the publisher.

Library of Congress Cataloging-in-Publication Data
Names: Buncololi, author. | Kantoku, illustrator. | Prowse, Alice, translator.
Title: Sasaki & Peeps / Buncololi ; illustration by Kantoku ; translation by Alice Prowse.
Other titles: Sasakitopichan. English
Description: First Yen On edition. | New York, NY : Yen On, 2022. | Contents: v. 1. That time I got wrapped up in a supernatural battle in modern times as I was trying to enjoy a relaxing life in another world -looks like magical girls are on deck-
Identifiers: LCCN 2022005660 | ISBN 9781975343521 (v. 1 ; trade paperback)
Subjects: LCGFT: Fantasy fiction. | Humorous fiction. | Light novels.
Classification: LCC PL846.U63 S3713 2022 | DDC 895.6/36—dc23/eng/20220203
LC record available at https://lccn.loc.gov/2022005660

ISBNs: 978-1-9753-4352-1 (paperback)
978-1-9753-4353-8 (ebook)

1 3 5 7 9 10 8 6 4 2

LSC-C

Printed in the United States of America

contents

Frontispiece, Book Illustrations
Kantoku

\<Invitation to Another World\>

With my fortieth birthday nearly at hand, my heart was lonely.

Which was why I'd come to a pet shop. One of my senior coworkers had adopted a cat, and the pure joy on his face when he brought up his beloved kitten had infected me. That cat was now plastered all over his computer and phone wallpapers. His every day suddenly seemed blissful.

Still, cats weren't exactly a beginner's pet.

Having one would catapult apartment-renting deposits into the stratosphere, and they needed a lot of space. To make matters worse, I'd been told the start-up fee for cats was in the hundreds of thousands of yen. Sadly, with my meager salary, that was enough to make me have second thoughts.

I wish I had money, I thought. That way, I could adopt my very own cat. Actually, even a dog wouldn't be out of the question. A golden retriever—the greatest pupper of them all.

But I didn't have that kind of money, so no dogs or cats for me.

And that brought me to today. For today, I was after a small bird.

My current home was a studio apartment with a separate kitchen, which limited the space I had to raise pets. That narrowed my options down to a bird or a rat. Unfortunately, rats had a heartrendingly short life span—I'd heard that most of them died within two to three years.

If I was to raise a rat, I'd be too preoccupied with trying to cherish our short time together, the dread that this year or the next might be our last together always lurking in the back of my mind. What I wanted was a pet to heal me, not add all that tension to my daily life.

When I thought about it that way, a bird was the only choice. If possible, I wanted one that was relatively quiet, smart, and able to handle a degree of stress.

Spying a golden retriever puppy in the shop, my heart longed for a big dog. It yearned to raise a golden retriever in a spacious single-family home.

"He's so cute…"

The puppy was dozing in its cage. I couldn't help but let my gaze linger on the adorable scene; it almost made me pause on my way through the shop. My eyes were drawn to the price tag, and I found myself comparing the number with my credit card limit.

But even if the limit would have allowed for it, this was one wish that wouldn't be granted.

My home, after all, was a tiny six-tatami room—only about a hundred square feet. More importantly, I still didn't have the money to shell out for it.

Letting the sweet little puppy pass me by, I continued toward the bird section.

"There they are…"

I'd already decided on the species: a Java sparrow.

As far as birds went, according to the internet, they were comparatively quiet, fairly smart, and lived for about seven or eight years. Plus, they were small—and easily grew attached to people. Once I'd learned that, I couldn't imagine getting any other type of bird, so I'd arrived at the pet shop with one goal in mind.

"Oh no, they're adorable."

Buying it. Already bought, in fact. But which to choose? The shop had more than I'd thought it would.

"……"

This was troubling. After all, I was about to choose my life partner for the next several years. Considering how most divorces happen within the first five years, I was basically searching for a marriage partner. I needed to adopt one that had values as compatible with my own as possible. Appearance was another important factor.

I went down the line of cages, carefully checking each. After a few, I heard a voice from one of them.

"Pick me, pick me!"

"……"

That sparrow had just spoken to me.

Though it surprised me, I *had* read online that a rare few of these birds could speak. Maybe this was one of them.

"Pick me, pick me!"

It seemed it wanted to go home with me.

Not that I believed it understood what it was saying. I was sure that was just a phrase it had picked up from someone. Besides, those were the only words it kept repeating. A conversation between a customer and a store clerk must have sparked something in this particular sparrow. Talk about slick self-marketing.

"......"

It had certainly piqued my interest. In fact, I was starting to feel like fate had a hand in this.

Well! My mind was made up.

"Excuse me! I'd like this Java sparrow..."

My new family member would be this chatty bird.

*

I left the pet shop and returned home. After cleaning the birdcage, I set it on a colored plywood box in a corner of the room. With that, the welcome reception was complete. Unlike with cats or dogs, I didn't need to set up a pen or somewhere for it to go to the bathroom, which was nice. The only other things I'd prepared had been bird food and a cloth to hang over the cage.

"You're so cute..."

Looking at the creature inside just warmed my heart. Golden retrievers were great and all, but so were Java sparrows. *Pleased to meet you—and welcome to the team.*

"Oh, that's right. I need to give you a name."

But what sort of name would be good? I wanted to give it a cute one. Preferably something that commented on its appearance somehow.

"My name is Piercarlo the Starsage, inhabitant of another world."

"......"

It had just talked. The sparrow had spoken to me. It seemed as though it already had a splendid name of its own—wait, no, that didn't make sense.

"Piercarlo?"

"Indeed."

"......"

Oh, great. I'd just communicated with a bird. Like a regular conversation. Didn't Mr. Yamada from the pet shop say this chick was only two months old? He'd told me if I acclimated it to human contact, it might even learn to sit on my hand. I'd headed home, vowing to make that happen.

"Peeps."

"*Peeps.*"

"Great. We'll go with Peeps."

"……"

For a moment, it seemed like his face got a little scarier. Was he unhappy with it? But he was so cute.

I decided to talk to him a bit more, just to make sure.

"Peeps, what would you like to eat today?"

"*I desire a Kobe beef chateaubriand.*"

"What? How did you…?"

"*The man named Yamada employed at the shop claimed it was the greatest thing he had ever tasted.*"

"……"

That did it. This was definitely a conversation.

Also, Mr. Yamada was sure eating some fine cuts of meat. Didn't chateaubriand go for, like, ten thousand yen per one hundred grams? And the famous brands were twice that, even, or three times…

"…You don't want these pellets here?" I asked, pointing to the bag beside the cage. It contained the comprehensive nutritional diet pellets I'd bought when I'd gotten him. The clerk had said they were packed with all the nutrients sparrows needed and that as long as the bird ate these, the only other thing it would require was water. It was a lifetime diet for a sparrow—kind of like a chain restaurant beef bowl for poor office workers.

"*Their taste is not to my liking.*"

"Oh…"

If they didn't taste good, that was that. If it were me, I wouldn't want to eat lousy food, either.

Ah, but wait. The beef bowl from chain restaurants was actually pretty good. Top it with a heap of red pickled ginger and mix it with a raw egg, and that sweat you got when eating it was just the best. Whenever I got off the last train and had some of it at the neighborhood beef bowl place, I felt like I could put in my best again the next day. Occasionally, I'd splurge and get a bowl of pork miso soup with it, too.

"I'm sorry. I don't think I can do chateaubriand."

"Why is that?"

"It's a very expensive kind of meat, and I don't have the money to buy it."

"...Is that so?"

"I'm sorry you had to be bought by a poor office worker."

"......"

For the time being, I set aside the fact that I was talking to a sparrow. An impulse flew through me to take a video of him and upload it to YouTube, but he was more human than I'd anticipated, so I hesitated to do something like that. For now, I decided to talk to him a little more.

"I have pork ribs. Would you like some of them instead? They're in the freezer."

"If you haven't the money, you need only earn it."

"Huh?"

Does he not like pork ribs? I think they're pretty tasty myself, but...

"I've thought about a great many things since being exiled from the otherworld and receiving new life in this form: How will I return to my former world? What do I need to do to accomplish that task? And what would I do if I did return?"

"...Is that right?"

All of a sudden, he'd started up a monologue. This sparrow had quite the backstory—more than I'd ever imagined. I found myself getting curious about the rest of it and had replied before I knew it.

"And I arrived at a conclusion."

The way his beak kept popping open and closed was so cute. It was like he was begging his mama bird to feed him.

"That I should, simply put, start living the way I wish."

"...I see."

Despite the big preface, his epiphany was fairly average. Still, the perspective was, in my opinion, precious. It isn't worth wasting your own time trying to fit in with everyone else. We all die alone; I figured it was better to do everything you wanted, to the best of your ability, while you were alive. As a corporate slave, I felt this keenly.

Anyway, was that why he'd been saying *Pick me, pick me*? He was starting to seem positively adorable.

"To that end, I require the assistance of someone from this world."

"I understand."

"*I'd like you to help me. You'll find it quite easy to make riches if you do.*"

"You know I'd do anything for my cute little birdie, but—"

"*Good. The contract has been finalized.*"

"What—?"

The sparrow cut me off by opening his beak and giving a squawk.

And then, suddenly, a magic circle emerged in front of me—the sort you see a lot in anime and manga. It floated in midair, glittering brightly. *I don't remember buying a toy like this*, I thought. Had Peeps created this?

"Peeps, what's this?"

"*I shall give you a portion of my powers,*" the bird said, the magic circle giving off more light.

Then with a quick flash, my vision went white. It was incredibly bright. Unable to withstand it, I shut my eyes and flinched. As I did, I felt a warm sensation materialize in my breast. It felt almost like someone had stuffed heating pouches inside me.

"Wait, I, uh, hold on…"

"*Calm yourself. It'll only last a moment.*"

"……"

If nothing else had convinced me, this little act had—Peeps was no ordinary sparrow. *Maybe I should have gone with the bird in the next cage over*, I thought in spite of myself. What if this magic circle produced short electromagnetic wavelengths? Like, radiation exposure? Maybe I'd have to make my next checkup a more thorough screening.

The brilliance only lasted ten seconds or so. Gradually, the glow from inside the cage subsided. The magic circle that had appeared in front of Peeps also vanished.

"*We are now connected by a path.*"

"What?"

I had no idea what a path was. It certainly didn't look like anything existed between us.

"*Would you open this cage for me?*"

"Oh. Right."

I didn't quite grasp what was happening, but I'd come this far—might as well see it through. I had a lot of things I wanted to say about whatever this was, but I was already too caught up in it to bother. I was also a little afraid of pissing off Peeps by complaining. Since we were going to be living in the same room, I preferred to stay on good terms.

I slid the cage door open.

"…Is that good?"

"*It is.*"

Peeps flew out of the cage and settled on my shoulder. A sparrow on my shoulder! How cute! He didn't even have to practice standing on my hand and positioned himself right next to my head. I was ecstatic— I'd done the right thing, picking this one.

"*I can now use my former power by channeling it through your body. Your flesh is quite frail, but it is better than this small bird's. Using magic should not cripple you, at least.*"

"Um, if this is going to be bad for my health, I'd like to refuse…"

"*Let us be off.*"

A moment later, my vision went black.

*

A few moments after the blackout, I noticed the scenery had changed completely.

To summarize, it was a fantasy world of swords and magic. The streets were lined with stone buildings, and the path was paved with bricks. The people going by looked just like the characters in a role-playing game. Here and there, I could see swords, spears, and armor— retro-looking items, every one. I even watched as a carriage clattered by.

We stood in an alley that opened up onto a main road, watching all this from the side.

"Peeps, where are we?"

"*The world in which I lived before my reincarnation into this form.*"

"Oh."

"*It is a provincial town in the Kingdom of Herz called Baytrium.*"

"By the way, I'm not wearing shoes."

"*…Indeed you aren't.*"

In fact, I still had on the sweatshirt and sweatpants that I only really wore at home. It made me very self-conscious. If I was going to be out in public, I at least wanted a pair of slacks and a collared shirt. Thanks to my age, it was hard to get away with jeans and a T-shirt these days. I felt like I couldn't expect basic human rights unless I had on at least a jacket and slacks.

Just going to a convenience store or supermarket in jeans and a T-shirt versus pants and a nice shirt made the clerks look at you differently. Maybe it was my imagination, but for a gross, poor older guy, it was a vital form of self-defense. A business card and a suit and tie—they alone would protect older dudes the world over.

"This certainly does seem like another world."

"Convinced?"

"Yes, I think I finally get you."

"Happy to hear it."

It looked like he hadn't been lying to me. A talking bird should probably have been enough to convince me, but the sensation of bricks beneath my feet dispelled every last doubt I had.

"But how does this connect to making money?"

"We can travel freely between this world and yours."

"...And?"

"We can do business between the two worlds. Things that are cheap in your world may sell for a high price in this one. And inexpensive items from this world may be valuable in yours."

"I see."

"And that should be enough to put Kobe beef chateaubriand on my plate."

"...I suppose."

I had figured out what Peeps was implying. I had the feeling, though, that it would take a lot of time to build a watertight system for it. After all, he was suggesting the possibility of exchanging items from this world with yen—which was synonymous with circulating stolen goods.

And it would be very hard work for any of this to actually get chateaubriand onto our plates every day. It would cost tens of thousands of yen per meal, which would be over ten million yen per year. That wasn't the kind of money you could ever take lightly.

"Peeps, that might be pretty difficult."

"Why is that?"

"Even if we did obtain valuables in this world and bring them to mine, we'd have no way to convert it into money. If anyone asked where they came from, I wouldn't be able to explain it."

"...Why not?"

"If I was honest and told them it came from another world, it would be a catastrophe."

"Could you not simply keep it secret?"

"I thought you'd say that—but no."

If an ordinary, lifelong wage slave repeatedly brought things to a pawnshop, the shop owner would, beyond a shadow of a doubt, contact the police. Pawnshops actually work with the authorities in secret pretty frequently. If they asked me where I'd gotten the goods… Well, I couldn't think of any way to get through that line of questioning.

Even if I was able to make the exchange, it would definitely be exposed on my tax return.

Japan, in particular, is very precise about managing currency circulation. Sex workers, for example, often get penalized with additional taxes by the government simply because they are self-employed and start working without understanding the system.

Even when your salary is paid in cash, it's surprisingly easy to get caught. Tax office workers have ways to check into the flow of our money, and they've only gotten more effective as the digital economy has become more and more normalized. A remarkable number of people don't know that one of the goals of a cashless society is so they have a perfect grasp of every single person's expenditures.

I knew that if I was to continuously exchange high-value items for money in the public market, they'd start wondering where the items were coming from. If a tax office investigated me via my dealings with a pawnshop, it would be over just like that. Still, that didn't mean I could ever make the decision to simply not pay taxes on public deals.

Japan has adopted a system of tax payment by self-assessment and a system of taxation by estimate. If they were to learn I'd been evading taxes, the tax office would force me to pay penalty taxes based on their calculations. To avoid that, I'd have to present a convincing legal case.

I could say a lot of things, but not that I'd brought treasures from another world. If I told them that, they'd interrogate me until I told them literally everything—and they'd take Peeps away from me. Plus, even if I went bankrupt, I would still have to pay the taxes.

Risks like that weren't something I wanted to take. That meant we needed some way to prevent them from happening—such as money laundering, the kind you see a lot in yakuza films.

Ideally, I'd just be able to exchange the goods for yen and pay the taxes, but that was simply impossible. The whole idea was predicated on otherworld commodities that would never add up in the books. To make these deals a reality, I would need to come up with a better solution.

I explained all that to Peeps.

"*Your world's financial systems seem quite troublesome.*"

"They really are."

"*But also incredible. It's a wonderful system, in my opinion.*"

Surprisingly, he was quite understanding. What a clever bird. I even thought, despite myself, that maybe recording us talking like this and uploading it to YouTube would be the quickest way to achieve our goal. I wouldn't do it, though—I'd feel too sorry for him.

"And if we got things anyone could get and sold them at auctions or in flea markets, we wouldn't be able to get your Kobe beef chateaubri-and for dinner every day. It may take some time to accomplish what you're suggesting."

"*Hmm...*"

"On that note. How do those pork ribs sound for tonight?"

Depending on how you cooked them, pork ribs could be quite deli-cious. They were the king of all stir-fry ingredients, and pork kimchi was the best of all—perfect with rice.

"*I suppose there is little choice. I must give up on enjoying myself in your world.*"

"Sorry about that. And after you went through all the trouble of sug-gesting it."

"*In exchange, we shall enjoy this world instead. That suits you, does it not? My curiosity pertaining to the food and entertainment of your world is boundless, but the road is long, and there's no rush. Sometimes, one can wait a short while, and the situation will change.*"

"Does this world not have systems like ours?"

"*Taxation exists, but it is nothing so strict.*"

"Oh."

That shouldn't cause a problem, then.

As it happened, I had been getting pretty curious about our sur-roundings. Watching from where we were in the street, everything I saw was completely new to me, and I was in the mood for some sight-seeing. If we could come and go at will, then it looked like my vacation plans for the time being were all set.

"*It seems we have settled on that, then.*"

"Sounds good to me."

With the two of us in agreement, we went back to my apartment.

✳

The next day was a weekday, which meant all good wage slaves had to go to the office at their assigned times. This day, however, it would be just a tiny bit different for me.

"Wow, we really *can* move here instantly..."

Peeps chanted a spell, and a magic circle emerged at my feet. A moment later, my surroundings had changed from the front door of my apartment to the back alley right next to where I worked. In the blink of an eye, we'd moved a dozen or so kilometers.

I had effortlessly evaded taking a packed train. What could possibly make me happier? That one man, older than me, who I fought for a seat every day—it frustrated me to forfeit my match with him, but on the other hand, it was kind of like moving into the major leagues from the minors. Thinking of it like that was satisfying.

"Didn't I say as much?"

"Well, sure, but you had to expect it would be shocking for me."

"You just experienced this yesterday."

"Yeah, but I thought that was a setup specifically for going to other worlds."

"The fundamental idea is no different."

I was whispering back and forth with Peeps, who was perched on my shoulder. Fortunately, the surrounding area was clear of people. He said he could use magic to bring me here instantly, so I figured we might as well test it—and now we were actually here. It was making me more excited than I should have been for my age. The possibilities of this spell were endless.

"Could I use it, too?"

"Currently, you have only received my mana. You may have the power needed to use a spell, but that alone is not enough. However, if you keep to your daily training, you will eventually be able to use magic just as I do. It may still take time, though, depending on several factors."

"Oh, is it possible for you to expand on that a little...?"

"Once you have returned from work, I will teach you."

"Really? Thanks so much, Peeps."

"I'll await you at home."

Suddenly, I was really looking forward to my after-work time. I'd have to finish up early and get back home.

"You'll go to the bathroom in the cage like you're supposed to, right?"

"Yes, I am fully aware."

With a brief answer, Peeps vanished along with the magic circle. What a clever bird he was, learning where to use the bathroom on day one. He only cost three thousand yen, too. What a bargain! I did still wonder why he was a little cheaper than the other birds, though.

✳

The workplace looked the same as usual. We weren't a very well-known business—just an average-size company, the sort you'd find anywhere. Bad sales meant bad wages. And naturally, I didn't get paid overtime, so I had been barely scraping by since I'd been hired.

Changing jobs was out of the question, since before I knew it, I had passed thirty. To someone like me who had experienced a job drought before, facing the market again was a frightening prospect, so I let my company work me to the bone. I figured they'd probably keep using me like that until the day I died.

"Mr. Sasaki, could you take a quick look at this settlement report?"

"Hmm?"

My colleague had spoken to me from the next seat over. He was a newer employee who had been here for four years now. He'd enrolled right out of his technical college, making him twenty-four this year.

Other companies might consider a fourth-year employee a key part of the team, and as a coworker, he was excellent. Unfortunately, those above him were nearly a decade older, so he was still being called the new guy. I felt kind of sorry for him. In my personal opinion, he was the best worker in our office.

"...Right. Yes, the language here does bother me a little."

"Oh, you thought so, too?"

"You know how the department head is. I think you should explain that part a bit more."

"Thank you, I will."

"You really don't need to spend your time on trivial things like this. Feel free to ask me whatever you want— In fact, you could just pass it straight to me. Then maybe you could get some work-work done, and we'd all benefit."

"Work-work?"

"You know. Stuff you could use somewhere else..."

"……"

"...What's wrong?"

"Nothing. I was just thinking you're absolutely right."

"Right?"

He was still young—there were better places that would let him shine. He didn't need to spend all his time working for a dull manager at this tired old company.

"Want to go have a smoke?" he suggested.

"No, no. I don't smoke."

"Then I'll buy you a soda or something."

"Well, I suppose…"

Accepting his invitation, I got up from my seat. Normally, we'd have gone to the vending machines on the same floor. This time, though, he led us right past them and outside. I followed him quietly, wondering where on earth he was going.

Eventually, we came to an alley next to our company's building. It was two, maybe three meters wide. No vending machines in sight. He picked a spot with no one around—what did he want to talk about?

My colleague, expression serious, spoke.

"Mr. Sasaki, would you be interested in going independent with me?"

"Huh?"

"I plan on quitting this job next month."

"…Oh."

This was a heavier topic than I'd expected. He filled me in on the details—he'd started planning a start-up half a year ago. He'd already been talking to several business connections he had, and that was apparently going well. As for his team, he'd called up some of his school friends and had gotten quite a few of them on board.

"I think having someone with your experience would really help us out."

"……"

It seemed like he'd asked me because he thought having at least one older person would round out their young team. I was extremely happy to get the invitation, but it was such a sudden offer it caught me off guard.

"Can I count on you? I think we can offer you more than you're getting now."

"Well…"

But I couldn't exactly answer on the spot, could I? I'd just adopted Peeps the previous day. I was pretty pressed for time right now.

"Would you give me a little while to think it over?"

"Yes, of course. You're even free to see how things go from the outside for a year or so. I know you're probably uneasy with a bunch of young people like me putting together a start-up. It's only natural."

"No, that's not what I meant. It's just that my, well, private life is a little busy…"

"Huh? Oh, are you getting married?"

"…No, that's not it."

"It isn't? I'm sorry; I guess I shouldn't have asked that."

"But I am really happy you invited me. Thank you."

"Not at all. I'll look forward to your answer."

"Okay."

He explained he would be the face of the company. I'd always thought he was talented, but to launch a start-up at his age—that was really something. Having him approach me so frankly was an unexpected and happy occurrence.

If there did end up being something I could help them with, I'd gladly give him a proper answer then.

*

I had just gotten back from work and was at the door of my apartment when I noticed a figure in front of my next-door neighbor's place. A middle school student wearing the sailor uniform of a nearby school was sitting with her knees up and her back against the door. A bag sat next to her—probably the one designated by her school. When I noticed her there and looked over, she glanced up at me as well, and our eyes met.

"Hello," she said in greeting.

With the temperature dropping down fast, I felt chilly just looking at her, hugging her knees and making herself seem even smaller. I didn't notice her wearing any cold-weather clothing under her skirt— only her socks were visible, pulled up all the way. The wind had been strong recently, including today. She must have been cold.

"It's been getting colder out. Are you all right?"

"…I'm fine."

This wasn't the first time I'd talked to the girl. I'd known her since she was in elementary school. She'd been living in the next unit over with her mother since before I moved here. From her seat on the floor, she claimed that her mother wouldn't let her into the apartment until she got home. This woman was either a toxic parent or a neglectful one.

At first, we hadn't had much to do with one another. Once, I'd put in an anonymous tip to a public agency. Since then, I'd just pretended I didn't see it happening. I hated that, but if I wasn't careful, talking to her could get me arrested. I figured this was a job for the authorities anyway.

"I've got a disposable heating pouch here, if you want it…"

"Are you sure?"

"They're cheap, and I bought a few too many."

"…Thank you."

However, I still saw no signs of things improving. How many months had passed like this? One day, I'd come home on the last train of the night after a company drinking party. Flecks of snow were visible on the rooftops, and she was sitting just as she was now, holding her knees in front of the door. Her stomach rumbling had drowned out the sound of my key in the lock, and I gave in. At the time, I guess I just pitied her. I'd grabbed a pastry from my apartment and given it to her—that was our first contact. Since then, I'd give her a little something now and then when we saw each other.

"Well, good-bye."

"Good-bye…"

Bowing slightly to my neighbor, I entered my apartment. I made no move to invite her in. Even if she'd accepted, letting someone under eighteen into your home would be kidnapping—a criminal offense. I'd done some research, and even for a first-time offender, the prosecution would just skip the probation and go right to the jail sentence. I couldn't take that much of a risk with a parent I already knew was guilty of neglect.

So I kept our conversations to a minimum, too. I was only giving her a little bit of help until she could stand on her own.

✳

That evening, I had arrangements to receive a lecture on magic in my apartment from Peeps.

I'd finished eating dinner and had a bath, and my mind and body were clean and clear. I sat in the chair at my desk, and Peeps perched atop his metal cage, positioned on top of some cardboard boxes in the corner of the room. It was a cramped apartment—a studio with a kitchen—so our current positions seemed likely to become routine.

"I see. So you chant the words and create an image in your mind, and it just comes out?"

"Now that I've shared my power with you, you don't need to worry about lacking mana. You will likely never need any more for most spells. If you can chant the appropriate words and construct a sufficient image in your mind, you can use magic."

"That's surprisingly ordinary."

"Ordinary in what way?"

"Sorry. Don't mind me."

This meant the issue came down to chanting. If the incantation was long enough to fill a whole page of notebook paper, there was no way I could memorize it. It would be nice if they were as short as the ones in fantasy games—I wondered if there were any like that.

"How long are the incantations?"

"It depends on the spell. Some are short; others are long. The shortest are just a few words in a row, but the longest might take up an entire book. Memorizing the latter would likely prove impossible."

"That's quite a range." More so than I'd expected.

I remembered having to read aloud in Japanese class during my school days—and how one time a kid named Ookawauchi had been called on by the teacher to read aloud, and brandishing his textbook in front of him, he'd started belting out the magic chant from a popular anime. *Wonder how he's doing these days.* If the bell hadn't rang as he was trying to sort out his failed prank, things would have gone a lot worse for him.

"You can also shorten incantations once you are accustomed to them. However, to do that, you'll need an even stronger, even clearer mental image. It's hard to describe, but spells will steadily sink in over the course of using them hundreds or thousands of times."

"Hearing all this makes it sound more like a practiced skill than I thought."

"Yes. And that is why learning magic takes time."

I'd been thinking magic was more of a specific technique. This seemed much more difficult. But it was basically like making an illustration, wasn't it? Beginners did plenty of rough drawings before starting their final draft. Professionals, on the other hand, could start from the draft, since they could tell what it would be like already. Depending on their level of skill, they could even skip all the way to the line work. Was that a good analogy for incantations and shortening them?

When I thought about it like that, it started to feel like this was going to be a long journey. *I'm pretty bad at drawing, too...*

"Personally, I'd like to use the spell for teleportation like you did this morning."

"That is a fairly advanced form of magic. The incantation isn't overly long, but it is extremely difficult to form the mental image. I cannot recommend it as a first spell, with you only just beginning your studies."

"I see."

I still wanted to use the teleportation spell, though. I could skip the crowded trains. I could make my commute time zero. Being a corporate slave working in the city gave that a value that was hard to substitute. I could rent a cheap place in Hokkaido for the summer and in Okinawa for the winter, then still work here in the city. It was like a dream—and this spell could make it reality. I very much wanted to learn it.

This morning, I'd shown Peeps the company's location and a picture of the area using a map application, so he could see what it looked like before transporting me there. He'd mentioned it was difficult to go somewhere you haven't already been, but even he was surprised at how smoothly it went. It was a fearsome combination of magic with satellite imagery and a street view.

"In that case, I'd like to learn two spells at once. Would that work? First, I'll learn whatever spell you think would be easiest, and at the same time, I'll study the teleportation one. How does that sound?"

"Quite ambitious, I must say. You seem quite curious about magic."

"Maybe not magic in general, but definitely the teleportation."

"I see. Then you will need diligence. I will teach you the spells. In the meantime, I can send you to work. It will likely make it easier for you to form the image in your head as you experience it over and over."

"Thank you so much, Peeps."

The night hours passed just like that. Peeps told me the incantations needed for the spells, and I wrote them down in a notebook. In contrast to the teleportation spell, which was about half a page long, the other spell was only the length of a haiku.

I'd read and memorize them during my breaks at work. It was best to go steady with everything. If you went hard right away at something you weren't used to, you'd quickly exhaust yourself. Good old daily practice suited my personality. Still, the idea of teleportation magic was attractive enough to make even *me* want to rush.

*

The problem occurred the next day in my office. And the cause was magic.

During my lunch break, I'd read out a spell, a notebook in one hand. Not the teleportation one, but one Peeps had explained to me as being simpler. I must have gotten the incantation and mental image right, because a small flame burst to life at my fingertips. Essentially, it was like a magic lighter.

I was in a bathroom stall at the time. When the spell triggered, it created a bigger flame than I was expecting. It was stronger than a lighter—it was more like what you got when you sprayed a flammable aerosol into a lighter's flame. The flame was so large that I started to panic.

A moment later, the smoke detectors went off, and things went down the crapper. I'd obviously be in deep trouble if they found me out, so I hurried out of the bathroom. Returning to the now-lively office, I joined up with my concerned coworkers and looked back at the restrooms, acting like I didn't know anything.

Fortunately, they never found the culprit and decided someone had lit a cigarette in a restroom stall. I was eliminated as a suspect right away since I never smoked, and things ended without incident.

When I got home and told Peeps about it, his reply was encouraging. *"It seems you have more of an affinity for this than I thought."*

"Affinity?"

"I didn't think you would succeed all at once. That is quite an accomplishment."

"Getting praised by you like this makes me kind of happy."

"And you should be proud. The day may well come when you exceed even my powers."

"Does that mean if I try hard, the teleportation spell will be possible?"

"I had thought at first it would take years, regardless of how fast you were. But if you keep this pace, it will probably happen much more quickly. It will still take more than a mere few days, however. Just never forget your daily diligence."

As a modern man born and raised in a society always surrounded by tests and exams—high school exams, university entrance exams, all manner of certification tests—I was used to tackling a single task over the span of years. Since picking up a guitar as a hobby, a few years had passed in the blink of an eye.

"I know it's early, but can you teach me other magic, too?"

"Indeed I can. Next…"

Peeps generously taught me more spells.

I took these and created folders on my PC, neatly separating them into such fantasy-esque categories as attack magic, healing magic, fire magic, and water magic. It felt almost like I'd become a novelist. Memorizing these spells would be my daily task, it seemed. One was over a page long.

Peeps, you're really something. How did you memorize all this?

I spent nearly an hour organizing the text files I'd be studying for now. Then once my magic studies were complete, it was time for a short stay in the otherworld.

"Now then, we shall hurry on to the otherworld."

"Oh, about that. Do you have a second?"

"What is it?"

"I wanted to know what happens here while we're over there."

It would be no joke if I ended up being late for work after returning. Today was Tuesday, tomorrow was Wednesday—for the next three days, I had to show up at my desk at the office at nine AM every day. Morning roll call was set in stone at my company, and they timed it very strictly. If I missed roll call, I'd immediately be marked as late. The management—led by the company president—seemed to have it a little easier, but it didn't take much for us rank-and-file employees to get a bad reputation. This rule has been instated five years ago, when our profits started to plunge.

"Time does not flow equally there. Last time, I calculated the difference. If my estimation is correct, the long needle on that clock moved about three times."

When had he figured that out? Peeps was just such a clever bird. I didn't have the disposition to think that far ahead. It felt like we'd been over there for a little under an hour to me. If that was right, three minutes in this world was one hour to theirs. In other words, an hour here was around twenty in that world. That was a bigger gap than I could have anticipated—almost an entire day.

"...Peeps, that place is incredible."

"*Is it?*"

If I ever collapsed or caught a cold, I could ask Peeps to take me over. I could get a few days' worth of rest and refreshment, and only a few hours would have passed here. That was literally out of this world!

But wait, wouldn't that mean my life span would be shortened at the same rate? In that case, I would probably be better off not doing it too often.

"There's still more than an hour before the date changes, so let's get going. Thank you again."

"*Mm. Let's be off.*"

His beak popped open adorably, after which a magic circle emerged in front of him—the same effect as before. And the next thing I knew, my body had been moved from my apartment without a trace.

✳

The first thing I did upon arriving at the otherworld was to start trading the merchandise I'd brought with me.

Since this world was lax about currency management and taxation, I'd carried along as much as I could. I put it all in a large backpack I'd bought a few years ago after deciding to make a hobby out of mountain climbing. I'd used it once, after which it had sat there gathering dust—until now, at least. Now it was packed full of goods.

I'd already had Peeps check the things I'd stocked up on. As an observer—and a former local of this world—he had pointed out last night what items would probably sell for a high price. Most were things I didn't have in the apartment, so on my way home from work, I'd stopped by the neighborhood superstore and bought them.

The goods included the following: ten kilograms of chocolate bars, ten kilograms of white caster sugar, one thousand sheets of printer paper, and five hundred ballpoint pens.

After having lugged it all here, I was struck by how insanely heavy the load was. The five hundred ballpoint pens, which I'd picked up last, were especially conspicuous. With one being ten grams, that meant five hundred weighed five kilograms. I never thought the day would come when I'd be measuring pens in *kilograms*.

All of it, though, would apparently sell at a high price in this world.

I wondered if it was all right not to quarantine the goods, but according to Peeps, that was likely not going to pose an issue. Since I had no familiarity with this world, I had little reason to doubt him.

Besides, these days, even common items get antibacterial treatment. Big manufacturers have clean, hygienic manufacturing processes. In that sense, my body was probably far more dangerous than any of my wares.

On the other hand, caution was probably advisable when I ultimately brought things back home. Even a single bug on my jacket could be catastrophic. A clothing brush, at least, as a precautionary measure would likely be a good idea. I'd have to grab one the next chance I got.

"The nobility has great influence in this world. If you wish to make large sums of money at once, you will be dealing primarily with them. Commoners form the majority of the population, but their total wealth is far less than that of the nobles."

"Not much different from my world, then."

As I walked down the street, I saw the same sights as before. If I recalled correctly, this was a provincial town in the Kingdom of Herz called Baytrium. Though night had fallen in Japan, it was still midday here.

"Still, it will be too difficult to trade with high-standing nobles right away. It will be easiest to form relationships with nobles of lower rank, then have them introduce you to others. Thus, I would like you to meet the lord of this domain."

"An acquaintance of yours?"

"Not precisely, but I can vouch for his character. However, I would like you to keep my return to this world a secret for now. This will be very important to help secure your own safety."

"Wait, does that mean…?"

"Do not worry. It is not what you are thinking."

"Are you sure?"

I didn't want to think about my pet having a criminal record. I wanted him to be clean in body and soul, so I could love him unconditionally.

"The world consists of many types of people. It's not possible to forge harmonious relationships with them all. Even simply maintaining a normal lifestyle is bound to produce unwanted discord. It was as a result of this that I had to cross over to your world."

"……"

Despite his looks, maybe Peeps has had a really rough time of things. Maybe I could splurge on some slightly more expensive meat for dinner the next day. Perhaps a roast?

"That building is home to one of the trading companies run by the nobility. If you do business there, word will spread quickly. You should be able to raise money to make a start using the items you brought today."

I followed Peeps's gaze to a large building made of stone. Five stories high, it had an extremely pretentious design, and its architecture was similar to the gothic styles I'd seen in social studies textbooks. At its entrance stood an armor-clad man holding a spear, overseeing those going in and out. It looked like some foreign embassy building you might find in a city.

Before the heavily ornamented facade, I hesitated over whether I should really be going inside. Most of those entering and exiting had a high-class look to them, beyond what the others I saw on the streets were wearing. This place was probably like Japan's Isetan or Mitsukoshi, both lavish, upscale department stores.

I had come wearing a suit, though, so while I did stand out from my surroundings, I trusted I wouldn't be in violation of the dress code. Peeps, perched on my right shoulder, however, still made me hesitate.

"Should I really be going inside with a sparrow on my shoulder?"

"There should be no issue if you refer to me as a familiar."

"I see— Those exist, huh?"

It looked like I'd have to study more than just magic—I'd need to acquaint myself with this world's rules and sensibilities, too. Taboos would be the highest on the list of things to learn.

"Let's go inside."

"What's this place called anyway?"

"The Hermann Trading Company."

"I see. Hermann, then."

Urged onward by the self-professed familiar, I let my steps take me inside the trading company.

✳

To sum up, my dealings went far better than anticipated.

"This is incredible…"

I had been shown to what seemed to be a reception room, where we'd started talking shop. On the other side was a man who called himself the vice manager of the company. He was probably about my age, but his facial features were very handsome, and he was quite tall, to boot—good-looking enough to make me think he'd probably never had issues finding women. His green eyes and green slicked-back hair were striking. He went by the name Marc. Apparently, as a commoner, he didn't have a surname.

"What do you think, Mr. Marc?"

Given that we had sat down for business, I decided to be formal, addressing Marc with *mister* and asking him his thoughts with a smile.

I certainly wondered why I even needed to sell products in another world. Somehow, though, given it was a request from my adorable birdie, I found that I was able to give it my all.

That didn't mean it wasn't difficult, of course. The reception room was even more lavish than I'd expected, and it had elicited in me unanticipated awe. Even the wooden frame of the chair I was sitting on had gold trim, and its cushion was soft enough that I sank into it. This had all conspired to put a slow, slimy sweat on my brow.

"I do believe I'd like to purchase everything you have."

"Thank you very much."

Peeps had clued me in to the prices for the items I'd brought, saying three hundred gold coins would be appropriate for everything. That broke down to fifty gold coins for the chocolate bars, fifty for the sugar, one hundred for the paper, and one hundred for the ballpoint pens.

In local currency, one gold coin was equivalent to one hundred silver coins; one silver coin to one hundred copper coins; and one copper coin to ten cents. For meals, lunch cost about ten copper coins, with a one-night, two-meal inn stay generally priced at about one silver coin. One copper coin seemed to be about the same as one hundred yen. Converting it like that gave three hundred million yen.

However, the price of crafted goods was terribly high compared to Japan, such as a new outfit costing ten silver coins or a kitchen knife— even a used one—costing around a dozen. So the real value probably had one or two fewer zeroes on the end, bringing the three hundred million yen to thirty million.

Also, this currency was only circulated in the nation that was home to the Hermann Trading Company, where I was presently doing business—in other words, the Kingdom of Herz. Adjacent kingdoms, explained Peeps, distributed their own forms of currency, with each weighed against the others according to relative strength.

"I can prepare four hundred gold coins right away."

"Four hundred?" Peeps had mentioned the number three hundred beforehand; this was one hundred more. It was far too much money to be a miscalculation.

"In exchange, I would like to secure your business in the future…"

"Ah. In that case, very well."

This *was* the shop my adorable little pet had recommended, so there couldn't be any harm in making friends. I didn't think this one trade would get my name around the lower echelons of the nobility; better to sell my things wholesale right here and build up business results.

"Thank you very much."

Peeps hadn't said anything at all this entire time. He just sat on my shoulder, still and patient. What a good-mannered sparrow he was. When starting my business, I'd simply explained he was a familiar and hadn't gotten any pushback. Apparently, familiars were commonplace in this world—just like he'd told me.

There was, however, a concern with Peeps's choice of perch. I remembered hearing from the pet shop clerk that birds would sometimes go to the bathroom very suddenly and being advised to be careful taking him out of his cage. I felt bad because I wanted to trust Peeps, but I couldn't do so completely. No matter how logical his mind was, wouldn't it be difficult for him to resist his biological imperatives? It seemed like a real possibility he might accidentally do his business right on my shoulder. The animal feces I saw littering the cages in the store spoke to some unfortunate accidents.

"Would you mind if I asked you a question, by the way?" the vice manager asked me right after our transaction was completed, his expression again turning serious.

"Not at all. What is it?"

"I understand the chocolate and the sugar. Their quality is positively mind-boggling, but even I could procure them given enough time. What I cannot understand are these pens and paper."

"I see, sir."

"Forgive my rudeness, but you appear to be from somewhere beyond our borders…"

"I'm terribly sorry, sir, but please allow me to keep my sources a secret. It may not be much in the way of compensation, but I won't sell the paper or pens to any other store. I'd very much like to maintain our good relationship."

"Do you mean that?"

"Yes, sir, I do."

A little lip service never hurt. Plus, I'd always wanted, just once, to try some of that self-important business talk, no contract in sight. Days spent bowing on behalf of my company's pathetic products flashed through my head. So this was how other company's sales reps felt. What a devious pleasure. I relished it all the way to the bottom of my heart.

"Understood. I would very much like that as well."

"Thank you so much for your understanding."

With all that behind me, four hundred gold coins found their way into my pocket. I knew it was a significant amount, but it still hadn't sank in. All I'd done was pass ten thousand or so yen's worth of goods from right to left. It felt as though I hadn't done any real work. I wondered if this was what it had been like for those who'd made a fortune from cryptocurrency during its genesis.

"Again, forgive my rudeness for asking, but are you lodging in the area?"

"No, I'm staying at an acquaintance's house."

"Oh, I see. I apologize again."

"I believe I'll be able to bring some more goods in the near future, so long as I have your permission."

"Of course—you're my guest, and you're more than welcome."

After parrying all sorts of questions with suitable answers, my first objective was complete. I was politely seen off, then I left the building behind me.

✳

Just like Peeps had predicted, my backpack had emptied in under an hour. The same went for the printer paper and ballpoint pens I'd been carrying in my hands.

I was finally able to take a breather. It felt like a burden had been lifted from my shoulders—which it literally had.

I had exchanged all those wares for one hundred gold coins and three larger gold coins. Large gold coins were, as their name implied, bigger versions of the gold pieces, apparently worth one hundred of them each. They were used mostly for major business deals, though, and didn't generally circulate in the markets.

Carrying around this fortune had me on pins and needles. Still, according to Peeps, there were no signs of anyone following me. That gave me some measure of comfort as I continued down the street. And physically, a job well done felt good, too.

Which all turned my attention to today's lunch.

"Peeps, what should we do for lunch?"

"I would prefer a shop with tasty meat."

"I wholeheartedly agree."

The only issue was that this world didn't have any restaurant review websites. Walking down the main road, I spotted plenty of eateries, but as someone who had been unlucky many times with places in the city, I was hesitant to charge in somewhere without knowing its reputation. Internet review sites were a must-have for the modern man.

"What say you to that shop there?"

"...It does smell good."

The fragrant scents of cooked meat were wafting from its doors. It was so wonderful to have a partner who took the lead and suggested a place to eat at. Peeps was very cool and macho—so much so that I bet he was all the rage with the ladies before becoming a Java sparrow. In contrast, I was the type to fret and worry about things.

"Okay, let's go there."

"Yes."

Time to sample some otherworld dishes. How exciting! Since I'd sold the chocolate bars and sugar at such a high price, my expectations were somewhat low. Still, I figured we could find one or two tasty offerings. Otherwise, there would be less point in me trying so hard in this world. Prompted by the sparrow's glassy eyes, we headed into the store.

Or at least, we tried to.

Just as we were about to try the door, the entrance burst open, and someone came flying out.

"You sure as hell ain't my apprentice anymore! Get out of here, now!"

The young man, who was either in his late teens or around twenty, groaned. He was tall and possessed some muscle. He seemed to be a cook, given the apron that was part of his outfit, but to me, he had more of a carpenter vibe. The sight of him being flung to the ground in front of the shop set my nerves on end.

The one who appeared to have sent him crashing outside was another man, also wearing an apron. This guy appeared to be in his forties. They were probably coworkers, one being the senior cook and the other a junior—or perhaps an employer and his employee.

Now, though, relations between the two of them weren't exactly looking very good.

"Don't ever show your face around me again!"

"Master, just…just hold on, please! I swear it wasn't me!"

"Enough lies! I have proof!"

"I was framed! I've worked hard for this shop—"

"Now you're going to lay the blame on someone else?!"

"Please wait! If you fire me, I… I'll have nowhere to go! I won't be able to provide for my parents, so please! Please, I'm begging you! I'll be living on the streets!"

"And you can die there for all I care!"

With a loud bang, the door to the shop slammed shut.

The man stared balefully at it. His hairstyle—long and bright red, with one side combed back—combined with his deeply inset features gave him a noticeably stern look. He kept his words mostly polite, but the sharpness of his eyes gave him the air of a low-grade punk. Definitely more the air of a carpenter than a cook.

Also. Had I just witnessed a firing?

＊

I suddenly had an idea and called out to the man on the ground.

Something along the lines of "Would you like to have a talk in that café?"

Which was, now that I thought about it, an incredibly suspicious-sounding invitation. But having just been fired, he was still in a daze and accepted with less fuss than I would have anticipated. You could even say he was like a zombie as he tottered after us.

We walked together to an eatery a little farther up the same road and settled into seats near the rear of the shop, with him, still in his apron, opposite me. Only drinks—hastily ordered—sat on the table.

"Pleased to meet you. My name is Sasaki."

"Oh yes. Hello. My name is French."

"All right, Mr. French."

"I, umm. What did you want to talk to me about?"

"Well, I happened to overhear your troubling exchange."

"…I'm ashamed to admit it, but yes."

After getting a look at this world, I had realized something. Just a few hours ago, I'd been overjoyed that one hour in Japan equated to one day here, but that wasn't necessarily advantageous. During weekdays, when I was at work, more than ten days would pass in this world.

That wasn't a time gap I could laugh away, especially if I really wanted to get something started here. Even if I came to do business during lunch breaks, several days of empty time would still pass. That would make my future dealings difficult.

What was I to do to make up for the time difference between our worlds? Obviously, I had to make some local friends.

"Excuse me, Lord Sasaki, but are you a noble?"

"A noble?"

"It's just that you're wearing such fine clothing…"

Oh my goodness. I just got complimented on my suit. Even this drab, bargain-rack outfit seemed fine enough that others mistook it for noble dress. Clothes really weren't cheap here. This sort of free status boost certainly wasn't unwelcome… I'd have to make sure I always wore a suit during my visits in the future.

"No, not a noble. I'm a merchant."

"Oh, I see. A trader," said Mr. French, his expression looking somewhat relieved.

Judging by his attitude, a big barrier must have separated nobility from the common folk. I'd have to ask Peeps about this when I got a free minute. I was the one being mistaken for a noble, so things had worked out—but doing it the other way around would be a terrible mistake.

"If it's all the same to you, would you mind telling me your story?"

"Huh? Um, I…"

"I may be able to provide some assistance."

"……"

Anyone would be suspicious of a first-time acquaintance saying something like that. I'd have left the shop already, personally.

But what he'd shouted in front of the restaurant certainly hadn't sounded like lies—that bit about supporting his parents and having nowhere to go. He seemed to be in a very tight spot; it only took a few moments before he started spilling everything.

To sum it all up, it appeared he'd been framed by a coworker.

Having worked as an apprentice at the restaurant since he was young, his culinary skills had—by his account—been growing rapidly in recent years. A coworker of his was jealous and falsely claimed French had stolen the shop's money—or something like that.

Then, today, his attempts to convince the shopkeeper of his innocence had fallen on deaf ears, and he'd been driven out. That was the final, decisive scene I'd happened upon.

"That is an awful story."

"I've been working there ever since I was little. Everything I did was cooking, so I don't know much about how the world works. I can't really write, either. Now that I've been fired, I have no idea what to do."

"……"

"At this rate, I won't be able to provide for my family anymore. One of my parents lost a leg and an eye as a soldier and can't do very much work anymore. I have a younger sister as well, but on top of being a woman, she also takes care of our parents, so she can't save up that much money."

"That sounds terrible."

I could sense the hopelessness oozing from Mr. French's tale. I even thought for a moment that if I left him alone, he might have been dead by his own hand the next day. It seemed this world had less of a social safety net than I thought.

"…I apologize. I don't even know you, yet I've gone on and on…"

"No, don't apologize. I was the one who asked."

We had talked for close to an hour, and he didn't seem like a bad person.

So I decided to make an investment—using the day's profits. It may have been a lot of money in this world, but with Peeps's support, I hadn't had to work that hard to make it. I'd only brought one backpack of goods, too, but I planned to bring some bigger gear starting next time. To me, it was like shoving a wad of bills into a street-side donation box.

"If you're interested, would you like to open a place with me?"

"…Huh?"

Mr. French's pupils shrunk in surprise.

If he really was an excellent cook, this proposition would benefit Peeps and me as well. Peeps loved meat, and pursuing flavors that could satisfy his taste buds went along with his ideal of living the way he wanted to. And of course, when a pet is happy, the owner is happy, too.

*

With Mr. French in tow, I went back to the trading company Peeps had pointed me to. After a brief conversation with the security at the entrance, I had them announce me to the vice manager. In blank amazement, I was shown once again to the reception room from before—with Mr. Marc already present and everything.

"Is something the matter? Did you have reservations about our business agreement?" he asked cautiously. My sudden return must have made him anxious.

"No, it's nothing like that. There was something else I was wondering if you could prepare for me, separate from that matter."

"I see. In that case, I'm all ears."

"Thank you."

The vice manager smiled back at me. I used that as a chance to launch into my proposal. "This may seem abrupt, but I'd like to open an eatery in this area. Can I ask you to procure a shop, equipment, and foodstuffs for it? I regrettably have no expertise in this field myself, so I wanted to know if the Hermann Trading Company would be willing to assist in this matter."

"We wouldn't mind, but what of your companion?"

"I plan to make this man the shop's manager."

"...What?"

Mr. French stared at me agape, clearly wondering if this was a joke. I'd already explained that much to him—had he not understood? Well, it didn't matter. I'd already talked to the vice manager about everything, so I was set on this course. Better than him wandering the streets.

"If you could stock the equipment and foodstuffs in accordance with his wishes, it would be much appreciated. I believe three hundred gold coins would be enough to cover initial expenses. If that is insufficient for anything, I'd like to pay the difference during our next deal. Would that be possible?"

I remembered seeing on the internet that you needed at least ten million yen to start up a restaurant in the city. Because of how expensive furniture and utensils were in this world, I felt like three hundred gold coins was just barely up to the task. If things seemed tight, I could supplement the payment in our next business deal.

"...Did you want to get into the food business here?"

"No, I wasn't planning on anything that big. And I have no intention of stirring up trouble with competitors. Some of the products I deal in

are food, so I thought it would be nice to prepare a simple location to test the market."

"I see— So that is your plan."

My explanation seemed to have convinced him. A frown crossed his face for just a few moments, but his expression quickly returned to normal—and then he smiled.

"Can I count on your support?"

"Yes, by all means. Please allow me to assist you with this venture."

"Thank you very much."

The unexpectedly eager response made me hopeful things would go smoothly even after I returned to Japan. Given that he was vice manager for a huge market like this, the level of support he could offer was likely significant.

"I have entrusted the matter of the shop entirely to him, so please ask him for all the details you need. He is a first-rate cook but somewhat unfamiliar with the more delicate parts of the job, so I would greatly appreciate it if your company could assist him on the business side of things."

"I understand—I'll send one of my people to help."

"Really? Thank you so much."

When I looked at Mr. French, who stood beside me with his face white as a ghost, I felt like I'd started up a temporary personnel agency. I did feel sorry for doing it to the guy, but if this fell through, it wouldn't really cause any issues, so I wanted to keep things easy and carefree.

"Don't worry too much about it, Mr. French. Give it your best."

"Um, yes, sir!"

And with that, I had taken my first step toward fulfilling my promise to Peeps.

*

After leaving the minor details to Mr. French and the vice manager, I left the Hermann Trading Company. Normally, I would have stayed with them until everything was hammered out, but I didn't have a choice. Something more important demanded my attention—lunch with Peeps, which I'd put off quite a bit. I didn't want to make him grumpy and end up stranded and alone in an unfamiliar world.

As planned, we headed for the place where Mr. French worked— well, used to work. With him set up for the time being, we could now return to our original objective.

Still-steaming meat dishes lined the table in front of us.

"*...Not bad.*"

"Yeah."

I'd gotten the day's special for lunch, which the manager had recommended. Peeps had ordered the one thing he'd smelled from outside, à la carte. It was some sort of animal meat cooked and marinated in a secret sauce, and the sauce was in the special, too. It was quite delicious. We were very pleased.

"Despite chocolate bars and sugar selling for so much, this is quite the variety of flavors."

"*That's simply because sugar and cacao are precious.*"

"Would pepper sell highly, too, then?"

"*Indeed. If you can procure it cheaply, it would be worth looking into.*"

The suggestion came naturally from me, partly since I hadn't noticed it on the list of ideas Peeps had given me. When it came to valuable commodities, pepper was a sure thing, right? Pepper is always a safe bet. In an Age of Discovery sort of sense.

"I've heard there was an era in my world when it was worth its weight in gold."

"*Yes, pepper is certainly valuable in this one as well. However, it doesn't fetch an astronomical price. In fact, I'm rather curious how it came to be worth its weight in gold, as you say. Why was there such a demand? It is a luxury item like sugar, is it not? And you can substitute it with herbs or other such things.*"

"I think they needed it to cover the stench when eating poorly preserved meats."

"*Why would they need to eat poorly preserved meats?*"

"Huh? Well, hmm. They didn't have refrigerators back then, so..."

At the time, the rotting of meat plagued both noble and commoner alike. It had been especially bad in early spring, after the preserved meat had already started to go bad. There must have been so many people with upset stomachs—or worse—from eating tainted meat.

I remembered reading on the internet once that Carnival, a holiday familiar to Christians, had started as a way to consume, all at once, the meat they had stored up during the winter before spring came and it spoiled too much. Whether that was true, I wasn't sure. But meat must have really been rotting badly back then to produce a story like that.

"*Ah, I understand.*"

"You do?"

"Magic exists in this world. To preserve meat, one must only prepare ice. Create a room filled with ice and store meat in it. Then you can eat fresh meat whenever, wherever you are."

"…I see."

"Spells to create ice are relatively easy to learn. Slightly more advanced forms can also freeze specific objects in ice. Prepared this way, you can preserve foods for long periods of time."

"I guess there was that icicle-flinging spell you taught me about yesterday. If you could gather the icicles instead of launching them, you could make a refrigerator, just like you say. I'm sorry—it seems I didn't think hard enough."

Man, magic was handy as heck. I doubted this world would have proper refrigerators for a long time.

"It is another world. You can hardly be blamed."

"It's also giving me a lot more ideas about things to bring here…"

"Mechanical goods would likely be an easy option. The metalworking technology in that world is extremely advanced. I would also suggest luxuries that haven't yet circulated or taken root here. And the other thing—plastic, you called it? I believe that would fetch quite a high price as well if you stocked it."

"Yes, I see."

I'd have Peeps come with me next time I stocked up. I got the feeling I'd be able to pick out the goods more efficiently that way.

✳

After finishing lunch, we went back to my apartment. Having spent half a day in the otherworld, we found upon arriving that a little less than thirty minutes had passed in Japan time. Peeps's estimation seemed about right; I could safely assume one hour here was the same as one day there.

Exhausted from our exploits, we went right to sleep.

The next morning, this corporate slave went to work, just like the day before. Curiously, the coworker who normally sat next to me was nowhere to be found. Other than that, though, nothing out of the ordinary happened. The little fire incident from the day before had apparently gone unsolved, with the culprit unable to be identified. Mr. Kikuchi, the general affairs manager, was really frustrated about it.

Finally, quitting time rolled around. Except it was after nine by that point. Having gotten home a little early today, this corporate slave decided to take Peeps to the big superstore near the house. The place was open until eleven, so it was popular with office workers of all kinds who returned home later.

Right after leaving my apartment, I spotted a familiar face outside the neighbor's front door—a middle schooler in a sailor uniform, sitting down with her hands around her knees. I hadn't seen her when I got back from work, so she must have returned a little later even than this corporate drone. Still, her mom wasn't home yet, so she was whiling away her time in front of the door.

"...Is that a Java sparrow?" she asked suddenly, looking in my direction—or rather, at Peeps. He was packed in a bird carrying case hanging from my shoulder.

"Yep, it is. I got him recently."

"......"

The case had a metallic frame base, with the cage part made of clear PVC pipe and a polyethylene mesh. It looked like a miniature travel bag with a perching tree inside. You could see Peeps resting on it from above or from the sides. I'd ordered it online around the time he'd started talking. Luckily, it had come in just as I'd gotten home, and I'd decided to put it to use right away for my outing today. A sparrow sitting on a man's shoulder while he was shopping would draw some stares.

"Do you not like sparrows?"

"No, that isn't it," came the laconic, indifferent answer from my neighbor, before her stomach gave a loud rumble.

I would have expected a girl her age to show some sign of embarrassment at that. She didn't seem to care one way or the other, though, and just watched Peeps. For her, this was simply another nonchalant moment in her daily life.

"Hold on a second."

"Actually, I'm just going to bed for today, so..."

Having an apartment made for a single person came in handy at times like these—the front door was very close to the kitchen. One of the cabinets was near enough that I could lean in without having to take off my shoes. I grabbed a pastry I'd had in reserve, then turned back to face my neighbor.

"It expires today, so here."

"......"

It was a lame excuse. With her mom coming home soon, I couldn't have a lengthy conversation with her. Anyone who saw me—a middle-aged man who, at a glance, had no women in his life—would probably interpret the interaction as somebody trying to bait a minor. Actually, they definitely would. That was why I really had to insist on a sense of distance between us. I seriously didn't want any rumors starting about me among the neighbors.

"We've got things to do, so good-bye."

Ending the conversation, I placed the bread on her bag, which was sitting next to her. It felt like I was making an offering of a few coins to a shrine's donation box—and wishing that, one day, the good deed would come back to me.

"...Thank you," my neighbor called after us as we left the apartment.

✳

Our destination was, as planned, the neighborhood superstore. They had food and everyday sundries in addition to books, bicycles, sports gear, and even home appliances. Basically, it was the kind of massive supermarket you find in the suburbs. We headed to the second floor to stock up for tonight's business.

"This seems good."

"Gotcha."

Following Peeps's instructions as he sat in the carrying case, I put one item after another into my shopping cart. I spoke softly and kept my mouth closed when passing people so nobody would overhear us. They would just think I was an eccentric owner who really loved his Java sparrow.

Oh, a frying pan. "Peeps, what about this?"

"How is it different from a normal pot?"

"It's incredibly hard to burn."

"This is good."

"I'll just throw it in, too, then."

I tossed the Teflon frying pan into my cart. It didn't feel like enough with just one, so I put in a few more. I also added several peelers—I had the feeling they were a more recent invention.

Thanks to my aggressive series of carefree purchasing decisions, the total price was significant. I was a little scared of next month's credit card payment. I still hadn't thought of any way to convert valuables from the otherworld into yen.

After quickly paying for everything, cart still fully loaded, we moved to a space that was empty of people next to the restrooms. It would be a pain to get all the way back to the apartment like this, so we'd devised a way to go straight to the otherworld.

"Let's be off, then."

"Okay."

After making sure nobody was around and no surveillance cameras were on us, Peeps activated his magic. As the magic circle appeared under my feet, our surroundings shifted.

The destination was right next to the trading company I'd visited last night, in the middle of a small alley coming off the main one. It was only a little over a meter wide, so nobody ever came through here. Taking advantage, I exited the alley and headed for the trading company.

The sun was high in the sky, so if it wasn't a holiday, stores would be open. Peeps returned to my shoulder from the carrying case as well.

It was a ton of fun walking a supermarket shopping cart down a fantasy road. Many other people were pushing their things along in a similar way, so nobody would pay much attention to me just for the cart. We were able to get right to our destination—the trading company.

The guard in front of the entrance was an acquaintance at this point. After I asked him for the store's vice manager, he happily nodded. I was then shown back to the reception room I'd been in the day before.

"It's been a while, Mr. Sasaki. It's good to see you again."

"And thank you for responding to such an abrupt request, Mr. Marc."

It had only been a day for us, but for them, it had been almost a month. We took our seats on the sofas, which might have looked relaxed, but with the low table between us, I could feel a bit of a difference in enthusiasm. Apparently, he wasn't as carefree as I was today.

"Forgive me, but would I be able to see the goods right away?"

"Yes, by all means."

I didn't want to put on airs, so I got straight down to business.

I'd brought sugar and chocolate again at the vice manager's request. More, this time—twenty kilograms of each. The lower rack on the cart was filled with sugar and chocolate, as well as a few spices and seasonings, new this time.

The main part of the cart, however, was absolutely packed with new products. The one I particularly wanted to recommend was the calculator. They were cheap at a hundred yen a pop, but according to Peeps, the abacus was in its heyday over here, so they would likely be worth a lot. With their solar batteries, they could work for years without any maintenance, too—that would spice up the deal. It was a really good thing this world's number system was base ten. Not to mention they already understood the concept of zero.

However, our characters were different, so they would need to convert from one to the other. Their digits were similar to our Arabic numerals but still not quite the same. Peeps had said, though, that they only had ten numeric symbols, so it shouldn't prove that difficult for them. On our way here, the bird had been fiddling with one himself as we walked. Seeing a sparrow poke at the buttons with its feet and beak was the most adorable thing ever.

"How do these work?"

"I can't explain in detail, but they use very complicated mechanisms. It would take several years just to understand the principles—and even more to develop similar ones. You would need decades, at least, and vast amounts of capital."

"……"

The vice manager kept a stony silence as he looked at the calculator in his hand. By that, I could anticipate a high selling price. I had also only brought three. If I was told the abacus was more convenient and they had no use for the devices, I'd be in trouble, so I'd kept it to a minimum.

"How is it?"

"…Does two hundred gold coins sound fair to you?"

Whoa, I felt like the selling price just went way down. Last time, I'd gotten four hundred gold coins for my trouble.

"That is somewhat less than before, isn't it?"

"Oh, excuse me—I meant just for one of these."

"Ah, I see."

That was far higher than I'd ever imagined. I stole a glance at Peeps, who was sitting on my shoulder. I made out a very subtle nod from him—the price must have sounded good. It was a godsend, having a local to help me out.

"Understood. Two hundred will do."

"How many of these do you have with you, by the way?"

"I have three…"

"I will pay you in cash for all the goods you've brought today. In exchange, could I purchase all three calculators?"

"Yes, of course you can."

Judging by his reaction, calculators would be my biggest earners for a while. I'd have to search for more solar battery–powered electronics on the internet later.

"May I ask how many of these you have in stock right now?"

"Let me see…"

It wouldn't be good to stock so many of them that I crashed their market value. I wanted to assume as much of an air of importance about them as I could and maintain the price at two hundred gold coins apiece. I was thinking about one per house for nobles and leading merchants was a good standard. Probably best to limit my supply to ten per month in that case.

"I believe I can bring you ten more for our next trade."

"Excellent! I would very much love to purchase those as well."

"Understood, sir. I will be sure to prepare ten more."

"Thank you very much."

The vice manager's face was a full smile. Praise the heavens for calculators. Industrial goods like these seemed to sell for higher prices more easily than food-related products. I could keep costs to a minimum buying them, too, and they weren't bulky, making them effortless to deliver. Seemed to me like the direction for my future business had been decided.

*

Ultimately, this sale brought me a total of fifty large gold coins. Not only did the calculators add a ton of value, but I was also able to sell the sugar and chocolate at a stable price. On the other hand, the Teflon frying pans and peelers didn't do quite as well. I supposed it was important to go for items the nobles would want.

The vice manager also gave me some advice: Apparently, hunting was becoming quite a major hobby among the upper classes. Hobbies were, in essence, trees that grew money. Maybe advanced, high-cost outdoor equipment would do significantly well with them. As we went over things like that, Mr. Marc's reactions were so encouraging that it really got me thinking about everything. If only doing business at my actual workplace were this easy.

"By the way, about the eatery…"

With our deal concluded for now, the vice manager steered the conversation in another direction—one I was curious about, too.

"How is it doing?" I asked.

"We have prepared a nice plot of land on the main road. It isn't a very big shop, but it's in a relatively good location and costs about two hundred gold coins per month for rent. Combined with things like labor costs and stocking supplies, think of it as thirty per month."

"Did you have enough for the initial expenses?"

A plot of land on the main road? That sounded more luxurious than I'd imagined. When I had said "in the area," he must have taken that to mean the entire town. I was shocked. He'd apparently already prepared the place, so I couldn't ask him to put it somewhere else. It was all on me for delegating the matter wholesale to them.

"Yes, that was no issue. We created the shop using our own products, so we were able to finish it up somewhat more cheaply than would have been possible had we entrusted it to someone else. In the coming month, we'd like to use the budget you provided and start up operations."

Judging by his remarks, it seemed they were doing more than a little work for no pay. I mulled over his words, estimating the coming month's portion. I would have to indirectly thank him somehow.

"Thank you so much for going to all that trouble. I really appreciate everything you're doing for me."

"Don't worry about it. I am enjoying it, myself."

"I'm happy to hear that."

"Not to change the topic, but would you like to pay it a visit?"

"Yes, of course. If you please."

I'd actually wanted to check on how they were doing during my lunch break at my office but couldn't find a way to get Peeps into the building with me, so it had to wait. The difficulty of going to work with a sparrow was not to be underestimated.

I had the option of renting an apartment closer to the company, but thanks to rent in the city center being so awfully high, I couldn't afford it with my current income. More than a few ways to mitigate this likely existed, but none were being implemented. Really made you feel how entrenched land ownership was in this nation.

"Then allow me to ready a carriage. It shouldn't take more than a few moments."

"Thank you."

You're getting me a carriage? You're so generous, Vice Manager.

Come to think of it, what was I supposed to do with the supermarket shopping cart I'd brought without asking? This kind of thing was exactly why stores were so sensitive about how people treated their carts. I felt endlessly apologetic about it.

✳

A few rattles of the carriage later, and we'd arrived at our destination.

They seemed to have finished doing all the interior decorating, and the view of the shop from the road was neat and tidy. It was like a decked-out, foreign-owned coffee shop. Built entirely of stone, too, which gave it a very cool, retro atmosphere.

When the vice manager and I entered, we saw Mr. French in the kitchen.

"S-sir!"

When he noticed us, he came running up. We met halfway down the hallway. Several other people, probably the kitchen staff, were visible inside. This world seemed to have that "all cooks wear white aprons" rule, too, because every last person in the kitchen had on the same exact uniform.

"I apologize for my long absence," I said.

"No, don't trouble yourself, sir! You entrusted this wonderful shop to me, after all..."

"Have you decided on a grand opening date?"

"I talked it over with the vice manager, and we thought it best to discuss it with you first. I'm deciding on the menu myself, but I figured it would be best to consult you at some point, sir."

"I see." Nothing special really crossed my mind, though. Except for one thing. "You can feel free to do what you will with the menu. As long as you are respectful to the customers, I don't see any reason to restrict you at all. Still, I do have one request apart from all that."

"Wh-what would that be?"

"I'd like you to re-create some recipes I'll bring with me next time."

"You can cook, too, sir?"

"Think of it as a dish from my homeland."

"Oh, I can't wait!"

"How long do you think it will take to get the shop ready to open?"

"The kind folks at the trading company have been handling all the food procurement, so just say the word, and we could open the day after tomorrow. Hermann Trading Company has amazing influence. Buying things wholesale from them is like a dream!"

"I see."

In that case, I'd need to get some recipes together for my next visit. If he was somehow able to reproduce them, Peeps and I could eat delicious food without spending any Japanese yen. A Kobe beef chateaubriand might have been out of the question, but if there were any similar ingredients here, a comparable flavor was likely possible.

"Oh, but I can't really read, so…"

"I'll handle that, so don't worry about it."

"I'm sorry. Thank you."

I couldn't read or write this world's characters, either. I'd probably have to ask the vice manager for someone to help me out.

"Also, I have your pay for this past month. Here, take it."

I took two gold coins out of my pocket and handed them to the manager. In this world, the amount of money someone could make by working from morning until evening without having any special skills or expertise was said to be about a silver coin to two. Considering my hire's position as manager of this eatery, I quintupled that. Then assuming I'd been away from things for thirty days, that made three hundred silver coins. I added a little something extra to arrive at five gold coins total. That would probably suffice, right?

Still, compared to my interworld trade profits, the amount seemed very small. I couldn't help but feel bad about it. Considering I was still a novice in this otherworld, I couldn't quite grasp the value of money as locals saw it. That was something I'd have to solve step-by-step.

"Huh? Is—is this really okay?"

"In exchange, I want to leave everything about this shop completely in your hands in the future. If that sounds fair, would you accept it? I can promise the same amount from next month on, too."

"Are you sure, sir? I'm not; I'm just a—"

"Please, take it."

"…Sir."

It seemed like he hadn't been paid very much at the last restaurant. He'd worked his way up from an apprentice, after all, so maybe

everyone else had been taking him for granted. Single-manager busi-
nesses seemed to always be cutting corners.

"I'll work like my life depends on it!"

"...Thank you."

As I watched Mr. French bow, I couldn't help but compare him to a
certain corporate slave. It hit close to home.

What was labor, really?

I wondered what kind of answer Peeps would have for me if I asked
him that question.

*

After we'd checked on the restaurant, Peeps and I went outside the
town together.

It was time to practice magic.

Peeps used his teleportation spell to warp us from town into a
nearby wooded area. The plains surrounding the town were apparently enormous, and we'd come right to the edge of them. There were
zero people in the vicinity, of course. There, I recited the incantations
to try to learn the spells.

After a short while of repeating the same words over and over, Peeps
asked me a question.

"What do you stand to gain by setting up a restaurant in town?"

"Huh?"

"I don't remember it being in our initial plans."

"I figured it would be helpful for when you needed to eat."

"Then, you did it for me."

"It's the first step in indulging in this world's pleasures. I did want to
use this for myself as well, of course. Oh, and there was one more serious reason for it: because purchasing so much stuff is putting a strain
on my finances back home."

"Ah."

"I'd like to reduce expenditures by eating here."

"Hmm..."

Each meal by itself didn't cost very much, but they still added up.
Buying sugar and chocolate in kilograms was surprisingly expensive,
and I was already scraping against my credit card limit. I had to be
frugal where I could.

The time difference between the two worlds only made this more urgent. Still, that difference wasn't purely a disadvantage. Since one hour in that world was a day in this one, a corporate slave could spend time here in relaxation. Once Mr. French's restaurant got on track, we'd be one step closer to the relaxing life Peeps wanted.

"Oh, water came out!"

As we were talking, water burst from my outstretched palm like a fire hose.

The magic I was testing was a spell to produce water from nowhere. I'd recited the incantation a few dozen times and had finally managed to cast it.

Peeps had mentioned the water was drinkable, so I figured I'd prioritize this one. Water sprayed like tap water out of a broken faucet from the magic circle that had appeared in front of my palm. A fairly powerful spray, too.

Keeping it going would probably soak my boots, so I hastily stopped it.

"*You're learning these spells at a considerable pace.*"

"Thanks to you."

Normally, using magic spent something called mana, so beginners couldn't use spells dozens of times in the same day. But since Peeps had shared a staggering amount of mana with me, I was able to overcome this and keep on practicing without getting tired. Hence my marked improvement. In just two days, after learning the lighter spell, I'd acquired a second.

Still, I was getting nowhere with my main objective: the teleportation spell. Its difficulty truly seemed to be on a different level than beginner magic, like Peeps had said. That was why I was coming all the way out here to practice.

"Peeps, I want to learn the teleportation one next, if possible."

"*What is your fascination with that spell?*"

"It makes it easier to get to work. Right?"

"*Do you truly wish to go to this company of yours so badly?*"

"Well, no. I'd rather not, actually."

"*Then you don't wish to go?*"

"I suppose I don't, but it's more that I'd prefer to avoid those shaking, jam-packed trains. I'm sure you'd understand if you tried it—ah, but you might get squished in your current form…"

"*…Well, I suppose it doesn't matter.*"

After that, I practiced the teleportation spell at length. I asked

Peeps to use the spell on me several times so I could experience it, hoping to feed that experience back into my training. However, despite persisting in my efforts until the sun went down, I produced no particular results.

I knew the incantation forward and backward, but it seemed this road would be a long one.

*

That day, instead of returning to my apartment, I decided to stay the night. Our lodgings were notably high-class; I'd been told they were mainly used by nobles and wealthy merchants. I'd given the vice manager a ring beforehand, so I was able to check in without much effort. A two-day, one-night stay with three meals would cost one gold coin.

"*Not a bad room.*"

"It's amazing…"

The place must have been over a hundred square meters. Aside from a master bedroom, there was a living space, plus separate rooms for the toilet and bath. Though I could see slight differences, it was almost the same as a hotel room in my world. The furnishings were expensive-looking, too, including the bed and the sofa set.

If I found a room like this in the city, one night in it would cost six digits in yen.

The rooms here all had their own private maid, too, who would see to the needs of whoever was staying there. She had introduced herself when I'd arrived—a very cute girl, apparently in her midteens. Right now, she was in a space close to the room's entrance made for her to wait until needed.

I hadn't figured out if she was an attendant or a companion. Peeps was with me, so I was reluctant to start anything like that. And I would rather pass on making a mistake and contracting a sexually transmitted disease.

A few years back, a superior at work had taken me to a brothel, and I'd picked up a case of chlamydia. After going through treatment, I decided I'd had more than my fill. If the alternative was going through such a wretched, painful experience again, I was fine with my right hand as my lover for the rest of my days.

According to some statistics I'd looked up afterward, among female high school students with sexual experience, one in eight had chlamydia; the ratio was three in ten for those age eighteen to nineteen.

Most of them apparently didn't even realize it. Incidentally, the ratio for male high school students was one in sixteen.

"Peeps, I want to live here forever."

"Go ahead. I'll accompany you."

"But we need to make money in my world to keep stocking goods."

"...No prospects for promotion, then?"

"Not at the moment. My pay hasn't gone up a yen in the last five years..."

"I see..."

Never thought the day would come when a pet Java sparrow would be badgering me to get a promotion. I'd heard nice-sounding stories about other companies and how they held evaluations for promotions anywhere from every few months to every year. My dead-end, midsize company, however, offered almost no opportunities to move up the ranks. The only ones who got raises were the managers' relatives.

My coworker's assertion that he'd quit next month and go independent was seeming more and more like the right choice. If it worked out for him, then I should probably follow his example and look for greener pastures myself. Unfortunately, given my skill set, the only jobs available paid less than what I was getting now.

My colleague had invited me to his independent start-up, but I didn't have the guts to give a response. I knew myself best. Maybe it would be different if I had a job in mechanical design or programming or something.

"Isn't there some way to make money over there?"

Sinking into the soft, fluffy sofa, I racked my brain. Peeps hopped off my shoulder and onto the low table in front of me.

"There is a spell called Charm. It charms a person to make them do as you bid them. However, a single Charm will only be effective for a few months at most, and their memories will persist even after it wears off. Would it be possible to solve the problem using this?"

"That's something to consider. But if we went for it, we'd need someone else to stand in for us. Or else we'd have to keep charming every single person we ever dealt with, forever."

The former idea would be to buy and sell valuable goods under another person's name to simply get the money from the sales. Or perhaps we could falsify a store's books. Either way, the person or pawnbroker whose name I borrowed, as well as whoever I asked for help using the money I got to keep stocking goods—in other words, all the targets of Charm—would be in deep trouble afterward. If I didn't care about said string of abuses, then maybe it was an excellent plan. Charm could wear off once the people had been arrested and their crimes proven without any issue. Without evidence, avoiding the false charges would be impossible. Basically, they'd be the disposable cell phones mooks used for scam calls.

The latter idea, on the other hand, had a way to protect Charm's victims. However, the number of targets necessary to Charm would keep on increasing, one after the other as time went on, so it didn't feel like a very realistic plan.

"With the second idea, the duration being only a few months would be the bottleneck. Ultimately, we'd have nobody but people we'd charmed around us, and we'd lose track of everything, wouldn't we? I can't help feeling like we would. And it might lead to the magic itself being exposed."

"*As you say, there are some who use Charm on too many targets and bring about their own ruin.*"

"Yeah, I thought so."

"*Why not charm a government official directly instead?*"

"The short version is that you can fool people, but you can't make it so the money never changed hands. False records are still records kept. And if there was anything suspicious in their books, it would be caught, and in the end, someone would have a fine dropped in their lap."

"*Which would force you to Charm other targets whether you wished it or not.*"

"I think so, yeah."

I didn't want to risk it if, the moment the spell's effects ended, I'd be hounded by additional taxes or criminal charges. No matter how much I wanted to build a place for myself in this world, my home would always be modern Japan. My position here was dependent on my life back home. I wanted to make my fortune peacefully and without anyone finding out, though I knew this was me being greedy.

"Still, I have solved part of the stocking issue."

"*Have you?*"

"If you use your teleportation to bring us to another country and buy goods there, in local currency, we could probably get away with it. Japan monitors visitors entering and exiting very closely, so if we just carry the goods straight to the otherworld, I doubt they'd catch on."

"*Then outside the country, you can make it so the money never changed hands?*"

"There are other issues with the idea, so it might take some time to figure out—like whether I'd have to disguise myself, for example. We'd also have to exchange for foreign currency. Still, I'm pretty sure we wouldn't have the tax office fishing around for us."

"*In that case, you could buy and sell precious metals overseas.*"

If there was any other problem, it was that I couldn't speak English. Peeps had gotten straight to the painful heart of the matter. "I certainly don't think it's impossible."

"*Truly?*"

"Unfortunately, I can't speak any foreign languages. I could maybe buy products at a local supermarket, but I wouldn't have the connections or skills to sell valuables of dubious origin. Nine times out of ten, the local police would arrest me."

"*...I see.*"

It would be best if we could start with untrustworthy currency and, in a roundabout way, convert it into foreign currency. But I was pretty sure I'd need some language abilities under my belt for that. But if I was able to make that sort of stable system, wouldn't that be a business of its own?

If I was able to pull it off, I had a feeling something even scarier than the Japanese tax office would be chasing me.

"Could I have some more time to think about it?"

"*I'll read up on the workings of your world as well.*"

"Thanks. I knew I could depend on you."

The more I thought about it, the more I realized how well put together money-related systems were in my world.

And so with a bit of this and that, the day passed.

*

After practicing magic for a few days in the otherworld, we returned to my apartment.

I'd been able to dedicate a big chunk of time to my studies, so I'd been able to learn several spells. Most were, according to Peeps, made for beginners. After the lighter spell and the faucet spell, I'd kept going, acquiring a spell that shot icicles, one that made the ground ripple, and another that shot a fireball.

Even those were apparently meant to be learned over several months or even years. Perhaps that was why I was feeling rather good about myself at the moment. However, I still had no prospects for the going-to-work spell. I really wanted to get that one quickly.

And so the next day, I went back to work.

It was a refreshing experience, thanks to Peeps—I skipped the loaded trains and ate breakfast at a beef bowl chain near the company before going to the office. A big part of it was having taken multiple days off in the otherworld.

"Anything good happen lately, Mr. Sasaki?"

As I was doing some clerical work at my desk, my coworker spoke up from the next seat over. Apparently, it was written all over my face.

"No? Not in particular," I said.

"You just seemed like you were in a good mood."

"I bought a new bed, so maybe I slept better."

"I see. That's excellent."

Compared to my tiny pipe-frame bed, the one I used while staying in the otherworld had been wonderful. I could stretch my arms and legs and still not reach the edges—that was how big it was. And so soft, too. Plus, the private maid changed the sheets every day.

Because of that, when I had gone to bed in my apartment last night, I'd really started to feel how cramped my room was. My body was getting more and more used to a luxurious lifestyle. I'd even started to consider not just eating over there but sleeping as well.

"Oh, right. Mr. Sasaki, are you coming to the company drinking party next week?"

"Actually, my finances are a little strained at the moment…"

"If you go, I'll go, too."

"I'm sorry— I just can't make any promises."

"Oh…"

My budget was incredibly tight now that I was stocking up goods for the Hermann Trading Company. I was quite sure I had no spare cash to attend the company's drinking party. Not having secured a way to make money here was quickly getting me in over my head.

"Heeey, Sasaki! About the school thing…"

"Yes, sir! I'll be right there."

Whoops, the section chief just called. I bowed to my coworker and rose from my seat.

I'd put my best into my job today—but in moderation.

✳

After finishing work, I set out for the superstore near my apartment to stock up, like always.

One day in this world corresponded to several weeks in the other. I couldn't afford to miss a single supply run. I already had a surplus of over a thousand gold coins, but keeping my relationship with the vice manager affable necessitated stocking up regularly. And I planned to go there with Peeps again today.

Like last time, I had him get into the outdoor carrying case. When I asked if it was comfortable, he responded that it was neither comfortable nor uncomfortable. I figured we'd keep using the case when going out together for the time being.

It was just after we stepped out the front door of the apartment.

"Good evening, mister."

I immediately heard a familiar voice right next to me. I directed my attention toward the source where I found my neighbor, sitting up against her front door, hands around her knees.

"Wait, is she still not home?"

The lights had been on in their apartment already when I'd returned from work. I'd thought for sure her mom had gotten back. So it seemed strange, seeing her sitting alone at the front door like this.

But her next words made everything clear. "She brought a man over."

"Ah…"

Was this her showing a modicum of parental concern, or did she just not want her daughter getting in the way? The reason was unclear, but whenever her mother brought a man to the apartment, as a rule, the girl would get kicked out. It was a scene I'd witnessed more than a few times before.

"By the way, can you drink black coffee?"

"…Yes."

Remembering something, I plucked my wallet from my pocket. Buried in between the receipts was a coupon to get a free can of coffee at the nearby convenience store. They'd held a lottery as a one-time service for any customer who bought more than seven hundred yen's worth of items, and I'd won it as a prize. I'd been saving it for something like this.

I held it out to her with the side labeled ONE FREE PRODUCT faceup. I'd checked the expiration date on it last night, so it should have been fine.

"It has a place to sit and eat inside."

"……" It seemed like this was her first time seeing such a thing. She stared at the paper.

In the past, I'd tried to give her cash and the like several times. It was more convenient and would put me at ease since I'd have to interact with her less often. Besides, if I gave her food, it might be some time before she got around to eating it, by which point it might have gone bad, upsetting her stomach.

But she stubbornly refused to accept any money. She'd probably set a hard rule against it. It did make things more difficult for me, but I wanted to honor her pride. Which meant that little things like these came in handy.

"Are you sure?"

"I've been avoiding black coffee lately—it gives me indigestion."

"It does?"

"Tossing it would be a waste, so will you take it?"

"……"

After thinking about it for a moment, she took the coupon apologetically. It would give her something to do until her mom finished her private business.

∗

Parting ways with my neighbor, we headed for the superstore as originally planned. We looked high and low, pushing our clattering cart all the while. Peeps rode on the cart like last night, tucked away nice and safe in his carrying case.

"What will you stock today?"

"I heard hunting was popular among the nobles."

"Indeed. It would be akin to golf in this world."

"You've really been studying hard, haven't you?"

"You are letting me use this 'internet,' after all."

As he said, I'd given him access to the computer in my apartment. Which was, naturally, connected to the internet. He was small, but using magic, he employed a magical creature called a golem to elegantly work the keyboard and mouse. I'd told him about a certain internet dictionary, so he had probably been perusing it all day long.

Magic of the sort that allowed one to go back and forth between worlds was apparently quite the ordeal. Though Peeps couldn't use that spell on his own, the one for creating a golem was relatively easy. No support from this corporate slave needed.

To create the golem, he'd used some dirt from the land on which the apartment building was built. At Peeps's suggestion, I went to check and found about two buckets' worth of dirt missing from beside the concrete block wall. Needless to say, I was more than a little surprised to find a strange automaton moving around my room.

"Right, so I wanted to stock up on some outdoor equipment they could use for hunting."

"You have an eye for this. You are sure to get a good deal for them."

Yay, Peeps gave me a compliment! If he's right, I can relax and just stock up.

The vice manager had once again requested sugar and chocolate. Sugar was fairly cheap, so that wasn't a problem, but purchasing chocolate retail got surprisingly expensive. I decided I'd deal with the problem by getting less chocolate for now and making up for it with more sugar. That left the goods I had promised specific amounts of, beginning with the calculators.

"I wonder how this would be?"

"What is it?"

"A small version of a telescope."

"Oh yes. That is likely to sell for a fair sum."

Apparently, the otherworld had telescopes and other similar items. Peeps gave a sparkling appraisal, so without further ado, I threw them in the cart. They weren't very expensive, so I could get more than one—I tossed in a few more. If they got good reviews, I could maybe buy some more advanced ones off the internet. But for that, I'd need a way to raise money in this world.

"By the way."

"What?"

"What is that metallic object? It looks awfully busy."

"Huh? Oh, that's a Swiss Army knife."

"A Swiss Army knife?"

"It's a knife with a bunch of stuff attached, like scissors, tweezers, and a bottle opener."

"It contains much despite its diminutive size."

"Well, we might as well grab one."

They were a bit pricey, but they sure looked impressive, so I decided to buy a few. It wasn't like anyone in that world would know what Switzerland was, so I doubted calling it that would cause an issue. I'd heard the really good ones had fifty or sixty tools attached. It was lunacy.

"*I'd also like a nice, wooden tree for my cage in your apartment. My claws have grown long.*"

"You can't make do with the plastic one you've got now?"

"*No, evidently not. I did research on the internet and found that Java sparrows cannot sharpen their claws using plastic trees. A wooden tree would seem to be the solution.*"

"I didn't know that. I'm sorry I bought you all that cheap stuff."

"*I only just learned of it myself. Do not worry about it.*"

"There's a pet aisle over that way, so let's look for one."

"*Yes.*"

I was very pleased to have a pet who could manage and report on the state of his own health. What a smart bird he was.

And just like that, same as last night, I filled the cart with all manner of items. Naturally, I racked up a considerable bill, as before. *If I keep on shopping like this, won't my savings hit rock bottom very quickly?*

*

After we finished stocking up and went back to the apartment, we headed to the otherworld. Peeps's spell took care of the interworld transportation.

We arrived in an extremely average room—the kind where commoners would normally stay. I'd paid its rent for the next few months, making it our base for moving between worlds. It eliminated the risk of someone witnessing the teleportation and getting suspicious.

It would also allow us to bring several shipments over, meaning I could bring more than just ten kilograms of sugar—I could get twenty or even thirty here at once. Because they sold for a high price compared to their low initial cost, they seemed set to become my main product for the time being.

Now in the otherworld, we went straight to pay the vice manager a visit. At the Hermann Trading Company, we entered the reception room and got down to business.

"Mr. Sasaki, you could sell this to the nobility."

"I'm glad to hear that."

"Viscount Müller, who controls this city, also enjoys a good hunt."

The load of items I'd bought were lined up on the table for our deal. I was getting the feeling my guesses had been right on the mark.

"I see. Thank you for the information."

"These were called binoculars and Swiss Army knives, right? I would think they'd be very useful in battle as well as for hunting. If you don't mind, my idea is to create similar items here at the company and sell them ourselves."

"Oh, you can go right ahead."

I never planned to prohibit imitation products. From what Peeps had told me, there was no patent-like system over here, so it wouldn't be possible to restrict them anyway. I could struggle all I wanted, but these wares were fated to be copied. The only exception would be a monopoly approved by the state, be it official or unofficial.

Either way, it would require organizational backing, so I gave up on that. Even with the strong framework of patents back home, modern society overflowed with bootleg products. Given this world's culture and civilization, it was really too much to ask. Instead, I'd been choosing things that were hard to copy.

Also, even assuming one of them *was* copied, there was a limit to the level of quality this world could produce. That made me think strategic branding was in the cards—I could provide higher quality and thus more expensive goods, bringing the value of those products up in general.

"In that case, will you not need them in my next delivery?"

"No, no, that isn't what I meant!"

"Oh?"

"And we'll promise you twenty percent—no, thirty percent of the profits on the imitations."

"Well, thank you."

Still, though, I'd figured it was a waste to simply nod and agree, so I acted a little grumpy about it. And what do you know, it seemed I'd be getting a better deal than expected. I'd wanted to discuss the sale price if possible, but since manufactured goods were so expensive here, it would be difficult to set a base price when I didn't know how much they would cost to manufacture in the first place.

Mr. Marc seemed to have no intention of deceiving me, either, so I decided to simply agree then and there. Peeps hadn't shown any particular reaction, so I assumed that meant the arrangement was suitable.

"Regarding this deal in its entirety," he went on, "the total price we've discussed comes to twenty-five hundred gold coins—but actually, since we will be studying them to our profit, would twenty-six hundred be amenable? I would pay in cash."

"Yes, that works just fine."

My total sales had risen even higher than last time. It was probably the outdoor goods being so attractive to him, though the fifty kilograms of sugar I'd brought no doubt helped. Combined with the sales from last time, I now had over four thousand gold coins in my pocket.

Since it cost one gold coin for a night and three meals at my previous lodgings, and assuming three hundred sixty-five days in a year, I could spend the next ten years here without working, doing nothing but eating and sleeping. Articulating it that way made it seem like a *very* charming prospect.

"There is one other thing I'd like to ask of you, Mr. Sasaki."

"What is it?"

"I have been entrusted with a message from Viscount Müller."

"A message?"

Oh-ho—it appeared a noble finally wanted to talk to me.

The name of this personage of interest was Müller. Casually glancing at Peeps, I made out a small nod. This was definitely the person he was after. Personally, I was fine just doing business with the vice manager, but if a noble willed it, I could only obey. Being on good terms with a noble would likely be a merit unto itself.

"He says he wishes to meet and speak with you."

"I see. In that case, I would be happy to oblige."

"Ah, then you'll accept?"

And so I ended up in a meeting with the town's bigwigs—just like we'd planned from the start.

*

We spent the first night of our stay at an inn. The next day, we paid a visit to Viscount Müller's castle. A carriage came all the way to our lodgings to pick us up, too. It seemed the vice manager had contacted the viscount in advance and relayed the name of our inn. As a result, we had no trouble finding our way.

In any case, we were shown to the castle's audience chamber. The vice manager and I stood side by side before the viscount, who sat in the highest seat. We were kneeling on the floor and bowing our heads.

Many others had congregated in the room as well—apparently nobles—and were lined up against each wall. It all looked exactly like the throne room you'd see in a fantasy video game. I'd imagined our host would come off more like a petty official given his low rank of viscount, but that wasn't the case at all.

Also, aside from the other nobles—who were essentially observers—several others stood around the room. They looked like knights, with swords in hand. And boy, were they glaring daggers at us. I felt like they'd come running at us if I so much as sneezed.

If this was how a viscount did things, what would a king be like? Just thinking about it terrified me.

"It is good that you have come."

I'd asked the vice manager's assistance in communicating with Viscount Müller. I had no clue about any of this world's standards of courtesy or etiquette. It was all I could do to just keep my head bowed in accordance with the instructions I'd received earlier.

"You may lift your heads."

"Yes, my lord!"

With a short response, the vice manager looked up. I followed his lead and returned my head to its previous posture.

"Is this the Sasaki we discussed?"

"That is correct, my lord."

The vice manager's voice rang through the room.

With that, I sensed the attention of everyone assembled there focusing on me. I felt like I'd turned into a panda in the zoo. The fact that my skin color, hair color, and features were all different was probably only making them even more curious.

"I have heard he deals in items that are quite delicately made."

"We have brought some along with us today, my lord."

"I see. I would very much like to see them."

Viscount Müller raised his voice. Two of the knights who had been waiting in the chamber moved. Between them, they carried a gorgeous pedestal bordered with gold. They lumbered over and placed it before the chair on which the viscount perched. Atop it was an assortment of items we'd given them in advance.

"What is this one called?"

"My lord. That one is…"

Among the objects on the pedestal, the viscount had picked up the Swiss Army knife. From that point on, the vice manager explained what everything was. Incidentally, these were all products already purchased by the Hermann Trading Company. According to the vice manager, it wouldn't have been possible for some nobody merchant like me to bring them straight here.

I supposed that made him sort of like a guarantor. He'd said that if things chanced to go extremely poorly, it would be his head on the chopping block, literally. Wasn't that a horrifying prospect? It seemed wise to be even more particular about the products I brought in the future. I couldn't afford to bring something like surströmming, even as a joke.

Once the vice manager had finished his round of explanations, the viscount spoke to me.

"Your name was Sasaki, yes? I had a question for you."

"Yes, my lord. What is it?"

This was the first chance I'd gotten to speak since setting foot in this place. Naturally, I was incredibly nervous.

"I have heard that you came from another continent. Is this correct?"

"It is, my lord."

I wasn't lying. It was probably safe enough. I'd explained the calculator numbers as being from that culture as well.

"Then allow me to ask you this. Do items like this regularly circulate in common markets on this other continent? Or are they special products, the sort that only a select few, such as the nobility in this country, would possess?"

Viscount Müller's concerns were reasonable. I had no idea how far away other continents were from this one, nor if it was even possible to travel between them. However, I could easily tell he was afraid of outside invaders.

"Only a select few possess these goods, my lord."

"Truly? Then, naturally, that would make you a man of high status in your own right. What of that? You may be from another continent, but I have misgivings about one-sidedly dealing with a noble or someone with equal status."

Upon hearing the viscount's words, the vice manager shuddered next to me. He seemed surprised at the revelation. If I pretended to possess too high a status, then if there was ever a chance to meet those from the next continent, my lie would be exposed, and that would probably be a disaster. Status fraud came with many kinds of punishments in Japan, too. I decided it would be best to settle on a suitable rank.

"I am a craftsman, my lord. I had left for a voyage on the sea before shipwrecking and drifting to this continent. The goods I've brought today are the ones I had with me as well as ones I have newly made."

"I see— So you are a craftsman."

Internally, I was distressed. What if he asked me where I was making them? I'd never been this nervous even speaking to our best customers at the company. It was mainly the knights waiting behind the viscount who scared me. I mean, they had swords and everything.

"Do you plan on working in this town for the moment?"

"Yes, my lord, if it so pleases you."

I didn't want to carelessly move to another town and fall victim to a bad government. I got the feeling such environments were relatively common. The lord of this territory—Viscount Müller in front of me— was good-natured enough, according to Peeps. I wanted to be in his care for the time being.

"Do you intend to sell your wares wholesale to the Hermann Trading Company?"

"I do, my lord."

"Then, in the future, when you sell to the Hermann Trading Company, you will also make a contribution to me. I will purchase them for a slight increase on top of what the company pays. Depending on the usage of the items you bring, they may greatly affect our lives."

"Understood, my lord."

"Henceforth, you are permitted to enter this mansion. If, while living in this town, you notice anything strange or strike upon anything that could benefit my territory, report it to me when you bring me your wares. I will also spread your name to the others of my house."

"You do me a great honor, my lord."

And with that, our conversation with Viscount Müller came to an end.

I felt better about how it went than I'd expected. I'd successfully gained a noble connection, just as I'd discussed with Peeps. Still, I could hear envy-laced mutterings from the other nobles who had congregated involving phrases like "just a commoner," so I knew I'd have to be on my guard when entering and exiting the mansion.

Additionally—and this I heard from the vice manager later— different viscounts would actually be higher or lower in status than one another. It was like a massive corporation, with head section managers and senior managers. This world probably had too many higher-ups for its own good, just like mine.

And the viscount who ruled this town was in a relatively high position compared to others.

＊

With the audience over and done with, we headed straight for the town's restaurant quarter to check on the store I'd left in Mr. French's hands last time. The vice manager said he had things to take care of at the castle, so just Peeps and I visited. He was probably still listening to Viscount Müller and working out other administrative tasks.

They'd provided us a carriage from the castle again, just like when we'd traveled there. The shop wasn't terribly far, but with my still-shaky understanding of the town's layout, I decided to gratefully accept the generosity. The vice manager had told the driver our destination—everything was done for us.

And so we arrived at our destination. Saying my thanks to the driver, I climbed off the carriage.

Today marked my second visit. I was apologetic to Mr. French for pushing everything on him, but I didn't really want to work in this world, *too*. I'd returned with the intention to at least pay him enough to make the venture worth his while.

When we entered, we saw a good number of customers inside. About 30 percent appeared to be nobles. They wore cloaks around their shoulders and expensive-looking accessories on their bodies. The rest appeared to be commoners, but most of them were of proper appearance. It seemed this shop's clientele had become comparatively upper-class.

"Ah, sir!"

I walked through the shop, heading for the kitchen. Upon doing so, I ran into a familiar face.

"Hello. It's good to see you again."

Mr. French, who was holding a knife, ran to me when he noticed me. I could see other staff members nearby—they seemed to be people he'd hired. Seeing the strange foreign man come in, they all stopped what they were doing and bowed to me. It seemed he'd already told everyone in his establishment about me.

After mildly telling them they could go back to work and didn't have to worry, I turned back to face Mr. French again. "I'm sorry for leaving you by yourself. How have things been?"

"Thanks to you, the shop is running smoothly. With the help of the vice manager from the Hermann Trading Company, we've been able to turn a profit from the first month. As you can see, even at this hour, our seats are filled, and we have reservations going forward quite a while."

"Wow—that is amazing."

"We tried using the chocolate and sugar you brought to make sweets, and now it seems like they've become our main draw. Of course, they say our regular meals are delicious, too."

The reason they were flourishing seemed to be the sugar and chocolate.

Having one star offering, the kind you'd put front and center in an ad, was the key to a restaurant's success, after all. As a shop, it was a little small, but the location was great, which surely helped. However, I never thought they'd end up being a reservation-only place.

"I brought the recipes I mentioned last time."

"Really? Thank you so much!"

I'd handwritten a bunch of recipes on printer paper, then stapled them together. It was a collaboration between Peeps and me. I'd checked recipe videos in my world and added a few minor points to them, then Peeps used a golem to put everything together in the local tongue.

Peeps was actually the one who decided what should be included, mainly things he wanted to eat. Wouldn't that mean we could eat my world's food here the next time we visited?

"Do you have any staffers who can read?"

"The one the Hermann Trading Company introduced can."

"Then please have them read it for you."

I handed the recipes to Mr. French. He took them reverently, like a student receiving his diploma or something.

"Also, here is your pay for this month."

"Huh?!"

Finding some cover so the rest of the staff didn't see, I held out about ten gold coins. I'd given him five before, so he'd just gotten a raise that doubled his pay in a single month. The exchange made me wish my company was as aggressive with promotions.

"Please, take it."

"No, I—I can't—"

"It's thanks for getting this shop on course."

Mr. French immediately began getting flustered. Acting that conspicuous would draw strange looks from the nearby staff. I didn't know how much anyone else here was working for, so having this get out would be a pain.

"I'll put it right here."

I tucked the coins into his apron's front pocket.

"Wait…"

"Please look after the shop like you've been doing. If you have need of additional equipment or anything, just tell the vice manager. I've already notified him about it—and the recipes as well."

"…I-I'll do my best!"

"Thank you."

The restaurant was packed, and if I stayed too long, it would bother the customers. For today, I decided to take my leave.

∗

Leaving the shop behind us, we headed for outside of town to practice magic. We used the same spot as last time—the outskirts of the plains surrounding the town, right next to a forest. Peeps had been kind enough to use his magic to get us here.

Then for a few days, while going back and forth between there and our lodgings in town, I practiced magic.

When I wasn't eating, sleeping, or bathing, I spent all day practicing, and I had managed to learn several more spells this time. Plus, I'd figured out how to cast the lighter magic and faucet magic I'd learned before without even chanting.

"You are progressing very quickly…"

"Really?"

"Yes. Perhaps even more than I. It is slightly vexing."

"I think that may be going a little far."

"No, it certainly isn't. You must be quite talented with the handling of mental images, though this is just my own thought on the matter. If you keep learning at this rate, you may be able to get to intermediate-level magic in the near future."

"I see."

Apparently, magic was categorized in several different difficulties— beginner, intermediate, advanced, and the really dangerous stuff above that. The last was a very loosely defined category, as the sheer span of spells above advanced was enormous, and so few people could actually use them that they generally were never even talked about.

All the spells I'd learned thus far had been beginner ones. The teleportation spell, though, was part of that "really dangerous stuff." It took so much mana to use that few ever learned it. Naturally, after hearing that, I was worried—but Peeps said the mana he was supplying would be enough.

"It's a lot of work memorizing the incantations, though..."

The number of spells I could use had been rapidly increasing, and keeping the incantations straight had become troublesome. I'd have to learn how to use the simple spells without reciting their incantations at an early stage, or else they'd turn into a complete jumble when I tried to learn more. I got incantations wrong several times during practice, too, causing my spells to bomb.

"Why not simply bring your grimoire and use that?"

"My grimoire?"

"Haven't you been writing the incantations down?"

"Huh? That's what a grimoire is?"

"Yes."

"Well, that's surprisingly simple."

I'd imagined a grimoire as more like... It would increase your mana when you held it—or something. The level of disappointment I felt at knowing a bunch of sheets of printer paper could be a grimoire was massive. Anyone else would have looked at that and seen an elementary or middle school kid fooling around, playing wizard.

"Many of the grimoires in this world have magic stones and magic circles embedded in them in addition to the incantations. It is possible to use one such grimoire to increase the power of magic. Grimoire *refers to all of them as a single group."*

"I see."

It looked like what I was imagining existed, too. Hearing that made me suddenly remember something the vice manager had told me— the printer paper and ballpoint pens would sell like hotcakes with magic users. Now I could easily understand why. They were probably using them to make grimoires.

Not only was the paper I brought thinner than this world's, it was also of higher quality. I bet it was handy for those who wanted to carry around a whole bunch of incantations. In that case, if I brought thick, unlined notebooks and sturdy leather covers to put on them, they could sell for a high price. I'd have to check on it the next chance I got.

"I'm thinking it's time to wrap things up for now."

"Hmm. I see."

"My biggest achievement was learning healing magic, I think."

I could cure wounds, as long as they were small scrapes and such. At higher levels, I would actually be able to regrow severed limbs. Beyond that, apparently healing magic could deal with most problems affecting the human body, such as disease and whatnot.

"Despite the high demand for healing magic, few are able to learn it. I'm treating the spell you learned as a beginner spell, but one could view it as intermediate given the degree of difficulty. Because of this, you should be careful when using it."

"I see."

I got the feeling I could make a lot of money using healing magic in modern times, maybe by starting a religion geared toward older, powerful folk. Still, secondhand religious corporations had been on the rise in recent years, which would make it difficult as a source of small-time cash.

Other than the healing magic, I'd learned a spell to shoot fire arrows, one to make objects float, another to create a gust of wind, and one to create light. Combined with those I'd learned last time, that made ten. It felt like a nice beginner magician's set of magic to me.

Each of the spells apparently had a version that was more difficult that corresponded to it. As Peeps had said, some of them would naturally be categorized as intermediate. I figured I could start learning them next time. It was way more fun than studying bookkeeping.

"The sun is setting anyway, so let's go back, Peeps."

"I would like meat for dinner."

"Didn't you just have meat yesterday?"

"I like meat."

"You sure eat a lot even though you're so small, Peeps."

"Is that bad?"

"No, I'm just a little surprised…"

"Then make more and more money and give me even better meat."

"Well, how can I say no to my adorable birdie?"

"That's the spirit."

With Peeps's magic, we returned to our lodgings. After taking dinner in the attached dining room, I slept the night away in a vast bed before returning to our apartment. We'd kept careful track of what time we came and went this time so that, upon returning to Japan, there would be a little under an hour before I had to go to work.

For the time being, it seemed I wouldn't have much chance to use my pipe-frame bed. My relaxing life in another world was really getting started now, apparently. And I felt kind of like... You know. Like the main character of a role-playing game who was fully geared and carrying as many healing items as he could. I'd gotten my level pretty high, too. Now I'd just have to follow the strategy guide, defeat the last boss, and take down the secret boss. Maybe I could even livestream it on a video website.

That was how I felt.

\<Encounters with Psychics\>

With several days of otherworldly vacation at an end, it was time to resume my life as a corporate slave.

I'd spent this particular day visiting clients with the section chief. Though autumn had deepened, and it had gotten quite a bit cooler out, it was still hard work taking the train to a million different places. To make matters worse, an annoying event always occurred after this type of tour: a company drinking party.

"All right, Sasaki. Let's get those drinks."

Once we'd finished greeting our last client, we left their offices.

Not a moment later, the section chief started in, a smile lighting up his face.

"…Um, Chief?"

"What is it? It's getting chilly, so how about some giblet hot pot?"

The man would turn fifty-six this year. He loved going out drinking after making the rounds with his clients. Everyone under him hated getting caught up with this and respectfully kept their distance. This time, it had fallen to me to accompany him.

"I bought a pet last weekend, and my finances are really tight—I can't afford a stick of yakitori from the convenience store, much less giblet hot pot. I'm really sorry, since you took the time to invite me, but could you let me off the hook this time?"

"What? You started raising a pet?"

"Yes, sir."

"I've got a dog of my own. Pets sure are great, huh?"

"Wait. You have a dog, Chief?"

"Yeah. It's a golden retriever—pretty big one, too. He was a tiny little thing when I first got him, but next thing I knew, he'd gotten gigantic. It's hard for me to even play with him now. If he jumped on me, my body wouldn't hold out."

"……"

Are you serious? This was the first time I'd heard the section chief had a golden retriever. I couldn't possibly be more envious. That's the greatest pupper of them all—the kind I've always wanted.

And it would jump on him to play? That meant the dog loved him, didn't it? Again, I couldn't be more envious. I wanted to be jumped on by a golden retriever I'd raised from a puppy. I was sure it would be an experience of pure bliss.

Peeps was cute, too, but he didn't quite have the same *mass* to him. You know—like, he had a smaller presence, if that's a thing.

"We got him because my daughter just had to have one, but I'm the one who ended up with all the responsibilities. For the last two or three years, I've been taking him for a walk every day after coming home from work. Solved my lack of exercise right off, and all the red marks disappeared from my medical exams last year."

"……"

"What's the matter, Sasaki?"

"Would you be able to, say, treat me to the giblet hot pot? I'd like to hear more about your dog."

"What? Did you get a dog of your own?"

"No, I actually got a Java sparrow."

"A bird? Birds are great, too. I used to feed the crows in the neighborhood as a kid. It was so much fun. All right, fine, you talked me into it. Today's my treat. You're the one who works hardest in my section, after all."

"Thank you so much."

Pet conversations at the bar—it sounded pretty good. Plus, my superior would be treating me. The guy wasn't so bad, after all. I'd use the opportunity to learn things in preparation for the future.

✳

I drank with the chief for about two hours. It wasn't until a little after nine that we headed out and said our good-byes.

Since the last client was relatively close to my apartment—only two stations away—I decided to walk home instead of catching a train. The chief had said you needed quite a bit of stamina to walk puppies, so this was to prepare for the days yet to come.

The chilly wind tickled my cheeks, sobering me up. I could still go around in a light jacket, but soon enough, I'd need a coat. With Peeps's magic helping me out, I felt like I could easily forget to bring one when I went to work—a scary thought. Maybe I'd have to keep a spare at the office.

"......"

Come to think of it, how did the seasons work in the otherworld? If the temperature changed the same as it did here, wouldn't nice, fluffy winter clothing fetch a pretty high price? Clothes was already expensive, so cheap synthetic fiber goods would probably work great.

"......"

I kept walking down the mostly empty street lost in thought.

When I was about halfway back home, I suddenly heard a shrill screech.

The sound had come from an alley perpendicular to the road on which I was walking. It was only a few meters wide—one of those tiny spaces wedged between two buildings. *Construction work, maybe?* While I walked, I peered into the alley's depths.

A moment later, something passed right in front of my eyes. Several strands of my hair, which had floated into the air, were severed and blown away.

I heard a grunt—then a few moments later, a loud impact.

When I turned to look at where *that* had come from, I saw several icicles, around thirty centimeters long, stabbed into the asphalt. They had whipped past me like bullets.

There was no mistaking it—this was magic.

In a fluster, I looked to where they had originated and saw two figures. One was a man, the other a woman.

The former was young and seemed to be in his late teens, wearing sweatpants and a sweatshirt. His somewhat long blond hair was striking, all pushed back. From his appearance and skin color, I assumed his hair was bleached. He looked like the local delinquent type.

The latter, however, was a lady, probably in her early twenties, wearing a suit. Her short skirt—and the thighs peeking out from under it—were charming. Her features were a little stern, her eyes almond-shaped. Combined with her short black hair, she had the air of an office assistant. She was also wearing thick makeup.

Of particular note were their relative positions. The man was strad-
dling the lady, who was lying faceup on the ground. And for whatever
reason, the man's right arm had turned into a blade from the elbow
down. It was pointed at his apparent victim's neck, about to come
down.

"Are you kidding me...?"

My feet immediately made an about-face, and I tried to run away.

But then I remembered something. Thinking about it, I had pretty
similar abilities. If I let this thug do as he pleased, that woman was as
good as dead. The front page of the newspaper would say KILLER ON
THE STREETS! It was bound to come up at the office, too, one way or
another.

It wouldn't have been hard, if I'd been powerless, to tell myself I
couldn't do anything about it or make some other excuse. I could rule
it an unfortunate accident and forget it within six months. However,
for better or worse, this corporate slave had recently come into some
mysterious powers.

An otherworldly power bestowed by Peeps, that is.

"......"

With no other choice, I aimed the same spell that had shaved off a
few bangs at the man. It was the icicle-launching magic I'd just learned
how to shoot without an incantation the other day.

"Gyah!"

The icicle flew true and struck the man in the shoulder. It hit the
arm that had morphed into a blade from the elbow down.

Immediately, there was a change. The sharpened edge dulled, then
returned to its original shape—a human arm, just like the man's left
one. It was like I was watching clay animation. At the same time, I heard
a crackling noise, and he began to freeze at the point of contact.

"Ack..."

That wouldn't go well if I left it alone. The affected part was near the
neck, so he was sure to die if I did nothing. But I had no way of dealing
with that right now. *What should I do?* If Peeps had been with me,
maybe he would have been able to handle it. But I was alone. And
about to become a murderer.

Crap. What do I do? What the hell do I do?

It was the first time I'd shot something living—I hadn't thought it
through. Still, though, all my other magic was even more lethal, so I'd
had no choice.

"…Guh."

As I was panicking, the woman in the suit moved.

No sooner had her hand touched the icicle stuck in the man's shoulder than… How was she doing that? The frozen spear melted into a liquid in the blink of an eye, then fell from the man's body. It had only taken a few seconds.

Right after that, the thug fell faceup with a thud.

Seeing that, the lady in the suit slowly stood up. Were they both magic users like I was? It wouldn't have been strange for someone else like Peeps to have crossed over. With that in mind, I wanted to have a word with her.

"Um, excuse me…"

At least, that had been my idea—but her reaction was incredibly harsh. She turned to face me. Then, without hesitation, she took a gun out of her inside pocket and pointed it at me.

"Another psychic? Where did you come from?"

"…What?"

Her attitude made it clear that it *definitely* wasn't a model gun.

Hearing the term *psychic* put me at a loss for how to answer, though. Was that different from magic? Meanwhile, she had pulled a device out of her pocket and started contacting someone else. She then walked over, heels clicking on the road, toward the icicle stuck in the asphalt.

This one, too, melted straight away, splashing to the ground when she touched it. The only things left were a fist-size hole in the pavement and the water dripping into it. Who looking at the scene now would imagine that an icicle had been stuck there?

"Um, what is a psychic, exactly…?"

"…You were the one who fired the icicle before, right?"

Given her outfit and the fact that she had a gun, she struck me as a police officer—or someone in that vein. Alternately, she could have been yakuza, or mafia, or some other kind of outlaw. Whatever she was, the situation was bad.

I didn't want to get shot, of course, so I decided to answer honestly.

"Well, I did, I suppose, but…"

"How long have you been able to do that?"

"Just a few days, but…"

Was there some kind of spell that would make me bulletproof? If there was, I'd need to have Peeps teach it to me the next chance we got.

I never, even in my dreams, thought the day would come when someone would point a gun at me.

Right now, the most I could probably do was conjure a whole bunch of icicles in front of me as a shield. Or maybe make the earth ripple and form a wall. Wait. But how would that work with asphalt? I could only hope it would rise up the same way dirt did.

"I can't believe I was just saved by some stray psychic…"

But when I gave her the honest answer, her expression changed. Now she seemed somewhat frustrated.

Psychic was the key word here. It seemed to me like something that corresponded to magic.

"I honestly cannot figure out what's going on here. What is a psychic…?"

"I'm sorry, but would you mind coming with me?"

"Huh?"

"And things won't go well if you refuse. I'd prefer it if you came quietly. I don't know what kind of powers you have, but they don't mean much with a gun trained on you, do they? I promise I won't do anything bad to you."

Wait. Was she hitting on me? No, no, that was impossible.

Actually, it *had* been quite a while since the last time I'd talked to a woman. Not only were there virtually none in my office but most of the client reps we talked to were men as well. My interactions with the opposite sex basically came down to the few words I exchanged with employees at restaurants and convenience stores—and my neighbor. Ever since I got that STI at the brothel years ago, I hadn't been back.

Without money, a distance had formed between women and me, and at some point, that had just become my default. Marriage was out of the question at this point, and if I was going to be paying money at a shop, it'd be at one where I could eat delicious food. Maybe that was how I'd gotten to this state.

I had a libido, but my chances to even think about actual, real-life women had become very sparse. This was probably how a person died on the vine. I figured it was the same as gazing at expensive clothing in a store window, knowing it could never be yours and then losing your very desire for it. It was the perspective of an amateur virgin.

"I'll go with you, but could I stop home first? It's right down there. I'm on my way from work, so I want to drop my things off. I also have a pet, and I can't leave it alone."

"I'll allow it."

"Thank you."

Maybe my honest answers had given her enough cause to lower the gun. Thanks to that, I was regaining the feeling in my limbs.

"…Also, thank you for your help," she said.

"Not at all. We should all help those in need."

Soon, a high-class black sedan appeared out of nowhere. The lady in the suit prompted me to get in, so I did. I was nervous about what I could do if she kidnapped me and they locked me up unlawfully. However, given that she still had a gun tucked away, I couldn't consider disobeying.

The car headed for my apartment a few hundred meters away.

✻

Upon returning home, I saw Peeps facing my laptop.

Next to him, I could see an object—the golem he'd created. It was about as big as a medium-size teddy bear. It sat on the desk, manipulating the keyboard and mouse. The first time I saw it, I'd been pretty shocked.

I'd asked the lady and whoever else she was with to stay outside. Thankfully, she hadn't strongly objected.

"…So I had a little incident on the way here."

In any case, I had to explain the situation to Peeps. He was a professional when it came to weird stuff, so I figured he'd be able to shed some light on it. When I finished, he flapped his wings and moved to the window.

From there, he peeked outside from between the curtains. There was a car parked on the road and a woman standing next to it.

"*That female wearing the suit?*"

"Yes, that one."

"*I can't sense any mana from her.*"

"Wait. You can't?"

Without mana, you can't use magic. Peeps had explained that to me several times in the past. But I'd seen her do something magical right before my eyes. She'd turned the icicles into water in less than a second.

"*You said psychic?*"

"That's what she called it, but…"

"*Perhaps it uses a different framework from magic. Hmm, that idea is interesting, indeed. Could it be that your world has a similar phenomenon but with a different logic from that of my own?"*

"If that's true, it's the discovery of the century."

"Interesting..."

Seeing Peeps peeking out the curtains was really cute, by the way. It made me want to take a picture.

It struck me that I hadn't taken a single picture of him yet. Everyone took pictures of their pets—it was the first thing they did when they got them, to cherish the memory. Just a little earlier, the section chief had been showing me photos of him with his pet dog. I was super jealous. Once this fiasco was over, I really had to take a picture of Peeps and me.

"You should probably listen to what she has to say—you may be able to learn something."

"Any chance you can come along?"

"Hmm. I do not see why not."

"You might be a little cramped. Is that okay?"

It wasn't really an issue to whisper back and forth in the local supermarket with the sound of store announcements as cover. Absolutely no one would suspect I was chatting with my pet Java sparrow. This time, though, that could be dangerous. It hurt me to say it, but I'd need Peeps to play the meek bird in the cage. There was no way I could introduce him as my talking pet bird from another world.

"I understand. I must only be silent, correct?"

"Sorry for always making things hard for you."

"It is no issue. It was I who involved you."

"Thanks so much."

I was truly blessed as a pet owner to have a sparrow who was so understanding.

＊

Following the lady in the suit's directions, I brought a change of clothes and a few other things and left the apartment. I made sure to bring Peeps's cage, since I was told I'd be spending the night.

When I said I had work again the next day, she responded that she'd take care of it. I thought that sounded pretty ominous, but not wanting to come off as being combative, I decided to just do as she said.

Right after stepping out of my apartment, I ran into a familiar face.

"Are you going out, mister?"

It was my neighbor. She sat in front of the next door over, hands around her knees, in that familiar sailor uniform.

"Ah, yeah. I am."

"It must be hard having to be out so late."

"Is your mom still at work?"

"Yeah, seems like it."

"I see…"

She appeared to have her own problems to deal with. I wondered if there was anything I could do for her. Unfortunately, I was in a rush just now and couldn't come up anything. Maybe I could reach back into my apartment and grab one of the pastry packages I had stocked in my kitchen.

"If you want, you can have this."

"…Thanks—and sorry."

It was something I'd bought last time I'd gone shopping with Peeps. My neighbor took it with an apologetic expression. This was an exchange we'd had tens, if not hundreds, of times, but she was always humble and polite. As a result, I, too, dragged on in the same fashion.

I'd thought a few times in the past that veering *off* the straight and narrow would put her in a happier place. It might have been rude of me, but I couldn't help thinking there were plenty of things she could do as a good-looking youth. Then the old dude living next door to her could finally retire from his post.

Nevertheless, she seemed to prefer this aesthetic.

"By the way, um, do you have a second…?"

"Who? Me?"

"Yes."

Wonder what she wants. Curious. But I didn't have time to entertain her right now—I already had someone waiting for me. "I'm sorry; I'm in a bit of a rush today."

"You are?"

"Can it wait until next time? I'll be back tomorrow."

"…Yes."

In this case, a phone call or text might have been the way to go in our modern era. But she didn't have a smartphone. Our little chats outside the apartment were our only means of communication.

On the other hand, even if she did have a smartphone, I wouldn't really want to exchange numbers. If worse came to worst and she got wrapped up in a crime or an accident, the thought of my name in her phone would be a source of pure terror.

"I'm sorry. I've gotta go."

"Okay. Be careful."

As she saw me off, I left the apartment behind me. The area around the front door to each individual unit was concealed by a wall from the main road. Consequently, there was no chance the lady in the suit could have seen or heard our conversation.

After seeing I'd returned, she opened the back seat of the black vehicle. At her signal, I got in. I put my things at my feet; Peeps's cage rode on my lap. My host climbed in next to me. When the door closed, the car wasted no time driving off.

Just then, I happened to glance in the rearview mirror at the scenery behind us.

Against the dark of the night and illuminated by weak streetlights was a vague, indistinct sailor uniform. It was my neighbor—she'd moved from the front door. Her eyes were locked in our direction.

"……"

"Is something wrong? You look distracted."

"It's nothing."

It was probably a coincidence, but for a moment, I thought I felt our eyes meet in the mirror.

*

Peeps's cage in my arms, I felt the rock of the car as it carried us. Our destination turned out to be a grand building in the city center. From there, we entered an office space that spanned an entire floor.

It was in what looked like a reception room on the same floor that I finally got an explanation from the woman in the suit. It was just us two in the room except for Peeps, perched in his cage, still pretending to be an ordinary Java sparrow.

"…I see. So that's what you call a psychic."

The first thing she did was explain the key word in question: *psychics*.

They were like magicians, but their powers occurred spontaneously. Their abilities varied wildly from person to person—from those who could reduce an entire town to cinders overnight to others whose abilities were so insignificant it was as if they had none at all.

In addition, once one of these abilities manifested, it was set in stone and would never change. Developing a second power was unheard of. However, through repeated use, whatever had manifested could grow in strength and scope.

My host's power, incidentally, was the ability to control water. She explained that both firing icicles like missiles and the ability to instantly melt ice were just different facets of the same ability.

"Naturally, many powers are dangerous, so we need to keep track of them."

"Is that your job, miss?"

"Yes, it is. And it's about to be your job, too."

"What?"

"I'll give you a few more details. First…"

She continued rattling off explanations.

According to her, every country was secretly keeping track of and managing these psychics. Since certain powers had the potential to cause widespread chaos in society, they were very strict in their treatment.

Thus, as a general rule, once someone manifested an ability, they would be immediately recruited to the country's organization for managing psychics. If they refused—well, she let me know that would be unwise. I was told there had been a big incident involving psychics in the past.

At that point, I was curious about how many of these psychics existed. It turned out that about one in one hundred thousand people manifested powers. In other words, there were likely over a thousand of them in Japan. Considering the low number, the authorities probably had eyes on every single one.

"Do you have any questions so far?"

"No, please continue."

"All right."

The rest of her explanation detailed the organization itself. It was treated as a government agency, so all the psychics who worked there were civil servants. They even received salaries. Depending on their ability and degree of success, they could make far more than was possible just working in an office.

The higher ups had probably decided it was better to shower them with money than be stingy and invite antipathy. However, it seemed there were also high expectations, as many an issue had been resolved through the deeds of psychics in the past.

But of course, there would always be those who rebelled.

What I had stumbled into earlier was a face-off between the organization and just such a person. The blond-haired man who had tackled my host was a member of a group who objected to this system. Apparently, several such groups existed throughout the world, and suppressing them was one of the jobs assigned to psychics in this organization.

I was taken aback by the level of danger. Psychics did get hazard pay on missions, but even so, I really wanted to avoid all that. That delinquent had overpowered this woman even though she had a gun. I didn't think I'd be any use against people like that.

"That's the short of it, I think."

"Thank you."

"Now then, I know it's sudden, but I need to confirm."

"……"

At this point, the issue was how to describe my ability. This stuff was completely different from the magic Peeps had been teaching me. I didn't want to do anything too dangerous, which meant I needed to set expectations low. I was looking for one that had as little versatility as possible and wouldn't help at all in battle. In other words, what she had already seen had to be *all* I could do.

"What exactly is your power?"

"Like you saw earlier, I can shoot an icicle. That's about it."

Just being able to shoot an icicle wouldn't make a very powerful ability. There was no need for an annoying, hard-to-handle clump of ice when you carried a government-sanctioned gun.

I did feel an attraction to the title of civil servant, so I'd certainly take the initiative and change jobs if I could do clerical work at the rear. I couldn't make any less than I already did.

"Would you mind showing me?"

"I suppose…"

At her urging, I produced a small icicle without chanting. It was about thirty centimeters long. It hovered and drifted in the air above the coffee table in front of the sofa.

"Just as I thought—you're able to create it from nothing."

"……"

The lady flashed a grin. I had a bad feeling about this.

"Um, what is it?"

"Your power is *very* compatible with mine."

"What…?"

"I can control water, but I can't create it from nothing. That means I have to carry my own water when I'm on the job—or else procure it on-site. If you were with me, I could use my power without limit."

"……"

Ah. The power to control water didn't involve creating it, then.

And the way she said it—I'd heard that same tone whenever working holidays came up. She was already fitting me into her next mission. And I got the feeling she was the type to volunteer for the dangerous ones.

"Normally, I'd carry a few bottles of water or buy them from vending machines near the site, but you can solve all that. I'll be able to use more water than ever before."

"Are you by any chance…the type who lives to work?"

"I told you, didn't I? Depending on how hard you work, there's no limit to a psychic's paycheck."

"Yes, but—"

"If I didn't give it my all, the higher ups wouldn't hand me such lucrative assignments."

"……"

It seemed a very dangerous person had set her sights on me.

✳

That same day, they gave me a physical and a fitness test. No real problems there. Nobody had said a word to me about Peeps, either. They seemed to regard him as a normal pet for the moment. Given all the things I was hiding, that deserved a sigh of relief, in any case.

Released from the examinations and question-and-answer session, we were sent to a hotel the woman had arranged for us. A posh one right in the city, too, with a room just as luxurious. It was probably an investment in our future relationship.

"Now, then…"

The events of the day had exhausted me, and I wanted nothing more than to go to bed right away. Plus, it was almost midnight.

However, there were a few things I absolutely needed to do tonight. Some very important tasks I still needed to cross off my list: stock up in this world, visit the otherworld, sell the goods to the vice manager at the Hermann Trading Company, see Mr. French and pay him.

But that wouldn't be easy.

The lady in the suit had arranged this room for me. If, by some chance, they had thought to put a surveillance camera in here, everything would be ruined. The one thing I absolutely wanted to avoid was Peeps's secret getting out.

There were people in this world who could accept such strange and mysterious things as a talking Java sparrow, and now I was finally realizing how terrifying that was. I might have to stop talking to him even in the supermarket.

"Peeps, just a little longer, okay?"

"Pii! Pii!"

When I spoke to him like a pet, he responded with adorable tweeting. *You can act like a bird, too, huh, Peeps? I think I just discovered yet another charming thing about you.*

As far as I could tell from his energetic response, he definitely understood my intent. *Thank you so, so much for clearly grasping a one-sided message like that.* I bet he'd been an insufferable genius in his past life.

"Want to go for a little walk, Peeps?"

"Pii! Pii!"

I moved Peeps into the shoulder carrier, then left the room. I couldn't recall them ever touching my clothes or my things, so they probably hadn't put a bug on us or anything. If we could get somewhere nobody was looking, we could probably spend an hour or so in the otherworld, thanks to the time differential.

I'd thought about it from a bunch of angles, but I'd have to give up on buying anything here. For today, I would explain the situation to everyone concerned and come back right away.

"We're being tailed, eh…?"

As I exited the hotel and started walking down the nighttime streets of the office district, Peeps murmured to me. His voice was low enough that only I could hear it. And what he said was, once again, disturbing.

Also, his fluent use of criminal lingo gave me a bit of a start.

"…Can't we do anything?"

"The time difference will cover our trip if we keep it short."

"Yeah, you're right."

I slipped into a convenience store in the neighborhood and headed toward the restroom. If I locked it from inside, nobody would try to come in. Given what the place was for, they wouldn't have surveillance cameras here, either.

One hour in this world was about a day in that one. That meant I could spend a little less than an hour over there, and only a few minutes would pass here. I'd just say I was so rattled by the unexpected series of events that it'd given me a stomachache and I *really* had to go to the bathroom. Perfect excuse.

"Peeps, if you please."

"*Mm.*"

Peeps moved from the bag to my shoulder. As he nodded, a magic circle emerged on the restroom floor.

✳

After crossing over into the otherworld, we headed straight for the Hermann Trading Company. Fortunately, the vice manager was in, and we were able to get a meeting with him right away. We were led to the same reception room we'd visited several times over the past few days. Its sheer opulence was a function of how rich they were, and I still hadn't gotten used to it.

"An issue?" The vice manager's expression clouded after hearing our explanation.

"I apologize, but I may need a little bit of time before our next deal. I came here today to inform you of the situation. I'm terribly sorry for letting you down."

Seated on the sofa, I bowed my head, making Peeps go crooked. He was very cute as he grabbed ahold of my shoulder and hung on for dear life.

"If we can be of any help to you, Mr. Sasaki, we would gladly provide assistance."

"I'm sorry, but this is a problem I'm going to have to solve on my own."

"…I see."

The vice manager made a lonely-looking expression as though concerned about me. He was a really good person, and for the sake of our future business relations, I wanted to smooth things over as much as possible right now. I couldn't afford to ruin his impression of me.

"Again, I apologize for these personal issues, but if things go well, I may be able to increase my stock in the future. I'm sorry for not sharing the details, but I hope you will take a long-term view of the situation."

"Aha, well, in that case."

His expression softened, just a little, upon hearing my response. I must have prompted him to consider the positives.

"I'm terribly sorry for this inconvenience."

"No, I know you have your own circumstances to deal with, Mr. Sasaki."

"I'm grateful to hear you say that."

Given this exchange, I could probably hold out for two or three months. If I did change employment and got paid more, I could anticipate stocking more product. If I could increase my offerings for our next deal, it would be more than enough to cover my absence. This incident wasn't purely disadvantageous.

"Thank you, and I look forward to working with you again."

"And you as well. I will pray for your good fortune."

Ultimately, he saw me off from the company in a friendly manner.

Right before leaving, I left Mr. French's pay with him, as well as some additional money in case the restaurant's operational costs dipped into the red. I had to rely on him because there was simply no time. He gladly accepted, for which I was incredibly grateful.

After leaving the company behind, I hurried back to Japan. My relaxing life lasted only a moment, no time to even sit down and eat.

✱

We returned from the otherworld, then quietly went back to the hotel and immediately fell asleep.

I'd wanted to talk a little more to Peeps, but timewise, that wouldn't have worked out. If we'd been in that world too long, whoever was tailing us would think something was up and ask how long, exactly, I'd spent holed up in the restroom.

At this point, all the things I had to discuss would have to wait until the next day. The same went for our original plan to practice intermediate magic. I'd really wanted to do that before starting my new job as a government employee, so it was truly disappointing.

In any case, the new day dawned and brought with it a very early visitor.

"…A job, is it?"

"Yes, a job."

As I was lazing about on my bed right after waking up, there came a knock at the door. Figuring it was the housekeeper, I poked my head out. But instead, the lady in the suit stood in the hallway. She was the one who had taught me all about psychics the previous day.

"Sorry for bothering you so early, but could you come with me?"

"......" I wanted to refuse if I could, but her smile wouldn't allow it. And she had on thick makeup, as usual.

"I don't know anyone else at this organization aside from you. I would be happy to go along with your invitation, but could I possibly talk to whoever is in charge, first? I'd like to make sure this is standard procedure for the whole organization, if that's all right."

"Not happy working with me?"

"Isn't it natural, if we're going to be working together, to want to objectively confirm what sort of position you hold within this organization? You seem like a field officer, and I'm a little hesitant to head straight to the scene without reporting to your immediate superior first."

"...Ugh, older people always make things difficult."

"If you want someone else to open up, you have to start by being honest with them."

"......"

Despite her coming off like a cool, collected office assistant at first glance, on the inside, she seemed more like a battle-crazed promotion shark. Passion for one's job was all well and good, but I would have appreciated her giving me a little more consideration. Were all psychics like this?

"Ah, Hoshizaki? Hoshizaki, do you have a moment?"

"?!"

Before we could continue our conversation, I heard someone else's voice from the hallway. I didn't recognize it, but the energetic career woman immediately scowled.

"...Section Chief."

"Since you burst out of the office first thing this morning, I got curious and followed you. So this was what it was about. I don't mind you being enthusiastic about your work, but maybe it's best not to involve the new guy."

"......"

Behind my would-be partner appeared a man in a suit. He had striking medium-length hair with flowing bangs, and his features were as attractive as any actor's. He was probably in his thirties. He was tall, too—probably over 180 centimeters. The suit he wore went very well with his height. Judging by the way she called him section chief, this must have been her superior.

"My name is Akutsu. You're Sasaki, correct?"

"Huh? Oh yes, that's me…"

"I heard about you from Hoshizaki, but this is the first time I've gotten to meet you. I'm a pretty busy man. I'm sorry, but I hope you can understand. For the moment, though, I'm the one who will be your immediate superior. I'm hers as well, of course."

"It's a pleasure to be working with you."

He'd come all this way to see me, it seemed.

And while it was a little late, I finally had a name for my career-obsessed new acquaintance. It was apparently Miss Hoshizaki.

If this man was our boss, that made him a government employee as well. I didn't know the division's name yet, since it hadn't been shared with me. If this place was on the level of other central government ministries, though, then the fact that he was a section chief at his age meant that he had been promoted *incredibly* quickly.

Even a liberal estimate of the man's age put him in his mid-thirties. Was he wearing makeup or something? Normally, a section chief was a post for someone over forty. Or maybe there were powers that could change your appearance to look younger. Whatever the case, I was definitely curious about this man's background.

"Hoshizaki, go back to the office and write up yesterday's report."

"Ugh…"

"Sasaki will be getting some training."

Oh, thank goodness. I had a lot of questions about this guy's backstory, but inside, he seemed more put together than I'd expected. I'd been secretly a little worried about what I'd do if he turned out to be just as gung ho as the water-controlling Miss Hoshizaki. I still had no idea about this company's rules and regulations—important occupational stuff, like how to use a time card or how to put in for overtime.

"Here, take this." He gave me a smartphone. It was a civilian model, too.

"What is it for, sir?"

"To contact you. The one in charge of your training will call you with instructions; please follow them."

"Understood."

Apparently, whoever was in charge of my training was elsewhere. For now, I was just happy it wasn't Miss Hoshizaki. She was looking pretty depressed after being told to go back to the office. With such an unsubtle reaction, I started to wonder exactly how high this pay she'd mentioned went.

"Make it a habit to carry it whenever possible."

"Even outside work hours, sir?"

"You may be called out in an emergency."

"…I see."

Emergency calls suck. When a company had a system like that, you couldn't fully relax even on days off. If they called me too frequently, I'd just leave the phone in the otherworld. The waves wouldn't reach it, and it would disable all GPS tracking.

"I apologize for showing up unannounced, but please consider this my formal introduction."

"Yes, sir."

"I have some other work to do. If there's anything you're confused about or any problem you can't resolve on the scene, just call me up or send me a text. My information is in the address book."

"Thank you for taking the time out to see me, sir."

After I gave a slight bow, he quickly left.

✳

Not too long after my boss and the workaholic left the hotel, I was contacted through the device. I followed the instructions and headed to the building I'd visited the previous day. Apparently, my training would be carried out there as well. Naturally, it would mean I'd be parting with Peeps for now. After stopping by my apartment and putting him back in his cage, it was time to go to work.

After announcing myself to the front desk, I was led to another area, gaping in amazement all the while.

They took me to a conference room about fifteen square meters large. Swapping out one after another, people who seemed to be employees gave me various explanations on what the work entailed—from how they managed attendance and the dress code to giving me the accounts I'd need and planning my schedule.

I was the only one undergoing job training, incidentally. It was tough, too—no time for napping.

The name of this curious organization was the Paranormal Phenomena Countermeasure Bureau. It was directly under the Cabinet Office headed by the prime minister, rather than being a peripheral government ministry or agency. Outwardly, though, this bureau didn't exist, and I was told very firmly that I was not allowed to speak of it to anyone outside the bureau. They probably wouldn't believe me if I did anyway.

However, that raised some problems for its employees. To maintain our cover, we were given business cards for the National Police Agency, under the jurisdiction of the Public Safety Commission, which was an outside bureau of the Cabinet Office. I was instructed to use that card when introducing myself to outsiders.

Our official position was listed as detective—part of the Criminal Affairs Bureau within the National Police. When Miss Hoshizaki had called her superior a section chief, that was because it was Mr. Akutsu's "official" position in the Criminal Affairs Bureau. Miss Hoshizaki and I held the rank of police sergeant. Now I finally understood why she was able to carry a firearm.

If anyone I knew heard I'd switched from an employee at a dead-end company to a police officer, I bet they'd be shocked. My pay was going to go up significantly even without the various benefits, such as hazard pay. I probably wouldn't need to worry about stocking up in the future.

With that out of the way, my next concern was the working conditions. I was told that, unlike other employees, psychics didn't have to clock in at a specific time every day. Some people even worked a second job concurrently, and it seemed relatively flexible in that regard. In exchange, you had to show up whenever they called.

The work itself covered a lot of ground, with everyone being assigned jobs that suited their powers. Some psychics were experts at tracking people down, while others specialized in sabotage—there were all sorts here, it seemed. Participating in such operations comprised the bulk of the work here.

Miss Hoshizaki's job, as it happened, was one of the more secretive ones. I sure had won the lottery. When the employee conducting my training heard who I was working with, he flashed me a sympathetic look.

Finally, I was given an allowance to cover any preparations for the job. The "allowance" was one *million* yen.

Some psychics needed money to use their powers, so an even lump sum was given to anyone who entered the bureau. The monetary benefits after that were affected by the powers' usage on-site. I personally didn't need anything in particular, so this was probably the only bonus I'd get.

I'd gladly use the extra money to stock up for the time being. With my credit card reaching its limit and my bank account scraping the bottom, it was a huge help. It seemed like I'd still be able to bring over plenty of stock while waiting for next month's paycheck.

The allowance probably also served to encourage loyalty to the bureau. Compared to those who entered after taking government employee exams, psychics were naturally less predisposed to patriotism.

And that was basically how my training progressed. From the next day on, I'd be on standby until contacted. Miss Hoshizaki had already assessed my abilities last night, so that seemed like the end of the orientation. I probably wouldn't be back at the bureau until my first job.

And so the workday ended.

*

I got back to my apartment to find Peeps acting strangely. Normally, my beloved pet bird would at least offer me a "welcome home," but it was as if he'd reverted to a wild animal and was tweeting his adorable little heart out. Almost like he'd forgotten how to speak.

"Pii! Pii!"

"Peeps?"

"Pii! Pii!"

"……" Coming to a sudden realization, I moved him into my shoulder bag to take him outside. If my supposition was correct, it would be incredibly dangerous for us to act as we always did here. As I changed from my suit into my regular clothes, I left the device the section chief had given me on my desk. Then, taking only my wallet along, I exited the room.

"Peeps, let's go for a walk."

"Pii! Pii!"

With a few energetic chirps, Peeps fluttered his wings. Seeing that, I casually exited the front door. Once I'd walked away from the apartment, he finally began speaking human words.

"Somebody entered our lodgings this afternoon."

"Figured as much…"

"They were rustling around and installed something. An acquaintance of yours? In case they were not, I decided it would be a poor idea

for my existence to be known. If my concern was uncalled for, then I apologize."

"No, you really saved the day. Thanks, Peeps."

"Very well, then."

"They probably installed a surveillance camera or a bug somewhere. They didn't see you or the golem using the internet, did they?"

"No. Thankfully, they woke me up from napping in my cage."

"That's good."

Considering the timing, they'd most likely come on the section chief's instructions. There was no way I could let this slide.

"Do you know where they put the devices?"

"I memorized all their locations."

What a reliable sparrow, I thought.

As I continued strolling around the neighborhood with my pet, Peeps told me where all the bugs were planted. He knew of five in all. Frankly, I wanted to go stock up right now, but for today, I'd prioritize getting rid of the bugs.

After a few minutes of walking, we returned to the apartment.

I then began an investigation of the spots Peeps had confirmed. Just as he'd pointed out, there were spy cameras and bugs and everything. They were so naturally placed that I never would have noticed them without some sort of tip-off—five of them, sure enough. I cut the power to each and made sure they'd stopped working.

Immediately, the device I'd gotten from the chief buzzed. Checking the display, I saw Akutsu's name. It couldn't be a coincidence. I paused for a few rings to gather myself, then pushed the call button, ready to engage.

"…Hello? This is Sasaki."

"You're a real talent, Sasaki."

"……"

What a way to start a phone call.

"I fully understand your apprehensions. However, could you refrain from setting up spy cameras and bugs in my apartment? If this sort of thing continues, it will make it more difficult for me to act in accordance with your wishes."

"Sorry about that. It was actually more like a rite of passage."

"…What does that mean?"

"That you passed, Sasaki."

"……"

I had no idea what I'd just "passed."

"*Normally, people can only find one or two. I never thought you'd destroy all of them. You're considerably more perceptive than you seemed. Lived long enough to pick up a few tricks, eh?*"

"May I hang up now?"

"*Wait, wait. I admit, it wasn't a nice thing to do. I'm sorry, and I apologize. It's just that there are many people who don't think very highly of our organization. This was both to confirm your stance and to test your skills.*"

"In that case, you haven't confirmed my stance yet, have you?"

I'd eliminated all of them before doing anything incriminating.

"*If you did view the organization as an enemy, you wouldn't have removed them right away. We've had several opportunities to catch informants, but all of them would either do something incriminating immediately or put on a show of not noticing.*"

"…I see."

"*You seem to be an honest, talented person. I think we'll get along quite well in the future. And this isn't flattery. Psychic powers aren't the only thing you need for this line of work. Please don't misunderstand that.*"

"……"

"*So many psychics rush recklessly into danger. You also see a lot who are convinced they're chosen ones. A person like you is perfect for handling and managing that. I hope you'll put those skills to good use working for me.*"

"I understand."

"*Thanks. All right, I'll talk to you later.*"

After my boss finished monologuing, he cut the call. It looked like I would have to keep my guard up around Section Chief Akutsu as well.

✳

Now that I was finished talking with my boss, it was time to stock up at the superstore. This time, I decided to go by myself. Things were getting dicey, so I would probably need to cut down on taking Peeps out of the apartment in the future. I also needed to pay more attention when other people were around. Talking to him outside the apartment was not an option.

I explained as much to the bird, who agreed with me. Stocking up would be a bit less fun and a lot lonelier now.

As I went out my front door with those thoughts in mind, I promptly heard a voice call out to me.

"Good evening, mister."

"Huh? Oh, right. Good evening."

I turned to see my neighbor. She was sitting against her front door, hands around her knees, in her sailor uniform. I'd only put one foot out the door, and she was already talking, which surprised me a little. Her outfit—her navy sailor uniform against the night—was something I thought I'd gotten used to over the past few months, but it still made a strong impression.

Until this spring, she'd been wearing the backpack used by elementary school students. All that had changed was her uniform, but it felt to me like she'd suddenly grown up. I wasn't her father or anything, but I felt weirdly sentimental about it.

"Did you finish your urgent business?" she asked, staring at me.

What was this all about? It took a few moments for me to remember. When I'd said good-bye to her the previous day, she'd said something. It was the night I'd first met Miss Hoshizaki; my neighbor had been outside her front door. We'd had a conversation—I'd promised to listen to something she had to say, hadn't I? I'd been so preoccupied at the time that I'd totally forgotten.

"I'm sorry. You did say you wanted to talk to me about something, didn't you?"

"You remembered?"

"I almost forgot, actually. I'm sorry."

"No, I'm sorry for bringing it up so suddenly."

She stood up straight and gave a quick bow. The way her black hair smoothly passed over her shoulders was oddly striking. Now that I thought about it, she'd had bobbed hair when we first met. At some point, she'd grown it out, and it was beginning to make her look more like a woman. And she'd started to fill out, bodywise, hadn't she? Probably only a matter of time before one of her mom's boyfriends snatched her up.

"What was it you wanted to talk about?"

"I had something I wanted to give you."

She took something out of her skirt pocket. Wrapped in a clear vinyl bag and sealed neatly with a bit of tape were several cookies. They were oddly shaped compared to store-bought ones, and their sizes were all different. She'd probably made them by hand without using a cookie cutter.

"I made these in my home ec class. Will you take them?"

"Wait, you're sure?" Food was a precious commodity for my neighbor, who was still a victim of child neglect. I hesitated to deprive her.

"You always give me food, so please let me return the favor."

This must have been another expression of her pride. If so, maybe it would be better to take them without objection.

"Thank you. I'll savor every bite."

"No, thank you."

This might have been my first experience getting something from someone of the opposite sex outside of my family.

I recalled my lonely past as I took the bag. Despite my age, I'd just received handmade cookies from a middle school girl. It felt like my experiences with women, which had been overwhelmingly in the negatives, had just reverted to zero.

With this, I'd checked the last box for life experiences with the opposite sex, right? When I had that thought, a sort of sense of accomplishment welled up in my chest. Like another piece of the puzzle of life had clicked into place.

"Also, could I ask you something?"

"What is it?"

"The woman you were with before—are you two dating?"

Was she talking about Miss Hoshizaki? If she was, then no—our relationship was nothing so wonderful.

"She's essentially my boss at work."

"Oh. She seems pretty young for that."

"It's one of those places where people are ranked by ability."

"Is it a foreign company?"

"Something like that, actually."

It was about as non-foreign as it could possibly get, but I stayed quiet on that point. During training, I was told about a thousand times not to tell anyone about the bureau. Even so, there were still newcomers who would let it slip and leak confidential information. When they'd offered a concrete example of the punishment that ensued, I'd broken into a cold sweat.

"Sorry, I misunderstood."

"No worries."

Young women liked talking about that stuff, huh? I'd have been happier if Miss Hoshizaki was just a little more restrained—like my neighbor. Not that I wanted her to spill her love life to me. It was just that happily plunging into situations with supernatural powers and bullets flying every which way was a little straining for someone like me, already past middle age.

"Anyway, I've got some errands to run, so I'll be going."

"Sorry for stopping you like that."

"No, don't be. It's perfectly fine."

We'd been talking for just a few minutes outside the front door. After saying good-bye, I headed off to the superstore as I'd originally planned.

*

Once I'd finished shopping, we used Peeps's magic to enter the other-world. The same old spell as usual sent us from the apartment right to our base. From there, we headed on foot to see the vice manager.

"...In any case, I've resolved the issues I mentioned previously. For now, though, I may be busy from time to time. I know it's a lot to ask, but would that be acceptable?"

"Thank you for taking the time to explain. First of all, I'm just relieved that you're safe, Mr. Sasaki. And regarding the future, I understand. I have no desire to inconvenience you, and I hope we can continue doing business long into the future."

"Thank you. That helps a lot."

"With goods as wonderful as yours, creating them must be a lot of work."

I'd basically told the vice manager that a problem had come up in my manufacturing process. I couldn't exactly tell him about every-thing that had happened in my world, so unfortunately, I had no choice but to lie about it. For now, I got by with the excuse that my production line was still unstable.

"Now then, on to other matters. What I have for you today is..."

Our exchange was taking place in the same reception room, with us seated on the sofas.

The goods I'd brought from Japan sat on the low table in front of us. I'd handed off my regular wares, like the sugar and chocolate, to another person when I arrived. Only the new items were left. Like last time, I'd gone for outdoor goods.

I'd brought a variety of items with me, but there were two high-lights. I'd learned that fishing was popular among the same groups of nobles who enjoyed hunting using bows and arrows, so I'd brought a full set of fishing gear. And for communicating locally, I'd included a set of transceivers and batteries.

I explained their usage and function to the vice manager. What excited him was the transceiver.

"…Mr. Sasaki, this is *amazing*."

"It is a convenient tool, but as I explained before, it needs fuel. You can use it for a little over a day with one of these small pieces of metal. If the power inside the metal runs out, the whole thing will be useless, so please keep that in mind."

"Even so, it's incredible. But is this not a tool for war, rather than for hunting? Even if the fuel you had cost one hundred gold coins per piece, it would be worth the price."

"Well, it was originally developed for war, yes."

"Is it wise to be selling something like that to us?" he asked with visible consternation. He was probably worried about whether it would become a problem down the road.

"They're limited in number, as is the metal that fuels it. Even if you did break it apart and tried to analyze it, it would be difficult to re-create. I concluded that if it was on a limited basis, selling them wouldn't cause a problem."

"I see…"

It was a cheap transceiver; the whole set only cost a few thousand yen. Still, it seemed to have value in this world. I mentally thanked those great figures of the past who'd helped develop such technology. Peeps and I would gratefully use it as a source of income for our extravagant life in this world.

Primitive items were one thing, but modern transceivers were installed with integrated circuits. There was zero possibility of anyone in this world reverse engineering it. They'd see what looked like pieces of chocolate inside, and there it would end.

My offerings aside from the transceivers and fishing supplies were deemed useful enough as well, and the vice manager decided to purchase the entire shipment at once. I was relieved I wouldn't have to carry any surplus.

The final all-inclusive price came to 5,600 gold coins. Three thousand were for the three transceiver sets and the fifty batteries needed to operate them. That made it my biggest haul yet, and the number of gold coins I had on hand ballooned to nearly ten thousand.

"Thank you so much for yet another wonderful exchange."

"No, thank you for responding so quickly to me."

We bowed over the low table, giving our parting words to round out the agreement.

And then, on a whim, I decided to ask something I'd been curious about.

"By the way, may I ask a question?"

"What is it?"

"Is the representative of this trading company present?"

It was always Marc, the vice manager, who dealt with me. I hadn't seen whoever was in charge even once. A few days in Japan were several months in this world, and I'd been worrying about whether I would be best served introducing myself.

"Hermann is our representative, but he's currently traveling to the capital on a major business deal. He doesn't plan on returning this year. If you need something urgent, we could send out a letter, if you wish."

"No, that's perfectly fine."

"Are you sure?"

"I just thought that I should say hello, if he was around."

"In that case, you will have the chance to do so once he returns."

"Thank you."

Since there were no forms of high-speed transportation like cars or bullet trains here, it probably took a long time to get to other towns. Peeps's magic might have been able to get us right there and back, but I'd put it off for now.

Let's wait until my life settles down into all that psychic business.

If I could just get used to my job, I would have more free time than I ever had working at my old company.

✳

After bidding farewell to the vice manager, I went to talk to Mr. French.

According to him, the restaurant's finances were still positive. He'd also learned most of the recipes, so we ended up eating there for the day. He'd prepared a private table for us in the back of the shop for when reservations ended.

Peeps and I sat across the table from each other.

"*This is quite good. I have never experienced this flavor before.*"

"Could be because there's so few spices in this world."

We were eating soup curry. In general, the curried rice popular in Japan didn't look all that good on the outside. It was possible nobody would eat it if they added it to the menu. Predicting that, I had instead proposed soup curry—and it was surprisingly popular now.

However, most of the spices came from the Japanese supermarket where I bought sugar and chocolate. They were limited and could only be used for ten meals in one day, apparently. In the future, I wanted to try re-creating it with local ingredients.

"*The meat is deliciously soft. And I like the tingle of the spices, too.*"

"You're not kidding. It's so soft, I can't get enough of it."

The level of quality was higher than I'd expected. I had wondered if it would end up being a soup that was spicy and not much else, but they seemed to have followed the recipe to the letter. I found myself excited, thinking about new foods and unknown recipes. Peeps's meal came with extra meat, incidentally.

As we were eating, Mr. French came to check on us. He was wearing his apron as usual.

"Um, how…how is it?"

"It's delicious. Just how I imagined it would be."

"Really?! Thank you so much!"

"No, thank *you* for re-creating it this wonderfully."

It really was thanks to him that I was able to begin to repay Peeps. My meeting with Mr. French had been bumpy to say the least, but in the end, I was glad I'd invited him to do this. He was working with the vice manager of the trading company on the shop's finances, too, so they were taking care of it all by themselves.

Naturally, I needed to show my appreciation. I held out a sleeve of gold coins I'd put together in advance. I'd bundled them and held them together with paper and tape. Even I would have felt bad giving it to him without something like that, so I did a little decorating. It was like the koban coins that showed up in period dramas about the Edo era.

"This is your pay for last month."

"Oh, I, thank you… Wait, this is—"

"It includes my own thanks for re-creating my recipe."

"Are…are you really sure I can have this?"

"Yes. Please go right ahead."

Thirty gold coins *was* pretty generous. At the trading company, the vice manager had given me joint ownership over the shop since I brought in so many goods—which then applied to its earnings and expenses. He told me they'd been a hundred gold pieces in the black last month. I wasn't even doing anything in particular, yet a hundred gold coins still found their way into my pocket. I couldn't bring myself *not* to reinvest it in the venture.

"I… I'll continue to pour my heart and soul into it!"

"Thank you very much."

"Yes, sir!"

"In addition, starting next month, I want you to delegate an amount based on the restaurant's profits for yourself. For the future, I will leave the entire management of the shop in your hands. You only need to give me a report once a month."

Having to come here to give him his pay every time was a pain. And things in my own life seemed ready to cancel my plans on short notice. Considering that, I figured it would be easiest just to leave everything to him. He had the Hermann Trading Company's support, so I was sure he'd be fine.

"Wait, but that's…"

"I really am sorry for making you do everything. Please take care of this place."

"Y-yes, sir! Thank you!"

Still, I hadn't done any work at all and felt uncomfortable being so profoundly respected. This was literally all thanks to Peeps. It gave me an indescribable feeling having the bird himself standing right in front of me while Mr. French thanked me so profusely. Though he seemed to take no notice whatsoever as he pecked away at his incredibly tasty-looking meat.

"Excuse me, but—would we be able to enjoy ourselves from here on?"

"Huh? Oh, uh, yes, of course! Please excuse me, then!"

Once I got the message across, Mr. French went back to the kitchen.

Seeing as how I'd been making Peeps do all the work lately, I hoped this meal would lift his mood. It wouldn't be an exaggeration to say this shop existed for him. With any luck, it would continue functioning nice and easily like it was now.

"I would like to keep eating here for the time being."

"You'll hear no objection from me."

"You gave him other recipes as well, correct?"

"I did."

"Are they as tasty as this is?"

"I think so."

"You really are something, you know."

"I'm just glad you're satisfied with it."

"It is a shame about the Kobe beef chateaubriand, but this is good in its own right. If a variety of dishes aside from this await, I will be able to enjoy myself for a while. Now, once our lives elsewhere settle down, we will be assured peace and security."

"Well, hopefully that happens soon…"

As I watched the delighted sparrow eat, I felt it warming my own heart.

✳

Once our bellies were full, we went to practice magic.

We chose the same spot as always: the forested region next to the plains around our base of operations, the town of Baytrium. This spot, on the border between the forest and plains, was our training grounds. It was fairly far from town, so we wouldn't be running into anyone.

Just like the last time we visited, I practiced muttering incantations over and over again, excited to learn new magic. I was just as absorbed in memorizing the incantations in my own world, too, and strove to do so whenever I had a free moment.

My efforts must have been paying off—because, somehow, I was able to use an intermediate spell.

"…I truly did not think you would learn intermediate magic in this short a time."

"It's because of the mana you gave me, right, Peeps?"

"No. Mana is certainly a barrier to entry, but you are still progressing very quickly. Usually, magicians in this world need over a decade before they can learn intermediate magic. Reaching that point after mere weeks of training is unprecedented."

"You're praising me so much I'm starting to get a little scared."

As for the spell—well, it launched lightning. It zapped out, crackling, from the magic circle at my hand.

It was conspicuously powerful. No sooner did it leave my hand at a blinding speed than it connected with the target and burst. Not only did the bolt send an electric current through the target, it also blasted away whatever part it struck last. If I set my aim carefully, I could kill a target with near certainty.

When I turned to a nearby tree and fired a bolt as a test, it easily broke the trunk at its base, toppling it. The point of contact was burned to a cinder, smoke hissing from it. What a dangerous spell this was.

"Barriers of a certain strength can easily nullify it."

"…I see."

Peeps didn't seem to perceive the spell as something to fear, but now I was a little scared of the sparrow perched on my shoulder. I was certain he'd never turn on me, but the possibility of others existing in this world who could use this spell was extremely high. I wanted to learn this barrier spell or whatever as soon as possible.

Actually, based on the way he'd said it, that was probably a requirement—in a fight against another magician.

Given the fact that there was a means of nullifying the spell rather than avoiding it, this world's magic seemed more like a contest of brute strength than I'd thought—one of those scenarios where each side would cancel out the other's spells, looking to land a single effective hit.

Considering the pure power of the lightning attack I'd just witnessed, you'd need more than a police officer's gear to overwhelm it. Even with modern weaponry, gear that wasn't top-of-the-line would be pointless in the face of magic.

"Wow. Intermediate magic is… How do I put this? Amazing."

"This may be intermediate magic, but it is still of the fairly low-level variety."

"Huh…?"

"We call it intermediate magic for convenience, but it still contains a vast range. Broadly speaking, we divide magic into beginner, intermediate, and advanced categories, but each category further contains easier and more difficult spells. Within the intermediate category, a higher-level spell can have considerable power."

"……"

If Peeps thought something had incredible power, it must really be something.

I would rather spend my time learning that teleportation spell than something that dangerous. But despite my unceasing practice regimen, I still showed no sign of improvement. It seemed like it was considered above the advanced level for good reason.

"For your information, magic above the advanced level is purely a matter of talent. No matter how hard they work, those who cannot use it cannot use it. However, that comes down to their store of mana, so you will not have that limitation. If you diligently apply yourself, you will be rewarded."

"Peeps, I'm kind of scared to be learning advanced magic."

"Oh, so you do intend to learn it?"

"……"

Oops, he saw right through me. I said I was scared, but I still wanted to master it.

"Don't let it worry you. This is the sort of creature man is. As I once was."

"…Is it?"

"You cannot afford hesitation now to begin with, can you? Together, I can protect you, but if we act separately, I cannot. If you learn advanced magic, we can live safely over there as well."

"Yeah, you're right."

Before I knew it, learning more spells had become a matter of life-and-death.

✳

The next day, as I was whiling away the time in my lodgings in town, the vice manager came to see me.

Apparently, he wanted me to accompany him to see the viscount, who wished for a contribution of the transceivers I'd delivered the day before. Hearing that, I quickly readied myself, and we headed for the same castle we'd visited the other day. He'd prepared a carriage to take us there. As a modern, stay-at-home man, his consideration was greatly appreciated.

At the castle, in deference to our previous successful audience, we were shown to the viscount without any suspicion. Though we'd greeted each other in a ceremonial space last time, today we were shown to what seemed to be a reception room.

"Ah yes. I can indeed hear your voice from this box…"

The vice manager had clearly already told the viscount about it. He'd probably come here while I was practicing magic. Because I'd prioritized learning intermediate magic to deal with the trouble in Japan, I'd left all the business-related dealings in the vice manager's hands.

"We at the Hermann Trading Company believe that you, Viscount Müller, are the right person to whom we should offer this product. It could create issues if we were to sell it indiscriminately. What are your thoughts?"

"Indeed, I thank you for your consideration."

The viscount nodded deeply in response to the vice manager's words. It seemed like we had a buyer for the time being.

Viscount Müller gripped the freshly imported transceiver in his hand. With the vice manager's help, he was able to test its functions and uses. Thus, he was able to understand it without issue.

"Sasaki."

"Yes, my lord."

"Do not circulate these...transceivers, did you call them?...any-where else. I'd like them all to come here. The same applies to the metal fuel you call a battery. I would also prefer it if you were to keep their existence a secret. Can you do that?"

"I see no problem with that, my lord, but..."

"I do apologize for interfering with your business. In exchange, I will purchase as many of these items as you have—at an increased price."

"Understood, my lord. If you would allow it, I accept."

"Indeed. Thank you."

These radios had more bargaining power than I thought they would. Still, my otherworld wallet had already gotten very heavy. I'd be set to live off it for the time being. Thus, there was no hurry for me to bring a lot of them. I'd let them trickle in and create more opportunities to meet with the viscount.

"I also have something to inform you of, Sasaki."

"What is it, my lord?"

"There may come a day when I will require your help."

"Huh? My lord, I..."

"I'm sorry, but I cannot explain in detail."

"...Understood, my lord. I will endeavor to humbly accept any requests you have of me should that time come."

Honestly, I'd wanted to apologize and turn him down. Unfortu-nately, he was a noble—I couldn't possibly refuse him. It was like a direct order from the company president. The man seemed like a good person, so I doubted he would criticize me for denying him, but who knew what those around us would think about that?

That was how my audience with the viscount ended.

On our way back, just as we were about to part ways, the vice manager stopped me.

"Mr. Sasaki, about the matter the viscount spoke of…"

"Oh yes. What is it?"

"I've heard rumors that our relations with a neighboring country have worsened."

"……"

"It may be wise to prepare yourself."

Well, that was disturbing rumor. If he'd chosen now to tell me about it, then it was probably true. The vice manager had a good head on his shoulders. He would never give someone specious information that might confuse them. The intel seemed pretty legitimate.

Learning barrier magic just jumped way up my to-do list.

For the next few days, I had Peeps help me study up on various types of self-defense magic. I also wanted to learn a more potent form of healing magic, if possible. Peeps had told me that I'd be fine as long as he was around, but it still made me uneasy.

✳

After finishing several days of magic practice, we returned to my apartment. With no end to the problems I was facing in either world, I was still somewhat anxious. Still, thanks to the high-quality sleep and delicious food I'd gotten in the otherworld, I was in pretty good physical condition. At this rate, I felt able to face the day energetically. Maybe I'd do some weight training—it had been a while.

Though it seemed that jinxed me, because right after I got back, the smartphone went off. Not my personal one but the one the section chief had given me. I checked the display to see it was from Miss Hoshizaki.

"Yes, this is Sasaki."

"*Can you come to the office right away? We've got an urgent job.*"

"Is that what Mr. Akutsu…?"

"*Yes, the chief gave the instructions. I'm counting on you, all right?*"

"…Understood."

That was a shame.

If Miss Hoshizaki was acting on her own again, I'd have a good supply of excuses to get out of it, but I couldn't ignore a directive from the section chief. She'd said *right away*, so I rushed like a madman to put on my suit and get my things ready.

"I'll be back later, Peeps."

"Yes. Take care."

Wow, it was…really nice to have someone to see me off like this.

✱

Being my second trip to the office, I had already learned the train route and was able to go there directly. In truth, I wanted to have Peeps use his teleportation magic. However, with my destination being what it was, I decided to refrain. I did, however, eagerly start scheming for how to fool them going forward.

"Good morning."

As instructed over the phone, I headed to the conference room in the office. When I arrived, almost a hundred people were already present. It felt like one of those TV dramas where the detectives on a case get together to discuss the details.

However, everyone here was extremely unique. There were teenagers alongside older people who must have been close to sixty, male and female, all sitting around tables lined up like bleachers in a theater. The hair colors were vibrant, from those with black hair to others with brown or blond. They didn't look at all like civil servants.

I saw a few suits like mine in the crowd, but unfortunately, they were in the minority.

"Oh, you're here," said the section chief, seeing me enter.

He was standing next to the huge screen set up at the front of the room. It displayed a series of what looked like human faces. Included here and there among the mug shots were a few photos that were clearly taken without furtively.

"Sasaki, come up here for a moment."

"Um, yes, sir."

I went to stand beside him as prompted. The conference room was intimidating. Everyone assembled was staring at me with curiosity. I had taken my previous job right out of college, and visiting that office for the first time had felt just like this. In fact, there might have been even *more* attention on me now.

"This is our new recruit, Sasaki. Today will be his first job, so I want you all to take care of him. His power was listed in the papers distributed earlier. I believe he will largely be working with Miss Hoshizaki, but he may team up with others depending on the situation."

The section chief gave me an introduction in his own words. He glanced at me, indicating I should say something.

"It's a pleasure to be working with you all."

Since he mentioned my psychic traits had been given to the others in a report, I probably didn't need to go to the trouble of explaining them. Instead, I simply gave a slight bow to finish my greeting. No one raised any questions.

"You can take any empty seat."

"Yes, sir."

I found an empty seat at his request and sat down. I was keenly aware of the people sneaking glances, but none of them spoke to me.

Once he saw I'd settled in, the section chief, still standing in the front, opened his mouth to speak again. His voice carried as he looked over the entire room.

"Since Sasaki is here, allow me to explain why I've gathered you all today."

Looked like he was getting straight to the mission. Everyone's attention turned to the screen up front. The section chief began his explanation with a detached tone, pointing at the photographs on the display. In his words, they were irregular psychics who had refused to join the organization.

For convenience, our bureau called psychics belonging to it *regular*, while those who didn't were called *irregular*. Those unaware of this state-run organization were called *stray psychics*.

Among the irregulars, several like-minded groups had formed. The photos on the screen featured members of two of the largest of these.

Naturally, our bureau wanted to expose them all. After tailing them day in, day out, we had acquired information that there would be a meeting to discuss a merger. If successful, they planned to join together to resist the regular psychics. We couldn't let that happen, which was what brought us here today.

Meaning that my first job was, in short, a raid. What a frightening occupation this was going to be. Would I get worker's compensation if I was injured?

"...Does anyone have any questions?" asked the section chief after talking for some time.

Several hands quickly went up. The section chief called on a man in a sweatshirt and sweatpants. He was a rough-looking fellow who seemed to be in his mid-twenties. His hair, dyed brown in an equally rough manner, left an impression. It looked like it had been a while since he'd dyed it, given that the black of his roots was starting to peek back out again.

"Is this everyone who will be participating?"

"Yes, this is everyone in the task force. We plan to have a dozen or so non-psychic bureau members providing support from the rear, but as a general rule, they don't participate in combat. They're armed just in case that does happen, but don't depend on them."

"But for real, will this be enough?"

The two of them exchanged words in front of everyone. This was something I'd been wondering about as well.

"We've determined it is, which is why we have gathered you here."

"Well, I hope so…"

It looked like only the people in the conference room would be going on this job. I doubted you could make a judgment based solely on numbers when it came to battles between psychics, but given how many pictures were in the slides, they had more than we did—twice as many, in fact.

After that was a short question-and-answer session between the section chief and other members of the bureau. They quickly covered everything I'd been curious about, so I didn't have anything to ask. Most of the questions were just confirming the current situation, and our superiors didn't reveal any new information.

＊

No sooner than our explanation of the mission was over, we were hurried out to the site. To travel there, we used cars owned by the bureau—black HiAces, to be specific. We split into several vehicles and headed straight there.

We were told our destination was an abandoned building on the fringes of the city. Originally a bowling alley, it had lost popularity and fallen victim to the Heisei-era depression and ceased operations. They'd put the plot and building on the market, but without a buyer, it had just been left to rot.

Once we arrived, we followed the section chief's instructions and split up to carry out our respective roles. Those ordered to make a direct confrontation went to the front, while those instructed to provide support moved into the shadows. We positioned ourselves based on a map distributed earlier.

And as for who I was with—well, this was a pain.

"I'm counting on you," she said.

"…I'll do my best."

I'd be on the front lines, supporting Miss Hoshizaki. This was a little much, wasn't it?

My task was to go with her as she charged to the front, replenishing her stores of water in the form of icicles from behind. Though it was explained to me that I wouldn't need to engage in any direct combat, it all depended on her actions, which were unpredictable. Every time she pressed forward, I would need to follow.

This was a big downer. It was why I'd practiced barrier magic so much—for exactly this sort of situation. However, I hadn't actually learned any yet.

According to Peeps, the only barrier magic with practical use started at the intermediate level. There was magic with similar effects available at the beginner level, but his view was that it was comparatively weak. It was simply a matter of the spell's capabilities.

The reason was that a beginner-level barrier could just barely stop a beginner-level spell. If the opponent could use anything more than that, they'd easily break through. It wouldn't be *pointless*, but it wouldn't be reliable in a real-life situation, either.

Plus, there were plenty of ways to deal with beginner-level magic without using a barrier. They only truly became indispensable in crossfire at the intermediate level or higher. Beginner-level barriers were, as he put it, a sprinkle of water in a drought.

Ultimately, even though there *was* a beginner version, I'd decided on learning more effective healing magic. I hadn't been sure then which was the correct choice, and I still wasn't. What I really wanted was to get by without using either.

"Go, go!"

Through an earpiece I'd been given came the chief's instruction. He had taken command of this operation. He, however, would be away from the planned battlefield—the bowling alley—in a van parked on the road. He had told us to use our own discretion once we were in the thick of things, which meant he'd probably foreseen a melee breaking out. As someone actually going there, it was yet another source of anxiety.

"Let's go!"

"…Right."

With me chasing after Miss Hoshizaki, we ran across the parking lot toward the building. I felt like an allied soldier landing on the beaches of Normandy.

At the moment, only my colleagues were visible. As we didn't know what might come flying at us, though, we couldn't drop our guards. We'd have to be cautious not only of powers but bullets from snipers, so we jumped from cover to cover.

Those who wanted it had been lent gear, so I'd gotten as much as I could. I looked like a special forces member of a police squad or something. I never thought the day would come when I'd be wearing body armor and a combat helmet. I even had a bulletproof shield in my hand.

The reason they were only lent to those who'd asked had to do with how an individual's powers worked. Most had, however, protected themselves. Miss Hoshizaki was wearing the same kind of outfit as I was today. She didn't have a shield, though. She said it would get in the way of using her powers.

According to what I'd heard, in the past, an employee who had mobilized in short sleeves and jeans had been shot in the head and killed by a sniper. Once they'd started mentioning that fact in training, equipment rentals skyrocketed. Training for its use was also done proactively and on a daily basis.

"…Nobody here," murmured Hoshizaki.

"Looks like it."

After barging in the back door, we entered the main area. It seemed like a long time had passed since the alley had ceased operations, and it was still a disaster inside. Graffiti marked several spots—delinquents had probably been here. Empty cans and bottles and convenience store bags littered the place; the garbage was awfully conspicuous. Even the bowling lanes were full of holes.

But nobody aside from those in the bureau could be seen. Had we gotten here too early? No, that wasn't possible.

As we looked around the interior, which was deathly quiet, I felt a dangerous presence. Miss Hoshizaki apparently did, too, because she immediately gave me an instruction. It was to turn right around and go back the way we came.

Right as I nodded, it happened.

"I've been captured; I'm sorr—"

The chief's voice came from my earpiece. Not a moment later, there was an explosion on the other end. It sounded like gunpowder going off.

"Ugh…"

At the same time, our own surroundings changed as well. All those building scraps, bowling balls, and leftover pins started floating into the air, one after another. There were so many of them—probably in the triple digits.

"It can't be…" Miss Hoshizaki's face tensed.

Actually, so did the faces of everyone with whom we'd arrived. Like students caught shoplifting, their expressions became a mixture of shock and terror. Of course, as a rookie, it had me very worried.

A few meters separated us from the front lines. Since this was my first outing, we'd been instructed to pursue targets from the shadows, but that didn't mean my legs weren't trying to shake free of my hips.

I had checked our intel beforehand and didn't remember any psychics who could make things float. At a glance, it looked like psychokinesis, or telekinesis, or something along those lines. Seemed like a pretty versatile power.

"Sasaki, run for it!"

The next thing I knew, Miss Hoshizaki had given me the order to retreat. I never imagined she would command me to withdraw without using my power even once. She seemed more like the type who would punch first and think later.

The psychics from the bureau scattered in every direction. A moment later, the floating objects moved. Suddenly accelerating, they flew toward the fleeing raid team. Those who noticed the change frantically put up their defenses.

One person tried to dodge and failed. The objects seemed to home in on their targets, and though the intended victim had avoided the barrage once, it had looped back around. Another got their bullet-proof shield up and tried to weather the onslaught, but the debris knocked their shield right out of their hands.

It made sense why only heavy objects had been made to float. The speed with which they flitted through the air was intense—one person took it to the head, and the contact destroyed everything from the neck up. Even those who skillfully tried to slow the debris down couldn't avoid injury.

People from the bureau were dropping, one after another. Only those holding shields were relatively safe.

But even for them, it was just a matter of time. The heavy objects didn't just ram into them once. They came back up, again and again, launching from all angles. A few could be blocked, but eventually, a person was overwhelmed, and one would get through, followed by an endless beating.

It was a simple power, and yet it was absolutely terrifying.

The only ones who could avoid the hurricane winds were those who had been near the entrance. That meant those of us, including myself, who had been on their way to support the front lines—those waiting in the wings. The power must have had some kind of range limit.

"Miss Hoshizaki, here's some water!"

"Thanks!"

In the meantime, I launched human-size icicles at my coworker, who was currently running this way and that, trying to escape. They were quite a bit bigger than before. I didn't just make one, either—I made ten, then another ten.

When they arrived at her hands, she touched them with her fingertips. The icicles then changed into water, becoming a wall of water that surrounded her. It was like a water tank in an aquarium, rising around Miss Hoshizaki in a cylinder almost a meter thick.

Several heavy projectiles rammed into it in the meantime, but they were caught by the wall of water and lost their momentum. By the time they made it through, most of that momentum was gone. It would still probably hurt if they hit, but they'd likely only leave small bruises.

Once I'd given her a few dozen icicles, she'd completed her wall from top to bottom. She looked like she was in a bowl all by herself. I suddenly had the urge to add fish.

"Good work, Sasaki!"

"Thanks."

What worried me were the heavy objects that fell to the ground, blocked by Miss Hoshizaki's barrier, coming back. However, she seemed to plan on dealing with them by moving quickly and leaving them behind. She dashed left and right, protected by her wall of water. For a time, it looked like we'd be able to operate even inside the maelstrom.

However, that assumption crumbled a moment later.

Because this time, Miss Hoshizaki's body floated up into the air.

"Ack…!"

Apparently, the hurricane wasn't picky—it could use people, too.

*

I had nervously come to face my first battle, and now I had a hunch it was going to be a disaster from start to finish.

Through some unknown person's power, all the nearby heavy ammunition—building material scraps and bowling balls—were speeding around through the air. It was like a localized hurricane had touched down right here.

Everyone who had charged in was wiped out. The section chief's drones had all been shot down as well.

The only ones still active were Miss Hoshizaki and me.

And in the end, she had become fodder for the hurricane herself, floating around like the building scraps and bowling balls. It had to be the work of a psychic in the enemy group—her body drifted higher, rising almost to the ceiling.

And then, suddenly, she was flipped on her head and sent hurtling down like a solo pile driver.

Still, she had her wall of water that followed her in every direction, so she wouldn't take a whole lot of damage from it. The water absorbed the impact, protecting her from the collision. The only real effect she suffered was getting drenched from the water.

When I thought about the situation abstractly, this woman's power to control water was itself a form of telekinesis. I naturally concluded that so long as I was there to serve as her tank, we had some fighting chance against the hurricane user.

Unfortunately, we couldn't even see our opponent, and Miss Hoshizaki was completely on the defensive.

"Sasaki… Run—run away!"

"But…"

There was no communication from above, so fleeing was probably for the best. But what would happen to Miss Hoshizaki, then? The other members of the support group who had been with me were already gone. It looked like they'd managed to escape. And I really, *really* wanted to follow suit. But as her partner, I couldn't do that.

Many of my fallen coworkers were clearly dead. If she lost her steady supply of water, she might join them. If I heard later on that

Miss Hoshizaki had died, it would put a massive strain on my mental state.

"You'll die! Just—just go already!"

"As your partner, I cannot leave you behind."

"Ugh…"

Above all, if it turned out desertion was a punishable offense—well, that would be terrible.

I remembered reading a book on the rules of the Self-Defense Forces. Fleeing in the face of the enemy would earn you at least seven years of penal servitude or even confinement. I doubted the bureau was the same, but it wouldn't be strange if a similar rule existed.

Actually, as a government employee, if there was hazard pay for on-site work, there would *have* to be such a rule. Now that I thought about it, I hadn't checked. There might be no actual law, but I didn't know about how it worked within the bureau.

If I decided to run, I'd need to think that over carefully first, and—

"My, this is more exciting than I'd thought."

But my mistake was worrying about everything too much. A new figure suddenly emerged from the corner of the space.

She appeared in the main area with the bowling lanes, on a path leading back to the restrooms. She was dressed in traditional clothing and, at first glance, looked like an elementary schooler. Her black hair reached down below her waist, and her skin was as pale as snow— both striking features. Was she the cause of this chain of hurricanes?

"What…?!"

A shriek escaped Miss Hoshizaki's lips when she saw the girl. An unusual response from the bellicose woman.

"Still, though, I suppose this is where it ends."

Miss Hoshizaki wasted no time creating icicles from her water wall and firing them. Each was about the size of a plastic bottle with a sharpened tip, and they were hurtling straight for the newcomer in front of us.

In response, the girl launched herself into a dash. Deftly, she avoided the icicles shooting her way, zigzagging as she closed in quickly toward Miss Hoshizaki. Her speed was unbelievable for a child. She was like a wild animal.

Eventually, reaching the wall of water, the girl swung her right hand up in a wide arc. Miss Hoshizaki turned the water to ice.

Paying no mind, the girl brought her fist back down, striking the thick sheet squarely.

With a huge *thump*, the ice crackled and broke. Miss Hoshizaki's face emerged from behind it, eyes wide with shock. She clearly hadn't expected that.

The girl gently drew a fingertip along Miss Hoshizaki's cheek. "I'm not going to kill you. Your ability seems rather useful."

I didn't really understand what that meant. However, as the girl touched her, the water and ice floating around Miss Hoshizaki dropped to the floor, lost its form, and became a large puddle.

At the same time, Miss Hoshizaki herself fell limp and stopped moving. It looked like she'd lost consciousness. She hung in the air like a puppet on strings at the end of the show.

"……"

Judging by this sequence events, a different psychic must have caused the hurricane. In other words, from our point of view, there was yet another enemy psychic to deal with. And what I'd seen so far revealed nothing about this one's power. Did it have to do with her superhuman physical abilities?

"…And it would seem a rat still hides here."

"Umm…" As if things couldn't get any worse, I was pretty sure she'd caught on to my presence.

The whole business with the two groups meeting up was completely out the window. The section chief had probably been fed false information. We'd walked right into their trap, and what was supposed to be a one-sided raid had turned into an ambush.

Even if I simply ran, I doubted I could escape that incredible leg strength. And somewhere else in this abandoned building hid the psychic who was the source of the hurricane. I would be better served trying to calm down and grasp the situation, rather than moving around carelessly.

Those were my thoughts as the newbie psychic who'd missed his chance to flee, then I took a step out from behind cover.

"I'm sorry, but I'd appreciate it if we could stop with the violence."

"Hmm. I haven't seen you before."

The little girl gazed up at me. She was actually adorable. The old-fashioned Japanese clothing suited her—she was like a doll.

"Pleased to meet you. My name is Sasaki."

"You appear to be with the bureau. Are you the source of that water?"

"Well, essentially."

"I see. Then it has a use when combined with this girl."

"……"

She'd figured out exactly what was going on. This wasn't going well. I had to somehow stay a part of this conversation and get information out of her.

"You two have awe-inspiring powers. One controls the area with flying objects, and then you clean up the survivors. For future reference and for my own benefit, could I ask your names…?"

"…Do you not know who we are?"

"Huh?"

Wait, was she famous or something? Either way, as a freshman psychic, I had no clue. I had exposed my inexperience. To make matters worse, the very first thing I'd said turned out to be a land mine.

"Ah, then you are new."

"……"

The girl's lips turned up in a smirk.

Help me, Peeps. I think I'm in serious trouble this time.

✳

I was totally overwhelmed on my first mission. Now my leader had been knocked out, and the only one left on the scene was me, a total rookie. Still radio silence over the earpiece. All pretense was gone—this mission was over.

"As you pointed out, I am new here. I was assigned to the bureau just yesterday. Hence, I would very much like to say hello to everyone else as well. Could I possibly have an audience with the other one? I have no idea where your partner is at the moment."

"You seem quite calm despite the situation."

"Ignorance is my only weapon right now."

"Optimistic, too."

As we exchanged offhand remarks, I glanced around the room. The regular psychics had been annihilated. Each of them, without exception, lay on the floor, not even flinching—either they were unconscious or dead. And the psychics who had been on support duty didn't appear to be coming back.

On the other hand, no matter how much I searched, I couldn't find the psychic responsible for the hurricane. I had to consider the possibility of a third psychic hiding them. If so, then I certainly wouldn't be able to spot them.

And so I was left with no other choice. "I'll ask again—may I have an audience with them?"

"Unfortunately, you may not."

"...That's a shame."

I switched my mic off. Fortunately for me, the lightning spell's incantation was relatively short. Having practiced chanting the incantations for days, my tongue had gotten very used to them, and I was able to complete the spell in only a few seconds.

"Hah...!" I stuck my hand out in front of me and fired the intermediate spell.

With a loud crack, a bolt of electricity shot at the girl's lower body. It went faster than the eye could track, making contact with the target and tearing through her. Blood and skin went shooting off, sending a splatter of red across the floor.

It had taken a chunk out of her lower-right leg. Her small body, losing its balance, crumpled. It was grotesque as hell.

"Ngaaah..."

I'd wanted to hold her back with a softer spell, but given that this was a life-or-death situation, I'd chosen what would reach her fastest. As I saw the scene unfold, I started feeling a bit guilty. That she was a young girl was *not* good for my mental health.

But considering this spell could topple a large tree in a single hit, the damage she'd taken was slight. Her bones were still attached—it had just blown some skin off. She seemed to have some kind of barrier set up. That made sense, considering how she'd broken through Miss Hoshizaki's ice with her bare hand.

Was it her own power or someone else's? I had a hunch she could take a bullet dead-on and keep fighting like nothing had happened.

As pained groans escaped the girl's mouth, something nearby moved.

"Tch..." The building scraps and bowling balls littering the floor around me rose into the air one after another and hurtled toward me. As I'd surmised, the psychic causing the hurricane was using some means to hide their presence and get closer to me.

Now inside the power's effective range, dozens of heavy objects were flying at me.

Chanting a spell would be too slow. Now that I'd used one in battle, I understood how important it was to be able to cast spells without incantations.

In the future, I'd have to put more effort into speeding up my spells in addition to learning new ones. Peeps could apparently cast all beginner and most intermediate spells without an incantation. What an impressive sparrow.

Pleading for it to work, I omitted the incantation and envisioned the spell. I chose the same one as before—the lightning attack. It was the most powerful weapon I had at my disposal.

And it worked. Talk about a fight-or-flight response. Multiple lances of lightning burst out with a crack, shooting down the targets before me, one after another. The shattered scraps and bowling balls passed by me, now nothing more than tiny fragments. I used the shield to block those heading directly at me, disabling them. A few did connect, but it only hurt a little. I'd managed to deal with the pressing threat by a hair.

"What…?"

Just then, I heard a voice from a point about a dozen meters in front of me. A man's voice. But I couldn't see him anywhere. He definitely seemed to be borrowing a third psychic's power to stay hidden.

"Around here, maybe?"

Getting a little carried away, I proceeded to fire a second lightning attack in the direction of the voice, aiming low. A series of crackling noises resounded, lights radiating out like a fan. One of them struck something, sending off a spatter of red.

It seemed I'd been correct. Where there had been nothing, figures suddenly appeared—a team of two.

The first was a man who looked somewhere in his late twenties or early thirties. Right away, I noticed his long blond hair, slicked back. He wore an expensive-looking suit, and at a glance, one might have mistaken him for a yakuza member.

The other was standing right up next to him—a girl who appeared to be in middle school. She had glossy black hair in a princess cut, and her gothic Lolita-style clothing only made her more conspicuous. Her features were fairly cute, and her clothes, though they might have seemed garish on some, suited her well.

My main concern was which of them I'd hit with the spell, and that turned out to be the man. The blast had taken out everything below his knees. The girl raised her voice, holding him in her arms as he lay faceup. Her shriek resounded through the room.

Unlike the girl a moment earlier, the man had been struck with the lightning attack's full force. Both his legs had been blown off. I was worried the others might have the same resistance as my first opponent, so I hadn't held back.

"Who exactly are you?"

The girl in traditional clothing spoke from below me, seeing that the tables had turned. She pushed her arms against the floor as she craned her head up to look at me.

Didn't her wound hurt?

"As I said before, I am a newcomer who just entered this business yesterday."

"……"

She glared up at me skeptically.

It might have been possible to end them all right here. However, the section chief's orders had been to capture the psychics, and judging by my previous conversation, these ones seemed to be celebrities. Whatever I did now would impact my future treatment, so I needed to tread lightly.

Another thing that bothered me was that the fallen girl's body had started to change. She was still on the floor, but her leg was—in the present tense—squirming. Somehow, the flesh and blood vessels were beginning to reconnect. It was like her leg was trying to reform itself with each passing second. It was so gross.

"I have a proposal for you all," I offered.

"…Go ahead."

"If you promise not to speak of what happened here to anybody, I'll stop attacking. Would you be amenable to considering this a draw? I'd rather not go too far and get hurt, after all."

"……"

It would be pretty miserable if they held a grudge, found out where I lived, and attacked me there. I was already wary of the section chief these days, so I didn't want to make any more personal enemies. Though I had the option of fleeing to the otherworld, my life in modern Japan was just as important to me.

"What do you think?"

"…Fine."

After seeming to consider for a few moments, the girl in traditional clothes gave a slight nod. Negotiations complete.

A moment later, another person appeared right in front of me. This new character materialized out of thin air next to the fallen girl and didn't make a sound—just like Peeps's teleportation. A similar power probably existed.

She looked to be about twenty. She had a big chest, a big butt, and was just overflowing with feminine charms. Her outfit—a white blouse, a beige jacket, and navy culottes—combined with her youthful appearance to give her the look of a new employee.

"You said your name was Sasaki?" asked the girl in traditional clothing.

"Yes."

Belatedly, I wished I'd used a false name. All anyone would have to do was check something like my mail to get my information. Realizing it was too late to hide, though, I pulled myself together and admitted it.

When I did, the girl came forward with a surprising proposal.

"Would you be interested in joining us?"

"Unfortunately, I'm the type who's more at ease sticking with the biggest player."

"...I see."

I was surprised she'd make such an invitation at this point. *If I didn't know any better, I'd say she was older than she appeared. Perhaps even older than me*, I thought suddenly. It wouldn't be strange for there to be a power that falsified your appearance.

"If ever the mood strikes you, we would be happy for you to give us a call."

"Well, if I ever have the chance. Thank you."

Before I'd realized it, the blond-haired man and the gothic Lolita had approached the girl in traditional clothes. The former, without his legs, had been dragged there by the latter. Thanks to that, the floor was a complete mess—stained bright red all over with blood.

"In that case, we will be taking our leave."

"Oh, just one second."

"...What is it?"

"What happened to our boss? He's in his thirties, very handsome. He was taking charge from outside until a little while ago. But I haven't heard a word from him since the fighting started."

"……"

"Is there something wrong?"

"Do you require his custody?"

"He is important, as my boss, so yes."

I wanted to avoid switching bosses on my first day. Those who took over positions like that tended to reject how the former boss worked. New employees recruited by one's predecessor were always the best heavy bags to vent stress on.

Government employee culture had a more feudal bent, so it was probably even worse at a job like this.

"…All right."

"Is he alive?"

"Our match ended in a draw, so he is only injured. We will return him to you."

"Thank you."

It seemed the enemy group had gotten their hands on the section chief. That meant they would have snatched him if I hadn't brought it up. It felt exactly like doing business with a shady company. No time for complacency.

"Until next time…"

"Yes. I look forward to working with you in the future."

"……"

The girl gave me a strange look as I left. Her brow had furrowed.

Did she not like what I'd said? I couldn't help it—as a corporate slave, those kinds of phrases were like a natural reflex.

The attractive woman's power was definitely teleportation. As we said good-bye, they all disappeared without a trace, withdrawing from the scene—including the two who had retreated to the little girl.

"……"

Now all that was left was the obliterated team from the bureau.

✳

After all that had happened, the evening passed quickly, and the next day, I had orders to return to the office.

Immediately upon returning from the site last night, I'd been confined in a nearby hotel at the organization's direction. I hadn't been able to go home to my apartment or see Peeps. Nor had I been able to go to the otherworld. I felt very guilty for leaving the vice manager and Mr. French hanging.

Yet I'd somehow managed to return alive. For that, at least, I was grateful.

I was the only one who was relieved, however. When I checked in afterward, I heard that 70 percent of all the psychics who had participated in the operation had died. Most of the ones who'd survived were the front-line support psychics. The losses we'd sustained during the incident had been massive.

The organization was in chaos.

Not every psychic working for the bureau had taken part, but we had certainly lost a good portion. Plus, participating in the front lines required psychics who were above average, both in terms of their powers and mental fortitude. That meant they were particularly valuable resources.

It was explained to me that we wouldn't be engaging in any more large-scale actions for some time.

And the section chief, who was both commander and responsible party during the incident, did indeed seem to have been kidnapped by the enemy group. They told me he'd been released—at the same time as I completed negotiations with the girl—for no apparent reason.

"...Then the enemy withdrew on their own?"

"Yes, that's right."

Thanks to that, I was subjected to some annoying questions during the debriefing.

I'd been called out to the office, and as soon as I got there, someone grabbed me. Now I was in a small conference room, no more than ten square meters in size, sitting across a desk from the section chief. No one else was in sight.

"......"

"Did you hear anything, Chief?"

"No, I haven't gotten any particular intel, either," said my boss, a big strip of gauze wrapped around one cheek. Several bits of white were peeking out from the sleeves of his suit jacket, too. He must have been embroiled in his own fight without me knowing.

"By the way," I inquired, "who provided the intel we relied on for the operation? I'm sure the other bureau members reported the same thing, but the enemy knew exactly what our plans were."

"...That was a failure on my part. I apologize."

"You can't give any more details?"

"Unfortunately, no."

"I see…"

This was one of the hard parts about being a government worker. Being in a section chief's position within the Cabinet Office meant he was a national bureaucrat. A single casual decision at his own discretion could affect hundreds, if not thousands of civilian lives. If he said no, then he meant it.

But I was going to keep pressing him anyway. After all, if I didn't, I'd be the one getting questioned. In order to keep my own situation hidden, acting offended seemed the best option.

"Were they investigating the bureau's psychics? Or perhaps thinning our numbers was the goal all along. Sorry to start making things up as a new hire, but still…," I speculated, taking the opportunity to toss in a bland remark or two.

"……"

He made a show of thinking hard about something. He was probably suspicious of my part in all this. Considering the timing, I *had* put myself in an extremely dubious situation. I wouldn't have been surprised if he thought I was an undercover agent for the enemy.

"Could it be that you're suspicious of me?"

"Yes, I am."

Whoa. That was a more straightforward response than I expected.

He stared at me dead in the eyes.

I couldn't afford to make terms like *otherworld* and *magic* into public key words. Without that, however, I couldn't explain why the enemy group had withdrawn. In which case, my only course of action was to come off as dubious of him as well.

"In that case, Chief, I also suspect you."

"…I see."

I learned after the fact that the girl in traditional clothes and the man with the hurricane ability were apparently big celebrities in Japan's psychic circles. Everyone in the bureau had been warned: If you encountered them, don't think—just run.

Of course, that hadn't been shared with me during the meeting beforehand. Their appearance had been completely unforeseen. If the bureau had considered it even a slight possibility, they might have tread more carefully—or so the others in the support group had lamented. I'd seen their faces in the back seat of the HiAce on our way out of the site. They were white as ghosts, and I didn't think they could be lying.

Psychics were apparently granted something like ranks depending on how their ability worked. Essentially, it was akin to a threat level. They used the letters A through F, which was a global index I was told other also countries used. My own rank was E. That had been determined by the tests I'd undergone at Miss Hoshizaki's request when she first brought me in.

Many things factored into this assessment, but one particularly easy-to-understand contributor was that any power that, unleashed in a city, proved difficult for police to control was ranked D or above.

The issue here was that the ones we'd encountered the previous day were a team consisting of mostly psychics of rank B or above. The girl in traditional clothing was A rank. The hurricane man and teleporter were B rank. The gothic Lolita princess's ability, some sort of optic camouflage, was rank D. Miss Hoshizaki, incidentally, was rank D like the goth girl.

Although the compatibility of certain powers would greatly affect things, I was told during training that a difference of two levels would make a matchup totally one-sided. And the highest-ranking psychic on our side on the previous mission was rank B.

Out of all those people, only one was B rank. Psychics of rank B or higher must be incredibly rare. Below that, we'd had a handful of rank Cs. Of them, over half had died in the initial onslaught. I could only pray there was no such thing as a rank-S psychic.

"I didn't see any of the psychics we were looking for," I said. "Instead, the ones who did appear—and I only learned this later—were a well-known group of very high-ranking irregulars; isn't that right?"

"I've received reports to that effect. All I can say is that I'm sorry."

"I doubt anyone would have emerged from that event unscathed. However, doesn't using a lone support psychic who was slow to escape as a decoy seem a little cruel to you?"

"No, no, I wasn't intending anything like that. Please calm down."

"Are you sure about that?"

"Psychics are too valuable. You work well with Hoshizaki, and on top of that, you have a sharp mind."

"Then I'd prefer that you trusted me a little bit, if possible."

My plan was to gripe like a subordinate to get him to compromise. If even *that* didn't work, I'd have to go into hiding with Peeps in the otherworld. Then I could learn a whole bunch of magic before returning. It might be the end of my life as I knew it, but a little Kobe beef chateaubriand wouldn't be out of the question. In the worst-case scenario, I could request employment with the girl in traditional clothes.

"...All right. I'll trust your account."

"Thank you."

"I apologize for putting you through all that on your first job."

"Don't be—it's in the past now."

"Right..."

I gave a slight bow and rose from my seat.

No one tried to stop me as I left the room. In the meantime, I was told operations involving psychics were being suspended—meaning it was time to do nothing but eat and sleep.

They'd still pay me, apparently, so for that, I felt fortunate.

✳

Once the section chief released me, I quietly returned to the office.

I passed by lines of employee desks. Since we'd had so many casualties, it felt like a wake. As a newcomer, I didn't know much, but it seemed like many of these people had been close or cared for each other as coworkers—there had been many human connections here.

A moment later, Miss Hoshizaki stopped me. "Sasaki, got a second?"

"Hmm? Yes, what is it?"

"I, er. I had something to talk to you about..."

I didn't have any real work to do after this. Given that I couldn't go home the previous day, I figured I'd just head back now. On the way, I'd need to stop by the supermarket—oh, and I'd have to remember to get Peeps a gift.

Since I didn't know when I'd be coming into the office next, though, I decided I should at least hear her out. For the time being, she was my coworker and partner, someone I would be working with both in the office and on-site. I didn't want to give her a bad impression.

"Did you need something from me?"

"Yes, er, well, I just wanted to, um, say thank you, so...," she started to say, scratching at her cheek. Her attitude was actually reserved for once—quite unexpected from someone who was usually so aggressive.

"No need to thank me. We both just did the jobs we were assigned, right? And ultimately, I wasn't strong enough and let you get hurt. In that sense, I should be apologizing to you."

I didn't want to get involved with her too carelessly; instead, I'd put some distance between us. If we started getting along, I was fearful I'd get dragged into something even more catastrophic. To me, the ideal distance was one where we were both a little reserved.

"...Yeah?" she asked.

"I think so, yes."

"But you did still save me."

"Please don't worry about it."

"If it's all the same to you, I'd still like to repay you."

"......"

And now she's causing me trouble again. I'd never experienced someone of the opposite sex being friendly with me except at that brothel, so I couldn't help but be skeptical. When I thought about what she would inevitably expect from me in return, it made me want to turn around and run straight home.

I really wanted to get back as soon as I could and have a soul-soothing conversation with Peeps.

✳

What ended up happening was that, after a great fuss, I went with Miss Hoshizaki to lunch. She was treating me as thanks for the previous day, after all.

If I'd had work to do, I could have told her I was busy and wormed my way out of it. However, we were both bureau psychics with the same orders to stand by at home. Since I'd already told them about quitting my previous job, using that excuse probably wouldn't work, either.

Ultimately, we ended up sitting face-to-face at an Italian place near the bureau.

"Thanks for coming with me, Sasaki."

"I was actually getting hungry anyway."

"I'm happy to hear you say that."

It was refreshing, seeing her relatively docile compared to the first time we met. I could tell she sincerely wanted to thank me.

Even so, I was restless.

"This is a gorgeous restaurant. Do you come here often?"

"Not really, no..."

A short while after we sat down, the waiter came over to take our orders. Befitting the stylish restaurant, he was a good-looking young man. He wore his closely cropped black hair in an undercut, with his bangs up and away from his forehead. His features were chiseled, and his beard was shaved into an anchor shape, which all went perfectly with the sharp restaurant uniform.

"Have you decided what you'd like to order?"

"I'll have the special, please."

"Oh, I'll have that, too…"

"Understood."

The way he respectfully nodded to us radiated refinement. I was totally jealous. Not only was he the lean, muscular type, but he also had long legs, and his crisp uniform just seemed to add insult to injury. He'd probably never had any trouble dating. Also, he was quite mild-mannered and really cool.

"We do have a selection of alcohol. Would you like anything?"

"Oh, in that case…"

Might as well go for the beer with lunch. I've always dreamed of doing this. If I had been an attractive older man and wanted to put the moves on Miss Hoshizaki, I might have considered the choice of *not* day-drinking. But for an ordinary man like myself, who had learned to evaluate the probability of such things, there was no reason to hold back.

No, I'd just have fun when I wanted, and to hell with everyone around me. That was the only way to enrich my life, considering my bad luck with women. I couldn't let the values of others sweep me away. After all, a young woman *was* treating me to lunch.

Having a beer with lunch now would be even better than usual. *I can feel it—I swear.*

"I'll have this beer, here."

"Today's recommended craft beer, then? Understood."

I wondered what Miss Hoshizaki would get. I wanted her to drink all she wanted and not mind me.

As I thought this, I gave her an encouraging look, and her expression became troubled.

"I'm actually a minor, so…"

"Wait. You are?"

I'd thought for sure she was at least twenty.

The waiter was surprised, too.

"In that case, feel free to pick something from our soft drink menu."

"…All right."

After we'd put in our orders, the hunky waiter went back into the kitchen. It was a little past eleven in the morning, and the store had plenty of empty seats. Our food wouldn't take too long to get to us.

A few moments after seeing the waiter go back into the kitchen, this old man asked the minor a question.

"Forgive me for being rude, but how old *are* you?"

"……"

"Oh, but don't feel like you have to tell me…" Wouldn't be good for me if she complained I'd been harassing her later.

Still, she answered more honestly than I'd expected.

"…I'm sixteen."

"What…?"

Sixteen? That meant she was, you know, just a high school kid. Asking her had given me a second shock. I never imagined she'd be in high school.

"You're, uh, not joking, right?"

"I get this look using makeup, and I go to school like a normal person."

"…I see."

I'd always heard that makeup could transform a woman, but apparently, you could use it to look older rather than just younger. Ever since we'd met, I'd been noticing how thick her makeup was. The way she always wore a suit only reinforced the illusion. I'd never really thought hard about how old she might be.

But she still didn't seem like a high school girl. She seemed like she was definitely over twenty at a minimum.

"People won't take you seriously if they think you're a child. That's why I change my appearance like this."

"Is that also why you talk the way you do?"

"……"

It looked like I'd hit the nail on the head. Thinking back to our past exchanges, when I considered that it was a high school girl leaving "mister" off my name, it felt strangely okay. It also made me helplessly curious about how she acted at school.

"You get along normally with friends, though, right?"

"…Of course I do."

That makes sense. If she spoke and acted like this at school, she would probably have a hard time making friends. Plus, she was hiding the fact that she had psychic powers. Her life must be one hell of a ride.

I was glad I didn't get roped into all this until later in life.

"Why do you work so hard at this job, Miss Hoshizaki? If you're in high school, there must be all sorts of other things you want to do, interests you want to pursue. There's no need spend all your time on something so dangerous.

"Like I said before, this job pays very well."

"I see."

Seemed like it was a financial problem for her. That made me hesitate to ask her anything more. It was possible she was in a much tougher situation than I'd assumed. Honestly, after confirming she was in her teens, I came to wonder if it was her youthful energy giving her the courage to do such risky work.

I would definitely need to maintain the distance between us very carefully from now on.

"Apologies for the wait."

As I was thinking, the waiter came over with our meals. After that, we spent our lunchtime quietly, exchanging idle chatter here and there.

✳

That day, after finishing lunch, I said good-bye to Miss Hoshizaki and went to stock up.

Because I couldn't go back to my apartment the previous day, I had to be very deliberate in my procurement, looking for things with as much value as possible. I also needed to remember a gift for Peeps. As an apology for leaving him alone for an entire day, I splurged on it.

That said, it was possible I was being tailed by a colleague of the section chief's, so I decided to forgo making any purchases they might consider suspicious. The receipt would tell a story: one of a middle-aged man with a sudden abundance of free time and a newfound interest in the outdoors.

I'd probably need to look into ways to stock up on things like sugar and chocolate, which I needed to buy in bulk. *Should probably hold off on buying them at the neighborhood supermarket, at least. Or online, since it leaves records linked to my personal account.*

Those were the types of thoughts running through my mind as I headed home. I proceeded down the road, a plastic bag hanging from my arm.

Moments later, my phone rang. I checked the display and saw my boss's name on it.

"...Hello, this is Sasaki."

If I'd had a choice, I would have rather not answered. I couldn't afford to ignore him, though.

"*It's Akutsu. Do you have a couple minutes?*"

"Sure."

"*Sorry, but I'd like you to come into the office tomorrow as well. We have work for you.*"

"Understood, sir."

I didn't have anything else to do, so I could probably manage that. They were paying me properly, too, so I didn't have any aversion to showing up. Compared to my former employment, where unpaid overtime was the norm, this was heaven. Still, I did wonder why he was calling me in.

He couldn't have been harboring suspicions about my past purchases, could he? A shiver ran down my spine.

The words that followed, however, were completely unexpected.

"*You're being promoted. Consider this an unofficial notification.*"

"…Oh."

A promotion? A promotion. That took me completely by surprise.

"*I'm sure you understand how many bureau members we lost in the incident. We'll need to fill those empty positions. This is extremely unusual, but psychics are particularly limited human resources. We've decided to prioritize HR as soon as possible.*"

His words made sense. Based on what Miss Hoshizaki had told me, out of the entire population, only one in every hundred thousand people were psychics. This was far fewer people than worked as government employees. At least when it came to the on-site players, there was probably zero leeway.

I had a hunch my paycheck would be seeing a windfall in the future.

"I understand, sir."

"*For the time being, it looks like your next mission will be to canvas for psychics.*"

"I suppose that was inevitable."

"*I'll give you more details tomorrow at the bureau. All right, I need to go.*"

"Good-bye, sir."

For now, I could only pray this psychic recruitment turned out to be safe work.

*

After I'd stocked up on my intended items and was on the way back home, something happened.

I was hurrying from the station to my apartment when I caught sight of something odd. Around the side of a convenience store, in a small conjoining alley, there was a child in a very cute-looking outfit adorned with frills and ribbons rummaging around in the store's garbage cans.

No matter how I looked at it, the kid had to be scavenging for scraps of food.

If it had been a shabbily dressed old person, I wouldn't have given it too much thought. But no matter how many times I looked—the child was definitely an elementary school student. And they were wearing clothes that looked like they'd jumped right out of an anime.

They had their face in the can, so I couldn't make out their expression. From the youthful, taut skin below their skirt, though, they didn't appear to be an adult who was simply short. And judging by the long pigtails, I assumed it was a girl.

"……"

Should I report this to the police? I wondered—and then I remembered.

Starting last week, I *was* a police officer. I'd been given identification and told to carry it at all times. Even now, it was shoved in my pants pocket. With it, even a middle-aged fogy like me could safely speak to a young girl. No danger of pepper spray or personal alarms. I could even bring her to the nearest police box.

"…All right."

I remembered struggling to eat as well, during my years of compulsory education. White rice provided by distant relatives out of obligation only. A time when stir-fry with wieners and cabbage or instant ramen with no toppings were special treats. Eating snacks at a friend's house was the highlight of my day.

Thanks in part to these experiences, my legs moved automatically.

"Do you have a moment, miss?" I addressed the girl fishing through the trash, readying my ID in one hand.

"Ah…!" When I spoke, her whole body gave a jolt of surprise. Her head quickly came up out of the bin, and her eyes locked onto mine.

To be honest, I'd always wanted to do something like this. Whip out my police ID and hide behind state power to act all high-and-mighty. I mean, it just had to feel good, right? But now that I was actually

doing it, guilt rushed in instead. I wasn't that impressive a person, and there wasn't really anything to gain from it.

Honestly, it made me feel a little empty.

"……"

"Could I ask what you're up to?"

As I'd expected, she was a girl who appeared to be of elementary school age. Her eyes were strikingly big and round, and her features were very cute. But her expression was far from childlike. This was because she had no emotion whatsoever on her face. What stared back at me was like a Noh mask.

Meanwhile, the rest of her—at a glance—screamed "magical girl." The kind you saw a lot of in anime. Her otherworldly pink hair caught the eye, and I doubt you could have fit more frills on her skirt if you tried.

That said, the clothes were dirty, coming apart, or outright ripped in spots. She smelled pretty awful, and without even being that close to her, it felt like I'd just walked past a homeless person. Her hair was greasy with skin oil, too. You couldn't get this way in a day or two. She seemed to be quite skilled and experienced at scavenging for leftovers.

"I'm a police officer. If it's all right, we can bring you to a police box…"

"Leave me alone."

No sooner had I asked the question than she'd turned back to face the garbage bin. She then resumed rummaging through its contents.

"……"

It was like watching a professional at work. She sorted through it silently and smoothly, seeming oddly determined.

I hesitated to say anything more to her. I didn't want to cause a scene and give actual police officers a headache. Despite having a police ID, my position wasn't exactly clear. Marching straight into a police box like I worked there would only cause trouble for the real officers on patrol. The section chief would also think less of me for it.

All of which gave me no other choice.

"You could eat this, if you want," I said, taking an ice cream out of the plastic bag in my hand.

I'd just bought it at the shop in front of the station up the road, planning to have it for dessert. However, seeing a girl rummaging through the waste of a convenience store made my body move on its own. I'd bought two—one for me, one for Peeps—so I was offering her mine as a present. If she'd been an adult, I probably wouldn't have done this.

"…You're not going to lecture me?"

Her question was odd. Was this a common interaction for her?

"Did you want me to lecture you?"

"……"

But her confusion over my words only lasted a moment.

"You shouldn't get involved with me, Officer."

"Huh?"

Suddenly, the girl's body floated into the air.

Her feet left the ground, and she drifted upward without any support. Naturally, I was shocked. I certainly hadn't expected to see *that*.

"See you."

And with a short good-bye, she somehow disappeared. As if splitting apart the scenery behind me, a jet-black crack had appeared in the air and swallowed her up. It looked just like when you saw black holes in science fiction movies.

"…Are you kidding me?"

I thought I'd run into an abandoned child wandering the streets—I would never have guessed she was actually a psychic.

✳

After the homeless girl left, I went quietly back to my apartment.

There, as I shared the events of the last two days with Peeps, I got dinner ready. I lined up the ingredients from the supermarket and turned on the burner. I worked quickly, parboiling the vegetables and grilling the meat.

And then dinner was served—on our plates were Kobe beef chateaubriand steaks. I'd finally gone and bought it.

"So this is Kobe beef chateaubriand?"

"You've done so much for me that I wanted to thank you."

If I hadn't learned that lightning spell from Peeps, I probably would have died. It was with that thought in mind that I'd naturally reached for the expensive stuff. I'd even gone all the way to a department store in the city instead of the neighborhood supermarket to get my hands on it.

One hundred grams had been thirty thousand yen. For both of us, the expense came to sixty thousand. And I hadn't bought it where they sold the fresh food, but in the gift corner on a separate floor. Thankfully, they'd had some in the storefront.

"How is it? I know Mr. Yamada at the pet shop was raving about it."

"It is good. Oh my, this is good."

"Glad to hear it."

It was cute watching Peeps peck away at the chateaubriand, which I'd cut into slivers and set up on the round dining table. One after another, the pieces of meat piled on the plate disappeared into his mouth. He was like a one of the pigeons at the park eating scraps of sweet treats some kid dropped. He was so cute—although, I was a little anxious as I watched him.

Thanks to that, I could feel his sincere appreciation for my efforts. It wasn't flattery—he seemed to think, from the bottom of his heart, that this was delicious.

My feelings were sincere, too. I was glad I'd bought it.

Next to the plates, I'd prepared salt, pepper, and steak sauce. Peeps would deftly use his beak to roll the meat in one and season it to his liking. What charming creatures Java sparrows were.

"I could eat this every day and never grow tired of it."

"Well, it cost about as much as an entire month of food…" My hands had been shaking while I was preparing it. An awful sweat had broken out on my back—what if I'd burned it?

"…Is it truly that expensive?"

"Yep."

"I see…"

Seeing him clearly deflate like that was also very charming.

That said, even though it was pricey meat, it wasn't so expensive that I couldn't buy it. Now that I'd successfully changed jobs, we could probably manage it once a month. If I only got enough for Peeps, that would halve the expense.

"We can't have it *every* day, but I think in the future we could occasionally splurge on it."

"Are you sure?"

"You do so much for me, after all."

"…I thank you for this kindness."

"You're very welcome."

As we ate the lavish meat together, I felt like we'd gotten a little closer.

✳

After finishing dinner, it was time for my scheduled short stay in the otherworld. With products in both arms, I went down to see the vice manager.

During the last several days, I'd gotten used to going to the reception room at the Hermann Trading Company and exchanging the goods I'd brought for gold coins. The flow of the process came easily to me now. For wares I'd brought in the past, all I did was verify the price. For new items, I explained their purpose and directions for use.

The prize items this time were battery-powered motion-sensor security cameras and bug repellent spray.

The motion-sensor camera came with an LCD screen, so you could check static images taken without needing a separate device. It made it a little tougher to use, but it would do the job. Originally, it was meant to link to the cloud, so you could see the pictures on the internet.

It was intended for use in areas without power by mountaineering clubs and the like. It had a low-power mode that took eight batteries, letting it stay on standby mode for, at most, an entire year. It really gave me a sense of how far technology was progressing—these sorts of products got more advanced by the day.

As for the bug repellent, I'd purchased it because Peeps had said no magic like it existed here. Hunting no doubt involved a lot of walking around in bushes and thickets, so they were probably swarmed with bugs on a daily basis.

Still, they apparently had a similar herbal solution, so it came down to how much more effective the spray was. Since today was my first time bringing it, I figured I'd limit the inventory and gauge customer reaction.

I'd also considered portable water purifiers, but after remembering you could make drinkable water using magic, I didn't bother. I didn't know how big a portion of the population were magic users, but rich nobles almost certainly took one along in lieu of a canteen.

The vice manager's response to both of the new items was positive. All in all, it came out to 2,300 gold coins—a fairly decent sale. We were both pleased with the transaction.

After business was done, it was time for me to practice magic as before. Once I'd checked in at our usual lodgings and dropped off my things, I could head straight out of town. My goals were to learn intermediate barrier magic and healing magic.

However, right after sealing the deal, the vice manager had something to discuss. Apparently, the viscount had called for me. If possible, I was to go to the castle with the vice manager immediately. He'd already prepared a carriage outside, so I couldn't exactly refuse.

We went directly to the towering castle in the center of town. The carriage bumped as it went, the Hermann Trading Company's crest emblazoned on the side.

We got through the gates on familiarity alone. When we informed those in the castle that we'd been summoned by the viscount, they happily escorted us to our destination. We'd been to the place a few times already, so they probably recognized us. We didn't have to wait very long before being shown to the reception room.

"I thank you for coming, Sasaki."

"I am most honored by your invitation."

When we arrived, Viscount Müller was already in the room. At his urging, the vice manager and I settled down on a sofa side by side.

After the usual greetings, we explained our contributions to him. He seemed to once again take an interest in what we'd brought— motion-sensor cameras and bug repellent spray—and like the vice manager, he wanted to buy everything I had. In addition, in accordance with our previous promise, I delivered a set of ten transceivers plus batteries.

With that, my otherworld wallet got nine thousand gold coins heavier.

When our deals were over for the time being, the count finally looked me in the eye and said, "By the way, Sasaki, I have another matter to discuss."

I couldn't help but tense up.

"What is it, my lord?"

The first thing that came to mind was a three-letter word I'd heard from the vice manager during my last visit—*war*. Since then, around fifty or sixty days had passed in local time. It wouldn't be strange if the situation had changed entirely.

"As a merchant, I am sure you have already heard, but about ten days ago, a neighboring country—the Ohgen Empire—attacked the Kingdom of Herz. Relations have been unstable between us for two months, but this incident constitutes an official opening of hostilities."

I was right on the mark.

"I, too, have been ordered by the Crown to lead troops against the enemy."

"……"

What was someone in my position supposed to say at a time like this? Definitely not "Good luck," and I doubted pleasantly saying "I see," was right, either. Naturally, my mouth stayed closed.

"The Ohgen Empire is powerful. Just comparing numbers, they have twice as many soldiers as we do. Given this town's proximity to the border, it is possible enemy soldiers will make it here. If that happens, the damage will be considerable."

"……"

The viscount's expression was grave as he spoke. I felt the excitement from my deal with the vice manager receding. In that case, it would be better to stay away from this world and wait it out in Japan. Ah, and first I'd have to exchange the local currency with that of the Ohgen Empire. The currency of a defeated nation would definitely decrease in value.

"And so, Sasaki, I must ask if you would be willing to help me."

"I deeply apologize, my lord, but I am only a craftsman—and no special merchant. I don't have any particular martial talent, nor am I accustomed to instructing others. I am certain I would be of little help to you, my lord."

"I feel guilty for asking this of you. However, the wares you have brought to my territory can support the war effort and will be extremely valuable. I would like to employ you as a wartime merchant."

"My lord, I…"

"I know full well that you are a craftsman of another nation and that you are a merchant. I don't mind you prioritizing your own profits above all else. In exchange, I humbly ask you to provide us with the goods we need to beat back the Ohgen Empire."

"……"

Just when I thought all the psychic business had settled down, too. What a mess this conversation was turning into.

*

(The Neighbor's POV)

Once again, I'm sitting outside the front door of my apartment, waiting.

For whom? For what?

For the older man who lives next door to come home.

"……"

How many years have I been spending my time after school like this?

It all started when my parents divorced. My mother took custody, and we moved here. That was a little after I started elementary school. Ever since then, I was disciplined harsher and more often, until things finally settled into the way they are now.

I've known the older man the next apartment over for several years. He first moved into this complex several months after my mother and I did. I still remember when he visited with sweets to greet us as a new neighbor.

I can recall exactly what my mother said: *Gifts from a man living in a cheap apartment like this? You obviously can't eat them. It's too dangerous.* And I vividly remember the way she looked as she threw the sweets in the garbage a second later.

I wasn't eating enough at the time. Even after having been in the garbage, those sweets were like a feast. They were the first solid food I'd eaten in days, aside from school lunches, and they helped clear the fog in my mind somewhat.

Ever since then, whenever he saw me sitting in front of the door, he'd give me something to eat. Most of what he gave me was relatively high in calories, like bread or rice balls; he must have been worried about how thin I was. The next most frequent were sweets. I only learned recently that most of the sweets he'd given me had some kind of extra nutrition in them, like vitamins.

And it didn't stop there. I remember him giving me all kinds of things: piping-hot meat buns on cold winter days and chilled sports drinks and ice cream on hot summer ones. He even gave me some school supplies at one point.

"……"

Child services has visited us a few times in the past. I don't know for sure, but I think the man called and reported us. My mother would always play the loving parent in front of them, though, so they never did anything. All the visits ended with a verbal warning, and my relationship with my mother never changed.

I don't know what goes through her head, but my mother has never changed. She doesn't let me, her child, into her home when she's away, and she doesn't feed me, either. When I graduated from elementary school and started middle school, things stayed just the same.

My mother knows about the gifts from the man next door but never says anything about it.

I still don't understand what she's thinking.

"…He's late again today," I say to nobody in particular, looking up at the night sky.

It's very clear out, and lots of stars are twinkling. It's a scene I've looked up at many times before. I think this night sky will be what sticks with me as I age, the scenery of my youthful memories.

"Come to think of it, he's said before that he works a lot of overtime."

On a different note, I've been starting to think about something else recently.

About my worth as a woman.

In elementary school, I didn't know anything about that stuff, and I was still impoverishedly thin back then anyway. All I knew was that I was starving, so I was wildly overjoyed at the food the man gave me. I never thought my body was worth any more than that food.

But that changed shortly after entering middle school.

I was blessed with more physical development than other girls my age. More and more boys started looking at me at school. I think I'm actually bigger than my homeroom teacher, too.

And while my mother did buy me a new uniform, she never got me any bras or anything for my periods. For the latter, I make do with the toilet paper in the school restrooms. But I can't do anything about the former. That only put more eyes on me.

Maybe that's why I started thinking about the natural progression of that attention. And wondering if the older man living next door was seeking that sort of thing as well.

I'd be lying if I said the idea wasn't repulsive. Even the men my mother brings home lately have started ogling me. If I was given the same thing, I very much doubt I'd be able to accept it. I think I hate everyone other than myself.

But when I consider thanking the man next door for taking this much care of me, I feel like maybe it would be possible, at least. I think he's older than my mom, but it doesn't seem like he's married. It wouldn't really cause a problem if he was to get me pregnant.

I can repay his saving me from starvation by fulfilling his sexual needs. It's the only way for someone like me—who owns nothing but the clothes on her back—to repay him anyway.

As long as he used a condom or took care of any abortions, I might be okay letting him have his way for the time being. It's probably also a reflection of my trash heap of a heart, wanting that kind of reassurance in a visible form.

I learned in class that too many abortions can ruin your uterus. But I doubt I'll be able to properly raise children in my future. Better to ruin it now before I ruin the life of some unborn child.

Ah, I'm so dirty it makes me sick.

How could I ever criticize my mother like this?

" ...... "

I'm alive right now because of the older man living in the apartment next door. I can't survive without the food he gives me. It'll probably keep going like this, too.

At least until I graduate middle school and become independent from my mother, it'll go on, and on, and on.

<Interworld Trade>

In the end, I decided to ask the viscount to let me think on it.

When I conveyed my decision, the vice manager next to me went white in the face. It seemed delaying one's response to a noble's request was very rude, and I was more or less told that on my way out.

Viscount Müller was likely a man of great character—he had seen me off with a smile.

And so we had a planning session after getting back to our fancy lodgings in town. The members of this council were two—Peeps and me. We hadn't really needed a maid attached to our room, but in any case, we had her do some shopping for us in town. She probably wouldn't return for a while. Thanks to that, we could discuss the matters at hand undisturbed.

"Peeps, be honest. How is this war looking?"

"In all likelihood, this nation will lose."

"I, er, I see…"

I'd gotten that feeling from the viscount's demeanor, but hearing it come straight from the bird's mouth was a shock. If Peeps thought we'd most likely lose, then it seemed like the best decision was to leave town immediately.

But if I said I had no reservations, I'd be lying. I hadn't known this world for long, but I had still developed friendships—first and foremost, Mr. Marc, the vice manager of the Hermann Trading Company. Plus, the eatery I had built for Peeps was here. It was not a good feeling to imagine all of that being stolen from me.

"…What do you want to do?"

"I'd like to do something if I can. But nothing good will come of participating in a losing battle, will it? In which case, I think it would be more constructive to figure out how everyone can be happy after we've lost."

"You are right—the way the situation is progressing, the end is inevitable."

"Right?"

"However, my magic holds the potential to turn the situation on its head."

"...It does?"

"My name is Piercarlo the Starsage, inhabitant of another world."

"Oh, that's what you said before."

The first time I talked to Peeps, that was how he introduced himself. I personally enjoyed the imposing air that contrasted his cute looks. Now I could understand that exaggerated, provocative title of Starsage.

"It would not be difficult to settle a quibble between nations. Destruction is easy. However, creating something takes time. You have formed a relationship with this town, and thus, we should endeavor never to lose that."

"I see."

"To that end, however, I shall require your assistance."

"You will?"

"This frail body of mine cannot withstand the burdens of repeatedly using advanced magic. Just as when we move between worlds, I must use your body as a conduit to cast it. In brief, I must remain on your shoulder like this."

"Ah..."

I didn't know for certain how we would settle this war, but if Peeps said he could do it, he probably had the skill. The problem, then, was our position in society. We couldn't afford to act publicly.

That would veer us off the course Peeps advocated—ignoring everyone else and spending your time however you wanted. We would be lionized by those around us and given strenuous jobs from those in positions of power. The life we'd have would be far from the "doing nothing but eat and sleep" ideal.

"We should think of a way to resolve things as inconspicuously as possible."

"Agreed."

And personally, I was happy with Peeps's position regarding the war. If trouble started in this world, it could lead to my life in Japan breaking down. Given how sharp my new boss was, I wanted to leave as much wiggle room in my life as possible.

Frankly, I wanted this world to be somewhere I could always take a break.

"Then whether we like it or not, you must learn more about magic. In addition to teaching you intermediate spells, I will give you explanations regarding advanced magic and higher. We can then decide together how to use it."

"Thanks, I really appreciate it."

And so for the next few days, I practiced magic and listened to Peeps's lectures.

✳

As a result of this otherworld sojourn, I succeeded in learning one new intermediate spell.

And it was, amazingly, healing magic.

Now that there was a possibility I'd be taking part in a war, I made barrier magic and healing magic my top priority for this practice session. Though I hadn't managed to learn the former yet, I'd squeezed out the latter on the last day of our practice, right before we wrapped things up for the day.

I tested it out a few hundred times on a wild rat that was near death. Seeing its wounds heal was soul-stirring. According to Peeps, while beginner-level healing magic could only cure small scrapes, bruises, and simple bone fractures, the intermediate-level version could completely heal missing limbs, serious burns, and complex fractures depending on how much mana was used.

Once you learned intermediate healing magic, you would never go hungry. That's what Peeps claimed, at least. As I watched the rat run off, his words seemed to make sense. Just moments ago, it had been on the brink of death, and now it was full of energy.

In addition, Peeps lectured me on large-scale magic. Several spells of this type, apparently, could change the shape of *mountains*. How on earth would that even work? The two of us decided further investigation was needed for any practical use.

Once magic practice was finished and we'd eaten and slept at our lodgings, we went home. Considering the summons from my boss, we couldn't let our stay drag on for too long. As soon as we returned, I had to race to the office.

My destination was a conference room in the bureau's city center office building. In that cramped, ten-square-meter space, the section chief and I faced one another.

"I'm sorry for calling you up so soon after saying you'd have a break."

"No, I don't mind at all."

"When it comes to government employees being promoted, there's usually an exam or something you'd need to take, but our workplace is a bit special in that regard. In the first place, our official titles don't even match what we do. Considering that, roles can change quickly, like now, based on the situation on the ground."

"Will my pay change?"

"No need to worry about that—we have a suitable amount prepared."

"I'm happy to hear it."

My expenses lately had been on the high side, and my next payday would be a long time coming. *I wonder how first-year employee bonuses even work...* My old job had had nothing like that, so I couldn't help but be curious.

"That said, the fact is that we just don't have enough people. I'm sorry to do this to you when you just joined, but I'll be having you stand by as part of our combat-ready forces. As I explained last night, I'd like for you to partner with Miss Hoshizaki to canvas for new psychics."

"I understand about needing to bring in more psychics, but..."

"Is there a problem?"

"It's just that teaming up with Miss Hoshizaki seems like overkill."

"There are several ways to persuade psychics to join us, actually. You might use information reported to the police to find stray psychics and talk to them, or you might try to bring active irregular psychics to the negotiating table."

"I see."

"Would you want to do all that by yourself?"

"No, sir. I'll gladly pair up with Miss Hoshizaki for it."

Getting into a fight with some other psychic on my own? You had to be joking.

Love you, Miss Hoshizaki.

"An excellent decision."

"Will I be receiving hazard pay in that case?"

"As a general rule, our work outside the office always garners hazard pay. You're better off assuming there are no safe jobs related to psychics.

Suppose a total amateur with no training was suddenly handed a cannon or a missile. That's what a psychic is."

"...That does make sense, sir."

Perfect sense, in fact, given what had happened at the bowling alley. Maybe that was exactly why they were going through the trouble of gathering these psychics, employing them with the government, and using *them* to solve problems caused by other psychics. Otherwise, you'd need to mobilize the police or Self Defense Forces en masse. And on top of that, it was the best way to maintain secrecy.

"However, incidents like the one two days ago are rare."

"I wouldn't know what to do if you'd said they were commonplace."

Incidentally, the new title on my business card was going to be lieutenant, apparently. Considering my age, it had a pretty good ring to it. By the same scale, the section chief was a chief superintendent—an awfully impressive-sounding position.

"I'd also like you to take care of Hoshizaki."

"Sir? I feel like she's the one who's been taking care of me."

"Despite how she looks, her personality is cause for concern. And she's young."

"...Understood, sir."

Now that I knew how old she was, I could easily agree with the section chief.

Still, she was someone from whom I wanted to keep my distance, if possible. She certainly pricked at my conscience in an "adult responsibilities" sort of way, but staying alive had to be my first priority. After all, she was a high school girl turned mercenary out to pile up hazard pay.

"You'll be contacted about the unofficial announcement in a little under an hour. Until then, stand by in the office."

"I will, sir. I'll be waiting at my desk."

And that was how my meeting with the boss went.

Ultimately, the whole idea of a promotion sounded pretty good. Nothing about me had changed, but I could feel a groundless confidence swelling within me. This must be why other wage slaves around the world suck up to their bosses so much.

And for this workplace, the higher up the ladder I climbed, the more freedom it seemed I'd have. That would, in turn, make it easier to go to the otherworld. As a government employee, maybe it wouldn't be a bad idea to put my hat in the bureau's promotion ring.

I'd probably never have it as good as those who passed the government exam, but it still got my hopes up.

*

After safely receiving advance notice of the promotion, I got my very own business card stating I was a police lieutenant. Miss Hoshizaki had been promoted along with me.

Without anything in particular on the schedule, I left the office. The boss had told me to take the next few days to rest and recuperate. The bureau seemed to have its hands full dealing with the aftermath of the incident anyway, and I was told that the on-site teams would likely be on break for a while. So for today, I simply took him up on his generosity.

I didn't forget to stock up at the superstore on my way home. That said, making purchases too far out of the ordinary could put the section chief's eyes on me. I picked out the transceivers and batteries Viscount Müller had ordered—and a few minimal spices.

Once I got back to my apartment, it was time for Peeps and me to teleport to the otherworld.

It was just a little after noon. I'd been out of the house for three or four hours. With the otherworld's faster passage of time, several days would have passed. I doubted the war with the Ohgen Empire had changed all that much in the meantime.

If I assumed my paid vacation would last about a week, that worked out to hundreds of days in the otherworld. For now, I could be active over there without worrying about the time. At the very least, I wouldn't have to stress about the town getting destroyed while I was out at work.

"Okay, Peeps, I'm ready."

"All right."

With everything I needed in hand, we moved from the apartment to the otherworld's inn.

The familiar flooring of my room was supplanted by the hard stone of the inn. As far as I could tell from checking the scenery outside window, nothing crazy seemed to have happened. It looked like the Ohgen Empire's invasion hadn't reached Baytrium just yet.

But I couldn't afford to be optimistic. We hurried off to see the vice manager.

*

After heading to the trading company, we were immediately taken to meet Mr. Marc. It just so happened that he had received word from Viscount Müller, and he was hoping to head to the castle as soon as we were ready. He explained it was almost certainly about the war with their neighboring country. It wouldn't do to ignore the request, so we left for the castle, carrying only the contributions I was to make to the viscount. And so, just like that, we now sat in the castle's reception room, facing one another.

"...I see, my lord—military provisions and raw materials."

"Indeed."

As part of the war effort, Viscount Müller had been given orders by the nation proper to construct frontline facilities and make sure they were prepared to feed the soldiers. This was his role as a noble of his kingdom and was separate from defending his own territory.

Such responsibilities applied not only to Viscount Müller but to all the nobles in the kingdom. Each had been tasked with various duties proportionate to the economic and geographical conditions of their lands. If any of them disobeyed, it was quite possible their noble house would be ruined.

Incidentally, the count of the next territory over had been ordered to mobilize fifty thousand troops and one thousand horses. As a freshman in this world, I couldn't tell which of them had been levied the heavier burden. In any case, it seemed quite difficult for both of them.

"We must deliver the goods needed for the war within one month. It will take two weeks by carriage to reach the front. Procurement is already underway, but the situation is grim. Excluding the two weeks for travel, we will have two weeks to gather all the items requested. It seems impossible."

"Is that so, my lord?"

"We've been making requests of the trading companies and merchants in this territory, not least of all the Hermann Trading Company. But even with all of them, we cannot meet the demand for supplies. The price of food has already begun to soar, and if we continue with force, this town's economy will collapse before the war is even lost."

"……"

It felt a lot more like war than I was anticipating. I could sense the full force of a nation here.

"I understand that making such a request of you, a citizen of a foreign nation, is misplaced. However, if you have any means, would you advise me? Even a small suggestion would be welcome. As you can see, we are desperate."

As he said that, he bowed his head deeply.

Beside me, the vice manager's eyes were popping out of his head. Nobles bowing to commoners must have been a *very* rare occurrence here. And that spoke to just how dire their situation was.

"...Advice, my lord?"

"Yes. Do you have any good ideas?"

I didn't know what to tell him. If I made Peeps's existence public, there might have been any number of ways to go about this. On the other hand, I was just a commoner without his assistance. I may have well-lined pockets at the moment, but I could only do so much as an individual.

Thinking back, however, Peeps and I had agreed to remain as inconspicuous as possible. It was probably best to avoid bringing him into the conversation. I needed to keep my dealings with Viscount Müller within the scope of what I could do alone.

And hey, every pet owner wanted to show off in front of his pet once in a while, right?

"There is one thing I'd like to confirm, my lord."

"What is that?"

"What was the root cause of this war?"

"Ah yes. Being from another nation, you would require an explanation."

You can never tell unless you try—the viscount was much readier to explain things than I would have expected. His face as he did so, however, was even grimmer than before. The reason rapidly became clear as he described the situation.

Only one hundred years ago, this nation had been an important power known for its excellence in magic. It didn't have much land to its name, but it had many talented magicians and was able to go toe-to-toe with the great nations that surrounded it.

But that prominence had waned over the years. According to the viscount, the cause was a deterioration of the nation's magical talent. Overconsumption by the privileged classes—royalty, nobility, wealthy merchants—had disgusted many talented magicians. Over time, they began deserting the country, taking its power with them.

"Sir Sasaki, do you know of the Starsage?"

"…I do not, my lord."

A term I was sure I had heard somewhere before spilled from the viscount's lips. That was the title Peeps had used for himself.

"Despite all this, the nation managed to remain at peace—all because a tremendously great and powerful magician continued wielding his powers for us from inside the palace. He was known as the Starsage, and it was thanks to him that our days continued to pass in tranquility."

"……"

I decided to stay quiet and hear what he had to say. Peeps had shown no particular reaction, either. He just sat perched patiently on my shoulder like always.

"However, that ended several years ago. The Lord Starsage was the beneficiary of enormous support from the current king, and a group of envious nobles had him assassinated. Since then, this nation has seen only deterioration and decay, collapsing ever further by the moment."

"I see…"

Peeps had been a way more amazing person than I'd thought. Now I felt even more hesitant about relying on him. I didn't imagine it felt too great to think about lending his aid to the country that had back-stabbed him. He seemed to have good feelings about this particular viscount, but that didn't necessarily extend to the others.

And then Peeps, having escaped his assassination by means unknown to me, had ended up in a pet shop as a Java sparrow. He had stayed there for two months, while several years had passed here, and his country had entered a tailspin. Now it faced an unprecedented crisis, under attack from its neighbor.

"Did the Lord Starsage have no apprentices, my lord?"

"I am told he was an extremely busy man and had no time to train any."

"So that's how it was…"

In that case, even if we held out this time, the Ohgen Empire was bound to keep pressing the attack. Why, the Kingdom of Herz was nothing but their prey now, wasn't it? Unless the Empire was truly made to understand there would be consequences, the problem would remain unsolved.

"Why was he called the Starsage, my lord?"

"Somebody once had the idea that he commanded as many spells as there are stars in the night sky, and the name remained. In truth, I know of no magician who maintains a repertoire as massive as his. Though the moniker did seem to cause him some embarrassment."

"I see."

Viscount Müller was correct: Peeps knew a crazy amount of magic. He'd memorized even the longest of spells down to the letter and taught them all to me with precision. And despite his alleged embarrassment at the nickname, he used it to introduce himself anyway. Adorable.

Lord Starsage—I think he might be quite fond of it, actually.

✳

The place: still the castle reception room. The conversation: still regarding wartime countermeasures.

I'd heard the gist of things from the viscount. Moreover, we were now expected to give the best advice we could.

"I am fully aware that suggesting this will be rude, my lord, but now that you have explained the situation to me, I cannot help but think the wisest decision in this case would be to give up the Kingdom of Herz. I feel negotiation with the Ohgen Empire to be our only means of survival."

"Mr. Sasaki!" cried the vice manager on hearing my words. It did seem an extremely rude proposition.

"No, I don't mind," interjected the viscount. "I, too, had considered it."

"But, my lord…!" Losing his calm, the vice manager started casting about his gaze. It would probably be a huge mess if anyone but us heard this.

"However, I cannot risk the lives of my people on uncertain negotiations. With only one month left before I go to the front lines, I decided it would be impossible to bring the Empire to the negotiating table. In no small part because troops from other territories will be marching through my own on their way to the enemy."

"That would indeed make it a very difficult undertaking, my lord."

Come to think of it, he was right. Compared to modern society, things in this world progressed rather leisurely. The lack of telephones and internet meant information traveled at a snail's pace. Like the viscount had said, just communicating with the relevant people and places would easily take more than a month. In this world, horses were still working hard to fill in for fiber-optic cables.

"But I cannot predict the future, and so I believe we should aim to minimize our risk by responding to the kingdom's requests to the minimum degree possible. If word soon spreads that we have suffered the greatest of losses, I'm sure others will arrive at the same conclusion."

"I see, my lord."

"Fortunately, I have received no request to mobilize troops. The financial strain we will face instead is great, but as long as the people survive, there will be other chances in the future. We should arm ourselves if and only if it truly becomes necessary."

Viscount Müller seemed to have considered this from many angles. Even the duty he'd been levied with was most likely the result of strenuous negotiation and compromise. Any careless proposals on my part would only display my own indiscretion. This man was very talented—much more so than a nobody like me. I sensed he was definitely the type of person meant to lead others.

"I understand your considerations, my lord. I will limit my own to provisions and other supplies."

"I apologize—I was the one who troubled you with all this."

"No, not at all, my lord. In fact, I apologize for making such a meddlesome proposal."

"What do you think, then? Any plans?"

"Hmm…"

It wouldn't be possible to bring anything from Japan. Not food to feed tens of thousands of people, at least. That would go way beyond my credit card limit. And if the section chief learned about it, he'd absolutely have questions.

Which meant I'd have to bring things in from other towns in this world.

It was possible, I supposed. I could use what money I'd saved with my business so far to buy things in bulk, then have Peeps use teleportation magic to bring it here. If we did that, we'd be able to deliver what the viscount needed to the site within the allotted time. We'd get good enough results even in just a month.

However, that plan didn't come without its obstacles. Who would I say was doing it and how? I needed to answer those questions so Peeps didn't end up front and center in all this.

"Come to think of it, my lord, I remember hearing rumor of a kind of magic that allows one to travel freely through space. Apparently, one can move to a faraway destination in the blink of an eye. Distances that would normally take days could be traversed in a matter of seconds."

"I, too, have heard of this. The Lord Starsage was known for his proficiency in the spell. However, I know of no other magicians who can use it. It is apparently a very advanced technique, and average magicians are unable to learn it."

"…I see, my lord."

The viscount had said transferring the goods to the site would only take half the month mentioned—two weeks. If, somehow, a storehouse within his territory was suddenly stocked with the necessary goods, as if they'd appeared out of thin air, that would fulfill his need.

And what if no one was there to witness them appearing?

I'd only talked to the viscount a few times so far, but he seemed to have an outstanding character. If I forbade him from speaking of it to others, then even if a nonsensical amount of provisions and supplies suddenly appeared in one of his storehouses, would he keep silent?

Not only about that, of course, but about *us* as well. I felt, at any rate, that he would be a lot more accommodating than my local tax revenue office.

"……"

I shot a glance at my shoulder, where Peeps was perched. He responded with a very small nod. The Lord Starsage himself had given me the go-ahead.

"Viscount Müller, let us assume that there is a warehouse within my lord's territory that contains enough provisions and supplies to fulfill your duties. Would it be possible to bring it all to the site within the month available?"

"It would. We have plenty of leeway when it comes to moving goods."

"In that case, my lord, regarding such a storehouse in your territory— would you be able to keep it altogether secret and not let anyone in or out of it until the goods are to be transported?"

"Are you saying you are able to use that…?"

"If I cannot have your word, my lord, then I will need to leave this town."

I had decided to put *myself* front and center instead of Peeps. Judging by what Viscount Müller had said, the title of Starsage was too serious to raise here and now. Simply suggesting that he was alive would influence the power balance so greatly that neighboring countries would cower in fear.

"Can I have your word, my lord?"

"You have it," answered Viscount Müller without wasting another second. His next words came in a graver tone than any before. "I will prepare such a storehouse at once. I also swear to tell no one."

"Thank you, my lord."

"I should be the one offering my thanks to you, Sir Sasaki."

And so, for the time being, I had my work cut out for me.

✳

The viscount did as promised and prepared a grand storehouse on the castle grounds for us.

The building was about the size of a school gymnasium. A craftsman had urgently converted the entryway into a two-layered construction, and outside the only door stood a knight—one of the viscount's close aides. The knights would be keeping watch all day and all night. These were the people who had been waiting in the wings during our audiences.

Not a soul was allowed in or out of the storehouse, including the viscount and ourselves. Those were the orders the knights had received. This way, we could do our work worry free. The only ones who could come and go were Peeps, who could use the teleportation spell, and myself.

In my hand, I held the shopping list from the viscount. Once I transported all the items written on it to our warehouse, my task would be complete. As for the sale price of each, in consideration of wartime need, the viscount would pay me rates a good deal higher than the market value.

Though it would depend on my purchase price, because of how incredibly much of it there was, I had the feeling I was going to make an absurd profit. If I failed, the risk to my relationship with the viscount was high. However, the financial merits for pulling this off were immeasurable.

And so we wasted no time heading out to stock up. Our destination: a town called Newsonia in the Republic of Lunge. I'd unlocked the name of a third country, after the Kingdom of Herz and the Ohgen Empire.

Peeps had been the one with the idea to come here. According to him, he'd visited several times on trade-related business in the past. With his teleportation magic to help accelerate the journey, we arrived with no difficulties.

"It's lively here. Seems like it's more prosperous than the viscount's territory."

"Indeed. This is a flourishing town of trade."

I exchanged words with my beloved pet bird as I gazed at the town roads stretching off in front of me. It was on a completely different scale than Baytrium. This place clearly had a much denser population and significantly larger buildings. Maybe it isn't a direct analogy, but it struck me as akin to the difference between a street of shops in a suburban city and a famous shopping district in the capital.

I also felt like the people coming and going were dressed in finer clothes, and there were quite a few more individuals here with horns growing out of their heads, wings sprouting from their backs, and so on and so forth. It stirred up memories of the first time I visited Tokyo and walked through Ginza and Shibuya. I could feel myself getting more excited at the prospect of stocking up in such a place.

"Peeps, do you have any connections here?"

"Let me see…"

The well-informed sparrow led the way through the streets of Newsonia. We walked for a little under an hour or so, finally arriving at a large building.

It was a store—so large as to dwarf the Hermann Trading Company's facility. All made of stone, it stood eight stories high. Comparing it to Mitsukoshi's flagship store in Nipponbashi only made it look all the more resplendent. Peeps's contact was far grander than I'd imagined. I was too poor for this—I was getting scared.

"…Here?"

"This place should be able to gather and supply a good amount of actual stock. Suppliers who deal in provisions sufficient to feed tens of thousands are limited, especially now, when the prices in neighboring countries are soaring due to the declaration of war."

"I figured as much."

"And since we are using currency from Herz for our purchases, I would like do business here as much as possible. When a large amount of currency suddenly flows into a market, it can cause all sorts of problems. I believe your nation's financial mechanisms would act in much the same way."

"I gotcha, Peeps."

If that was his take on it, I'd just have to do my best right here. I needed to be resolute in my negotiations, to prevent them from sizing me up and taking advantage.

I had to say, this was one worldly sparrow, remembering the lay of the land across nations. The more he showed off his extensive knowledge, the more curious I became about what he had been doing with his life before his reincarnation. I bet he was the type of person who'd end up in textbooks down the road. If there were any portraits of him left, I wanted to go and pay my respects. There must have been at least one if he'd been so distinguished, right?

"……"

No, wait. That was a careless wish. What if he used to be a handsome older man with a chiseled face? That would definitely make me more self-conscious in our future conversations. Feeling his weight on my shoulder and imagining a dapper man—that would be kind of rough on me. But in that case, what look *would* I be able to accept? And so I thought for a while about this and that, leaving my own worthless appearance to the side.

I realized I was starting to get sidetracked, so I decided to focus on the problem in front of me. Peeps was Peeps. He was my adorable pet sparrow—nothing more and nothing less.

"*…What is the matter?*"

"I was just thinking. How far is it from the viscount's place to here?"

"*If a wagon was to make the journey at leisure from Baytrium in the Kingdom of Herz to Newsonia in the Republic of Lunge, it would take several weeks without interruption. Riding a swift steed would still take several days.*"

"That's pretty far."

"*And yet if we were to use one of those…airplanes, or what have you, that are so prominent in your nation, it would be but a few hours. In some places, they are attempting to domesticate certain subspecies of small dragon with low intelligence to use instead of horses.*"

"Would probably be faster to fly, huh?"

"*Indeed—they would far outpace horses.*"

So it looked like dragons existed here, too. If I was ever able to adopt one as a pet… Well, let's just say I was as interested in that prospect as I was with getting a golden retriever. I mean, how cool, right? Soaring into the air on its back would be beyond my dreams.

"What's this place called, by the way?"

"*The Kepler Trading Company.*"

"Got it. Kepler Trading Company."

With one hand on my leather bag lined with large gold coins, I steeled myself and walked right up to the front door.

✳

After catching the attention of a store clerk who was making the rounds, we were shown to an upper floor. Here, too, I simply introduced Peeps, riding on my shoulder, as my familiar, and nobody questioned it. It seemed this was common knowledge internationally as well. What on earth *was* a familiar anyway?

"Pleased to meet you. My name is Joseph, and I handle the foodstuffs for our company."

"My name is Sasaki. Thank you so much for agreeing to meet with me."

The reception room at the Hermann Trading Company was grand in its own right, but this one was beyond that. It might even have surpassed the one at Viscount Müller's castle.

And don't even get me *started* on how comfortable the sofa was. The moment my butt hit the cushion, my hips practically gave way and sunk deep into it. I wanted to sit there forever.

"I hear you're looking to stock a large amount of food."

"Yes, that's right. I wanted to ask for what's on this list here."

No sooner had we exchanged greetings than I handed him the list containing a description of the goods we needed. It had been written out in accordance with Viscount Müller's request and included our suggested price. As it happened, Peeps and I had collaborated to draft the list.

According to him, the Kepler Trading Company was like one of Japan's big five general trading companies, such as Mitsubishi or Itochu. It was also an international business, with branches in many countries.

Here in Newsonia, it had an enormous warehouse where various wares from all over the world converged. Because we needed to purchase a large variety of goods, Peeps had suggested this location.

"You're looking to order quite a lot, aren't you?"

"I assumed your company would have this much in inventory."

"Yes, we can indeed supply what you're looking for, Mr. Sasaki. However, as purchasing them all at once would create shortages for other customers, it is not a simple decision for us."

"In terms of remuneration, I believe what's written here is sufficient."

"We have many clients with whom we've been doing business for a very long time. No matter how much you offer us, if it was to cause trouble for them, we cannot easily accept."

"I see…"

"And looking at this list, it's as if you're planning to start a war. Now that I think about it, we did receive reports from a branch to the south that the price of food had gone up there—and that relations with nearby nations had become dubious."

Yikes, they're already onto me. If possible, I'd wanted to procure everything in secret, but that was quickly proving difficult. This was definitely going to affect the major players in business circles and the market.

Now I became curious about how well-informed the man before me actually was. Still, I doubted he'd tell me directly if I asked. In that case, I'd have to pull the conversation along myself. In my opinion, momentum was crucial in deals like these.

"Exactly—it is astonishing how fast a certain nation has declined."

"……"

If transceivers were so sought-after, then it seemed to me this world had no common form of high-speed information transfer—including magic. That said, if they'd used dragon mail as Peeps had mentioned, they could have gotten wind of things within a few days.

The viscount had said they'd confirmed an incursion from the Empire about ten days ago. For these negotiations, it seemed wise to assume news of the Ohgen Empire going to war with the Kingdom of Herz had reached them. Even if they didn't know, they would have heard that things were already very touch and go.

"And you are correct in that these will be supplies for war."

"Well, you've come from quite far away. If that is the case, though, would it not be difficult to bring the stores back even if you did purchase them here? If the war situation changes in that time, the losses could be staggering."

"That isn't the case—they will definitely help."

"A reassuring judgment, indeed."

As he spoke, Mr. Joseph's face brimmed with a relaxed confidence. Watching him brought to mind the face of a certain representative at a large company with whom I had worked at my former job. The company had been a valued client, and I specifically remembered the man's conspicuous pride and self-assured manner. How many times had he put me through the wringer?

"I've already arranged a means of transport."

"Very quick of you. I doubt you could have done such a thing without preparing fairly far in advance. That must mean it will begin for real very soon, doesn't it?"

"Yes, that does seem to be where things are headed."

"...I see."

"And so I respectfully ask for the cooperation of the Kepler Trading Company."

I sincerely doubted I could purchase the goods if I directly mentioned the Kingdom of Herz. Considering the level of national decay and corruption I had heard about from the viscount, it wouldn't be strange if the surrounding countries were unsympathetic. After all, it was the type of country that would assassinate a man like Peeps out of envy.

"I apologize, Lord Sasaki, but you don't appear to be from these lands..."

"The situation lets someone like me move around more easily. And we believe that what is needed to assure a merchant's loyalty is neither position nor honor, but profit."

"Would you be reaching out to any other companies?"

"No, we are very much set on the Kepler Trading Company."

"How were you thinking of paying?"

"As it says on the order form, we've prepared Herzian gold coins."

"...Hmm."

After my answer, Mr. Joseph began thinking about something. I wondered what sorts of scenarios were going through his mind. We watched him in silence, still sitting on the sofa, my heart pounding out of its chest.

A few moments later, he gave me his response.

"All right, understood. I'd like to go forward with this deal."

"Thank you so much."

And so we were able to obtain his approval without trouble. Relief washed over me. I'd been worrying over this and that just in case he turned me down, but all that quickly vanished from my mind. Out of respect for Peeps introducing me to this place, I was reluctant to go knocking on some other trading company's door.

"In return, I would like to maintain a special relationship with your country. You will likely need many things after the war is over. When that happens, I would very much appreciate you coming straight to us."

"I couldn't ask for anything better. However, regarding this purchase, would you be able to keep it a secret for the time being? We have made a very big investment of our own, so I wanted to know if you could keep our dealings within the company."

"Of course, yes—I understand."

I felt this when talking to the vice manager at the Hermann Trading Company, too, but I loved how quickly and promptly deals with merchants ended. It wasn't like talking to nobles—there was no particular etiquette to be observed, and we didn't take very long greeting each other.

This deal, too, was a straightforward and simple affair.

✳

Our biggest problem was receiving the goods. I dealt with it by borrowing a warehouse in the town of Newsonia, then having everything I'd purchased delivered there. Once it was all inside, we would use Peeps's magic to send the lot to the storehouse in Viscount Müller's castle. Ultimately, we finished transporting everything within a few days.

"*Until the very end, that man mistook us for messengers of the Ohgen Empire.*"

"That's what it seemed like."

We were conversing in the Newsonia warehouse, gazing at its now-empty interior.

"*And you planned for exactly that, did you not?*"

"Well, I hadn't thought about it precisely like that, but…"

My idea had been to try to get him to think I was a war profiteer from an unrelated nation. The misunderstanding was actually because the other party read too deeply into what I was saying. Doubtless the large gold coins I'd brought so many of had also added to my credibility.

"*We likely would not have had such an easy time had we been forthright and told them we were from the Kingdom of Herz. Its deterioration would be common knowledge in the Republic of Lunge. Any merchant worth his salt would shy away from investing in a nation like that.*"

"I wonder if the deal worked out *because* we used gold coins from the Kingdom of Herz."

"How do you figure that?"

"Suppose that when the Ohgen Empire decided it was going to invade the Kingdom of Herz, it wanted to first unload its stores of enemy currency before opening hostilities. It's just an idea I had, but I think maybe the Kepler Trading Company's representative took it that way."

Nobody would think someone from the Kingdom of Herz, hated as it was by those in nearby nations, would ever grab a wad of their own country's currency and attempt to visit a third nation to purchase military provisions. I assumed that such treatment would be even more prominent since this world's culture regarding commerce lagged so far behind. That was part of why I hadn't exchanged the currency for something else before trying to make a deal.

Peeps's answer, however, took a different track.

"That was dangerous. That viewpoint is based on your own world, with its banknotes and national debts and bonds."

"Wait, then how do you see it, Peeps?"

It gave me a start to hear words like *banknotes* and *national debts* come from his beak. How much knowledge had this sparrow gained during the few days I'd given him internet access? I felt a chill run down my spine. Had I allied myself with a more dangerous being than I thought?

"Gold coins from the Kingdom of Herz are high in purity. Compared to those of other nations, they are simply worth more."

"Yet another thing that doesn't sound good for a nation rumored to be on the decline."

"I ordered them to be made like that. It can't possibly have changed in just a few years. Setting silver and copper coins aside, gold coins and large gold coins can be melted down and reused. That is why the Kingdom of Herz still maintains an equal position in its dealings with other nations."

"...I see."

Peeps really was frighteningly formidable. I hadn't thought he'd be helpful even on this topic. No wonder I had received no warning about bringing in Herzian money. Everything had been under this ultra sparrow's supervision.

That's a little frustrating. I'll have to try harder next time.

"Another major factor was whether you had thought of a way to bring the purchased goods back by yourself."

"The representative was impressed by that, too, wasn't he?"

"The flow of goods in this world is yet immature compared to that of your own. A considerable distance separates the Republic of Lunge from the Kingdom of Herz and the Ohgen Empire. If this has been prepared in advance, it becomes an investment he simply cannot ignore."

"But now I'm scared of him finding out."

"You haven't told any lies. It should pose no issue."

"Is that how it works?"

"There is no point in worrying over it. It is the fault of he who was deceived, not you."

What a plucky sparrow he is. As someone who is timid, I envied the way he spoke with absolute confidence about everything. Still, he *had* been assassinated as a result, so maybe it was best to have a little restraint. As a comparatively average man, I figured I'd continue my unassuming existence in the future.

"If we had slightly more time, we could have diversified our purchase options."

"We barely had enough time for this as it was, so this will have to do, Peeps."

"Indeed…"

"I guess that means we should get back to the viscount."

"Yes. I only hope this will lighten his burden somewhat."

We'd have big problems if we stayed too long and the Kepler Trading Company uncovered the truth. It was time to take our leave of the Republic of Lunge.

✳

With Peeps's help, we safely got all the provisions and supplies transported. After verifying the work was done, we were ready to open up Viscount Müller's secret storehouse. The door, which had been closed tight for several days, was opened by the hands of the knights protecting it. Naturally, it was only the viscount and us two in attendance.

"I cannot believe this storehouse has filled in just a few days…"

"What do you think, my lord?"

Upon seeing the stacks upon stacks of provisions in person, the viscount was shocked. As the one responsible, I felt pretty good. Even though Peeps had done most of it.

"Sir Sasaki, I don't know how I can possibly thank you for the work you've done. This will give us another chance, and these supplies are likely to save the lives of an inestimable number of people."

"I'm happy I was able to carry out my duty, my lord."

"You have saved us. Thank you, Sir Sasaki," answered Viscount Müller, bowing his head to me.

The knights with us began to look visibly ruffled when they saw that. They immediately gave their opinions on the matter, telling him to raise his head—or that he mustn't do such a thing toward a commoner. Apparently, the knights were themselves a noble class. It felt like I was growing quite accustomed to this sort of exchange.

The payment, which I had been wondering about, put us overwhelmingly in the positives. We'd made a profit—no, an absolute *fortune*. Because of Viscount Müller's consideration for us, he'd bought everything at a significant markup. Of course, it was still low compared to the skyrocketing prices this area was seeing, but the wholesale price was still plenty high.

I now had close to a thousand large gold coins in my wallet. That worked out to about one hundred thousand gold coins. It had dropped to zero when we stocked up, but the viscount's payment had increased our initial holdings severalfold.

Lodging at the fancy place where I'd been staying for the last few days cost one gold coin for a one-night, two-day stay. Revisiting a familiar calculation, if I assumed one year to be 365 days here, then I could do nothing but eat and sleep for the next two hundred years.

In other words, financial worries had all but disappeared from my life. In this world, anyhow.

"We will be departing shortly for the front. It is thanks to you that we can bring these goods along with time to spare. We will not have to run our horses ragged."

"I understand, my lord. I'll be praying for your safety."

"Thank you."

With his knights in tow, the viscount disappeared.

Seeing them off marked the completion of my mission. For the time being, I'd be watching and waiting for a report from him. Regarding payment for the goods, I'd received the full amount in cash from Viscount Müller. While we'd been struggling to stock all the provisions and supplies, he had apparently been selling off many of the valuables

and higher-priced household effects to manage things. He was probably imagining the worst-case scenario.

As a nobleman of the Kingdom of Herz—well-known for its striking
level of corruption—he must have been one of the very rare men of
outstanding character. He was such a good person that it made *me* feel
guilty as I gazed at his lonely mansion, bereft of its furnishings.

＊

After bidding farewell to the viscount, we headed straight for where
Mr. French worked—to have a delicious meal. The CLOSED sign was up
in preparation for afternoon service, but I ignored this and headed
inside, making my way to the kitchen. It was then that I saw the
employees arguing over something with a person I didn't recognize.
Among them was the one we'd come looking for.

"Mr. French, what seems to be the commotion?"

"Ah, s-sir!" he cried out when he noticed us.

The rest of the gathering turned their attention to us as well. I actually remembered several of the ones in aprons. These had to be the
staff members Mr. French had employed. I had seen them moving
about the kitchen in a bustle during my last visit.

Standing opposite them were several men whose clothing marked
them as townspeople. I didn't recognize most of them, but the one in
front, facing down Mr. French, was a little bit familiar... Who was he?

"And who do we have here?"

"I-I'm sorry, sir! This is my master and the cooks from the restaurant where I used to work..."

"Ah, I get it. You're all from that restaurant?"

Now I remembered—he was the one who had been fighting with
Mr. French outside that shop. What business could someone like him
have here?

As I was thinking about it, Mr. French's former master asked, "Wh-
what reason does a noble have for being in a place like this, if I might
ask?"

My business suit must have confused him. I recalled that I had been
asked a similar question by several others—Mr. French as well as
people from the Hermann Trading Company.

"I am this restaurant's chief investor. What do you need with my
manager? There are many customers waiting to enjoy this shop in the

afternoon. If you need something, I would be more than happy to help. And to clarify, I am not a noble."

"I see—you're the owner of this shop, then?" Once he knew I wasn't a noble, his attitude worsened. At the same time, he offered a smirk. "There is something we absolutely must discuss with this man. This is a good chance, in fact—we would like you to hear it as well, sir. It would be for everyone's benefit."

"…What do you have to say?"

"This man has a criminal record—he has stolen from our restaurant's proceeds."

"……"

Come to think of it, I did remember Mr. French saying something along those lines. He, however, claimed he'd been framed. Considering how hard he'd worked these past few months, he was probably telling the truth. The people handling the store's accounting were dispatched by Hermann's vice manager. If Mr. French had done anything wrong, I'd have been told right away.

I didn't know what Mr. French was like before, but ever since I'd met him, he'd proven to be an extremely diligent worker, and he was certainly in Mr. Marc's good graces. If he said he was innocent, then there was nothing for it but to believe him.

"If that's what this is about, he's already told me."

"…What?"

My honest answer put a look of blank surprise on the man's face. He must have thought I had teamed up with Mr. French without knowing.

I didn't see much of a reaction from the assembled staff, either. It seemed the story of his origin had already made the rounds. Maybe the vice manager had laid the groundwork for this exact situation.

"He also insists he was falsely accused."

"Well, we know that's not true. After all, the money is gone."

"That sounds like a problem for your shop, not mine. His work here, at least, has been nothing short of spectacular. I don't know what sort of history he has, but to me, he is a valued friend."

"Sir…," said Mr. French, tearing up upon hearing my frank opinion.

I was pretty sure I had understood the situation. They'd seen someone they'd driven out doing well somewhere else and had come to pick a fight. I could sense it from the way the man had brought several cronies in tow.

"Then you're fine with employing thieves at this shop?"

"No, not at all."

"Well then, why have you—?"

"I hire no employees here. He and I are on equal terms. He receives financing from me, which he then uses to run this shop. That puts him on the same level as you—a manager. All I did was provide the funds to get this restaurant started."

At this, the man seemed taken aback.

For a few months now, I had let Mr. French pay his own salary. Basically, I'd told him he could have at it as long as it didn't affect the business. If this could be a place where Peeps could relax and dine on some delicious meals, that was enough for me. Mr. French and the vice manager could do as they wished otherwise. We only supplied the ingredients they needed to prepare, plain and simple.

"Is there anything else?"

"Well, I—I mean, there's plenty of…," the master stammered, starting to trip over his words suddenly. He must have had other complaints lined up.

"Did you pay us a visit to discuss something with him?"

"……"

"I would be more than happy to hear you out, if so."

"Er, well, I…"

I'd gotten curious and asked—but he fell silent. I'd just have to ask my colleague in that case.

"Mr. French, I'm sorry, but do you know what he's talking about?"

"Yes, sir. It's about—"

"H-hey!" cried the man as soon as Mr. French opened his mouth.

Mr. French continued, ignoring him and taking a determined attitude. "Our owner may have kindly placed me in charge, but I could never pass ingredients to other restaurants. I do feel an obligation to you for nurturing my talents, but I have one to him as well for helping me when I was down. I can't ignore that."

The man had no response.

After that, Mr. French launched into a detailed explanation.

And as he did, things gradually became clear. The source of the problem was the huge leap in food prices as a result of the war. Apparently,

Mr. French's former employer had been in the red for several days in a row now. At first, they thought they could just reflect the rise in costs in the price of their food, but when they did, the customers stopped coming. It seemed that the taste and the price were no longer in balance.

As far as our place was concerned, we were way in the black. Mr. French explained that, at the vice manager's suggestion, they'd made some bold changes to their menu. They now offered more expensive ingredients and meals, which had brought along a change in the clientele. Before now, they'd been catering to those of modest wealth—but now the main customers were *really* in the upper classes. With richer customers, they were able to raise the prices and still maintain a margin of profit, thus surviving the extreme inflation in costs.

I was struck by the vice manager's keen decisiveness. I'd have been too scared to do something like that. That must be why he held such a high position, despite being a commoner.

They were also able to keep older customers through a takeout service with a cheaper menu. This group saw the restaurant they had patronized becoming recognized by the upper classes and were not too displeased.

On top of all that, after hastily setting up some benches out front, they'd had to start taking reservations for those, too.

"I think I understand the situation now."

In other words, Mr. French's former master had come here to say he'd forgive Mr. French's past transgressions as long as he'd sell food to them on the cheap—or something along those lines. Considering their former relationship as master and apprentice, I could understand this somewhat.

After all, they still believed he had embezzled from their shop. If Mr. French's position would rise even a little after hearing the man out, I was more than willing to lend them some of my stores. I really wanted to avoid my manager getting chased out of town by the authorities or anything like that.

"Still, I don't think that will be possible."

"But…but why not?!"

"The food we have here is all geared toward nobles and other wealthy people. Even if I gave it to you at the previous market prices, it would still be quite expensive. Since your restaurant caters to the general public, wouldn't it be difficult for you to make use of it?"

"I…"

Their clientele was different. Couldn't do anything about that. To be honest, I wished they'd done a little research before barging in here.

"I'm sorry, but I must ask you to leave for today."

"……"

After hearing our explanation, the man and his staff left the shop dejected. I couldn't help feeling just a bit sorry for them.

*

After seeing off Mr. French's former master, we spent the next few days in this world.

During the day, I'd go outside of town and practice magic with Peeps. When the sun set, we'd return and have dinner at Mr. French's shop. Finally, at night, we'd take a load off in the big-shot hotel, enjoy a bath in a spacious tub, and fall asleep in a big, fluffy bed.

Aided by our luxurious living conditions, I was fit as a fiddle in both body and mind. Thus I could face my magic practice in tip-top condition. With all that to support me, I learned another new intermediate spell: the barrier magic I'd been after—and the intermediate version to boot.

According to Peeps, learning it finally made me a fledgling magician. Though according to the vice manager, even just learning beginner healing magic would put one in great demand wherever one went, so it seemed to me like opinions varied. Personally, I thought I'd adopt Peeps's attitude and continue my hard work.

The day after learning the spell, we returned to our apartment in Japan.

The sum being what it was, we'd deposited the large gold coins we'd earned from our deal at a bank. I couldn't let the section chief get so much as a glimpse of them. Mr. Marc had introduced me to a good bank, that would surely handle my money with care.

"All right, then. I'm gonna go out for a little bit."

"*Do be careful.*"

"Thanks, Peeps."

We'd returned to Japan so I could finish up the process of switching jobs. More specifically, I needed to go have a talk with my previous employer and have them issue the required documentation.

The bureau had apparently gotten in touch with them about my intent to resign. I'd been told during my training that I likely wouldn't draw any suspicions when going through the process. If a problem did occur, I was to immediately contact them and not try to resolve it myself.

I decided to take the train instead of relying on Peeps's magic to get there. It was about two hours after morning rush hour, so I was able to arrive without getting caught in any congestion.

When I saw the general affairs manager and explained the situation, he said they'd already heard about it and had drafted documents for me. Those that would take longer to issue would be mailed to me in the next few days, and I'd need to check them over.

The process went more smoothly than anticipated, probably because of some kind of government pressure. Normally, the personnel department head would have come around to make an unpleasant remark or two, but neither him nor my section chief showed up. As a result, everything went without a hitch.

Finally, I headed for my desk in my assigned workspace. My colleague—the one who sat at the desk next to mine—was there to greet me.

"Mr. Sasaki, it's true you're really becoming a government worker, then?"

"I apologize. I know it's pretty sudden…"

Just a few days ago, he'd invited me to go independent with him. I had no idea that I'd end up leaving the company before he did. I'd been totally certain I'd spend the next twenty years of my life here.

It was moving on a few levels. I'd worked here for a dozen or so years now after graduating, after all.

"I was really surprised. I didn't realize you could go into government work at your age! Er, I didn't mean to be rude. It's just that I was shocked you'd decided to go in that direction."

"Apparently, they have a framework for employing nongovernment workers."

"I'm really sorry for inviting you like that when you must have been so busy."

"No, don't be. It made me happy."

Now that I thought about it, ordinarily, you could only find employment as a police officer before the age of thirty-five. I could probably get myself in trouble for saying too much; it seemed a better idea to conclude my business here quickly. I figured I'd be fine but didn't want to goof up and cause trouble for my new workplace.

I wanted to at least say good-bye to my boss—but he was off-site.

Out making the rounds again, it seemed, and he planned to go straight home afterward. Our pupper-related conversation over giblet hot pot struck me then in an oddly nostalgic way. Thinking back, I'd met Miss Hoshizaki right after that.

"Once things settle down with you, hit me up. We'll go get a drink."

"Yeah, that's a good idea."

I hadn't thought anyone would reach out to me like that when I left. It warmed my heart.

*

From my former workplace, I headed straight for the neighborhood superstore. There, I did the day's stocking up. I mainly stuck with seasonings and sugar this time. I'd bought quite a bit, but I could maybe, possibly, get away with the excuse that now that I had free time, I'd taken to cooking curry or baking cakes as a hobby.

Nah, that wouldn't work. Or would it?

I couldn't tell. Either way, it was better than buying dozens of kilograms of chocolate.

To cover the wartime use of transceivers, I also bought several packages of alkaline batteries. I would have preferred to get nickel metal hydride batteries or solar generator panels, but considering their use would be out of my hands, disposable was best. Not far in the future, I was thinking about heading overseas for a large-scale wholesale purchase.

In any case, I finished up, left the supermarket, and hurried on home. After walking for a little while, I came into view of the convenience store. Over on the side of it, in a small alleyway, I saw a figure rummaging around. It was where I'd run into the young homeless girl before. I remembered her pink pigtails and frilly clothing being very striking.

"……"

Doubting myself, I couldn't help but look as I got closer.

And what did I find but that same girl, fishing through the convenience store's garbage bin. No matter how many times I checked, she looked young enough to be in elementary school. Despite that, she had her head stuck in the store's wastebasket and was rummaging for scraps of leftover food. She wore the same clothing as always—straight out of an anime. Her pink pigtails were no different, either.

"……"

The brown stains were still on her frilly skirt from when I'd met her a few days ago. Last time, I'd sensed she was accustomed to this—and now that we'd met a second time, I was certain she was professionally homeless.

"...What?"

As I was staring at her, she reacted. It seemed she'd noticed me. We were a few meters apart.

"We've met before, haven't we?"

"We have, Officer."

"......"

Her response was strangely unconcerned. I would have assumed a kid her age wandering around would have tried to look down and away if someone tried to talk to them. What inspired her totally straightforward behavior?

Also, she called me officer and not just mister, which made me happy.

"Where are your parents?"

Standing around on the road doing nothing would have seemed unnatural. After making sure no other passersby were watching, I slowly walked over to her. She didn't seem to respond, keeping her hands thrust into the wastebasket as she watched me approach.

"They both died."

"......"

I knew I was the one who'd asked, but that was a pretty heavy answer to just drop on me like that. The way she said it, like it was completely normal, hit me right in the heart.

Her grime-covered face and dirt-stained hair lent credence to her claim. She was still expressionless as she stared at me. Her cute features, too—including her big, almond-shaped eyes—were clearly mottled with grime, probably a result of persistent homelessness. It occurred to me that she'd be really adorable if she was cleaned up.

"If it's all right with you, I'd like to introduce you to a facility where children like you can live together. Would you be okay coming with me? You won't go hungry, and you might be able to make friends, too."

Last time, she'd floated into the sky. She was probably a stray psychic. If I could negotiate with the section chief and get her into the bureau, she'd probably live a much more accommodating life than most orphans. And these days, they were clamoring for new recruits. Maybe I was being a bad adult, but I decided to invite her.

Actually, to be honest, her life was at risk like this. I doubted she'd last the winter if her circumstances persisted. Even a handful of adults die from exposure every year.

"I can't live a normal life."

"Why can't you?"

"Because I'm a magical girl."

Yet another strange response. The clothing she wore was certainly magical girl in style. A cute dress with loads of frills. Her hair was pink, which wasn't natural for a Japanese person. If she said she was a magical girl... I mean, it made sense. She probably didn't know anything about psychic powers, so she'd arrived at the term *magical girl*.

"Can magical girls not live normal lives?"

"No."

"Why not stop being a magical girl?"

"I can't."

"Why can't you?"

"Because that's just how it works."

"Could you tell me who made it work like that?"

"...No."

"Do you know more about how it works?"

"A little."

"Who told you about it?"

"......"

After I asked her some questions, her expression grew troubled.

Now what? I was getting uneasy watching her. And then, suddenly, I remembered.

"I'm sorry for asking so many questions."

"It's okay."

In the plastic bag I was holding was a treat I'd bought for Peeps: a small cake they were selling near the station. The otherworld had cake, too, but this world had far greater variety. Plus, this one came from a pretty popular place. Apparently, it had been covered by some kind of social media, and now it always had a line of customers. Unusually, there had been no line today, so I'd seized the opportunity to buy one.

I held it out, still in the bag, to the self-professed magical girl.

"Would you like some cake?"

"...Why are you giving me cake?"

"Once you eat the cake, we can go to a police box."

"Is this like feeding pigeons in the park?"

"……"

What an awful conversation. Her question was very sharp, though, and she was right—it probably *was* like that. Well, less like a random pigeon and more like feeding a creature with which I had some connection. It felt the same as giving food to Peeps or my neighbor.

"I'm sorry for teasing you, Officer."

"It's all right. I'm more worried about you…"

"I'd like the cake, but I can't go to a police box."

"Why is that?"

"Everyone who gets involved with magical girls gets bad luck."

"…Bad luck?"

The girl turned away from the wastebasket to face the pseudo police officer. With both hands, she took the paper box from the plastic bag. In response to her activity, I got a whiff of that horrid stench. She was *really* smelly. It was an unbelievable stink. I literally almost threw up.

She was cute, but she smelled like a veteran derelict. When walking around the city, sometimes you'd get a whiff off a passerby—and it was especially bad in the summer. The stench was exactly like that, and the moment it entered my nostrils, I nearly lost my lunch.

If I pulled a face, though, I'd lose any trust I'd earned. Instead, I kept my expression neutral.

To this desperate old dude, the girl declared suddenly, "Thanks. I really like cake."

"Oh—"

But not a moment later, her body floated into the air. It was the same as the last time I saw it. There was a creaking noise, and next to her, the background scenery distorted. It was like a black hole had just appeared; a pitch-black space opened up immediately beside her. It was as though the world itself was being torn open.

The girl slipped inside. When she did, she began to disappear, as if the black space was swallowing her up. As always, it set my danger alarms blaring.

"Bye-bye, Officer."

Then with a brief word of parting, she vanished entirely. She was gone, swallowed up by that dark space.

"……"

She'd gotten away from me again.

But what *was* that power she was using? At a glance, it seemed like she was using two at once—one to call forth that black hole thing and the other to fly. That wouldn't fit the definition of a psychic, though. Apparently, psychics could use only a single power.

I wondered if the section chief or Miss Hoshizaki would be able to figure something out. I'd have to check with them about it the next time I found myself at the bureau.

✳

After parting ways with the homeless girl, I went straight back to my apartment. It was only a few minutes on foot from the convenience store. I had been able to finish my work errand while the sky was still bright, and seeing my neighborhood scenery in the daytime held an indescribable freshness.

In front of my neighbor's front door, I found a familiar face.

"Hello, mister."

"Hello there."

As always, she wore her sailor uniform and sat with her hands around her knees against the door. Her greeting was flat as she bent her neck up to look at me. Seemed like her mom wasn't home yet.

Which made sense, I supposed—the sun was still up. She was probably just back from school. I thought back to my own school days, which had already grown vague and indistinct. If a middle school girl like her was home already, that meant she probably wasn't involved in any clubs. Maybe that was inevitable, though, given club expenses and the like.

"You're home early today."

"Yeah, work ended early."

"Welcome back."

"Thanks."

Maybe if I was married and had kids, this kind of homecoming greeting would have been a regular occurrence for me. For a second, I entertained that ridiculous thought. Unfortunately, with my fortieth birthday fast approaching, I had long lost that kind of vigor. Besides, I had Peeps now, so I never felt lonely at home.

"…Um…"

Just as I put the key into my front door lock, my neighbor called out to me.

"What is it?" I replied, turning around and seeing that she'd stood up.

"If it's all right, do you want me to give you a shoulder massage?"

"A shoulder massage?"

"You always give me so much. I want to repay you."

I remembered being on the receiving end of similar suggestions many times in the past. Once when I mentioned my feet hurt from doing the rounds, she had offered to give me a foot massage. Another time, when I'd had lower back pain from all that desk work, she even offered to do some chores for me.

Either way, I obviously couldn't agree to it. We were just next-door neighbors. If I even *thought* about letting a minor touch me, my social life would probably fall to pieces faster than I could blink. And letting her into my apartment would be asking to get arrested for kidnapping. So I refused all her offers.

"Thank you, but the thought is more than enough."

"Is that a no?"

"To be honest, I've actually been feeling really fit lately."

"…I see."

Maybe the healing magic Peeps had taught me had something to do with it. I'd been using it here and there when I stubbed my toe on a shelf or suddenly felt tired. It seemed to be having quite the effect on muscle pain, too—a very handy tool, indeed. Using it on a daily basis must have been healing other parts of me as well.

"Oh, right. You can have these if you'd like."

Instead, I offered her some of the food I'd bought while stocking up. It was a plastic bag filled with several pieces of dressed and sweet breads.

"What? But it's so much…"

"The company that makes this bread has a rewards program. I got carried away and ended up buying way too much. I'd really appreciate it if you could help me finish them."

Middle schoolers were right in the middle of puberty. She would be needing high-calorie foods now more than ever, wouldn't she? I'd heard of girls that age who were so self-conscious they wouldn't finish their lunches even if they were hungry. I didn't know whether my neighbor was that type, but I figured it was always best to be prepared.

"…Thank you."

"No problem. All right, I have to go."

Guilt struck me—it felt like I was playing one of those video games where you "raise" a character. How did the parents of the world feel when they raised children? I couldn't even guess.

And so this single man hurried into his apartment, as if trying to escape these weird feelings.

\<Otherworld Battlefield\>

Setting aside my encounters with the homeless magical girl and my neighbor, I resumed my everyday activities.

First, I had a little meeting with Peeps in the tiny ten-square-meter space that was my apartment. Like the previous day, we'd be going to the otherworld to trade. I couldn't afford to miss even one of my daily visits, considering one day here was equal to a month there.

Before leaving for the front, the viscount had told me the supplies could be delivered in two or three weeks. In other words, given a month, a messenger on horseback might have gotten the initial word back to Baytrium about whether they'd arrived.

Plastic bags from the neighborhood superstore hung from both my hands, with the products for our trip stuffed haphazardly inside.

"You have less today."

"If I buy too much, the section chief will catch on."

"You refer to the man who planted the...surveillance cameras, they were called?"

"He didn't do it personally, but he *did* give the order, so yeah."

If worse came to worst, it might be a good idea to rely on the Charm spell, as long as it stopped with the section chief. Since we worked in the same building, we'd probably be meeting at least once a month, and I could reapply Charm each time.

That said, considering his social status, even one Charm spell meant I would have to keep it up for the rest of my life. It wasn't a choice I could make lightly. Better to think of it as a last resort.

"Is he a troublesome opponent?"

"He has authority, that's for sure."

A section chief in a regular company was only slightly higher than an average employee. It wasn't much different even at large corporations. But a section chief in the Cabinet Office was a government official. If he'd gotten promoted to the position at such a young age, he was sure to climb even higher in the future.

The presence of supernatural powers made it all seem a little less real, but if he was progressing along a proper career path, it wouldn't take all that long to happen. I couldn't afford to get on his bad side. I wanted him as an ally, even if I had to lick his boots to make it happen.

He was the sort of guy who could control the lives and careers of others without even dirtying his hands.

"All right, you're up, Peeps."

"*Yes.*"

As Peeps nodded, a magic circle appeared at our feet. Weightlessness washed over me—I was still getting used to that part.

✱

Now in the otherworld, we headed straight for the Hermann Trading Company.

The same clerk as always stood guard at the door. When I asked for Mr. Marc, he hastily rushed me into the reception room. The items I brought were barely glanced at before I was shown through.

Has something happened? I wondered as I walked to the reception room where I met the vice manager. It had been a month since my last visit.

His face looked like the world was ending. He looked like Mr. Yamazaki had—a temporary worker from several years ago who had been fired just before the three-year rule would have made him permanent. That was a terrible one—even for our company.

"Mr. Marc, are you all right? You look unwell."

"No, no, there's no problem with my health."

"Oh?"

"It's just that—how do I put this…?"

"Has something happened to the Hermann Trading Company?"

"No, not with the company."

"Is it a personal issue? If so, then I apologize for being nosy."

"……"

Despite my repeated questions, the vice manager's miserable expression remained. He wasn't giving me a clear answer.

His behavior was all the more peculiar since I knew him so well. This was very inappropriate for a place of business. It made me very curious to know what was going on.

Hearing the next thing out of his mouth, though, it all made sense.

"...Mr. Sasaki, Viscount Müller has been slain."

"What...?"

That was the last thing I'd expected.

It took me a moment to respond.

When I tried to speak, I couldn't find the right words, so then I'd try to say something simple like "Oh" and stumble over that, too. Eventually, I managed to squeeze out a remark that meant nothing in particular.

"That is, um, wow..."

Hadn't his sole responsibility been resupplying the rear and constructing bases? I recalled him taking very few soldiers. How could that have led to his death? Was this country at such a disadvantage that even they were suffering losses even behind the lines?

On my shoulder, I felt Peeps give a brief start.

✳

Mr. Marc filled me in on the details regarding Viscount Müller.

It seemed I'd been right—the war was proving to be a one-sided affair and remained firmly in the Ohgen Empire's hands. Enemy soldiers had been allowed to advance all the way to the rear, where the viscount had been providing support.

The vice manager had apparently just gotten word a few days ago. They hadn't found his remains, but his chances of survival were, as he put it, hopeless. Incidentally, this news had come from an agent of the Hermann Trading Company who had infiltrated the rear lines. He'd barely escaped with his life on a swift steed.

"This could spell disaster for the future..."

"It is as you say—the town will be thrown into chaos."

It seemed news of the viscount's death was still being kept from the townspeople. Only the family had been informed. Still, if both the front and rear lines had collapsed, it was only a matter of time before word got out. Other groups were probably reacting much the same as the vice manager.

"How are things at the castle?"

"If you can believe it, despite everything, they're arguing over the succession."

"In *this* situation?"

"Yes. I suppose it's what you'd expect from the Kingdom of Herz…"

"……"

The vice manager looked apologetic. Viscount Müller had been a man of outstanding character, but apparently, that didn't extend to his family. Or maybe something had occurred that was forcing the situation. Whatever the cause, it was clear his house was in disarray.

This meant the town's future was bleak.

I was worried about Peeps; I wanted to get some private time and strategize with him right away. I wasn't that close to the viscount, so it wasn't a huge shock for me—but I didn't know how Peeps felt about it. The way the bird talked about him implied that they had been at least on friendly terms.

"I'm sorry, but could I have a few moments alone?"

"Unfortunately, we've actually been summoned to the castle…"

"Wait, including me?"

"The summons is from Viscount Müller's butler; he was begging us to come."

"…All right, then."

I couldn't afford to make trouble for the vice manager after everything he'd done for me. With no other option, I ended up heading to the castle.

✳

A few rattles of the carriage later, and we'd arrived at the viscount's castle. We were shown to the reception room I remembered from past visits.

Opposite us, on the sofa, sat a girl who looked thirteen or fourteen. She had charming pale skin, blue eyes, and very pretty features. What stood out more to me, though, was her blond hair, which sat like a mountain atop her head.

In Japan's recent history, there had been a time when hostess bar culture had broken into mainstream fashion. This girl's hair rivaled even the tallest bump hairstyles that were all the rage back then. As a middle-aged man worried about his own hair, it was an enviable display.

To put it simply, she gave off serious street fashion vibes.

Behind the pile-hair princess sitting on the sofa was an old man who looked to be in his sixties, standing at attention. *Probably Viscount*

Müller's butler, who contacted the vice manager. Despite his age, he was quite tall—and muscular at that.

"…You seek our protection?"

"I apologize for making this request of someone from outside the family, but I respectfully ask that you hear us out. The other day, a conflict began regarding who would succeed the master of the house. Its effects are wide-reaching enough that they might extend to the young lady, who has nothing to do with the succession."

"I believe this is our first time meeting, young lady…?"

It was mainly Mr. Marc dealing with the situation. Peeps and I sat next to him, observing the conversation, not saying anything ourselves. The topic was complicated, so an outsider like me with little knowledge of this world's customs was better off not speaking.

"Say hello to the man from Hermann Trading Company, madam."

"…Hmph."

At the butler's urging, the princess gave an uninterested snort. She didn't seem to be in a good mood. As her head tilted, it caused the ornaments in her hair to sway to and fro. Her locks stretched tall above her forehead, and the summit shook at even the slightest neck movement. Those of us watching were on pins and needles expecting an adornment to fall off at any moment.

"Why should I have to give my name to some commoner?"

"It is for your own safety, madam. You should stay with the Hermann Trading Company until things settle down at home. Have you forgotten the poison snuck into your food the other day?"

The girl was caught out. It seemed like she was in a pretty difficult spot. Poison in your food? That would traumatize me, no questions asked. An anisakis parasite in my sashimi one time put me off raw fish for *months*. Whenever I ordered raw squid after that, I always made them use the frozen stuff, since I'd learned there was a greater chance of running into the little guys the fresher it was.

"…You may call me Elsa Müller."

"I'm pleased to make your acquaintance, Lady Elsa. My name is Marc, vice manager of the Hermann Trading Company. The man sitting next to me is another frequent visitor to the castle—he is the merchant Sasaki."

"Pleased to meet you. As he says, my name is Sasaki."

"……"

The pile-hair princess just stared at us, looking bored. She didn't seem especially interested in any of this. The fact that we were commoners and she was a noble was probably part of it.

"Because Lady Elsa is quite close to the eldest son, Lord Maximilian, she has been targeted by the second son, Lord Kai, who is vying with him for the inheritance. Each has a faction of nobles supporting them, placing us in a very difficult situation."

That was a slew of new names. Since her brothers weren't here, I'd probably forget them right away. I might have been able to imagine the characters had they been Japanese, but western names were more difficult. For now, I'd try to remember that the longer name was the elder brother and the shorter name the younger.

"Then the madam's presence is influencing the succession dispute?" asked Mr. Marc.

"Lady Elsa and Lord Kai have been on bad terms since childhood, which may be partly to blame. Many in the estate favor Lady Elsa, which doesn't help our cause. We must also consider that everyone's nerves are frayed as a result of the dispute."

"Kai's a fool. If he was to inherit the estate, it would fall apart."

"We shouldn't speak like that in front of guests, madam…"

"But it's true!"

"Why not ask others in the house for assistance? Our trading company certainly has what's needed for the task, but we are still only commoners. It seems to me that you would have more reliable protection if you asked other nobles."

"It is, in truth, quite complicated. We do not know how far anyone from House Müller can be trusted. Even one such as I, who has been serving the family for many years, cannot judge too carefully when it comes to the current dispute."

"I see."

Were she not directly involved in the succession conflict, it wouldn't be terribly difficult to help her. The Hermann Trading Company would probably be able to secure a tightly guarded facility. The power of their amassed wealth made it difficult for the average noble to intervene.

What's more, safely completing this task would put the Müller family greatly in their debt.

The vice manager seemed to have the same thing in mind, and his next words were amicable.

"I understand. We have always benefited from Viscount Müller's favor. Should we have it in our capacity to provide even a modicum of assistance during your family's crisis, we will gladly do so. Though it may be less convenient than your lives here, you are more than welcome to come to us."

"Thank you very much. Madam, express your gratitude as well."

"...Thanks."

The pile-hair princess, with her brusque demeanor and apparent middle school age, came off exactly like a young lady in the middle of adolescence. It would have sounded totally normal to hear her say something like "Don't you dare wash my clothes in the same load as Papa's underwear."

"I will have someone from our store secure a place for you to stay at once," continued the vice manager plainly, still smiling.

He seemed pretty used to dealing with nobles. This must not have been the first time he'd been faced with the child of someone with influence, either. I didn't know how social rank played into things, but it seemed the power balance—including economic influence—put them on surprisingly even terms.

"I apologize, but I had one more request."

"What would that be?"

"I have heard Lord Sasaki deals in some very unusual wares. According to a conversation I had previously with the master, he carries tools that enable people to converse over long distances, as well as ones that allow a person to see far into the distance."

Suddenly, the butler had turned to me. This was probably why the vice manager had brought me along.

I replaced Mr. Marc in his role of question-answerer. "Yes, I do have devices like that."

"I would like one of each of these things."

After my honest answer, the butler immediately put in an order. What did he plan on using it for?

"One of them is a very limited product..."

"I am aware. It seems the tool for speaking over long distances has a limit on how far away it can be utilized. And it requires a special metal to fuel it, which is very expensive."

"Yes, that's right."

"Would you still sell one to me?"

"...Let's see." Considering he was Viscount Müller's butler, it seemed safe enough. He'd only ordered one, after all.

"I understand, sir. I will stock one in the near future."

"Thank you ever so much. I greatly appreciate it."

With that, our exchange in the viscount's castle came to an end.

✳

After we had finished our conversation at the Müller residence, the vice manager immediately headed off. He mentioned something about preparing living quarters for the pile-hair princess. The butler, too, had requested it be done as soon as possible. Naturally, Mr. Marc had no time for chitchat. He might even have to pull an all-nighter.

And so, as usual, we went out to practice magic. Like before, I was still endeavoring to learn new intermediate spells. I'd learned both intermediate healing and barrier magic for defense, so next up, I wanted to get my hands on some new offensive spells. The only intermediate spell I could use to attack was the one that shot lightning. It was an extremely directional spell, so right now I was working to supplement it with more wide-ranged magic. Peeps had taught me several incantations, which I was repeating over and over.

After some practice, I heard Peeps mutter softly beside me.

"...*To think that he would be killed.*"

He wasn't on my shoulder right now but atop my backpack, which I'd placed on the ground. Perched there, he was watching over this guy in his late thirties trying to practice magic. A sparrow who was both adorable *and* reliable.

"Were you friends with Viscount Müller?"

"*Not friends, exactly, but I do remember having drinks with him several times.*"

"...Oh."

Ever since we'd gotten the news of his death from the vice manager, I'd had the feeling that Peeps was depressed. To him, the man was probably like a colleague who worked in the same company.

"*I thought he'd live just a little while longer.*"

"......"

Having only met Peeps recently, I couldn't think of the right words. Instead, I just stopped practicing and studied him.

Keeping quiet for so long was making things awkward, though, so I took advantage of my otherworld freshmen status to make an appropriate interjection.

"Is there any magic in this world that can bring a person back to life?"

"Not strictly. However, there is a method that can accomplish something similar."

"Wait, really?"

"Unfortunately, it hinges on many conditions being met and would not put everything back the way it was. At minimum, the person would have to give up on their past life and deeds as a human. The technique is abhorred as heretical by society."

"…I see."

"Does a method exist in your world?"

"I'm sorry. I don't think we have any technology that could help…"

"No, you need not apologize. To live is one day to die. Many other people perished along with him. Caring for each and every one would destroy a person."

If Viscount Müller's words were to be believed, this Java sparrow was surrounded by a society of outrageously corrupt nobles and yet remained a heroic character who worked for the sake of the nation. The sound of resignation in his voice, combined with everything he'd revealed to me when we first met, gave his words an incredible gravity.

"If there's anything I can do to help, don't hesitate to ask."

For my beloved pet, I was prepared to take on some risk. I also wanted to repay him for all his goodwill in the past.

"After all, I'm an owner who cares for his pet."

"Heh. You are gifted with words for one who makes so little money."

"Look, I'll try my best!"

"…Yes. I will look forward to it."

Considering how quickly he stopped fussing about it, Peeps must have mentally already taken a step back from this world. I got the sense it wouldn't be right for me to move ahead of him and act on my own, so instead, I turned my attention back to my magic.

Unfortunately, despite practicing for a few more days, I wasn't able to learn any new spells. Maybe it was because everything on my mind was muddling my concentration. Mental image was everything when it came to using magic, after all.

*

With my magic practice dragging, I decided it was time for a change of pace. So we headed over to the Hermann Trading Company.

My idea was to check in on how Viscount Müller's daughter was doing and to have a light chat with the vice manager. We, too, would probably be better off knowing her current situation. Given that we'd already met the butler, I didn't want to be caught unaware and have to make up pathetic excuses if something happened.

If I was able to see the young lady, maybe I could ask what her interests and favorite foods were. It'd be a personal test—paying a courtesy call to the pile-hair princess. She was about middle-school age, so if I bought her a cake or something from a famous shop, that might make her happy.

What I really hoped was that my talking with her might lighten Peeps's spirits a little. He hadn't said much in detail, but he seemed to have been on friendly terms with the viscount.

For those reasons, we paid a visit to the vice manager.

When we did, he gave his usual bright smile and showed us to where the princess was—on the upper floor of the Hermann Trading Company's main building. After much consideration, they'd decided their headquarters was the safest, most comfortable place for her.

It felt…kind of like the top floor of a high-rise apartment building.

Given this was the Hermann Trading Company's main branch, there would always be guards posted, even in the middle of the night. After hearing that, I decided they were right—there would be no better hideout than this. They'd also be increasing the amount of security for the princess, including plenty of armed guards.

Her living space was very extravagant. It must have been about thirty square meters, and I could see a canopy bed and a luxurious sofa set inside. Did those furnishings belong to the company, or had they brought them here from the estate? Each piece struck me as having cost a *lot* of money.

"Hello again."

"…What?"

I'd figured I would give a nice, breezy greeting, but her response was harsh.

She sat on her bed, glaring at me.

Had the vice manager been with us, perhaps he could have handled the situation more deftly. Unfortunately, he was busy again today, so it was just Peeps and me. He probably had a lot on his plate now with the viscount's defeat.

"I just wanted to stop by and say hello."

"Yeah, well, just so you know, you won't find me very useful. My brothers are in charge of everything back home, so doing something to me would bring you no benefit at all. The most I could possibly do is ask for an extra helping of dinner."

"I see. Are you something of a gourmet, Lady Elsa?"

"...Are you making fun of me?"

"Oh, no, not at all. I know someone who runs a ritzy restaurant in town. I figured I would ask if you wanted a little diversion. But if it's too much trouble to go about outside, I could have some food brought to you."

I was sure a brief escape would be fine as long as Peeps was with us. According to what Viscount Müller had told me, the Starsage was the most powerful magician in the land. He was probably enough to protect a single person. But if it still seemed like a concern, I had the option of asking the vice manager to lend us a bodyguard or two.

In my opinion, staying shut up for long stretches was bad for your mental health. I once holed up in my room for an entire month. It very quickly messed up my autonomic nerves, gave me heart palpitations, and caused me trouble sleeping even when I was tired. Tiny things concerned me, and I was racked with a strange sense of anxiety.

After that, I made sure to wake up when the sun was out, immediately take a hot shower, and get sufficient sunlight in my field of vision. Repeating that process for a few days finally led to my recovery. Human bodies weren't made to stay cooped up in dimly lit places—this I knew personally.

"What do you think, madam?"

"...What is the restaurant called?"

"It's..."

Crap. I didn't actually know the name of Mr. French's shop. Now what? This was yet another side effect of pushing all the work into his hands.

"Its name isn't well-known, my lady. It's in the best part of the shopping district—it has benches out front, and customers will even reserve those. Does that spark your interest?"

"Are you talking about French's place?"

I tried for a minute to describe it, and she seemed to know the place—and the name of the store manager. "Ah yes, most likely."

"You know the manager?"

"Is this manager's name French?"

"Yes, it is. The restaurant is famous for its sweets and amazing food."

"That's definitely the one, then, madam."

"And it doesn't have a name, either…"

"It doesn't?"

Thank goodness. Managed to get through that one in one piece. Actually, I was surprised the place was doing such good business without a name. The rules here weren't as strict as modern Japan's, but it was still impressive. How did the customers who went there talk about it?

"I ask all the time, but they keep saying they haven't decided. Everyone who goes there just calls it French's restaurant. That's basically become the name at this point, really."

"Ah." I hadn't realized it was like that. Still, I was saved. Thank you, Mr. French—truly. "What do you think, then, madam? I could get you something to eat from there within the day without having to go through any of that troublesome reservation business. Are you interested? I was thinking I could procure something to your taste, if you like."

"Why are you trying to put me in a good mood? Papa isn't around anymore."

"I have no ulterior motives, I promise. I just hoped it would be a welcome diversion."

"……"

"Or would you rather it be a different restaurant?"

This was the daughter of someone Peeps thought of as important to him, if even only a little. I wanted to make things better, as much as I could. An owner always shared in his pet's sadness.

"That restaurant treats everyone equally—they don't even let nobles barge in on reservations. I heard it's caused a bunch of issues in the past, but the Hermann Trading Company sponsors them, so nobody can really say much."

"It will work out, madam. I give you my word."

Wow, was Mr. French's shop really that amazing? I was technically going there every day, but Peeps and I always went in through the kitchen door and ate in a private room in the back. Because of that, I never had the chance to gauge what others thought of the place.

"…Well, if you really insist, I can do you the favor of going with you."

"Thank you, madam."

We always ate in a separate room anyway. It probably wouldn't be a huge issue if we brought one extra person along.

✳

With the princess's approval, we headed straight for Mr. French's shop. Mr. Marc had prepared a carriage for us—and a number of bodyguards from the company for our defense. They surrounded us in the carriage, making the riding conditions a little cramped.

Not long after the carriage got moving, we arrived at our destination. As always, we went in through the kitchen door and were met by the manager.

"Sir! You're earlier than usual today!"

"Sorry for coming so suddenly. I have one extra with me today. Would that be all right?"

"A guest? Of course! Please come right this way."

"Thank you."

"No, I should be thanking you! Take your time and relax."

After a reverent bow of the head, Mr. French took us into the private room in the back. It was where Peeps and I always ate, so no other patrons would come here. It was a nice little isolated space.

The princess, after seeing our brief exchange, regarded me in shock. Though I'm not proud of it, it kind of made me feel good.

From there, we ate our food together and talked. She seemed to really like the cuisine here, and eventually, she was in a better mood than when I had first met her.

"This curry dish is superb. I could eat it all day."

"I'm glad to hear it."

She spoke eagerly as she lifted the soup curry to her mouth. It seemed to be a popular menu item. If this kept up, I'd have to give Mr. French a recipe for curry and rice in the near future. Personally, soup curry was okay, but what I really liked was pouring the thick roux over rice, Japanese style—especially with something fried on top.

Peeps, who had jumped down from my shoulder, was enjoying his own meal on the table. Seeing him peck away at the tiny cuts of meat on the flat plate—prepared just for him—was such a lovely sight. I was filled with the urge to take an HD video of it.

Perhaps realizing what I was looking at, the princess said, "By the way, that familiar of yours is very cute, isn't it?"

"Yes, madam. He's very precious to me."

"Let me pet him."

"……"

A rather abrupt request. Was Peeps okay with that? In fact, I couldn't remember ever really petting him myself. Curious, I looked over. He gave an energetic response and pointed his beak away from the meat-filled plate and toward the girl.

"*Pii! Pii!*"

Knowing who he really was, I felt a little apologetic. Still, getting a cute girl to pet you was basically the desire of every man, wasn't it? When I was a kid, I remember one of my classmates, a girl, petting the crew cut of a boy on the baseball team, going on about the texture. It had made me really jealous.

Peeps hopped across the table. When he got to her, she brought her arm out. Scooping him up, she gently lifted him, then used her other hand to pet the tiny sparrow's head, stroking it softly.

"Hee-hee. He's really cute."

"*Pii! Pii! Pii!*"

"He feels really nice and fluffy when you pet him."

"*Pii.*"

His tweeting sounded somehow comfortable to me. Should I be petting him like this on a daily basis? Come to think of it, Mr. Yamada at the pet shop said it was important to touch your pets to build a relationship of trust. Still, no matter how adorable he was, he was the Starsage on the inside.

"He's really used to people. Is that because he's a familiar?"

"*Pii! Pii!*"

"One day, I want a pet bird that's this friendly."

"*Pii! Pii! …Ow—*"

"Huh?!"

"……"

Peeps, I don't think that was a good idea.

The princess's nail must have hit his eye as she was petting his head. It looked like it really hurt. I didn't blame him for crying out. All creatures, no matter how well they trained their bodies, were always vulnerable in their softer spots. Thanks to that, his yelp sounded very human.

"What…what was that…?"

"……"

"...It sounded like he just said something."

"*Pii! Pii! Pii!*"

Peeps was desperately trying to pretend to be a normal sparrow. I found the sight of him, admirably struggling, also quite charming.

But deceiving the princess now would be difficult. The hand she was using to pet him had frozen. Her eyes were open wide in surprise as they stared directly at the bird she was holding. I could see the words written in them—*Is this really a bird?*

"He definitely talked just now, didn't he?"

"*P— ...Pii!! Pii!! Pii!!*"

It looked like small birds understanding human speech was an exceptional occurrence even in this world. Peeps was doing his absolute darnedest to make bird noises. I could almost feel the desperate abandon drifting from him, and it was adorable. He may have been idolized as the Lord Starsage or whatever, but his unexpectedly human qualities engendered a feeling of kinship in me. I wanted to tell him to calm down a little bit so he wouldn't hurt his throat.

"You, um, heard that just now, didn't you?"

"Heard what, madam?"

"When my fingertip hit his eye, he cried out, and..."

The princess stared down at the bird in her hands suspiciously. Slowly and deliberately, her fingertips reached for his eyes. Was she seriously going to poke him again to test the reaction? That was a bit too much for this poor animal, wasn't it?

"?!"

Sensing the danger, Peeps flapped his wings and fluttered into the air, landing back on my shoulder.

"Ah..."

"Please don't tease him too much."

"...I wasn't teasing him."

I had thought letting her touch an adorable sparrow would be a bit cathartic after her father's passing, but now Peeps was taking damage instead. I'd have to set aside a little time to use my healing magic.

We continued our meal together for a while. Suddenly, the door flew open. I turned, wondering what business could be so urgent, and saw Hermann's vice manager at the door. He was out of breath as he looked into the room. As soon as he spotted the princess at the table, he cried out to her.

"Lady Elsa, it's terrible! Your brothers have passed away!"

"Huh…?"

"I'm terribly sorry, but you need to return home at once!"

The reports of their deaths came out of nowhere. I almost cried out "What the hell?!"

It seemed her two brothers, who had been fighting over the family inheritance, had taken each other out.

✻

In this world, the succession of noble titles generally fell to men. While conflicts over succession between an eldest son and a second son were nothing unusual, it was rare for the eldest daughter or anyone else born a girl to get involved. However, depending on the circumstances, there were times when a woman would succeed.

The princess's current situation, for example.

"I… I can't take over the title…"

"But there are no others who suit the role."

"……"

In the reception room of Viscount Müller's home, aside from the princess, were the butler, the vice manager, Peeps, and me. We had rushed via carriage from Mr. French's shop to the castle and been directed here.

Right then, everyone was sitting on the sofas in the middle of a heated conversation.

"Madam, please!"

"But I…"

The butler was the main one addressing her. He was beside the sofa set, the only one standing. The vice manager and I were facing them from the other side. I couldn't help but wonder if outsiders like us should be privy to such an involved discussion. It would be rude to just leave, though, so I sat in silence and watched.

For the vice manager, this was a golden business opportunity. From what he'd told me on the way here, a woman's succession was a temporary thing, and it was the norm for the estate to be given to whomever she married in the future. Still, however temporary the situation, she would still be the leader of the viscount's family. Choosing a marriage partner would probably take quite a bit of time anyway.

Being in the position of guardian for someone like that must have seemed too good to be true.

"If nobody succeeds, the family will fall to ruin."

"……"

Incidentally, her brothers had died when each claimant had poisoned the other, sending both on a journey with no return. This was something we'd heard from the butler immediately after our arrival.

The culprits were the other nobles supporting the two brothers, making it a very unfortunate situation. The siblings had apparently not been on unfriendly terms—as the butler explained, they had likely just been dragged into a fight among greedy relatives. In that sense, the biggest victims were the departed brothers themselves.

"If you do not succeed, madam, a great many people shall lose their livelihoods."

"Even so, I don't have what it takes!"

"We shall fully support you in your role. So won't you please succeed the family, if only in name? We will treat you well and take over all business aspects of the position."

"……"

"Please, madam. I, Sebastian, do solemnly swear to support you to the best of my ability."

The butler dipped his head, bowing deeply.

When she saw that, she nodded reluctantly. "…Fine."

"Thank you so much, my lady."

From today, it seemed this castle would belong to the pile-hair princess.

This also automatically made her my business partner. Of course, as the butler said, she wouldn't be bearing the brunt of the job. I didn't mind that. Still, I had doubts as to whether she'd be able to properly control those who led all the different departments she'd just inherited.

Naturally, any deals I had with Viscount Müller would be dissolved. For the time being, I couldn't say one way or another if I'd be able to continue making the same sort of clean, straightforward deals I had up to now. Depending on the situation, I might have to contend with nobles who *didn't* like to listen to other people.

The situation was making me increasingly anxious.

✱

Once he'd gotten the girl to acquiesce, the butler rushed out of the reception room. He must have had a lot of formalities to go through and groundwork to lay.

The only ones left in the room were Peeps and me, plus the princess and the vice manager. We were still sitting on the sofas, glancing at each other, wondering what to do next. It was suffocating.

"...Why did it have to come to this?" The girl muttered to no one in particular. Her voice was weak, like she was about to fall to pieces.

The vice manager responded with a question.

"Is inheriting the family a burden?"

"Of course it is."

"But Viscount Müller loved this house."

"And that's why it'll be so hard to watch it fall apart as I make one mistake after another! Even my father found it difficult, you know. How can I be expected to take control and do a good job?!"

"You don't know that..."

"Yes, I do! It would have been better for *Kai* to inherit than me!"

The words flooded out of her pretty mouth; she must have finally reached the limit of her patience. I'd heard she wasn't on good terms with her brother Kai. If she suggested *he* would be better, how little confidence did she have in herself? Her insistence gave a glimpse into what seemed to be a complex.

"I'm not smart like they are, and I don't have any martial *or* magical talent! I'm just average! So average it hurts! No matter how hard I try, I'll never catch up to the ones with talent! I'm just mediocre!"

"......"

The vice manager, too, took on a troubled expression at this.

In direct contrast to her piles of hair, her self-confidence was modest, to say the least. Having lived around so many exceptional people must have affected her poorly. Her father, Viscount Müller, for example, was remembered by such a pillar of the nation as the Starsage.

It made me think—she probably hadn't had many satisfying brushes with success in her life.

"The only thing anyone ever compliments me on is my appearance, which I got from my mother and father. I always thought that, to be of some use to my father, my purpose was to marry into a high-ranking family. How did I end up inheriting this one...?"

She seemed like she had so much pride, but she spoke so fervently to us—commoners. Her lack of talent must have been undeniable.

Personally, I thought she was on the wrong track. Having excellent looks essentially made you the most powerful of all. Intelligence, martial prowess, magical talent—they were all merely icing on the cake. It was just how the world worked: As long as you were attractive, most things in life would work out somehow. Especially given how young she was.

Before I knew it, my mouth was moving.

"In that case, you already have a weapon of your own, my lady."

"...What's that supposed to mean?"

"Good looks are the single most important thing when it comes to positions of power. Being smart or having martial or magical talents aren't actually that necessary when it comes to taking control of a town as its lord or lady."

"Are you trying to insult my father and brothers?"

"Of course not. I'm only stating a fact."

"It's not a fact; it was an insult!"

"Are there any bards in this town?"

"What? Of course! There's, like, a million of them!"

"All the popular bards are attractive, aren't they?"

"...So what?"

"People, in general, aren't very smart. They have their hands full keeping themselves alive day to day. They don't have time to learn refinement or patience. They need someone to make it easy for them— something to indicate where they should throw their support."

"S-Sir Sasaki..." Next to me, the vice manager was growing uncomfortable.

Peeps, on the other hand, remained silent.

Trusting that all was fine, this busybody of a guest continued his argument. If she didn't succeed her inheritance more optimistically, it would cause trouble not just for her house but for everyone in town. I couldn't bear to watch if those other nobles—the ones who could just *poison* acquaintances—were to show up.

"When the masses see someone as beautiful as yourself doing her best to wrestle with town administration, they will give you their support, and that will give you more strength than anything else. It doesn't matter who's actually *doing* the work. They'll be taken with you, so they'll help and cheer you on."

"...This is ridiculous."

"In my homeland, a bard will occasionally end up leading the city government, put there by support from the masses, in a vote where they defeated those who studied economics, law, and education."

"Leaving a town in the hands of a mere bard?! Why the hell would anyone do that?!"

The princess's retort was perfectly understandable. But this was the truth, and that was that.

"As I'm sure you know, my lady, gaining the support of the masses is the most important consideration when running a town or city. If a bard is beloved by the masses, don't you think having one in that position would be extremely efficient? They could just let other talented people do the real work."

"...Should I not be acting as a representative of the people, then?"

I thought she'd come at me angrily, asking if I intended equate her with some lowly bard, but she was clearly more intelligent than I'd guessed. That made things *very* easy for me. Doing so might have been rude, but it was time to give her the final push.

After all, this was the daughter of Peeps's acquaintance we were talking about. I, too, was invested in her fate.

"If a peaceful reign is the goal, the situation is rare when the representative of the people can *act* as such. I think your father, Viscount Müller, was one of those rare exceptions. But people like him almost never appear. As such, my opinion is that you should divide the work and delegate it."

"But I..."

"If a leader can't do that, and instead overworks themselves, wouldn't that lead to bad government? You seem to have a firm grasp on what you can and can't do, and I think that's wonderful."

"......"

She may have had a bad temper, but deep down, she seemed like an honest, straightforward girl. Thus, it was probably best for us to sway her before every single noble with a connection to her family tried to abduct her. We should do enough, at least, so that if something happened in the future, she'd listen to our advice. Otherwise, our own standing would become quite precarious.

"You see, my lady? You already have more than enough to inherit the family. You need never look down on yourself. If you hold your father dear to your heart and remain sincere when dealing with others, I'm sure those around you will choose to follow you."

Other than the vice manager's face turning white as a sheet, I believed everything would be fine and waited for her response.

And after a few moments, she gave me one.

"…I understand."

"Truly, my lady?"

"And out of respect for your lecture, I will forgive your rudeness."

"Thank you, my lady."

"However, I will not tolerate such behavior in the future. Normally, a commoner talking down to a member of the nobility warrants a beheading. No—they deserve to be burned at the stake in public. I hope you're thankful for how magnanimous I'm being right now."

"I am, my lady."

And then, finally, I realized why she had kept all that gorgeous hair growing for so long.

Aside from her appearance, she wasn't proud of a single thing about herself.

∗

For a few days, the house of Viscount Müller was in an uproar.

After a short while, the news of the viscount's death in battle and his replacement was announced to the domain. When the townspeople heard of it, they seemed to become restless and uneasy. Here and there, I even saw some of the more impatient among them leaving town in large, two-wheeled wagons.

What *wouldn't* wait around was the war with the Empire. Now that the front line had collapsed, the Kingdom of Herz had been placed in a very dangerous position, and the repercussions had finally pressed down on Baytrium, where we were making our home.

"What? A Hermann carriage was attacked by enemy soldiers?"

Several days after the princess inherited the family, we were in the Hermann Trading Company's reception room having a conversation with the vice manager. I had been getting ready to go out and practice magic when a messenger from the company contacted me.

"Yes. It seems they're becoming active in this area."

"I see."

This town appeared to be the Empire's next target. That wasn't to say it had been directly attacked; the enemy probably didn't have the troops to spare for an invasion. Apparently, they were planting vanguards on main roads in the vicinity and having them disrupt our supply routes.

They were like a group of thieves made up of regular soldiers. The vice manager said their goal was probably to exhaust the town before their main force came in and took over. With that happening, we'd need to decide *our* next move.

"What will you do, Mr. Sasaki?"

"Hmm…"

"I am considering leaving for the capital as early as next week."

"What about Viscount Müller's daughter?"

"We plan to have her accompany us," he said completely seriously, staring me dead in the eye. He must have decided this town was a lost cause.

"Would you like to come as well, Mr. Sasaki? We already have skilled bodyguards for the trip. Even if we encounter the Empire's regular troops, if it's only ten or twenty of them, we should be able to hold out just fine."

That said, I'd already talked this over with Peeps—and I couldn't go with him.

"I'm very happy you wanted to invite me along, but I still have a bit more to do here. I am well aware of your concerns, but I'm going to stay a while longer."

"…Is that so…?"

"I'm sorry."

"No, no, don't be. But if you do change your mind, come to the store again. We're making preparations to send as much of our stock to the next town over as time permits. If you were to go with them, you should be able to get travel somewhat more safely."

"Thank you for your consideration."

I'd be saying my farewell to the vice manager, too, for a while.

*

After parting with Mr. Marc, we headed straight back to the lodgings we used as a base of operations—the affluent inn that cost one gold piece for a one-night, two-day stay. The place: the living room area with a sofa set. I was sitting on the sofa, and Peeps was standing on the low table across from me. Each of us faced the other with a serious expression.

"*I apologize, but can I count on you?*"

"I'd do anything my adorable little pet asked."

"*…Thanks.*"

"No, thank you. You've been the one helping me this whole time."

"*So you say, but if you had never met me, you would have had no struggles.*"

"In my opinion, what you've done for me outweighs my own hardships. It's fine."

"……"

Peeps wanted two things: to preserve the town that Viscount Müller had presided over and for the young lady he had left behind to survive. It seemed like their friendship had been far from shallow—enough to change the mind of Peeps, who had once determined to leave this world behind.

Considering his strong feelings, I wanted to help him that much more—as his owner.

"When will we be leaving?"

"As soon as tonight, if possible."

"Will we be walking or using the usual spell?"

"Flying, I believe, this time. Without knowing how close the enemy forces have gotten, being spotted by anyone at our destination would be troublesome. I would like to start and finish this task without being noticed, if possible."

"But, Peeps, I don't have wings like you."

Come to think of it, how far could Java sparrows fly anyway? He fluttered around very gracefully indoors, but he'd never had a chance to fly for very long outside. I'd heard some birds, like pigeons, were relatively powerful and could easily fly dozens of kilometers.

"You have misunderstood. We shall fly using magic."

"Wait, what? That's amazing."

The hope for such a spell had always been hanging out in the back of my mind. Being told it was real started getting me excited. I'd wanted to do something like this ever since I was a kid. I couldn't even count how many dreams I'd had of flying. The closer you get to waking up, the less you're able to fly.

"Oh. I have not told you about this, have I?"

"Won't you please teach me, Peeps?"

"Depending on your mental image, you can fly around at a considerable speed. I'd been holding it back until you'd at least learned intermediate-level healing magic. Inexperienced casters will often fall— or run into trees. If they cannot heal their own wounds, they die."

"…I see."

"In addition, you will need to use a barrier spell simultaneously if you want to go over a certain speed. When you fly fast enough, even collisions with insects or birds can bring grave injury. This magic cannot be

used as if you are carelessly rushing about on the ground. You will need to practice beforehand."

Peeps had a point. Basically, it was like a Birdman Rally. Depending on where you got hit by something, you could die before even being able to cast healing magic on yourself. If a beginner was to learn it right off the bat, they would have a terrible time, just as he said.

"Thus, I will be the one to use it this time. I will teach you at a later date."

"I can't wait."

If that was how things were, I'd listen to what my master said without argument.

Those words of the great Starsage, after all.

✳

That night, we arrived close to the national border with the Ohgen Empire.

To get there, we had used magic to fly, just as Peeps had suggested, and our airborne trip through the dark of night had taken a little under an hour. We had traveled at a tremendous speed; we could have been going faster than a bullet train given how quickly the ground zipped by far below us.

Oh, Peeps. Despite your cute face, you're a real speed demon. Regardless, I had felt almost no air resistance since he was using a barrier spell—nor any shortness of breath or chill. I was extremely comfortable for the entire trip.

That made it all the more terrifying to think about what would happen if you hit something without a barrier. It felt to me like zooming down a highway or a bypass on a motorcycle wearing a half helmet. A pebble that bounced off a car in front of me could spell instant death.

"There they are."

"Oh, you're right…"

Far into the distance, all the way to the horizon, was a stretch of grasslands called the Rectan Plains. Right in the middle of it, you could see a mass of people gathered in something like a campground. From a few kilometers away, it was difficult to even tell they were people, yet we ascertained it was a cluster of soldiers. They appeared to wriggle and writhe, surrounding some temporary facilities that looked to be movable.

Peeps and I were flying pretty high in the air. With the night's darkness at our backs, they wouldn't be able to notice us. We, on the other hand, could clearly make out the lights illuminating the camp. It was an intimidating sight, with over ten thousand soldiers.

"What should we do?"

"Let us blow them all away."

"……"

Man, sometimes Peeps suddenly blurts out really scary stuff.

But I agreed that would probably be the safest option.

"If they lose this many troops, they should behave themselves for a time. Even if they do launch a new offensive, they will be more careful out of fear of similar retribution. In the meantime, Herz can rebuild its national power. I suppose I have no way to prove the latter will happen, though."

"You're gonna use one of those advanced spells you told me about before?"

"Categorywise, it is a step above that. It is possible to deal with them using advanced magic, but against so many, it is possible I might miss some. No, I want to end them all with one powerful attack. It will also bring them the least suffering."

"Oh."

"Now watch closely. The day may come when you learn this magic."

As he spoke, a magic circle emerged in front of him. It was more complex than any thus far. It was big, too—it must have been three meters across. Since he was perched on my shoulder, I got a direct look at the thing, too. My ears picked up a long string of words—the incantation, no doubt. Though I listened closely at first, it ended up being extremely lengthy, so I gave up on memorizing it partway through.

So I waited for a while.

Then Peeps spoke.

He opened his cute little beak wide and said, *"It is ready."* At the same time, the magic circle gave off a radiant shine.

A moment later, an immense light shot forth.

It stretched far away from us as we floated in the air, rushing toward the Ohgen Empire's forces below. As it traveled, it fanned out to the left and right, widening its range. By the time it had finally reached the ground, it had grown large enough to engulf the entire area.

The light pierced an area of the plains several kilometers square. Everything lit up like it was day.

A low, pulsating sound shook the atmosphere, almost causing me to recoil. I couldn't understand the details, but I could sense that an incredible, massive phenomenon had just occurred. It didn't feel like something caused by a single person but more like a typhoon or some other natural disaster.

"Peeps, uh, to be honest, I have no idea what is happening."

"*Understandable.*"

"It's like, uh, a beam cannon or something...?"

"*Think of it as something similar.*"

Peeps immediately understood what I meant by beam cannon. Must have been yet another result of his studies on the internet. The other day, I had looked through my computer's browser history—Peeps was going through internet dictionaries at an enormous speed. What a diligent sparrow. That said, regrettably, he hadn't looked at any adult sites. I wondered if he had lost his sex drive after becoming a bird.

After another twenty or thirty seconds, the light faded.

The blinding illumination was replaced once again by darkness. Immediately after, by the last remnants of the flash, I was able to make out a fearsome gouge cut into the entire area, as though it had been dug out by a giant excavator. It was so deep I couldn't see the bottom.

"...Peeps, that was very scary."

"*One can also focus its area of effect. Surprisingly, it is quite versatile.*"

"......"

If he had fired that in Tokyo, in one of the smaller areas like Chiyoda, or Chuo, or Minato, it would have wiped out everything in a single hit, right down to the metro lines running underground. Perhaps even more force than the nuclear bombs dropped on Hiroshima and Nagasaki.

"*You would do well to learn it as another option for your defense.*"

"...Yeah."

When I thought about over ten thousand people dying from that one attack, I felt a sense of desolation. That said, there wasn't much guilt, really. Of course, Peeps was the culprit here, and I was only watching. More than that, though, none of this felt *real*. It was more like I was watching a movie.

"*In any event, let us ret—*"

Just then, a glimmer of light shone from one corner of the gaping hole. Not a moment later, a magic circle emerged in front of us.

"Ngh..."

At the same time, from the point that had produced the flash, a ray of light came shooting up at us from the *ground* this time—like a beam cannon. When it struck the magic circle in front of us, the impact sent our bodies reeling backward.

"What…?"

"*Urgh…*"

The familiar sensation of Peeps's claws on my shoulder, pinching through my suit jacket, had vanished. I immediately scanned the area for him, finding the bird a few meters in front of me. The way he was frantically flapping his wings was quite unlike a Starsage—and very striking.

I noticed an unknown figure rapidly approaching Peeps from below.

"That spell seemed kind of familiar."

"*No… It's you…,*" came a voice I had no recollection of.

Like Peeps, the figure was floating in the air using flight magic. From their silhouette, our assailant seemed human—or at least a humanoid creature. I could see their clothes flapping in the wind, too. For whatever reason, their skin was purple. However, in the darkness of the night, I couldn't discern their gender or age.

Heck, I didn't have time to try because my body had begun plummeting toward the ground.

The next thing I knew, I'd already fallen a dozen or so meters. The impact seemed to have broken Peeps's flight spell. I gazed up at the super sparrow overhead in prayer—only to see him locked in battle with the figure who had just appeared. It didn't look like he had time to help.

"Are you kidding me…?"

He hadn't taught me the flying spell yet. In less than a few minutes, I'd crash into the ground.

Unlike the plains, where the enemy soldiers had been staying, I could see a dense forest covering the area below me—a wooded region bordering the grasslands. If I could get the tree branches to cushion my fall… No. I could see no way I was going to survive this.

I needed to be more proactive.

"…Oh, I got it."

I had that spell to shoot water from my hand. What if I fired it out at full force? No, there was no time to wonder about it. I had to use it *now*. The spell was just for making drinking water, but this time, I conjured the image of a fire truck hose and released it. Without a chant.

Then, a few dozen meters above the ground, all the water came rushing out. As it met the ground, the speed of my descent dropped significantly. I could feel my organs shifting upward.

Pressure slammed into me as though I were riding a roller coaster. For a moment, I thought I'd pass out. But I endured, continuing to fire the waterspout downward. To anyone witnessing the spectacle, I would probably have looked like a rocket launching in reverse.

After a few moments, I was soaked as my body caught up with the water. With a splosh, I sank in, and a moment later, my feet touched the ground. It seemed the trees had been toppled by the stream; my body hadn't gotten caught on any leaves or branches.

Presently, the water withdrew. With the sensation of my weight settling onto my feet, my vision opened up.

"I thought I was dead…"

It looked as though I'd been able to land without injury. My entire body was soaking wet, but well, that was one thing I couldn't do much about. I was happy just to have my life. It was a good thing we'd been flying so high—otherwise, I wouldn't have had time to use magic before crashing.

As I shook myself off, I heard a burst from overhead. It was a low booming sound that resonated in the pit of my stomach.

"……"

When I looked into the sky, I saw flames blooming across it. They were like clouds—expanding, red-colored fire. The scene was overwhelming. It made me anxious—if any of that hot stuff fell, I'd be dead. Fortunately, the flames scattered and vanished without scorching the surface.

Had a fight broken out between Peeps and the person targeting us? If someone as strong as Peeps didn't have time to help me out, whoever it was must have been a whole heap of trouble.

What should I do? I really wanted to help Peeps, but I had no way of getting aloft. Besides, if I marched in recklessly, I could end up getting in his way.

As I continued to fret, I suddenly heard someone call my name.

"Is that you there, Sir Sasaki?"

"What?"

I gave a start; that wasn't something I'd been expecting. I whipped around as if I'd been scalded and directed my attention to the voice I'd just heard. When I did, I saw him among the trees, staring out at me: Viscount Müller.

All around me were fallen trees from the water-producing spell I'd fired. The view was fairly clear for several meters around. That must have made it easy for him to spot me even in the dim light.

"Viscount Müller. What a coincidence that we should meet in a place like this."

"What are you doing here...?"

"Well, I've been wrapped up in something ever so slightly troubling," I said, obviously unable to give him an honest explanation.

This was huge news. Wasn't the viscount dead? The vice manager had told me he was. When I looked at him, I saw bloodstains speckling his body here and there, and he was altogether covered in wounds—but he was still on his own two feet.

Next to him stood a young man in his mid-to-late teens.

"Viscount Müller, who is this?"

The armor he wore looked even more expensive than the viscount's.

He was just as beaten and bloodied as the viscount, too. His armor was flecked with dirt and grime, with some parts broken entirely. Especially bad was the area around his stomach; dried black blood covered his gut.

It must have been too hard for him to walk as he was barely standing, leaning on Viscount Müller. His expression was pained. His face was a constant grimace and had lost a lot of its color. It seemed evident that he'd suffered a grave injury.

"The second prince of the Kingdom of Herz—Adonis."

"A prince?"

I hadn't expected royalty. No wonder the viscount was trying so hard to hold the man up.

"Viscount Müller, who is this man?"

"A foreign merchant who has been doing business in my territory."

"What is a merchant doing all the way out here? And why is everything wet?" asked the prince, surveying our soaked surroundings.

"...I apologize, Your Royal Highness, but I am having difficulty understanding, myself."

"......"

I had to say, this was a *really* suspicious place to show up. Soldiers from an enemy nation were massing just outside the forest. I wouldn't blame them if they suspected me of being a spy. From their point of view, just approaching me like this was putting their lives on the line.

However, facing this dodgy middle-aged man, Viscount Müller continued speaking.

"One thing is certain: He is not our enemy."

"...Is this true?"

"Yes."

He had spoken without a hint of hesitation.

I hadn't expected he'd trust me even at rock bottom. It filled me with happiness. I didn't remember talking with him *that* much, but the way he looked at me now was no different from our prior encounters.

Perhaps that was why I was able to continue the conversation without much thought.

"Viscount Müller, would you let me check on His Highness's condition? I actually have some knowledge of magic and may be able to help him."

"You? You can use magic, Sir Sasaki?"

"Not very much, but yes, sir."

"In that case, yes, please do!"

With Viscount Müller's approval, I tried out my intermediate healing spell. I'd learned how to cast the beginner version without an incantation just the other day, but for this one, I needed to chant. As I brought my hands closer to the prince, I murmured the longish string of words.

A magic circle appeared at the target's feet. As light rose from it, the prince's expression changed completely.

"I... The pain is leaving me..."

The magic circle was up for a dozen seconds or so. Based on my experience practicing on wild mice and such, I decided on an appropriate duration and lowered my arms. With that, the magic circle that had appeared on the ground vanished, and the light subsided.

"How do you feel, sir?"

"...Such wondrous skills. Those wounds were grave, and in the blink of an eye, they are gone."

"Does it hurt anywhere?"

"No, I appear to be fully healed. I think I'll be able to keep walking now."

The prince replied energetically, checking himself.

His shirt flicked up, and underneath, I saw lean muscle. Not only were his features attractive, but he was blessed physically, too. It was envy-inducing. Based on his physique, I could clearly tell that he trained on a daily.

"Still, I had not expected you to use healing magic at such a level..."

"I'm honored, sir."

"Would you please heal Viscount Müller as well? He is wounded."

"Yes, sir."

At the prince's instruction, I used the healing spell again, this time with the viscount as the target. The places I could see, like his face and fingers, healed immediately. I didn't want to leave anything amiss under the skin, though, like broken bones, so I kept it up for a dozen or so seconds to give it enough time, just as I had with the prince.

After a moment, the viscount called out to me.

"That should be enough."

"My lord? All right."

In accordance with his self-assessment, I ceased casting my healing spell.

Spurred on, no doubt, by this exchange, the prince's face had become somewhat more peaceful compared to the scowl he'd worn when we first encountered each other. I figured I could probably have a calm conversation with them now.

"Your name was Sasaki, yes? You've saved us. I give you my thanks."

"No, the honor was all mine, Your Royal Highness."

"And I will refrain from prying too deeply into why we met you in a forest so close to the battlefield. I'm sure you have your own work. In exchange, might you be able to assist us in escaping from this place?"

Having lost Peeps, I was in a pickle myself. Now that it would be difficult to meet back up with him, working with the prince and the viscount to escape danger instead was an extremely attractive option. There could always be remnants of the obliterated enemy forces hiding nearby.

"Understood. I would be glad to accompany you, sirs."

And that was how I formed a party with two very good-looking guys.

*

Viscount Müller, Prince Adonis, and I were headed back to the Kingdom of Herz through the nighttime forest.

They explained that the prince had been targeted by an enemy soldier on the battlefield, and stepping in to his defense, the viscount had become separated from the main force. The situation at the time had been desperate, and the Hermann Trading Company's messenger simply assumed the viscount was dead.

But they had miraculously survived and had been trying to get back to town ever since. For me, having already been informed of the viscount's death, it was a joyful reunion.

The area we were in was called the Niekam Forest. It was adjacent to the Rectan Plains, where the Empire's troops had been stationed, and moving away from the plains and through the forest would bring you to the town of Baytrium.

"By the way, Sasaki, it seems there is some kind of magician's conflict occurring above us..."

Prince Adonis appeared concerned about what was happening in the sky as well. He kept glancing overhead.

Sparks were still flying between Peeps and the unknown magician. The intermittent bursting noises made us feel like we were in danger even on the ground. I was extremely worried about stray shots reaching us.

"It seems that way, Your Highness."

"Do you know anything about it?"

"I'm sorry, but that is truly beyond my comprehension."

"...I see."

I couldn't exactly answer honestly, of course, so I ended up feigning ignorance.

Peeps had just obliterated an innumerable amount of Ohgen Empire soldiers in an instant. If someone was taking this much of his time to deal with, then if we ran into them, they'd kill us in seconds.

What frustrated me most was my distance from Peeps. As his assistant, without me there, Peeps couldn't use magic above a certain level—the world-hopping spell, for example. But if I tried to get closer to their battle, I'd probably get in his way. The surprise attack had stolen the initiative from us, and it was having a huge effect.

"If they can use such large-scale magic in quick succession, then if we do happen to encounter them, we wouldn't stand a chance. I appreciate your concern, but I believe we should focus on getting out of this forest and back to Herz."

"Duly noted."

"Thank you, sir."

Incidentally, this prince was quite convivial despite his title. I was a complete stranger, yet he spoke to me as an equal. Interparty communication was going better than I'd ever hoped it would. I was hugely grateful for it.

"Your Royal Highness, Sir Sasaki, please stop for a moment."

"...An enemy?"

"It seems that way, sir."

Meanwhile, the viscount had announced an enemy encounter.

He stared through the trees, his expression harsh. He then pulled his sword from his hip and took up a combat posture.

It wasn't clear what the enemy was armed with, but regular soldiers would at least have bows and arrows, right? I used the intermediate barrier spell, and it unfolded around us, including not only me but the viscount and prince as well.

A moment later, arrows were raining down on us from the side.

Several struck the barrier and fell to the ground harmlessly.

"Sasaki, you can not only use healing magic but barrier magic as well?"

"I was blessed with a talented teacher."

"I see. They must be very skilled, indeed."

Not a moment after his eyes had opened wide with surprise at the arrows, they shifted to me, and his expression switched to one of admiration. Being able to use both healing magic and intermediate magic at this level seemed quite valuable. I couldn't thank Peeps enough.

"Sir Sasaki, how long will this magic hold?"

"A while, I believe, but did you have some sort of plan, my lord?"

"Our situation will get worse and worse this way. I'd like to take the initiative, cutting into their forces."

"Isn't that a bit dangerous?"

"Do you have any other ideas?"

"I can fire magic at them from here."

"You can use attack magic as well?"

"Not very many kinds, but yes."

"In that case, please go right ahead."

Similar to when I had aimed at the invisible psychic in the bowling alley the other day, I fired the lightning magic toward the source of the arrows. I had some apprehensions that it would start a fire, but I didn't have the luxury of that concern right now.

I omitted the chant, and the bolt zapped forth without an incantation. A moment later, we heard several screams from what must have been enemy soldiers. Something told me I'd hit the mark.

At the same time, there was a change up ahead. Men with swords at the ready rushed out at us from between the trees. They'd probably realized their opponent was a magician and decided to close the distance. That put me, someone absurdly weak at melee combat, in a bad position.

"Leave this to me!"

Perhaps catching on to my hesitation, Viscount Müller leaped forward. Crossing the barrier, he charged the enemy soldiers.

And then, against a group of swordsmen, he plunged into a straight-up sword fight. This seemed to be his specialty. Despite being outnumbered, he showed no fear. Within moments, he'd already cut down his first.

Wow! Viscount Müller is super strong. Well, I can't just stand around watching, either.

Firing another lightning spell, I brought down more of the soldiers still at a distance from the viscount. I focused especially on bow- and staff-wielders for my shots. Since there could have been troops lying in ambush in the trees, I also spread my shots toward the vicinity of where our assailants had emerged.

The struggle lasted a few minutes or so. With Viscount Müller's swordplay and my sorcery, we safely defeated the enemy.

"Sir Sasaki, I am incredibly impressed that you can cast intermediate magic without an incantation."

The blood-drenched viscount returned to us, smiling. *That's a little scary.*

"It is your skill with the sword, my lord, that deserves special mention here."

"There are plenty of others more talented than I."

Prince Adonis seemed a little more resigned.

"You both did wonderfully. I find myself frustrated at my own powerlessness."

He'd watched the fight go by without any real chance to participate. His disappointment was clear as he stared at his feet. Given how attractive he was, it painted a pretty picture. I wished I'd been born with those kinds of looks.

"You have a more important role to fill than fights such as these, do you not, Your Highness?"

"Even so, there is no better leader than a strong one."

"Well, you still have plenty of time to learn and practice, sir. Your

Royal Highness is yet young and can recover from anything. The true path of the sword begins only when you have passed twenty and your body has matured fully. It is nothing to be worried about."

"Really?"

"I made little progress at your age as well, sir."

"...I see."

Seeing the prince talk with Viscount Müller, who was just as attractive, was like a scene out of a movie. It seemed like a sin to involve myself, so I naturally hesitated.

"Sir Sasaki, your magic has saved us."

"I am honored I was able to be of some help, my lord."

"You are quite skilled to have noticed their men lying in ambush. It is thanks to you I could move about freely. The most fearsome thing in melees like these is the presence of archers and magicians. Both can completely tip the balance of power in one direction."

"I see, my lord."

From how Viscount Müller was talking, it seemed safe to assume the threat had passed. I, too, felt like myself again.

"Sir, we need to move before beasts or monsters are lured here by the scent of blood. I know you are tired, but we should get moving. We're covered in blood, so I'd like to do so as soon as possible."

"We will do as the viscount says. Please lead the way."

"Thank you, sir."

Sensing that Peeps, too, was doing his best up above us, we resumed our march.

＊

How long had we walked? The sky was slowly whitening. It seemed daybreak was near.

I hadn't kept track of the time, but my body was saying we'd been trekking through the forest for three or four hours. Because of that, I'd naturally stopped talking as much, but even the locals, Viscount Müller and Prince Adonis, had grown quiet as well.

Yet it still didn't appear we'd be getting out of the Niekam Forest soon.

According to the viscount, we'd reach the nearest village before too long. Right now, I walked in silence, trusting in those words. Fortunately, we didn't have to worry about drinkable water. I could make as much as we needed using magic.

Meanwhile, as for what was happening in the sky, we could still hear plenty of thumping and booming noises. Peeps was still holding out. I couldn't begin to imagine what kind of opponent he was up against who would take that much time, even if the sparrow *had* been separated from me.

Our formation as we proceeded through the woods consisted of the viscount in front, me at the rear, and Prince Adonis between us. The viscount had said he'd trade his own life to protect the prince's.

"Your Royal Highness, are your legs doing well?"

"What I lack in martial talent I think I more than make up for in stamina."

Viscount Müller asked the question of the prince out of consideration. How many times did that make it?

"I am pleased to hear it, sir."

"More importantly, Sasaki, are you all right? This must be difficult on a magician."

Whoa. The royal just asked *me* a considerate question. Getting that kind of attention from someone in a high position made me 30 percent happier than normal.

"I can lighten my exhaustion with magic, sir, so I'm still doing fine."

"Ah, is that so?"

"Your healing magic," interjected the viscount, "must be quite powerful to cure even exhaustion."

The two of them had strong, healthy legs, so I'd been using magic here and there to help my own in order to keep up with them. For a modern man used to trains and automobiles, hiking like this was unimaginably taxing. Without the healing spell, I'd already have collapsed.

Thanks to that, though, I'd managed to abbreviate the incantation a bit when I used it.

"We will arrive at the settlement shortly," said Viscount Müller, encouraging us from ahead. "I recall visiting this area on an orc hunt once, so I have some sense of the terrain. Your Royal Highness, Sir Sasaki, this is the last spurt. Let's all stay alert and—"

It happened just then. From behind us, we heard a long, ragged roar.

I couldn't imagine that voice coming from a human. Actually, I wasn't even sure whether to call it a voice at all.

"Viscount Müller," noted the prince, "I just heard something that sounded dangerous."

"…That was an orc's cry, sir."

"An orc…"

"One may have been whipped up due to the Empire's advance."

"Would that not mean the nearby village is in danger as well?"

"It is as you say, sir."

The prince and Viscount Müller shared a disquieting exchange.

I'd heard several times from Peeps that this world was home to creatures that were called monsters. They spanned every sort you could imagine—from weak ones the size of the sparrow itself to huge ones the size of a large whale.

"Viscount Müller, Sasaki, given the situation, I apologize for asking you this, but can we not go and check on the village? If they have sustained damage, I would like to bring the information back and dispatch a team of knights."

"Understood, sir."

The viscount agreed to the prince's request immediately. That meant there was no way I could refuse.

Personally, I wanted to strongly insist on a detour. Peeps was still battling up there in the air, and I believed it would be best to get out of the forest as soon as we could. However, with the two of them acting like Braveheart, I didn't have the gall to say no.

Besides, if I was to refuse, they'd probably go on their own. If I truly wanted them to stay safe, they'd need my healing and barrier magic. For now, I'd strive to continue my role as their mysterious magician.

"I would be honored to come along as well, sir."

"I'm sorry for putting you through this, Sasaki. I promise to make up for it."

"No, sir, you don't need to bother yourself with me."

And so we rushed straight toward the source of the roar.

*

Ultimately, there *was* a monster in the forest. Many of them, in fact.

Plus, they were in the middle of an all-out attack against the village Viscount Müller had mentioned.

As has been explained to me, they were creatures called orcs. They were anywhere from two to three meters tall with muscle-bound bodies. They seemed somewhat intelligent, and they gripped weapons in their hands, swinging them as they rampaged. They looked pretty much like what you would get by searching *orc* on the internet. It was all very overwhelming for this otherworld freshman.

"Well, they *are* quite fearsome creatures," I noted.

"Is this your first time seeing an orc, Sir Sasaki?"

"Yes, my lord, it is."

"Then be careful. Most knights and adventurers tend to treat them lightly, but in force, they are very troublesome to deal with. And when they've formed a band like this, we must tread very carefully."

"Ah."

Right now, we were a short distance from the village, looking out from a vantage point hidden in the foliage. On the other side of a small fence, we could see the villagers running about, trying to escape. It was a gruesome sight, the orcs killing and violating the townspeople as they wished. Most of those being assaulted in the latter sense were women, but here and there, a man could be spotted.

"Viscount Müller, there are more orcs than we anticipated. The village will be wiped out before the knights can be dispatched. I am once again sorry to ask this of you, but is there no way to save the town?"

"…Hmm."

I couldn't believe it— In a situation like this, the prince was thinking of the village. Not only that, but Viscount Müller was also entertaining the idea. Such a sense of justice flowed from these two men!

"With Sir Sasaki's backup, perhaps."

"Truly?!"

The next thing I knew, they were looking at *me.* Not only the viscount but the prince as well—and there was fire in their eyes.

"Sasaki, would you please assist us? If we are able to return to the castle safely, I will guarantee a proper reward. I do not wish to forsake this village. I'm begging you—please help us."

"……"

"I have seen the Ohgen Empire's forces on the battlefield. This nation will one day be invaded and destroyed. I, too, am fated to die on the guillotine in the near future."

The Kingdom of Herz was heavily deteriorating, but it seemed the second prince, at least, was an exception. The earnestness with which he looked at me made his sincere care and concern for the villagers quite evident. Much of it was probably due to feeling his own death near at hand.

And with the viscount's attention on me, they were really making it hard to refuse.

Perhaps he harbored the same feelings as the prince. When a person became aware of their own mortality, they tended to want to leave something behind—like a reason for having been born or a legacy.

"Umm..."

After thinking about it carefully, however, their proposal wasn't all bad. We had walked a long distance, so in terms of securing a place to sleep for a while, this village was very important. We also had the food problem to deal with. Water I could summon with magic, but we needed to acquire food through some other means.

There was a lot to be gained from saving this place.

"I understand, sir. Please allow me to help."

"Thank you so much, Sasaki. You are a dependable man."

"After seeing your spirit, I feel my own energy welling up within me."

In any case, I may as well put them as far in my debt as possible.

After a firm nod, we began our orc hunt.

*

Our strategy for fighting the orcs would be the same as when we drove off the Ohgen Empire soldiers the night before. Viscount Müller took the front while I took the rear.

This time, though, Prince Adonis would be involved. Positionwise, he was at the fore.

As the one tasked with healing and defense, this made me very anxious. If the worst happened and he was wounded, what would other big shots say about it? I could fix him up with my healing magic, but the thought was enough to put me in a cold sweat. If he died or something... Well, I couldn't bear to think about that.

Therefore, our advance saw me pouring a significant amount of mana into my defensive magic, hardening our defenses as we went. The others were concerned about my mana running out, but I told them not to worry. I couldn't afford to be stingy on this.

No sooner had we set foot in the village than an orc attacked us.

A significant number of them seemed to have been hiding indoors. At a glance, there must have been close to twenty of the things swarming around. When my lightning magic hit their group, they all showed the same reaction—one after another, they swarmed us at the village's entrance.

For a moment, it was my time to shine. I continuously shot off lightning spells at the orcs that entered my range, whittling down their numbers. Peeps had told me this magic was one of the lower-level intermediate spells, but it sure packed a punch. One hit to the head or chest basically killed them. Even when my aim was a bit off, they collapsed to the ground with wails and moans.

Not long after the battle began, I'd successfully taken out about ten of them. A few, however, made it past my attacks—and it was those that the viscount and prince engaged.

The two of them, swords in hands, worked together to send the orcs to their graves. As always, the viscount was a powerhouse. It was no different from when he'd fought people—he would calmly and accurately pierce their vital points. The way he dodged by a hair the axes they were flailing about was incredibly cool to watch.

In his wake, His Royal Highness was embroiled in a struggle of his own. That said, in terms of his skill... Well, he definitely got points for effort. More than once, I glimpsed a scene that sent a chill down my spine, but we managed to hold out with the viscount's blade and my barrier magic to support him.

"Sir Sasaki, over there— It has a bow!"

"Understood, my lord."

Following Viscount Müller's warning, I aimed around the corner of a house and fired a lightning bolt. One seemed to have been targeting us from a hiding place behind the building.

As the viscount had advised earlier, orcs did indeed seem to be very difficult monsters to deal with when in a horde. The bows and arrows they held were far bigger than the ones humans used, too. One clean hit, and it would open a huge hole in any of our human bodies.

Without my Peeps-approved magic, we never would have stood a chance.

Between my attacks, I also cast healing magic on any villagers lying in my range of sight. Even if we took down the orcs, I couldn't let the village be wiped out—that would be too sad. I needed to do everything I could.

"...Sir, these orcs are behaving oddly."

"What do you mean?"

"Hordes of orcs are usually smaller in number," advised the viscount. He must have caught on to something abnormal.

"Normally, orcs live in groups of about ten, led by a single boss orc. There are over twenty-four in this village—actually, with just the ones I can see, they number over thirty."

"Is that right?"

"They may currently be led by a much higher-ranking orc…"

Gazing at the monsters, Viscount Müller was just forming his next word when it happened.

We heard a long, loud roar from somewhere.

It was the cry of an orc, which we'd been hearing incessantly throughout the fight. However, compared to the others, this one sounded several times more powerful. Its boom shook me, causing my stomach to vibrate.

"This is bad!"

Viscount Müller's face changed. His confidence was gone.

"Viscount Müller, was that bellow an orc?!"

"Without a doubt, sir, but it is most likely an elite. I have no way of knowing how powerful it is, but given the size of this horde, it must be suitably strong."

"I've heard of this, too. When one is born with the blessing of mana or coincidentally acquires it, it will live longer than others, and we refer to them as elites. I recall a lecture from the Lord Starsage on the topic."

"That is correct, sir. Unfortunately, I am going to have to ask you, as well as Sir Sasaki, to withdraw. If this *is* an elite orc, it will be a very difficult opponent. It may not even be possible for us to kill it alone."

"I've been curious about this—is it different from a high orc?"

"They are orcs as well but a different species than normal orcs, like the ones active here. Elite versions of high orcs exist just as they do for orcs. Humans would need an entire military force to fight an elite high orc."

"I see. Ever the wellspring of information, Viscount Müller."

"Sir, I know of it only because of the Lord Starsage's lectures myself."

In response to the viscount's words, the prince withdrew to my position. He had cuts and scrapes here and there, so I used my healing magic to cure him. I couldn't remove the blood stuck to his skin and clothing, but the wounds underneath vanished within a few seconds.

"Thank you, Sasaki. You've saved me."

"Sir, it is an honor."

"With any luck, we will be able to fell the fiend painlessly…"

After making sure Prince Adonis was physically fine, I turned my attention back to the village.

Our immediate surroundings were much calmer now, after I'd fired lightning magic at each and every orc I saw. They'd kept appearing from farther into the village, but it seemed like we were finally getting somewhere.

Orc remains lay scattered among those of the villagers. I couldn't see any of them moving.

At this point, the issue was the elite whatever the viscount had mentioned. With a nervous stance that belied the reverence with which he'd spoken of the creature, he faced the direction from which we'd heard its cry.

With nothing else to do, I continued imbuing healing magic to the villagers from the rear. Couldn't do anything about the ones already dead. The intermediate-level healing spell was kind of amazing, though—as long as they were alive, they were able to recover.

"Viscount Müller, Sasaki, over there!"

Meanwhile, the prince gave a shout. I turned to where they were looking to see an orc thumping along the village road, running at us. It must have been hiding in the forest on the other side of the settlement.

And this was an *awfully* large orc we were talking about. It was close to twice the size of the others—far bigger than the houses it passed along the road. How the hell had something like that kept hidden?

Witnessing the thing had nearly left Viscount Müller dumbstruck.

"Wha…? How—how is it that big…?"

"Viscount Müller, I'm going to head it off with magic!"

"Do it, Sir Sasaki!"

As one of those standing in the way of its approach, I was trembling. I couldn't bear the thought of this thing getting anywhere near me. Squeezing out all the magic power I could, I fired my lightning spell.

Faster than the eye could see, a burst of electricity rushed forth. The end of it was aimed directly at the orc's gut. With a brilliant *crack*, the bolt struck. A moment later, the orc fell to the ground headfirst.

This happened a dozen or so meters in front of us. I watched the fallen orc, praying it wouldn't get back up.

Unfortunately, praying didn't help.

"Grooooohhhhhhhh!"

With an earsplitting roar, the orc picked itself up.

The monster had taken the lightning bolt to the stomach, and the burn mark was clearly visible. The wound was not fatal, however, and the orc rose its feet. It seemed to have lost none of its fighting spirit as it proceeded to glare at me.

It was *livid*.

"……"

Peeps, my ray of hope, was still devoting all his attention to his business up in the sky. Perhaps death had finally come.

What were my options? The designated magic user of the party was at a loss as to his next move.

In the meantime, Viscount Müller sprinted toward the orc, raising his sword vigorously in a bold and daring charge.

It was a frightening scene, like watching a small sedan attempt to run a fully loaded ten-ton runaway truck off the road. The taller the creature, the stronger its muscles, and this monster was so big, its finger was as thick as a human limb.

"Hrrrrgh…"

The orc swung down its fist.

Dodging past this peril, the viscount laid into the orc with his sword. His strike went for the blood vessel in the monster's wrist. However, he must not have gotten deep enough—or maybe he didn't have enough oomph in his downswing—because it only made a shallow slice on the skin.

A moment later, the orc's leg moved. Its foot whipped upward, aiming for the viscount. The thing was nimbler than I'd thought.

"Gah…"

The viscount attempted to launch himself backward to slip out of the way. Unfortunately, he was unable to escape his opponent's incredible reach. The orc kicked him away, and his body flew in an arc through the air until it finally landed at our side.

"Gack…"

As his back hit the ground, blood spurted from his mouth.

It must have connected with his internal organs. That was not good.

"Viscount Müller, I'll heal you right away!"

In a panic, I started to chant the healing spell. However, our opponent wasn't going to let me do that. Feet thumping along the ground, it bore down on us. For a giant, a dozen meters or so could be covered in a few seconds. Must be nice to have such long legs.

"Sir, take care of the viscount!"

"Will do!"

With that, I directed the prince to drag the viscount into the magic barrier.

I had to hurry. Otherwise, the orc would flatten all three of us.

I canceled the healing spell. Instead, I poured my mana into the barrier spell encircling us. I didn't know how effective it would be, but it was better than doing nothing. It was a good thing I'd kept it active—I had zero time to chant anything.

"Groooohhhh!"

A moment later, the orc's fist hit the barrier. A bright, loud *thwack* echoed around us.

I had thought we'd be on our way to the next life after that one, but the barrier managed to bear the orc's strike. Being within its protection, we were safe as well—physically anyway. Mentally, maybe not so much. I actually pissed myself a little. I mean, a giant orc fist was literally right in front of me!

"Sasaki!"

"Please calm down, sir. I need to heal the viscount first."

I glanced the prince's way—and saw he'd soiled himself as well. He had it much worse than me, though. It was like a flood. *So nice not to be alone.* I was weirdly relieved to have a companion in this, but in the meantime, I used my healing spell on Viscount Müller.

Outside the barrier, the orc was in a rage-fueled frenzy. He punched and kicked at the semitranslucent wall, over and over and over again. It was so scary I almost fudged up the incantation. It was nerve-racking as hell.

Peeps would have been able to cast all this without chanting at all.

"Guh… Thank…you, Sir Sasaki."

"Please save your thanks, my lord."

The viscount was breathing properly again now that he'd been healed. I happened to glance at his pants—and he, too, had wet himself. I'd seen stats released by the military once that said about half of all soldiers who experienced a fierce battle soiled themselves. I thought we should be proud there weren't more potent scents drifting through the air at the moment.

But what would we do now?

"Taking on this orc will be difficult with only us…"

"Yes—we lack an offense."

Inside the barrier, the "we pissed ourselves" gang of three held a strategy meeting.

In the present situation, the lightning spell was our most powerful weapon. Not only had the orc already taken a hit of this head-on, though, but Viscount Müller could only make shallow slices in the beast's skin with his sword. We were running out of options to take this orc down.

"I am sorry, Sasaki. It is my fault for proposing something so unorthodox."

"We haven't lost just yet, sir."

"But…"

I knew now that my intermediate-level barrier spell *was* effective against an elite orc. We had enough in the way of defense, at least. Which meant that, in the worst case, I could lob a few dozen or a few hundred lightning attacks at it.

Fortunately, I had plenty of energy—mana—left in reserve, probably because Peeps had so willingly given me so much of it. Apparently, when your mana supply started to run dry, you'd feel increasingly sluggish.

During the course of my practice sessions in the past, I'd fired spells several dozen times in a short period, but I'd never experienced anything like that. It was safe to assume that while the monster had the strengths of an orc, we had an advantage over it in at least one way.

That said, watching it pound away at the barrier was bad for my heart. I had apprehensions—what if, in the next moment, my spell broke and the creature punched us with a fist the size of an excavator's shovel?

Just to be sure, I decided to erect a second barrier inside the first. After running it past the prince and viscount, I set up an inner layer to serve as backup. Unsure of the magic's durability, I decided to use this two-layered construction for the time being.

"Sir Sasaki, you have the use of very solid barrier magic."

"Perhaps, but I'm still worried about how long it will last."

"It's already impressive that you've been able to stop an elite enemy for this long—and on your own, without even combining efforts with other magicians. I wouldn't be the least bit surprised if you said you were a court magician."

"Magicians cast spells in groups, my lord?"

I'd spotted a bit of information in the viscount's compliment. Peeps hadn't told me about this, either.

"I have heard that magicians will form groups to cast spells of intermediate level and above. When it comes to advanced spells, there are only so many who can cast them on their own. Which is why I've been helplessly curious about what's still happening above us."

"Ah, I see what you mean."

"No matter how I look at it, those spells must be in the high-intermediate range—no, that must be advanced magic."

"……"

I got the feeling there was a vast ocean between the ABCs of magic as taught by Peeps and the world's general impression of magicians as told by Viscount Müller. Going by the former, you weren't even a full-fledged magician until you had learned intermediate-level barrier magic.

"I would like to whittle down his stamina using my lightning magic, my lord. Do you mind?"

"No, go right ahead. It frustrates me to say, but my blade will not be enough to slay him."

"Understood, my lord."

"But I want you to be cautious as well, Sir Sasaki. It may be an orc, but at this massive size, it would be above even a high orc. Elite monsters with many years behind them can even exceed higher creatures within the same species."

"I understand, my lord."

The monster hadn't emerged totally unscathed from the first shot I'd fired. You could still see the burn mark on the surface of its skin. If I added to that, it was likely I'd be able to weaken it quite a bit. It would then be possible to defeat it with Viscount Müller's help.

"Well, then…"

I aimed my magic at all the parts where my target's skin seemed thin—its eyes, its leg joints, and its crotch. Finally, I sharpened my awareness and prepared to fire—and then it happened.

All of a sudden, a humanoid figure fell from the sky and hit the orc dead-on.

With a loud *thud*, the giant creature toppled backward.

The collision seemed to have a ton of momentum behind it, and the fallen orc's body broke the stone pavement and ended up half buried in the ground. It was almost like it had been hit by a meteorite. The whole thing took no longer than a moment.

Having seen this collision up close, we were utterly shocked. I thought I might soil myself again. The prince had—a lot. The stains were growing.

"Wh-what is it this time?!" cried out Prince Adonis in total panic, his voice reverberating around us.

✳

The falling object had crashed down into the supersize orc, inflicting a one-hit KO.

My attention shifted skyward. A natural reaction, given the series of events leading up to this. Until just now, the heavens had been alive, as though burning with fireworks. Viscount Müller and Prince Adonis were craning their necks upward, too.

What greeted us was a cute little bird descending from the firmament.

"My apologies. I was delayed in coming to your aid."

It was Peeps. He fluttered through the air and landed on my shoulder. He looked the same as always, perched in his usual spot.

For some reason, this calmed me down a lot despite the two of us having only been together a few weeks at this point.

"Peeps, something, uh, fell from the sky…"

"Yes, it took longer than I anticipated. And I am deeply sorry for abandoning you in the air like that. You could have died. All fault lies with me, and I truly apologize."

Peeps went so far as to lower his little head as he spoke. It was just too cute, seeing a sparrow bow to me.

I did still worry about the viscount and prince watching us talk to each other like this, but something else was bothering me more: the reddish fluid stuck to the bird's body. Blood?

"Wait, are you injured? Are you okay?"

As his owner, I was beside myself with worry. He was a small Java sparrow on the outside, so even a little cut would make me uneasy. Mr. Yamada at the pet shop had told me that bird wings were extremely delicate, and even a tiny wound could render them unable to fly. Peeps could use healing magic, so he was probably just fine, but I was still concerned.

"It is nothing. Most of this blood is not mine."

"If you say so…"

"I apologize if I soil your clothing."

"Aw, don't be. The health of my pet is more important."

"And your health concerns me. Were you injured by the fall?"

"I managed with one of the spells you taught me."

"Yes? I see. Good…," he said, relieved—another emotion that looked adorable on him.

I was so happy to be able to talk to him like this that the conversation just kept going. Peeps really was a balm for the soul.

In the meantime, the fallen orc began to stir—it seemed to have regained consciousness. It propped up one hand on the ground, slowly standing. With its other hand, it plucked the fallen object off its body and flung it aside like a piece of trash.

I caught a glimpse of the meteor's skin, and it was the same purple I had noted on Peeps's opponent in the sky.

Whoever had attacked Peeps was not normal.

"An elite orc?" observed Peeps, staring at the giant creature now on its feet. Was this thing strong enough that even *he* would struggle against it?

I only had a moment to consider the possibility before my lovely little sparrow's wings moved.

From right to left, a whooshing flash of light.

The orc's head slid off its neck, sending massive amounts of blood spewing everywhere. Its body remained upright for a few scant seconds before crashing to the ground once more.

This time, it was facedown. It didn't move so much as a muscle after that.

Peeps, you're crazy strong! Our own fierce battle had been totally upstaged.

"The creatures of this world, through various means, can sometimes gain magic, which grants them a longer life span and allows them to grow into much more capable members of their species. We call such specimens elite."

"Ah."

Viscount Müller had taught me the same thing. For now, though, I'd just nod. It was very much like Peeps to start a lecture like this right after a real-life experience— I loved it.

"Such individuals come in all strengths. For example, an average orc, if it has acquired magic powers and lived a long life, may even exceed the abilities of a high orc—the next-strongest order of orc. In fact, the one lying there was likely more powerful than a high orc."

The viscount had said something similar, too. He said he'd heard it from the Starsage, so he'd probably learned it the exact same way I was now. Given that Peeps had been the original source of the information, his explanation was more detailed.

"And this phenomenon can also occur among humans."

"Wait, really?"

This was the first time hearing that tidbit. Apparently, the rule applied to more than just monsters.

"In that sense, ones such as you and I are elite humans."

"…Oh."

Without knowing it, I'd apparently taken a step beyond the realm of humanity.

Now I was scared of my next checkup. What if I suddenly got taller? The health exam at the bureau hadn't revealed anything in particular, but who knew what would happen in the future? I'd welcome some nice, thick hair—come to think of it, I hoped that would happen.

"Still, an elite creature can be very weak or very strong. Should you ever find yourself in a fight with another, be wary of this point. There are elite orcs with power greater than a dragon's."

"I heard you mention dragons before, too. Are they just, like, commonplace around here?"

"Yes, they exist, and certain areas are home to a great many of them."

"If it can happen to humans, does that mean it could happen to livestock or pests, too?"

"It does, indeed. The phenomenon is not limited to animals and can even manifest in plants."

Now, I didn't know whether cockroaches, centipedes, or spider crickets existed in this world. That said, creatures like them *could*, depending on the situation, suddenly get gigantic and threaten humans. Elite creatures seemed quite the force to be reckoned with.

"Thanks for the information, Peeps. It was helpful."

"Still, I do seem to have wasted all the effort you have expended thus far…," said Peeps, glancing over at the viscount and the prince.

Naturally, they'd heard everything we'd just said. I also knew from the viscount's daughter that a small bird being able to understand human speech wasn't typical. Plus, this sparrow had just sliced the orc's head off in one breath. They must have had questions.

Nevertheless, without Peeps's help, we would have been hard-pressed to take that enemy down. Nobody could argue that point. Peeps understood this as well as anyone, which was why he'd come to our rescue, even if it meant speaking in front of others.

I was overcome with joy at being able to rejoin Peeps here. Judging by his explanation about elite creatures, his sudden appearance must have been out of concern for us. Peeps was the one who would be most inconvenienced if anyone discovered his identity. Our current situation notwithstanding, there was no doubt he, himself, would have been the one who most wanted to keep it concealed.

"Sir Sasaki, what…is that bird?"

The question came from Viscount Müller. Next to him, Prince Adonis seemed primed to ask the same thing.

"This would be my master of magic."

"What?! Ah, so this is Sir Sasaki's master!"

Now that we'd already shown them all this magic, I decided to explain the bare minimum. The viscount, at least, seemed earnest and tight-lipped. Given his position, he was the perfect person with whom to share a secret—that was the optimistic way I wanted to think about it, at least. I still had my concerns about the prince, but there wasn't much I could do about that.

"*I apologize for my sudden arrival and late introduction.*"

"N-no, I don't mind that at all; it's just…"

Viscount Müller fumbled for words after the Java sparrow spoke to him. He and Prince Adonis were both glancing back and forth between Peeps, the orc, and whoever it was who'd crashed into the beast.

As for the last one, I was extremely curious myself. It was probably the person Peeps had been fighting until just a moment ago.

From the looks of the fallen enemy, they didn't seem human. They were humanoid, with arms, legs, and a head coming out of a torso, and their features were much the same as ours. They wore expensive-looking clothes, indicating a cultural level not far from our own.

That said, their skin was purple. They also had sheeplike horns coming out of their head.

"*As you can see, it appears that demonfolk have infiltrated the Empire,*" Peeps remarked offhandedly.

"Wh-what?!" cried Viscount Müller.

Demon was a new term for me. Though similar, it sounded like something separate from monsters.

"Peeps, what are demons?"

"*The demonfolk are a race of people with appearances akin to that of the one you see lying there. Just as we humans are considered our own race, these people are considered to be of the demon race. They possess superior magic power, physical abilities, and life spans compared to our own.*"

"Ah, I see."

It would probably be enough to keep in mind that such creatures existed. I wouldn't want to disrupt the flow of conversation by asking this and that. Having to wait for an otherworld freshman like me to understand everything would be an inconvenience. After all, Viscount Müller and Prince Adonis were here, too.

"Ordinarily, they live in the northern continent, where they have their own nation. However, some do come south to meddle in the business of others. This one, in particular, frequently causes riots involving the affairs of man. I know her personally."

As Peeps spoke, he gazed at the purple-skinned demon lying on the ground next to the orc. Her limbs were twitching, so she didn't seem dead.

"Wait, you do?"

"Yes, though I believe the name people generally refer to her by is the Blood Witch."

"The Blood Witch?! You don't mean one of the seven great war criminals?!"

Viscount Müller was all but flabbergasted. Next to him, Prince Adonis's eyes widened in shock as well. This woman must have been pretty famous.

"She must have grown too fond of her diversions in the world of man. Demonfolk are normally more self-disciplined creatures, but once one gets a taste for the easy life, they can lapse into indolence. She is likely involved in some way with the current disturbance."

"How could this have…?"

If I thought about her from a modern perspective, she seemed comparable to a soccer player or professional entertainer. It was no wonder Peeps, who fit into that same frame of "celebrity," had trouble with her.

"She, incidentally, is an elite of the demonfolk."

"It's starting to feel like there are elites all over the place."

"It is because of their superior abilities that they are more often in the public eye. When you look at an entire species, certainly not many exist—hence the struggle to deal with them when you meet one by chance. The orc there surprised you, too, did it not?"

"You're right—I was shocked."

"Among humans, some have been giving names and ranks to elite creatures such as these to do biological research on them. For especially violent individuals, encountering one is, many times, equivalent to a natural disaster. If this interests you, you would do well to research them."

I had been making light of this world a little bit, just because it was some fantastic place of swords and sorcery. But it seemed that people in this world, too, were devising cultural structures at all levels. Peeps might have already been categorized, for all I knew.

Something like *Starsage, rank A*.

"Sir Sasaki, may we have a word?"

While I was thinking, Viscount Müller piped up—probably because I was hogging Peeps all to myself.

"Oh, uh, yes, my lord. I'm sorry for getting so involved in the conversation."

"No, I don't mind that; it's just...," continued the viscount, seemingly struggling to choose his words. I purposely waited in silence for him to continue.

"The other month, when you procured those supplies—which I apologize for putting you through, by the way. Could your indecision at the time possibly have been due to needing your master's assistance?"

That was another question it would be difficult to answer.

Viscount Müller probably thought this cute little sparrow perching on my shoulder was somehow related to my having filled that gymnasium-size storehouse in just a few days—and to the teleportation magic used to accomplish that feat. And he was 100 percent correct.

Had I been able to use teleportation magic myself, we wouldn't have had to make such a difficult trek through the forest. I would have just warped the viscount, the prince, and myself back to town.

But I hadn't—so his hunch had become a near conviction. Were our positions reversed, that would have been my very first question. He, however, had kept quiet on that point until now. And even when he had asked, he'd phrased the question indirectly so as not to break his promise.

I'd said it before, and I'd say it again: This was truly a man of outstanding character.

"Yes, that's correct, my lord. I'm sorry for hiding it."

"Don't be. I apologize for sticking my nose in this business."

"If possible, my lord, I would prefer if you kept it a secret, along with my master's existence itself."

"Of course. You have my word. Your Royal Highness, might you be able to give yours as well?"

"You have all saved my life. I will speak of it to no one."

"Thank you, sir."

And with that, via Viscount Müller, I'd silenced Prince Adonis as well.

I didn't know how far I'd be able to trust the prince. That said, just from having traveled with him, he seemed to be a pretty earnest guy. The image of him bravely rushing to save the village from orcs was still fresh in my memory.

Not to mention, he, too, was a very important person within the Kingdom of Herz. He was a prince, after all. Royalty seemed to be higher than nobility. I wanted to avoid making a big deal out of this and that and ruining his impression of me. Probably best to make this my only request.

"But there is one last thing I wish to confirm," continued Viscount Müller, his eyes on the lovely little sparrow on my shoulder.

"*What is it?*"

"Could you possibly be the Lord Starsage?"

"……"

Uh-oh. I'd let my guard down, and he'd gone right for the jugular.

✳

From a modern perspective, a person turning into a bird would have been an unimaginable concept.

However, in this world—where magic was a recognized phenomenon—perhaps it was the kind of idea that *would* just pop into your head. Viscount Müller's expression was incredibly serious as he stared at the sparrow perched on its disciple's shoulder.

This didn't seem to be a situation where we could joke around or deflect. It wasn't the same as when he'd accidentally said something in front of the viscount's daughter. No. This time, even Peeps wouldn't be able to get out of it just by chirping—though I admit that personally I really wanted to see him make the attempt.

Evidently gauging the atmosphere, the revered sparrow gave a deep and solemn nod.

"*What made you think that?*"

"The way you speak—I remember it."

Well, he *did* have a peculiar way of talking.

And it *must* have been my imagination how he'd given that little chirp before speaking. For the sake of the Lord Starsage's dignity, I'd pretend I hadn't heard that.

"……"

"It is exactly the same as the one whom I respect above all others," the viscount said, his eyes clinging to hope. It was the first time I'd ever seen him make a face like that.

"Am I correct?"

While Peeps waxed on about this and that after arriving, Viscount Müller must have sensed in him the shadow of the Starsage. There must have been quite a lot in common between the two.

Hearing the viscount speak to him in that imploring tone, Peeps responded.

"*It has been a long time, Julius.*"

"Ah…"

The viscount's expression immediately broke.

It looked like he might burst out weeping at any moment. Given his handsome features, it was like a scene out of a movie. His long blond hair, parted down the middle and subtly swaying, completed the picture.

Julius, incidentally, was Viscount Müller's first name. It seemed as though the viscount had borne much deeper affection toward the Starsage than I'd thought. As I looked at his face, pregnant with emotion, I started feeling guilty about lying to him all this time about Peeps being my familiar.

"*I am sorry for taking so long to contact you.*"

"No, there is no need for you to feel that way, Lord Starsage. It was all the fault of the nobility of our kingdom. And all I could do was watch—I am just as guilty. I am unworthy of such kind words."

"*You needn't say such things—as you can see, I am safe.*"

"…You honor me more than I deserve."

Tears forming in the corners of his eyes, the viscount knelt on the ground and hung his head.

His attitude toward the Starsage seemed to carry even greater reverence than he showed Prince Adonis. His intensity was such that, if we let him continue, he'd keep bowing for an entire night or two.

It had been no mere whim or fancy that had prompted Peeps to choose Viscount Müller's town for my first steps in this world, back when I was just a sullen, almost-forty office worker at a midsize company. I now understood the strong feelings that had underpinned his decision.

"*What's more, I am now no more than this man's pet.*"

"…A pet?"

"*The Starsage has died. For now, I would like to rest—and live at ease.*"

"……"

"*Again, there is no need for formality. Stand, Julius.*"

The viscount's face took on a tinge of sorrow as he looked up at Peeps and let his words sink in. Peeps must have been even more amazing in his prime than I imagined.

Meanwhile, Prince Adonis asked a question of his own.

"But why is your body like that, Sir Starsage…?"

A reasonable inquiry.

"I will spare the minor details, but circumstances led me to cross over into another world. I was forced to take on this flesh as a vessel. To my great fortune, however, once there, I chanced to meet a like-minded collaborator, and now I am able to live without hardship."

"Are you referring to your pupil?"

"Yes, something like that."

Even the prince spoke respectfully to Peeps. The Starsage's influence was pretty incredible.

I understood a little how the nobles who had plotted to kill him must have felt. Though he was the most steadfast and reliable of allies, if interests were reversed, just having him nearby would have been a source of constant anxiety.

Maybe it would be best if I spoke to him a little more formally, too. Our interactions being what they were, bit by bit, I'd been losing all sense of distance when talking with him.

"Lord Starsage, would you return to our nation?"

"I would like to spend my time in leisure for a while. I have recently acquired the means to travel between worlds. For now, I desire to use it to study more about other ones. The universe is much, much larger than we ever could have imagined, Adonis."

"I see…"

Unlike Viscount Müller, who was genuinely happy to have reunited with Peeps, the prince seemed a little disappointed. Now that I thought of it, we never explained to them about the annihilation of the Empire's soldiers. As a member of the royalty tasked with ensuring the future of his native country, he must have wanted the Starsage's assistance.

After hearing Prince Adonis's words, the viscount quickly interrupted.

"Your Royal Highness, I fear it may be inappropriate for us to entreat the Starsage like this."

"I am well aware of that. Still, when I think about the people of this land…"

"Shall we discuss that formally upon our return instead, sir? I have no intention of giving up on the people, either. If you would be able to honor me with your assistance, I believe we could save many more."

"Truly, Viscount Müller?"

"Yes, sir. I promise it."

"That is reassuring to hear. Yes, in that case, please call upon me."

"Thank you, sir."

The viscount must have been referring to the plan about switching sides, which we had heard alongside the vice manager some time ago.

With the second prince on his side, his options would expand considerably. In the worst case, they could secure the Ohgen Empire's backing to stage a coup d'état and set up a puppet government. In that scenario, at least, they'd have a future—better than simply being overtaken and robbed of their land.

"Viscount Müller, regarding that, I'd ask that you please wait."

"Why is that, Sir Sasaki?"

Peeps had just done so much for them, I couldn't have the viscount rushing things. No—I needed to share a tiny bit of information with him right now.

"I have reason to believe that relations between the Kingdom of Herz and the Ohgen Empire will improve after a short while, my lord. I believe you will be informed of the details by the soldiers from the front lines, so I would beg you to please refrain from making a move until then."

"Improve…?"

"Yes, my lord."

"But that's—the Lord Starsage, he…"

The viscount, seeming to suddenly realize something, stared at Peeps.

The bird had no answer for him. He simply sat perched on his disciple's shoulder, looking quietly into the sky. *Looking pretty cool there for a sparrow, eh?*

Of course, with that face, he was probably just wondering what to ask for at dinner tonight. Recently, I'd been getting to know his various expressions.

"Viscount Müller, Prince Adonis, I know it's rude of me to ask something like this, but could I possibly request that you keep the Starsage's survival a secret? He strongly wishes for that as well."

"Yes, I understand. I swear to tell no one."

"Considering what was done to him, I fully understand…"

Viscount Müller happily obliged. The prince nodded and similarly agreed without argument.

For a while, that would be enough to safeguard our peace and quiet. Now we just had to get these two safely back to town, and we'd be able to close the book on all this war business. Perhaps this was just the beginning of the true battle for the politicians—the royalty and nobility—but that had nothing to do with Peeps or me.

"Shall we be getting back to town, then?" suggested Peeps, sounding a little tired.

Tonight, I'd have to ask Mr. French for something really extravagant.

<The Count and the Knight>

Our trip back to Baytrium was instantaneous thanks to Peeps's teleportation magic. We arrived in the courtyard of the viscount's castle. Even though I understood why, I got a little dizzy thinking about all the work we'd just put in hiking through that forest.

It reaffirmed my determination to get my hands on that spell one day.

As for the treatment of the purple-skinned woman called the Blood Witch, Peeps said he'd already told her off enough—and that things should be fine now. I trusted him and let the matter drop.

I didn't know what sort of relationship the two of them had, but as a pupil with little practical knowledge of this world, I simply went along with my master's wishes without a fuss. Peeps had said he knew her, and if they weren't total strangers, that made it harder for me, or anyone else, to object. The same went for Viscount Müller and Prince Adonis.

All kinds of ideas floated through my mind—perhaps she was a troublesome person he kept on running into, or an ex-girlfriend, or a younger stepsister. Not only did they call her a witch, she also had long hair, so she certainly *seemed* like a woman rather than a man. I'd be lying if I said I wasn't curious about what had happened between Peeps and her.

That said, she'd managed to escape while we were chatting, so there was nothing I could do about it now. Partially as a result, we were able to avoid disagreement.

Then a moment after we'd teleported, I suddenly remembered something. Our return wouldn't be met only with good news. In Viscount Müller's absence, some terrible things had happened at this castle. Not only had a dispute over the succession broken out—his eldest son *and* second son had died, leaving his eldest daughter to accept her fate and temporarily take over stewardship of the family.

When I thought about what a shock it would be for the returning viscount, I couldn't even walk.

I hadn't cared all that much after we'd wiped out the Ohgen Empire forces, none of whom I'd known personally. Of course, not only were they strangers, but they were also from an enemy nation. Plus, I hadn't been the one to personally hand down judgment.

But these were the children of someone I knew. It was human nature to be worried about something like that, especially if they were the sons of one who had been so good to me. I may not have ever met them, but it made me start wondering whether there was anything I could have done.

"What is it, Sir Sasaki?"

"Well, to tell the truth, several things have happened in your absence, my lord."

"Does this have anything to do with those fool sons of mine?"

"...You were aware, my lord?"

No, wait, that wasn't possible. The succession dispute had only started after they'd been informed of the viscount's death. Obviously, he was still alive, but timewise, it didn't add up. By the time they'd started fighting, he was already wandering the forest.

Which all meant he must have seen this coming.

"You needn't concern yourself over it."

"But, my lord—"

"I will talk more about it at a later time. Please, for now, do not let it bother you."

"...Yes, my lord."

Maybe there was more to the viscount's family circumstances than I was aware. Either way, it made us too hesitant to say anything more about it.

∗

Upon the viscount's unexpected return, the castle flew into an uproar.

They'd taken him for dead, so it was only natural. Everyone was rushing around and screaming like they'd seen a ghost in a grave-yard. It may have been improper of me to think so, but the sight was kind of hilarious.

Add Prince Adonis to the mix, and the entire place was in utter turmoil. It seemed the prince had *also* been reported killed in battle. When they heard the viscount had risked his life to save him, everyone started talking about what an amazing honor it was and so on.

This brought the once mournful castle into full-blown celebration mode.

With all haste, we were shown into the guest lounge and told to take a nice, long rest. The viscount and prince had left, saying they had several other matters to attend. Viscount Müller told us he'd probably see us again that night.

With time to ourselves, Peeps and I headed over to the Hermann Trading Company. When we asked for the vice manager, we were brought to the reception room.

There, we informed him that Viscount Müller was alive and well—and that he'd rescued Prince Adonis from the battlefield—*and* that the Ohgen Empire's forces had vanished in a single night. I left out anything about Peeps and the business with the Starsage but told him everything else I knew.

I'd figured a merchant would appreciate the news. When I finished, the vice manager showered me with gratitude, his hands shaking.

"Mr. Sasaki, thank you so, so much!"

"Hey, I only happened to be there by coincidence."

"The business opportunities will be massive! I will capitalize on this—you have my word!"

"I'm happy to hear it."

He said he'd be setting off for the capital next week, so I was glad I was able to catch him beforehand. If he'd already left, I would've had a hard time reaching him. Literally everything outside this town was unfamiliar ground for someone like me, who'd still just come to this world.

"I know it's sudden, but I think I'll send a post horse to the capital straight away."

"I'll just see myself out, then."

"Please wait. I need to repay you for this information."

"No, that's fine. Viscount Müller should be announcing it all very soon. Then everyone will know."

"Yes, but this little bit of extra time is vitally important."

"I see."

"In which case, how does this sound? I will profit heavily from this opportunity. I'll pay you, Mr. Sasaki, a suitable percentage of that profit. It wouldn't be fair for me ask you for a price—not when you're still unfamiliar with the way our nation does things."

"Thank you for the consideration."

"In any case, I must hurry off…"

"Oh, right. Would you be free tomorrow?"

"I'm sure I will be. Was there something urgent you needed?"

"Tomorrow, I plan on seeing Prince Adonis and Viscount Müller to the capital. I can't furnish you with any details, but if you'd like to send a letter with me, I can do you the favor. I believe it would reach its destination faster than by horse."

"Wouldn't that be the same as sending a post horse of my own?"

"Actually, we plan to *arrive* in the capital tomorrow."

"…By the end of tomorrow?"

"Yes, that's right."

"Wait. That's not…"

"Otherwise, the information will lose its freshness."

"…I see."

He seemed to have caught on to what I was implying.

Peeps had already told me about a subspecies of small, unintelligent dragons being domesticated for use in place of horses as a faster means of transportation. Even someone without access to magic could probably move pretty darn fast through the sky on one of those things.

Still, one of them arriving there in the day seemed like a fairly tall order. That said, the vice manager was someone who would keep his lips sealed regarding any mysterious methods—especially if it benefitted the Hermann Trading Company's bottom line.

His resulting profits would benefit Peeps and me, too. And with Viscount Müller and Prince Adonis—a member of the royalty—along for the ride this time, it could easily be assumed we had help from a third party—an impression that was extremely convenient for us.

The letter would arrive in the capital by the end of the next day. That was all that mattered to the Hermann Trading Company.

"Will that work for you?"

"If it is possible, then yes, please do me the favor." The vice manager smiled and nodded. His grin covered his whole face.

"All right, then, I will."

"I'll get the letter prepared right away. It won't take long."

With those words, Mr. Marc dashed out of the reception room.

∗

Just after parting ways with the vice manager and exiting the reception room, the pile-hair princess called me over. She'd been waiting for me in the hallway in front of the door. That's when it hit me—she'd been separated from her home this whole time, staying on the top floor of the building. Now that Viscount Müller had been confirmed alive and well, her confinement no longer made sense.

"H-hey, you!"

"Ah, Lady Elsa. Is there something I can do for you?"

"We're going to the estate!"

"What?"

She practically threw the words at me before I could even think. Why did *we* have to go with her?

"Look, we're going! My father is alive!"

"Yes, he most certainly is, but why am I going with you?"

"Because I heard you saved him when he was wandering on the battlefield! What the heck are you doing here, wasting time instead of being at our estate?! You must go and let them reward you properly!"

It seemed the information had skipped over the vice manager of the company and gone straight to her. She'd probably received an urgent message from her family. *They must really love her over there*, I thought.

"But, my lady—"

"Stop fussing and come!"

She was brimming with energy, as usual. Her hair was still piled atop her head, and she looked like a trendy teen girl puffing herself up—it was adorable.

"In that case, I would be glad to accompany you."

"I have a carriage waiting below! Let's hurry!"

"Yes, my lady."

She must have been bursting with excitement to see her dad again.

∗

The carriage rattled along until we had once again returned to Viscount Müller's castle. The pile-hair princess called it their estate, but it certainly *looked* like an entire castle.

"Father!"

No sooner had she spotted her father than she'd run over to him and given him a powerful hug, leaping into his arms. The good-looking dad wrapped his cute little daughter in an embrace. What a beautiful scene. If I'd taken a picture and posted it on social media, it would've gotten a ton of likes.

We then moved to a room in the castle for receiving guests. Accompanying the princess, I was allowed another audience with Viscount Müller.

I'd spoken with both the viscount and the pile-hair princess in this spot several times in the past. It was nearly empty now, since they'd sold off many of the furnishings to pay for military provisions. To anyone who remembered its previous extravagance, it would appear a little sad and lonely by contrast. Still, for today, that didn't matter much.

After all, Viscount Müller and his daughter were together.

"Elsa... I'm sorry I caused you so much trouble."

"No, you didn't cause me any trouble!" protested the pile-hair princess, tears in her eyes as she smiled widely. She seemed as happy as could be.

"I'm so glad you're safe and sound. I'm so glad."

"Thanks to Sir Sasaki over there, I managed to escape with my life. He was also the reason we were able to save Prince Adonis. Had I been alone, I couldn't have done so. We would have certainly died."

"I heard that from the others, too."

"Yes—it is no exaggeration to say I owe my life to him."

"But I don't get it. Sebastian said he's a merchant..."

"He is at once a merchant and a talented magician."

"......"

The Viscount choosing this moment to sweet-talk me had been the last thing I'd expected. And with others in the room, it embarrassed me a little.

All this was a result of the magic Peeps had given me. My gaze was naturally drawn to my partner, who sat perched on my shoulder. It made me feel like I needed to splurge on some even higher-grade meat for him tonight.

"I still have a long way to go," the viscount said. "From now on, I must study even harder."

"Even you have more things to learn, Father?"

"A person's life is an endless series of lessons."

"...I see."

"You must strive to keep up your own studies as well, Elsa."

"I... All right!"

For Viscount Müller, worshipper of the Starsage, there was likely no more difficult position than this. It was only for a moment, but I thought I saw him glance at my shoulder before a look of bashfulness flashed through his eyes. Now everyone was embarrassed thanks to Peeps.

A moment later, we heard a firm knock on the door.

"My lord! My lord, you're all right!"

From the hallway appeared the butler. His name was Sebastian, I think.

"Yes. I managed to return alive."

"Nothing could possibly make your humble butler happier, my lord! And if what I heard from the other servants is correct, you rescued Prince Adonis on the battlefield. Why, we must gather everyone and make preparations for a grand feast!"

"Yes, that would be very welcome."

"Understood, my lord! I will make this feast one to remember!"

"However, Seb, I have something to discuss with you first."

"What is it, my lord?"

Viscount Müller, untangling himself from his daughter's arms, turned to face the butler. Our attention shifted to them as well, and the pile-hair princess regarded them with a puzzled expression.

"Upon my return to the estate, I heard that you were considering introducing the second son of Count Dietrich as Elsa's husband. This is good timing. Elsa, is it true that Sebastian raised this with you?"

"Count Dietrich's second son?"

"That's right."

"I heard from Sebastian that I would inherit temporarily to prevent the house from falling, take a husband, and then rebuild. He told me it would be what you'd want, Father. But I didn't hear anything about my potential husband being the second son of House Dietrich."

"......"

Upon hearing Viscount Müller's remark, Sebastian's face had stiffened. I felt the mood in the room change.

"Sebastian, is there something you need to tell me?"

"......"

The key term here was *Count Dietrich*. Being an outsider with no knowledge of how nobility worked in the Kingdom of Herz, I had no idea what any of this meant. If there was anything I *could* be sure of, though, it was that counts were higher up than viscounts. I glanced at Peeps casually, but he was playing the sparrow as usual.

Meanwhile, Viscount Müller clapped his hands and announced, "You may all come in now."

In response, another door, different from the one that went to the hallway, opened. It seemed to connect directly to the next room over. With a click, it swung wide, revealing two young men in their teens on the other side, both wearing very fine noble clothing.

"What...? Lord Maximilian! Lord Kai, how...?"

I was pretty sure those were the names of Viscount Müller's children. The longer name was the elder, the shorter name was the younger.

"For a long time now, I have had doubts regarding you and some of the nobles. I used my deployment as an opportunity to enact a certain plan. If her prospective husband was to be the second son of Count Dietrich, then it was Viscount Döhl moving behind the scenes, wasn't it?"

"Ah..."

With a soft grunt, suddenly, the butler moved. He pivoted on his heel and tried to dash out of the chamber. Contrary to his previously placid demeanor, this response was quite aggressive.

Where did he think he could run? In the blink of an eye, knights appeared at the exit. A few of them piled in and surrounded the butler. I got a glimpse of even more guards outside—they must have been positioned there beforehand. Now it was all but impossible for the man to escape.

"Ugh..."

"Sebastian, you will tell me everything later."

The butler, bound with rope by the knights, was taken away somewhere. *They're probably hauling him to some kind of holding cell*, I thought—an easy assumption given everything that had just happened.

But anyway, what was going on? Viscount Müller's sons were alive?

Right now, just knowing that fact made me extremely happy. It was probably the happiest I'd ever felt about another person's life before.

*

We remained in the reception room where Viscount Müller explained things to us.

It seemed he had arranged things with both of his sons beforehand. Essentially, if they were to receive word of Viscount Müller's death, they were to hide themselves away from the rest of the family for a time.

His sons had loyally followed his instructions and made it look as if they had both died in the succession dispute, exactly as I'd heard it from the vice manager. According to the sons, they never thought for a moment the viscount had actually died. They were wise young men, just like their father.

On the other hand, the butler had simply believed the news of the sons' deaths and begun advancing his own plans, under the orders of this Count Dietrich, to promote the surviving princess and thus take care of the Müller family. Considering all this, Count Dietrich's family must have been something of a rival to the viscount's house.

Having to account for not only the war against the Ohgen Empire but internal conflicts between families as well... This kingdom's noble society was really something else. It made sense to me why someone as exceptional as Peeps wouldn't want to go back.

As for the whole matter of the poisoning attempt on the pile-hair princess, that had apparently been Sebastian's work—after which he'd played the victim—to distance her from the nobles who were friendly with Viscount Müller. And the Hermann Trading Company had been totally exploited.

"I see—so that's how everything played out."

"I've caused you some distress, Sir Sasaki. I apologize for getting you involved with our issues."

The viscount turned to face me and bowed his head.

As always, his children gathered there looked at us in shock. It really was a rare thing for a noble to lower his head to a commoner. The pile-hair princess, sharp-tempered as ever, immediately opened her mouth.

"F-Father, what are you—?!"

"Elsa," he interrupted, "I have caused trouble for you in particular. I am sorry."

"Mgh..."

He took his hand and stroked the piles of hair on his daughter's head. It was so voluminous, and soft, and fluffy, and there were ribbons and other decorations here and there, so it seemed quite difficult to pat like that. Nevertheless, he did his best.

"...Father, why didn't you tell me about this?"

"You're a very honest girl, Elsa. You know you're bad at hiding things."

"B-but I was so worried!"

"And that is precisely why I was able to force Sebastian's hand. You really helped me out there. In that sense, your actions have also given me great strength. Thank you, Elsa, my beloved daughter."

"Ah..."

It was yet another picturesque scene. With her dad smiling so gently at her, Elsa blushed. Had I done what he was doing, it would only have been notable to the prosecution.

After waiting a few moments for his daughter to calm down, Viscount Müller turned this way again. The pile-hair princess was in a better mood now that he'd given her head a good pat. She, too, regarded us with a docile gaze.

"What I did *not* expect was to truly almost die. At first, I had intended to return immediately after sending out the news of my demise. Before I could even send a notice, though, I had already been reported dead. My diligence was insufficient."

"I think you would have saved the prince on your own even if I hadn't helped, my lord."

"That is not so. At the time, I was certain we were done for. The prince was severely wounded and barely able to walk, and I had exhausted all my energy. When you made all that water fall from the heavens using your magic, it not only wet our throats but gave us hope."

I was pretty desperate back then myself, as it happened. I seriously thought I was gonna die—well, from falling anyway.

"Come to think of it, there was something I wanted to talk about regarding Prince Adonis, my lord."

"I would answer any questions you have."

"Thank you, my lord. I will do so at a later time."

"All right. Understood, Sir Sasaki."

For the moment, it seemed the disturbances in the viscount's family had been settled.

✳

That day, we ended up staying over at Viscount Müller's castle. He insisted on it.

Prince Adonis would also be spending the night, so the castle was in a great commotion. Although the viscount had already asked me not to inform anyone aside from the Hermann Trading Company of the prince's visit, it was doubtful how long they'd be able to keep it a secret at this rate.

And so, that evening, the extravagant feast began.

Because we'd returned so early in the morning, Viscount Müller and Prince Adonis had gotten the chance to rest while everyone else was preparing. When I saw them, the color had returned to their faces—they even seemed *energetic*. Peeps and I had been invited to the party as well.

Nobles were constantly swarming around the main players: the viscount and the prince. For commoners like us, it was difficult just to get close, much less have a conversation. And since we'd already talked quite a bit anyway, we figured we'd devote our attention to the food right from the start.

It was a standing buffet and all-you-can-eat. Chances like this didn't come along often, so we needed to chow down.

"*This meat is quite delicious. The sauce is very good.*"

"Really? I'll have to try some myself, then."

At a table in the corner of the hall, I kept my hands—and the food— moving as I talked to Peeps. All eyes were on Viscount Müller and Prince Adonis. They wouldn't notice as long as we kept our conversations quiet and discreet. I could see others who seemed to be commoners, so we didn't stick out like a sore thumb while we ate.

"Doesn't this dessert look like something Mr. French made?"

"*I believe it may be just that.*"

It was so much fun talking to Peeps about this and that as we ate. Part of it was being in a different place than usual. The variety of cooking arrayed before us was staggering—enough to make me think we wouldn't get to it all in a single night.

A short stretch of dinner merriment later...

"H-hey, you! You there!"

As I was seeking my next dish, empty plates in hand, I suddenly heard a familiar voice. My attention swiveled from the tightly packed buffet table to the source of the sound.

And what should I see but the viscount's daughter—the pile-hair princess. It seemed like she had some business with us and was staring in our direction.

Noticing her presence, the nearby attendees also shifted their eyes our way, wondering what was going on. She may have looked like a teen fashionista, but she *was* the viscount's beloved daughter, so her words carried weight here. Since she had addressed us, now everyone was looking at us.

"Ah, if it isn't Lady Elsa. Is there anything I can do for you?"

"...I heard everything from Papa."

"You did?"

What had he told her? This was such an abrupt conversation that I couldn't help being uneasy about where it might go. Peeps remained silent on my shoulder as well, waiting for the princess's next move.

Casually, I moved my eyes to seek out her father. However, he was busy in his own right with a gaggle of nobles jamming together around him—a little too far for me to request assistance.

"He said you rescued him from the Ohgen Empire's soldiers."

Ah—she was referring to what happened near the front. The viscount probably had probably been unable to fend off her questions and had ended up talking. I didn't know *how* much he'd divulged, but these things weren't matters I particularly wanted made public. I especially needed to keep Peeps's identity a secret.

"Oh, I didn't do very much. I happened to run into them and simply provided some support from the rear. Viscount Müller and Prince Adonis were the ones who stood at the front and fought. I can still see how heroic they looked in my mind..."

"I don't care about that stuff!"

"......"

I figured I'd dodge the whole thing by showering *them* with praise, but she cut me down quite cleanly.

She took just a few steps toward us. And then, with a somewhat apologetic expression, she continued.

"Um, thank you...for saving Papa."

"...Lady Elsa?"

In complete contrast to her always-angry-about-something demeanor from before, this behavior was gentle. It seemed she hadn't come to press me about what had transpired—only to offer her thanks.

"And I'm sorry for being so harsh with you in the past."

What had Viscount Müller even talked to her about? To think he could get such a strong-willed girl to say all this.

"No apologies necessary. Again, I only helped them a bit. In fact, I was the one who was saved. But if it helped everyone even a little, well, that would make me very happy."

"You're acting a lot different than when you were putting on airs before."

Crap. Looks like she's holding a grudge from when I lectured her.

It was extremely difficult to have her say this to me with so many others watching. And ultimately, since Viscount Müller was in fact alive, it was *especially* embarrassing. I never thought I'd still be doing things I'd want to bury in the past at my age.

"I am terribly sorry, madam. I had the chance to learn more about how this country works after that, which allowed me to deepen my understanding of the relationship between nobility and commoners. Thus, as a commoner, I have felt quite keenly the courtesy you, a noble, have given me, Lady Elsa."

"Really?"

"Yes, madam, really."

"...In that case, there will be more relearning."

"What do you mean by that, madam?"

"That's all I wanted to say. If you'll excuse me."

"I am honored by your visit, madam."

After saying what she wanted and not allowing any argument, the pile-hair princess left us. The way she walked with such long, stomping strides was very much like her.

With that, the other attendees lost interest in us as well. We hadn't exchanged many words; they probably assumed she had come to politely greet a commoner on behalf of Viscount Müller, who was quite busy welcoming everyone.

"......"

Speaking of thanks, I recalled my lunch with Miss Hoshizaki. I'd spent quite a lot of time in this world. I'd have to make a point to return to my former world soon to check up on things. I was worried about my work phone's call history, which I'd been neglecting. *The boss may have already contacted me.*

*

After the feast ended and the next day dawned, we all gathered in the castle's reception room. Our group of four included Peeps and me, as well as Viscount Müller and Prince Adonis. Nobody else could be seen in the room. Thick, light-blocking curtains had been drawn across the windows, making the interior dark despite the daylight. In the midst of all this, we had stood up from the sofas and were standing around the low table.

"Lord Starsage, thank you for doing this. We are ready."

"*Very well.*"

In response to Prince Adonis's words, Peeps cast the spell.

A magic circle emerged at our feet, scattering light into the dim room. The next thing I knew, the scenery in front of me had darkened. For a moment, I felt weightless. I'd experienced this spell many times before, but that moment in particular was something I still wasn't close to getting used to.

My vision was only black for a few seconds. Eventually, when light returned to my eyes, I saw an expanse of blue sky overhead.

"I felt the same way yesterday, but this spell really is wondrous," remarked the prince, staring up at the heavens high above.

We were on a street surrounded by stone buildings. It was about two or three meters wide. It seemed to be a smaller alley that fed onto a larger road, so nobody was around. We could see the hustle and bustle of pedestrians at the intersection several meters ahead of us.

"Judging by our distance to the castle, could this be the western edge of the noble district?" speculated the viscount.

Off in the distance, one could see a gigantic castle. Viscount Müller gazed at its soaring towers.

"*That is correct. I would not have wanted to arrive too near and risk being seen. I apologize, but please arrange a carriage or walk from here. We will be returning now.*"

"Please wait a moment, otherwise I won't be able to forgive myself."

Hearing Peeps's intention to depart, Prince Adonis immediately raised his voice. Looking at the Starsage perched on my shoulder, he continued without pausing.

"At least stay the night at the castle. I want to show both of you my thanks. It was only on your account that I was able to return to the capital. It would be incredibly rude of me to use you for transportation and then send you back home."

"*Would strangers like us be allowed?*"

"You're important guests. I won't let anyone object."

As the prince spoke, he wore a serious expression. Perhaps that was why Peeps then turned to me.

"*So he says. What do you think?*"

"What? Me?"

"I do not mind either way. I shall abide by your decision."

It seemed like he was going to let me choose. In that case, I couldn't exactly say no. Peeps was asking me purely out of goodwill, but I basically had no choice in the matter—not unless I wanted to pick a fight with Prince Adonis. It is in the nature of all wage slaves to be incapable of refusing an invitation from someone higher up the chain.

"If you insist, I would be glad to, sir," I said with an honest nod.

"Yes, then leave it to me!" answered the prince with a full smile.

✳

Leaving the narrow road, we headed off for the royal castle. As we walked, Viscount Müller and Prince Adonis explained Allestos—the capital of the Kingdom of Herz. Normally, royalty and nobility showing a commoner like me around town would be inconceivable.

For starters, the prince would definitely stand out, whether he liked it or not. There was little doubt we'd soon have military police all over us. To remedy this, the prince and viscount went so far as to visit a clothier and procure robes and hoods, all to act as tour guides to this foreigner in an unfamiliar city.

"This place is absolutely flourishing. It seems so vivid and full of energy."

"By one account, the population numbers over a million."

"That's amazing."

The prince sounded boastful as he talked about his city. I'd heard a lot of unhappy things about the kingdom deteriorating or collapsing, but he must have been proud of his family's many generations and the homeland they had supported.

That said, there *was* one person who kept interrupting: Peeps.

"Adonis. The town this man calls home consists of over ten *million people."*

"What?! ...Is that true?"

"Peeps, the prince is being very kind telling me about these things, and you keep interrupting. It's not nice to compare. Besides, the total population is different here than it is there, so there's no point comparing individual cities."

"I see. There is truth to your words."

He'd definitely learned that while surfing the Net. And he probably wanted to show off his knowledge to the others. I understood the

feeling. Recently, Peeps had been doing research on the internet whenever he had a free moment. It was becoming a bit concerning to me as
his owner. This must be how parents felt when they were worried
about their kids staying cooped up inside.

"I would like to hear about your land someday as well, Sasaki."

"Yes, certainly, should we have the chance."

It was with that type of friendly banter that we continued up the
street.

This being the capital city of the Kingdom of Herz, it apparently
boasted the greatest size in the nation. In the center of it sat the castle
where the royalty resided, and ordinarily, the prince lived there as
well. The building was of massive; it was overwhelming to look at,
even from afar.

Surrounding the castle were rows and rows of noble estates. Apparently, the higher ranking the noble, the closer their estate was to the
castle. That said, many nobles had a house in their own domain as
well, to serve as their main residence. It was similar to how daimyo
would maintain residences in Edo.

This was all on a much larger scale than Baytrium, the town Viscount Müller governed. We were mainly walking through streets
where the upper classes lived, like nobles and wealthy merchants.
These roads were paved and well-kept, and the buildings lining the
roads were all beautiful. It was reminiscent of the Little Italy area in
Shiodome, Tokyo. The place really felt like a gorgeous sightseeing spot.

"You can see over there the Hermann Trading Company's Allestos
branch."

"Ah, so they have a branch in the capital as well."

This name, offered by Viscount Müller, was one I knew. I looked to
where he pointed and saw a relatively large building. A sign hung out
in front of the shop, letters in the local language written on it. I had no
problem talking to people, but given my hopelessness when it came to
reading or writing, I couldn't determine what the letters meant.

"Mr. Marc mentioned moving the main branch to the capital soon,
didn't he?"

"Is the Hermann Trading Company's manager's long absence from
Baytrium related to that, my lord? I'm embarrassed to say I've never
actually met him before."

"Yes, most likely."

I was holding a letter from Mr. Marc, the vice manager. Maybe it was time to stop by and deliver it.

"My lord, could I possibly have a moment to conduct some business?"

"I wouldn't mind it, but did you need something from this branch?"

"I have a letter from the Hermann Trading Company's vice manager."

"Ah, I see."

After getting approval from my guides, I headed over to the shop. Compared to the one in Baytrium, it was much posher construction. They must have really put a lot of work into it, especially if they wanted to move their main location here. As someone who didn't come here to buy anything, though, and was instead just delivering a message, I felt a bit hesitant about going inside.

But being timid wouldn't get me anywhere. The viscount and the prince were with me, so I completed the task quickly.

After catching one of the employees walking around inside, I gave him the letter I'd received from the vice manager. I told him I was an acquaintance of Mr. Marc's and that he'd asked me to deliver it to the manager here. During that exchange, Viscount Müller removed his hood and added a few words.

Matters progressed quickly after that. The employee seemed to shrink at the viscount's presence and handled the letter with the utmost care. Finally, we were asked if we wanted a cup of tea. We mildly declined, then left the shop. It hadn't taken long, all in all—not even thirty minutes. We wouldn't have wanted to stick around so long that someone accidentally recognized Prince Adonis.

We then walked for a little under an hour before the three of us—plus a bird—arrived at the royal castle.

*

Immediately upon entering the castle, the reactions of those who caught sight of Prince Adonis were nothing short of remarkable. It seemed his family had already received word of his death in battle. Learning of his survival sent the entire place into a frenzy.

Viscount Müller's estate had experienced a similar uproar, but that had been nothing compared to what was happening here.

Naturally, they had no time to bother with some commoner they didn't know, so Peeps and I, at the prince's urging, were brought to a guest room in the castle, giving us a bit of free time. We were told to ask the maid stationed there if anything troubled us.

The prince had taken the viscount off somewhere. It seemed like they would be busy.

It wasn't as though I hadn't expected this outcome. Still, it had turned into a bigger to-do than I'd imagined, so we ended up with some time to kill.

"Peeps, what should we do?"

"My only piece of advice would be to refrain from walking about the castle."

That was coming from someone who had worked in the court's service and then been assassinated. I would make absolutely sure I didn't leave this room alone.

Viscount Müller's castle had its own supply of knights on watch. They glared at everyone they saw. Even when I was with the lord of the place, the stares from those around me never waned. Seeing as this was the royal castle, I was afraid even to *imagine* what would happen here. It was like an action game on the highest difficulty setting—one tiny mistake on the controls would get my little ship, with no lives remaining, blown up for certain.

"Guess that means we should bide our time here."

"Yes. That is for the best."

Fortunately, the guest room was *very* extravagant. The high-class inn we'd been staying at in the town of Baytrium had been plush, too, but so much more money had been poured into this place. First, its size—shockingly, it was over twice as large. The furnishings all looked very expensive, too.

The sofa I was sitting on was incredibly soft in its own right; it felt like my rear end was stuck in it. As for the room service, they'd actually been considerate enough to prepare a little tree for Peeps to perch on. Now his position had risen to a special stage made just for him atop the sofa table.

Even if we were staying over, it would only be one night. In which case, it didn't seem like a bad idea to enjoy the accommodations to their fullest. There was a restroom and bath adjacent, so I'd be able spend my time in comfort while still heeding Peeps's advice.

Eventually, there was a knock at the door. I called out to respond, and a maid appeared. She was probably in her midteens and had pretty features. Her blue eyes and short blond hair really made her stand out. She wore a skirt on the shorter side, giving a view of her thighs. Big boobs, too.

"Please excuse me. I have brought refreshments."

She took the liquid-filled glass from the tray she held and placed it in front of us. Also included was a longer dish, modified so a sparrow would easily be able to drink from it. I got the feeling I could ask for just about anything, and it would appear.

"Thank you very much."

"If you need anything else, please don't hesitate to ask me."

"Hmm..."

I had the chance to make a request, so why not? I wanted something to help pass the time.

"I would love it if you had any board games."

"Understood. I will bring one immediately."

"Thank you."

I didn't know how long it would take before Viscount Müller and Prince Adonis returned. Settling in for about a half-day wait, I figured I'd absorb myself in whatever games this otherworld had to offer.

*

After waiting a little while, the maid returned. Unlike when she'd left, she now had someone else with her—a second woman, also dressed in a maid outfit. This one was quite a bit older than our original attendant, though, and seemed to be in her midthirties. Her age wasn't that different from my own.

She had smooth blond hair that reached her waist and calm, gentle features. Her maid uniform, perhaps taking her age into consideration, consisted of a long skirt that went down past her knees and exposed less of her chest.

"I've brought several games."

They were both carrying a few objects that looked like wooden boxes in their hands. The younger had probably gotten the older to help her bring what she couldn't hold on her own. I felt apologetic—she probably had other work to be doing right now.

"Thanks, and I'm sorry for all the trouble."

The wooden boxes—which must have had games inside—were placed in a pile next to Peeps's tree on the low table in front of the sofa.

The packaging lacked decoration compared to modern board games, so I couldn't tell at a glance what sort of diversions were inside.

Perhaps catching on to my concern, the young maid continued. "If you'd like, we can teach you and serve as your opponent."

"Are you sure?"

"That was why I brought someone with me."

"I see. In that case, by all means."

Apparently, having one more person was best for these games. This was some thoughtful room service. Two was better than one, and three was better than two. You could play a lot more games when you had more people. It all made sense to me, as someone experienced in analog games.

Even for two-player games, having someone on my side to help out was very reassuring.

"Excuse me—do you mind?"

"Go ahead."

The older maid sat down next to me, while the younger—the one stationed here who'd been with us from the start—took a seat across from us. Personally, I would have preferred it the other way around, but there was no helping that.

"Pii! Pii! Pii!"

What was that about? Suddenly, Peeps started chirping. He was looking at me, too, tweeting as if prodding me about something. Did he want to join us?

In that case, we could continue playing by ourselves once the two women had left the room. This was someone known as the Lord Starsage—I was sure he was no amateur at these kinds of games.

"Then I will play alongside you and provide explanations," said the elder of the two maids.

"Thank you."

In the meantime, the younger maid set up the game board. She must have been familiar with it because the board and pieces were all arrayed on the low table in a flash.

"Well then, let us begin."

The younger maid signaled the start of the game and began moving the pieces.

This game seemed similar to shogi, pitting one player against the other. The elder maid, sitting next to me, explained how to play in thorough detail, telling me about rules that existed in certain situations—or how to move pieces to gain an advantage. She was like a real-life video game tutorial. Once she'd finished the basic explanation, we played several more times.

"By the way, I heard you aren't from these lands…"

"Yes, I came from another continent."

"Forgive my rudeness, but is the way you look characteristic of that other continent?"

"It is. I look a little weird, huh?"

"Oh, no, not at all."

While we were enjoying the board game, the elder maid sitting next to me would ask me all sorts of questions. My appearance probably struck her as unusual, my skin being a bit more on the olive side and my face flatter and somewhat differently constructed than her countrymen's. It was likely a point of curiosity.

"Have you been in this nation long?"

"No, I haven't even been here for a year. I floated to this continent after my ship was wrecked. The first place I visited was the town Viscount Müller governs. Anyway, that's why I don't really know left from right here. I've never even seen this game before."

"I see. Oh, you can't move that piece there."

"Whoops! Sorry about that."

We enjoyed the otherworld board game for a while longer. Spending this time in peace and quiet, making casual conversation with two maids in a super-high-class castle guest room was really not bad. The sweets and tea they provided while we were playing were delicious, too.

If I wanted to do this in modern Japan, it would cost me at *least* a few tens of thousands of yen. The labor cost for the women alone would be considerably high. Because of that, I felt I was definitely getting my money's worth having accepted this invitation to stay at the castle.

Eventually, the maids withdrew, and dinner was brought into the room. The food was even grander than in Baytrium's high-class inn or Mr. French's restaurant. They'd even prepared a special menu full of meats just for Peeps. Viscount Müller or Prince Adonis must have put in a word about it.

Naturally, I quite enjoyed the food, but the day had passed without my ever seeing either of them. There was nothing much we needed to discuss, so it wasn't a *problem* per se, but having agreed to stay on their invitation, I found myself without anything to do.

They were probably busy handling the aftermath of the incident.

Before I realized it, night had fallen, and it was about time to get to sleep.

"Now that I think of it, you were making noise when we started the game, weren't you?"

"*...I was.*"

"Did you want to play with us?"

"*No, and the time to worry over it has passed.*"

"Oh?"

"*Yes, you need not concern yourself with it, either. Let us just go to bed.*"

"Well, if you say so, I guess..."

That was a pretty vague response, but if Peeps told me not to concern myself with it, then I was more than happy to do just that. He was much better versed in the affairs of this castle than most. There was no point making myself uneasy by absorbing information I didn't need.

✳

The next day, soon after I awoke, Viscount Müller paid us a visit. It was good timing, too. I'd just been worrying about what I was going to do with myself that day. However, the first thing out of his mouth when he stepped into the chamber absolutely bewildered us.

"I will now be going to have an audience with His Majesty. I apologize for how sudden this all must seem, but would you mind coming with me, Sir Sasaki? You may feel a little uncomfortable, but it shouldn't take that long, at least."

"What? You want me to attend as well, my lord?"

"Could I possibly count on you?"

"It's just that—this is pretty, um..."

I never thought the "audience with royalty" event would pop.

This discussion was taking place in the living area of the guest room. We were sitting on the room's sofa set, exchanging words. Peeps was there, too, perched on his little tree atop the low table in front of us. The maid had left the room when Viscount Müller entered.

"His Majesty wishes to express his appreciation to us for saving Prince Adonis's life. I know this is all very one-sided, but please. Could you grant us your presence for but a short time?"

"My lord, I'm a commoner and a complete stranger..."

"*You should agree to do this.*"

Unexpectedly, Peeps gave me some advice. It was rare for him to go along with someone else on a point like this.

"Huh? Peeps?"

"Should you refuse a summons from the king himself, there is no telling what could happen."

"I see…"

It seemed we never actually had a choice to begin with. Considering Viscount Müller's apologetic and imploring attitude when requesting my presence, the circumstances implied in Peeps's comment were no doubt at work. Thinking of it that way, I felt very apologetic.

"I understand, my lord. Please allow me to accompany you."

"I deeply appreciate you taking the trouble."

"Don't worry about it. Thank you for all the consideration you've shown me."

And so my first scheduled item for the day had been determined.

＊

The viscount guided me through the castle until we arrived in a small room that connected to the audience chamber. Apparently, any outsiders having an audience with the king needed to pass through here first. The rules required a physical inspection to check, among other things, that no dangerous items were being brought inside.

Incidentally, while I called it small, the room stretched over fifteen square meters.

The construction and furnishings were both as posh as could be. It seemed they'd spent even more money on this room than the reception room in the viscount's castle.

For a short time, people in knightlike dress examined my body here and there before I finally received the go-ahead. Viscount Müller had endured the same inspection I had.

I would, however, be parting with Peeps temporarily. Apparently, bringing familiars in was forbidden. I had taken the perching tree from the guest room and placed it on the sofa set's table, and I told Peeps to wait there. Perhaps because he had once participated in the court, he raised no objections. He probably remembered rules like these. In fact, with our audience awaiting us, he regarded us with concern.

A few moments later, someone appeared to lead us inside. The preparations were complete, and it was time to make our appearance.

Following our guide's directions, we headed for the audience chamber. Leaving the antechamber behind, we walked down a hallway. Knights equipped with swords and armor escorted us from the front and rear. Viscount Müller seemed used to this, but being a freshman in this otherworld, I was on pins and needles—every little thing was new to me.

The whole experience was even more imposing than my first visit to the viscount's castle.

As we traversed the awfully spacious castle hallway, my eyes caught sight of a portrait hanging on the wall. It sat in a picture frame with a very showy design—gold edges—and was placed so that everyone who walked through this passage would see it.

The picture showed a young man with blond hair; he looked about ten or so.

It was a full portrait, depicting the crown of his head all the way down to his feet. He wore majestic clothing that reminded me of what Herzian nobles wore, and he stood proudly, not only wearing a cape but holding a staff in front of him with both hands. These combined with his sharp expression to create a very powerful image.

That said, no matter how much of a stern, powerful touch the artist had given him, his youthful features seemed to hold him back just one step short of true intensity. His slightly long hair, too—done in a braid that hung at his side—didn't help, either. He looked quite androgynous.

"Viscount Müller, this painting…"

"The figure in that painting is someone you know quite well."

"Someone *I* know?"

I could count my acquaintances in this world on one hand. When it came to nobility or royalty, I was acquainted with only two—the viscount and Prince Adonis.

"That is the Lord Starsage."

"What…?"

The answer was so unexpected and shocking that I stopped walking.

Owing to the positioning of the painting, I thought for sure this was a picture of a young king or one of his beloved sons and had expected an answer along those lines. To my utter shock, though, it was Peeps. I'd always envisioned him as a harder-faced old man, but he was really just a little boy!

"He looks quite young in the portrait, my lord."

"Oh? Were you not aware, Sir Sasaki?"

"Aware of what?"

"Though the Lord Starsage looks like this, he has lived for hundreds of years."

"Wow, I didn't…"

"His appearance remained unchanged since I was a boy. It was probably an effect of the vast magical powers within him; he is possessed of a completely different life span than normal humans. Even I don't know his exact age. He is a person surrounded in mystery."

"Come to think of it, the same topic came up on the battlefield."

I was pretty sure Peeps had given us a lecture when we first encountered the giant orc in the forest. He was going on about "elite individuals" or whatever. Apparently, creatures invested with large amounts of mana would gain much longer lives and much more power than other creatures of the same species.

As it happened, Viscount Müller got talkative whenever the conversation came to the Starsage.

"The first time I saw the Lord Starsage was when, like now, we were at war with another nation and he had been deployed to fight. He commanded tens of thousands of soldiers, even personally standing at the lead and scattering the enemy with overwhelming magic. I can still picture it in my mind, clear as day."

"…I see."

"At the time, I so admired him that I devoted myself to magic. Unfortunately, I just didn't have the talent. Or the mana. With no choice, I took up the sword. Not a story that paints me in a very good light, is it?"

"……"

Still, what was up with this? Hanging his picture in the passage to the audience chamber? I could feel the king's ardent admiration radiating from it.

You really were beloved, huh, Peeps?

✳

After leaving the portrait of the Starsage behind us, we quickly came to the audience chamber.

We passed through the pair of double doors in front of us. As Viscount Müller proceeded through the room alongside me, I mimicked whatever he did. Once we'd gotten halfway to our destination, we knelt on the floor and bowed our heads. I was positioned with my gaze fixed on the rug laid out below me.

This was no different than my first audience with the viscount. That said, the stage was so much bigger this time. Large crowds of nobles lined the walls, watching us. I could hear whispers being exchanged here and there. *Wow, this really is a ton of people.*

From the sheer number of attendees, the size and decor of the room, and even the equipment of the knights standing guard—everything about this was on a completely different level. My heart had been pounding painfully with nervousness ever since we'd set foot in here. The stress was going to give me a stomachache.

Before too long, we heard a voice in front of us.

"Raise your heads."

It seemed the king had taken up his position. Sensing Viscount Müller move, I lifted my eyes while remaining kneeling. I focused my gaze on a raised platform a few meters ahead of us, slightly higher than everything around it and topped with thrones. These were the two magnificent chairs that had been empty upon our entrance.

Two people had taken their seats there without me realizing it—and one of them was, surprisingly, a familiar face.

It was the maid who had played board games with me the previous day.

"Ah…"

I very nearly cried out but frantically swallowed it back down. What was she doing there?

No, wait, that goes without saying.

She wasn't a maid at all—she was clearly the queen.

The one sitting next to her, in contrast, *was* a new face. *That one must be the king of Herz.* He seemed to be in his midfifties and possessed deep-cut, sternly handsome features. I imagined he'd been incredibly popular with the ladies in his youth.

He *also* was likely about twenty years older than his queen. It seemed that when you presided over an entire nation, you had your pick of the litter when it came to the opposite sex. I was certain he had plenty of other mistresses and lovers. As a man, I'd have been lying if I said I wasn't jealous.

"Viscount Müller, I would like to sincerely thank you for saving my son on this occasion. I have heard he was separated from his knights and was alone on the battlefield when you lent him your aid. It would seem you further drove off many enemy soldiers on your way home before safely delivering him back to me."

"Your words do me too much honor, Your Majesty. I met His Royal Highness by chance, and I only had the privilege of aiding him a little in his return. I am sure the prince, talented with both the pen and the sword as he is, would have been able to return to your side hale and hearty without my assistance."

"Come, you needn't be so modest. I heard all the details from my son himself last night. I, too, dispatched you all knowing full well how difficult a war it would be. I am incredibly thankful for what you have done, Viscount Müller."

"It honors me to no end to hear those words, Sire."

The conversation had begun between the viscount and the king. The atmosphere gave me the impression it was reward time for the former. Considering how much the latter was grinning, it didn't *seem* like he would do any scolding today. The king's features were intimidating, so it was even more moving to see his joyful smile.

"Your accomplishments are great, Viscount Müller, for offering everything to protect Adonis, even on the rear lines, when so many other nobles fled in the face of the enemy out of fear for their own lives. I would like to grant you a new title—that of count—as well as a reward."

"Once again, Sire, you do me more honor than I deserve."

"I look forward to what you will do for the Kingdom of Herz in the future."

"I would do anything for this kingdom, Sire, even if it meant giving my very life."

Looked like Viscount Müller had just been promoted to Count Müller. The assembled nobles raised excited voices when they heard the king's words. Apparently, this was a pretty amazing event. Without knowing very much about any of this world's systems, I couldn't even begin to judge the importance of the exchange.

Maybe like a section chief becoming a director? I'd have to check with Peeps later.

"Now, Count Müller, according to what I have been told, we have another among us who protected Adonis alongside you on the battlefield—and who actively gave his help to assure the prince's return. If it is no trouble, I should like to hear more about this man."

Uh-oh. I got the feeling the conversation was going to include me very soon. As the topic steered my way, my whole body tensed. My armpits were already soaked with sweat.

"As you have so keenly pointed out, Sire, this incident was not my work alone. I could have only accomplished it with the assistance of this man, whose name is Sasaki. He is possessed of a rare magical talent, and it is he who healed the wounds the prince suffered on the battlefield."

"My, that is excellent work. He can use healing magic?"

The viscount—*er, I guess he's a count starting today*—explained this and that to the king on my behalf. As someone who had no clue what kind of courtesy to show royalty, I was really grateful. I honestly doubted I could have carried on a proper conversation here.

"He can use not only healing magic, Sire, but he has enough skill to cast intermediate-level attack spells without any incantation. As you can see, he is of another nation. However, by my estimate, his abilities are at least on par with those of the court magicians serving the palace."

"And this evaluation is coming from a count himself."

"Forgive my straightforward assessment, Sire."

"Not at all. In that case, I must grant him a reward as well."

It seemed it wasn't only the count being rewarded—I'd get a little gift, too. What could he give me? I never turned down a gift when offered, so I was happy for a chance like this.

"It is an honor to hear Your Royal Majesty speak my name aloud."

"I have heard of your deeds not only through Count Müller but from Adonis as well. He told me that his entrails were spilling out after being caught in the side with magic, and he could not so much as walk properly until you saved him. This aligns with Count Müller's testimony."

I figured if I spoke carelessly it would backfire, so I received his words in silence. When I did, the king started chatting about this and that.

"And the bit about you casting intermediate magic with no incantation is certainly no empty boast, I am sure. It is for that reason that I would like you to put your strength to use for the Kingdom of Herz. And so I wish to grant you the title of knight of our nation and have you serve in the court."

Immediately after the king spoke, there was a reaction among the nobles gathered in the audience chamber. They were making far more noise than when Viscount Müller had been promoted to count. Here and there, I heard a few people saying things like, "How could such a commoner be—?!" I'd been treated like I was invisible before, but now countless noble eyes were on me.

Which made me panic.

A lot.

I had no idea I'd be getting my hands on a noble title. I'd even told Count Müller and Prince Adonis beforehand that I had no desire for such a thing. Furthermore, it was against the wishes of the Starsage himself.

My eyes drifted to my side. Count Müller looked shocked as well. His whole face was saying "For real?"

It looked like the powers of the court had moved without any input from us.

*

After our audience with the king concluded, I returned to the waiting room with Count Müller, where he immediately apologized.

"I am so sorry. I had no idea things would turn out this way..."

It seemed this turn of events had caught him off guard as well. He'd known some reward awaited me at the end of the conversation but hadn't thought it would be a knightly title. With my own appearance being clearly foreign, the count's judgment couldn't be faulted. I had also thought the matter would be settled with gold coins.

From things I'd heard him say in the past, the nobles in this country were extremely feudalistic. I very much doubted they'd welcome a total stranger into their ranks as one of their own. Everything, from the way my face looked to the color of my skin, was different. I had also explained to the count and prince that I was from another continent.

"Sir Sasaki, I'm sorry, but could I have a brief word with you?"

"Yes, of course, my lord."

"Thanks."

Other knights and officials—they must have worked in the king's court—could be seen in the room, and their gazes were probably the reason for this suggestion. I could hear people whispering even now at the sight of Count Müller bowing his head to this freshly appointed knight.

I had plenty of things to ask, too, so I was grateful for the opportunity. Despite having received a new peerage and becoming even busier because of it, he still made time for me. Count Müller was truly a good man.

*

I returned to the palace's guest room with Peeps and Count Müller. With the maid nowhere in sight, we seized the chance to lock the entrance door. I hadn't been able to bring Peeps into the audience chamber, but he seemed to have overheard our conversation from the waiting room and quickly commented:

"Sounds like yet another inconvenience," he muttered, sounding frustrated.

At this, Count Müller rose from the sofa and bowed even deeper than usual. Ever since he'd learned this sparrow was the Starsage he'd loved and respected, his attitude toward Peeps had been getting humbler and humbler.

"I am terribly sorry. This is all my fault. I told Prince Adonis many times not to let this happen, but someone must have overridden him. I really do apologize for how this turned out."

"Well, no helping what's done."

"I'm terribly sorry."

"Anyway, what about territory?"

"The idea was for him to work in the court."

"Ah, so that's what he went with?"

Seeming like they were on the same page, Peeps and Count Müller quickly carried out their conversation. With me being an outsider, I was losing track of what was happening. *I'm sorry, but I need a more bite-size explanation.*

"Sorry, my lord, but could you explain this in more detail?"

"Oh, that's right. Well, it isn't that big a deal, but…"

According to Count Müller, there were many different kinds of nobles. Some possessed territory within the nation and governed it while others had their own positions in public agencies, the court being first and foremost. It seemed I was to be one of the latter.

There were several other less common noble positions, such as those who simply received a yearly stipend. For the ones with territory or jobs, those positions could be inherited by the next generation. What the other nobles in the audience chamber had been so surprised about was probably this point.

The king had just created a new noble family in the kingdom.

"I see—so that's how it works."

"Which means the issue at hand is what tasks he'll be given…"

Depending on the job's specifics, it could pull me away from a life of just eating and sleeping. That would be a heavy blow to both of us.

"I actually haven't been told a word about any of it, which has me confused. When things like this happen, it's generally after the groundwork has been laid in advance. By the time things progress to an audience with His Majesty, in almost every case, we would already have been informed."

"Ah."

That made a lot of sense. Everyone had strengths and weaknesses—and of course, whatever work they'd been doing before. It would make sense to have a job that was a natural extension of those. Someone with no experience becoming a knight was exceptional.

"Sir Sasaki, have you noticed anything odd since arriving at the palace?"

"Odd, my lord?"

"I can't think of anything, either. Rushing things like this is very rare. The only case I can imagine is if something like a royal mandate was issued from very high up—much higher than we were aware of."

"……"

"To repeat, I made your viewpoint known to Prince Adonis several times. The prince is not a man who would treat such debts with anything but gratitude; he wouldn't have broken his word. I believe perhaps there are yet other powers at work here."

After hearing that, I naturally thought about what had happened the previous day. For some reason, the queen had come dressed as a maid to play board games with me.

"There is one thing, my lord."

"If it's all the same to you, would you mind telling me?"

"It's astonishing to think about now, but yesterday evening, the queen visited my room. I had asked the maid for board games to pass the time, and the queen arrived and accompanied me as we played. She was dressed as a maid and didn't say a word about her name or rank."

"Wh-what…?!"

The count's face tensed.

Now I understood why Peeps had been tweeting away like that the previous day. He'd formerly worked in the court himself. He would have recognized the queen's face. After seeing her, he'd done his very best to be a warning siren for me. I had been oblivious and had just enjoyed the distraction.

The games in this world were no less interesting than the ones in mine, so I'd gotten pretty worked up about them. Given that they were in the palace, their handiwork was amazing, too. It had been so long since I'd played a game with anyone, I'd had quite the time.

"I only realized all this today when we went to the audience chamber, my lord."

"You didn't do anything careless with the queen—"

"No, no, of course not. We just enjoyed the board games, that's all."

"……"

"But now that I think about it, enjoying games with the queen must itself be highly improper. If there is a possibility they might use it as a reason to accuse me of a crime, I had better leave the country immediately."

After hearing my explanation, Count Müller fell into thought, a difficult look on his face.

If I were the hottest guy of the century, I could imagine the kind of daytime soap opera twist where the wife falls madly in love upon seeing my face. However, no matter how you looked at it, my looks were that of an unattractive middle-aged guy, so there was no such possibility. And naturally, I hadn't laid a hand on her.

Lately, I was too tired to even pay attention to women's charms. Romance—real or fake—had a terrible return on investment. The amount of happiness you could derive from doing a good job and eating great food was much higher.

But in that case, what *had* caught her eye?

"No, I'd like you to hold off doing that."

"I understand, my lord."

"However, not knowing the reason does make it difficult for us to act."

The count and I mulled this over.

After a short time, there was a knock at the door. The voice that spoke was one with which I'd become familiar these last few days.

"It's me. Can I come in?"

It was the subject of our discussion's child—Prince Adonis.

＊

The prince had brought with him information about our predicament and had taken the time to come all the way here to explain in person.

After welcoming him into the guest room's living space, along with

Count Müller and Peeps, we continued our discussion. By his account, my time enjoying board games the previous day had indeed played a role.

"My identity, sir?"

"Yes. It seems my mother wanted to pay a visit in order to get to know you as a person, Sasaki. To put it plainly, she wanted to see if you really had no connection to any other nobles of this kingdom—if you were a brand-new face and a brand-new magician here."

"Ah, I see."

"Peeps?"

Peeps gave a little nod at Prince Adonis's words. The total lack of dignity in the act made it absolutely adorable.

Now that I'd seen the portrait of him, I was feeling a little weird about it. Still, this was this, and that was that. I wanted to maintain our current relationship—with him as my cute little pet sparrow. Anyway, if I let it get to me too much, it would probably only cause him problems. I sincerely hoped we could continue on friendly terms.

"The same as the Müller family. Though that ended up being a lie."

"What about it was the same as…?"

What suddenly sprang to mind was a single word: *inheritance.* Without thinking, I had turned to face the prince and opened my mouth.

"A dispute over the succession, sir?"

"Yes, I believe so."

The prince nodded and gave a solemn answer. His face was apologetic throughout.

"I think my mother wanted to rope you into my faction. Not only can you use healing magic to fully cure fatal wounds, you can even cast intermediate attack spells without an incantation. To make the deal sweeter, you are unattached to any faction. Such a convenient magician almost never comes around."

"So that's what it was about."

It seemed the skills I'd learned from Peeps were being appreciated. I'd be lying if I said I wasn't happy about it. Still, it had worked against us this time.

It was true she'd asked me all sorts of things during our board games. Like where I came from, whether I knew a noble named this or that… At the time, I figured she was just making conversation, but this made all the pieces fit together. In essence, it had been the prince's mom's chance to interview me.

That actually made the *other* maid, the one assigned to the room, seem incredible. Her attitude had remained unchanged even with the queen consort right in front of her, and she'd been indifferent as she presided over the board games we played. Internally, she must have been an absolute disaster. Despite her youth, she was really something.

"Now, my mother is most certainly the official wife of my father—the current king. However, I am not the eldest child. One was born before me, to my father and another woman. Since before I was born, he was treated as an unwanted child and hidden away until a few years ago."

"And he's the first prince, sir?"

"Yes, that's right. As time passed—well, I'll spare you the minor details, but he has begun to show talent. Ultimately, that led to my title becoming second prince, creating a somewhat odd situation in the court."

"Wait. Then could your deployment have been...?"

I'd always thought it was ludicrous that the prince of a kingdom would be sent into a losing battle. Now that I understood more about the prince's personality, I'd started to think maybe it made some sense, but that there still must have been a good reason for it.

"The truth is that the first prince's faction did play some part. However, I personally asked to be sent to the front this time. So many of our citizens were willing to give their lives if necessary to benefit the kingdom. Without royalty leading their charge, how could we call ourselves the heads of the state?"

"I see."

This guy really was an Adonis—in body and mind both. That probably led to hardships for his supporters. And yet his character was so honest and straightforward that those who *did* like that sort of thing would end up absolutely loving him—or so I imagined.

Personally, I felt like putting a bit of distance between myself and such a person was for the best, but anyway.

"For that reason, everything has been my fault. Getting you involved in our affairs—I really apologize. But a noble title, once given, is not easily returned. I know it may not be everything you wanted, but I have a suggestion for you and the Lord Starsage as well."

"What is it?"

"I've been tasked with assigning your work, Sasaki. I directly negotiated with my mother to exempt you from your responsibility to the knights and related court organizations, as well as the duty to govern land. We also decided that your duties as a knight will be communicated through either Count Müller or myself."

"Then he's a royal guard, for all intents and purposes."

Peeps gave me a new term to chew on. Sounded kind of cool, actually.

"Peeps, what does that mean, exactly?"

"Knights of the royal guard are those assigned directly to royalty. They're a level higher than other knights and are handled differently. That said, you are a knight and not a royal guard, so you have no duty to join the official group. In other words, you can move about at will."

"I see."

That was a pretty convenient position to have. Joining the knights sounded like it would force me into a group lifestyle similar to an athletic club, and that was *not* happening. Just adopting a pet had had me debating for some time. Ultimately, I'd ended up living with Peeps, but this would have been *nothing* like that.

"Am I correct in my assumptions, Adonis?"

"You are. I should have expected as much from the Lord Starsage," the prince answered, nodding deeply.

It seemed I was going to get to spend my time pretty freely.

"And for you, Sasaki—for the days to come, I'd like to request that you manage my personal funds. I have heard from Count Müller that you are not only a talented magician but a merchant in your own right; is that so?"

"Manage your personal funds, sir…?"

"It will be for appearances' sake with my mother and those around us. You don't need to actually manage them, but you can. But with this setup, you would be able to continue your usual life under Count Müller as you have thus far."

"I get it, sir."

"It was my mother's scheme to grant you peerage—she wants to have you as an asset. Perhaps it is more correct to view it as us marking our claim to you before my elder brother's faction tries."

Considering Prince Adonis's mother's position, I could understand that judgment.

Just like in Reversi, only black and white existed in this world. If you didn't belong to either, one of them would try to convert you. If a piece was taken by the other side, it could only lead to your disadvantage. In that sense, it was fortunate that the prince's faction was first to rope me in.

Had I kept plying my trade under Count Müller, an invitation might still have been extended to me. In that case, it was much more meaningful to have a significant position under someone who knew me, like Prince Adonis, than to be treated as the lowest rung on the ladder by the *first* prince, about whom I knew nothing.

"All that said, I don't have anything I need from you right this instant. If my mother tries to force you to do something unreasonable, I promise I'll stop her. With that in mind, would you be able to simply accept this title?"

He'd apparently been taking my circumstances into consideration quite a bit. He must have sincerely felt apologetic about all this.

"Of course, if you *are* interested in managing my private funds, you may feel free to do so. The monies I refer to are my own, separate from the palace finances. Even if you were to lose them, nobody would blame you for it."

"I understand, sir. I humbly accept the rank of knight."

"Again, I'm sorry for always putting you in situations like this. And…thank you."

And so my position in this world had been determined for the time being.

I'd not only gone from a vagabond with no ties to a knight of the Kingdom of Herz, but I'd also been promoted to the prince's financial adviser—and bodyguard in case something happened. If I wanted to stick to my all-fun, no-work plan in this world, learning about its finances really wouldn't be a bad idea.

Whether I decided to *actually* manage Prince Adonis's pocket money, it would be worthwhile to think about what I'd realistically do with it if I so chose. Because, as I now recalled, I had quite the bank account myself.

"In that case, sir," said the count, "I will take care of Sir Sasaki for the time being. Though I don't know if it will be necessary, given he is already a talented merchant with the Lord Starsage's assistance, I believe I can still be of help to him in certain ways."

"If you insist, Count Müller, then I'd be glad to leave him in your hands."

"Thank you, sir."

And so, for a time, I ended up learning about the nobility under Count Müller.

*

The same day I received noble peerage, I toured the palace for all the formalities and procedures that entailed.

For the occasion, Count Müller was kind enough to stick with me the whole time and help me out. Thanks to him, we finished all the necessary tasks without any particular difficulty. If I'd been on my own, it would have taken the entire day.

In the palace hallways, I received critical remarks from nobles on numerous occasions. Had Count Müller not been with me, things would have gotten dangerous. He was giving off a real aura of protectiveness. Had I been a young lady, I'd have fallen head over heels.

By the time most of the procedures and explanations were over, the sun—which had been high in the sky before—had already set. It had taken nearly the whole day to go through the formalities and lectures on how I should conduct myself as a noble and the like.

According to a story I'd heard during the process, Peeps himself had held the rank of count before his reincarnation. Unlike Count Müller, who had just been promoted, he'd been a high-ranking one—very close to a marquess, in fact.

He *should* have become a marquess, too, according to his number one fan, Count Müller. Anything marquess and above was considered a tremendous position within the Kingdom of Herz, and apparently, Peeps's promotion had been held up by a faction of objecting nobles.

Given the portrait hanging in the audience chamber hallway, the royal family obviously had a high opinion of the Starsage. If his promotion had been delayed despite this, then the nobility must have had quite a bit of leverage against the royalty.

In that sense, my own rank of knight—gained only the previous day—might help contribute to my life in this world, depending on how I used it. Peeps looked sour at the prospect, but I'd decided to be optimistic. This was exactly the sort of time to split the load and work together to succeed.

In any case, we stayed that night in the guest room. We would be going back to the town of Baytrium the next day.

However, Count Müller did have a few things left to do in the capital. Word of the obliteration of the Ohgen Empire's forces by the Starsage's magic would arrive soon from the front, and the count wanted to handle things around the palace in advance.

He insisted he'd gloss over Peeps's role in the affair, and we assured him it was all right to make it out to be his own accomplishment. That would make things a lot easier on us than having the Starsage's name on everyone's lips.

Because of all that, Peeps and I would be the only ones going back.

After a quick bit of teleportation magic, we'd returned to our hometown. In other words, the town of Baytrium, ruled by Count Müller, formerly Viscount Müller.

Incidentally, now that he'd become a count, it seemed he had a new job in the palace. According to him, though, the promotion was a reward, so he'd probably just get the title and the salary. That said, this was a rank passed down to the next generation, which made it pretty significant.

"We were only away for a little while, but it feels like it's been so long."

"So much happened, after all."

We made our way to our lodgings in the high-class inn upon our return, like we always did. It wasn't as nice as the palace's guest room, but it was still way beyond my lame old apartment. I'd already paid my lodging fees for the next six months, so I was using the place as if it was a rented home.

At the moment, I was relaxing on the sofa in our leased living space.

"Let's take it easy until Count Müller gets back."

"That would be nice. I'm a bit tired myself."

"From your fight with that demonfolk woman?"

"For the most part."

They were probably throwing Count Müller a party to celebrate his promotion right about now in the capital of Allestos. We'd been invited to it the previous day, too, but politely declined. Considering my position, I just knew the other nobles would try something and make it difficult for me. Hurrying back home was partly a way to evade all that.

I was perfectly fine holing up in Baytrium for a while, at least until the excitement died down. Even if I did end up heading to the capital again, it would only be once the war was over. It would probably be quite the scene in the palace anyway when they received word of the Empire's soldiers losing so badly.

It was terrifying just imagining it. Peeps had advised me to stay far, far away from it as well.

"That purple lady won't come trying to attack you again, will she?"

"I think I dissuaded her. She's no fool, so we'll probably be fine."

"Are you sure?"

"If you're with me, I won't have nearly as much trouble as I did this time."

"Oh."

I remembered him telling me about how he cast spells using my body as a conduit. Seemed important for him to be perched on my shoulder. That was the only way he could conjure more advanced forms of magic, such as the one to go between worlds.

"I'll have to learn the flying spell soon, then."

"Yes, it would be somewhat difficult without that. I had the same thought after what happened."

"Maybe it's sudden, but can we start practicing that tomorrow?"

"I think that would be a good idea."

Whatever the case, all signs pointed to the war with the Ohgen Empire drawing to a close.

✳

The day after saw a return to my usual routine.

I woke up a bit late, then had brunch in the inn's dining space, followed by setting off from town to practice my magic. When the sun began to set, we returned to town and enjoyed dinner at Mr. French's place. At night, I'd go drinking in a nearby tavern or just go back to the swanky inn and play with Peeps in the living room.

A place in Baytrium was selling the board games I remembered from the palace. When I challenged Peeps, he beat the pants off me. It was really frustrating. No matter how many times we played, I could never win. *Couldn't he go a little easier on me?*

I visited the trading company several times as well, but as the vice manager was always absent, I never got to see him. He was probably preoccupied with a massive workload, what with the news I had brought of the war situation, Prince Adonis's survival, and all those other details regarding the dispute with the Empire. Instead, I just told an employee to pass on the message that I'd delivered his letter to the manager in the capital.

After a few days of this schedule, my efforts bore fruit, and I was able to learn the flying spell. Like Peeps had warned me beforehand, I almost crashed and died several times during practice. In spite of that, I continued to study and practice and could eventually fly somewhat deftly.

Flying magic was a beginner spell, and its usage, at least, was simple. On the other hand, you needed time to get up to speed or set your course properly. Hence, practice wasn't over immediately after learning it. Soaring the heavens at a practical level took me a lot of time.

It also wasn't a very fuel-efficient spell. Most mages, with their relative lack of mana, had a difficult time staying aloft for too long. Peeps told me that even the best could only manage it for a few minutes to maybe half an hour. This also meant they typically needed way more practice time.

Without the magic power Peeps gave me, I'd probably have run out of fuel in midair.

In my case, I never felt tired once during my flight training. I was able to fly for a little under an hour without any inconveniences. According to my master, I could probably manage it for an entire night.

Then again, now that I'd spent several days entirely on this spell, my progress in other areas was lagging. Of course, I was still showing zero signs of progress with the teleportation spell. It looked like anything of an advanced level or higher would require way more effort than any of the stuff I'd already learned.

If possible, I did want to have more attack options using at least intermediate spells besides the lightning magic. We'd have to leave that for next time, though. Still, knowing the flying spell was a big step forward—it let me flee much more effectively.

By pairing the flying spell I'd just learned with the intermediate barrier spell from before, I could probably even escape that hurricane psychic's power without getting hurt. Or if things really got bad, I could probably grab Miss Hoshizaki and make a break for it.

"All right. Should we head back?"

"*Yes.*"

"It'll be a month later when we come back here next, huh?"

"*With that much time, this incident with the Ohgen Empire should have settled down for the most part.*"

"Hope so."

At my request, Peeps returned us to our apartment for the first time in quite a while.

*

(The Neighbor's POV)

I haven't seen the older man living in the next apartment over for a few days.

Normally, he's only ever gone for a day or two. I haven't seen the lights on in his apartment at night, either, and the meters for his electricity, gas, and water usage haven't changed much.

It doesn't seem like he's been by his apartment at all.

In the few years since we met until now, I can't remember a single time he was away from for more than two days. He seems like a workaholic—he's even busy during New Year's. And I've been watching from the front door of the neighboring unit almost every single day.

On sunny days, on rainy days, on snowy days.

"……"

The man's residence feels utterly empty.

As I gaze at his undecorated front door, I think about this and that.

He must have gone on vacation.

Could also be a business trip, like for training.

Or maybe something unfortunate happened with his family.

"He did say before that he works at a small company, didn't he?"

I feel like that rules out the possibility that it's job training.

And New Year's and the *obon* festival are one thing, but we're well into autumn now. Doesn't that make it hard for him to take time off? I hear midsize companies like his are really bad when it comes to vacation time for employees.

It seems fair to assume some sort of trouble in his private life.

"……"

But he didn't *seem* any different the other day when he left home. Whether it's good news or bad, if something happened to make him leave for so long, I would think he'd have been different somehow.

Maybe it's too soon to rule out a vacation.

If it is a vacation, that brings to mind a bunch of different scenarios.

The first thing I consider is a solo vacation, the sort where you're with friends and acquaintances. Beyond that, there are honeymoons.

Well, that last one seems pretty unlikely. He's the same type of person I am. The kind who would live alone in an inexpensive apartment and grow old quietly, without anyone knowing.

That's why I feel close to him.

Yes—he's the same kind of creature as me.

"...A vacation..."

Come to think of it, I've never really gone on a vacation.

I've never gone to any school events, like the graduation trip or any day excursions. In fact, since moving here, I don't think I've left this town. I just go back and forth between home and school every single day. It didn't change a bit after graduating from elementary school and starting middle school.

He must be the same as me that way, too. He just goes back and forth between his job and his apartment every day—we're identical.

We really are two peas in a pod.

"......"

If I was a little more grown-up, a little older...

If I invited him to go on a trip...

Would he say yes?

It doesn't matter where—it could be some nearby park, for all I care.

Even just walking a couple minutes away from the apartment and sitting on a bench for a while.

"......"

Then, at night, after our trip, he would invite me to his place.

I'd accept, and we'd make love over and over.

How much time would the two of us have together?

A few months? A few years?

Eventually, with my sexual desires fulfilled, I would kill him, then myself.

We would be released from our worthless existences in this world and be free. We would die beautiful, without growing old and bitter, forever in that ideal relationship. The goodness inside him would remain within me. He has nowhere else to go, and I can accept him, body and mind.

An ideal relationship—where each of us could make up for all those things the other lacked.

"...You agree, don't you, mister?"

When did I first start thinking like this?

The more I think about it, the more real it all feels.

Now I imagine his body in my dreams sometimes. I wonder how long his member is. Whether my body could take it in. I think about my own rapidly maturing figure and imagine that final moment.

So please, mister—come back to me soon.

Afterword

First, I'd like to sincerely thank you for picking this book off the bookstore shelf when there were so many others to choose from, so—thank you, from the bottom of my heart, for reading *Sasaki and Peeps*.

This novel won an award at the 4th Kakuyomu Web Novel Contest, and eventually, MF Bunko J decided to make an actual book out of it.

MF Bunko J is the *bunko* label with a conspicuous green cover design.

Among those, I wondered why this book would be published in a larger format like their new literature.

The reason really comes down to how the story was constructed. Because I needed to have all the different worldviews and perspectives exist independently—the otherworld, psychics in modern Japan, the magical girl—this book ended up having a *lot* of text in it. It was very difficult fitting it all into the *bunkobon* format.

It was my editor, O-sama, and all the editors at MF Bunko J who were kind enough to tackle this problem head-on. They gave me the option of publishing this in *tankobon* format, in contrast to their usual *bunkobon*-format books. Despite being busy handling many hit works, they really went the extra mile, taking extra care with even the most minute details, and for that they have my utmost gratitude. Thanks to them, this book was able to go into the world in an even better form.

With regard to Volume 2: In addition to the content currently on Kakuyomu, the volume will be half original content. It'll be pretty thick, amounting to two light novels. One novel's worth will be completely new text. Its release date has already been determined, too—so please look for it on March 25.

Incidentally, since a *tankobon*-format book is bigger than one in *bunkobon* format, the cover illustration is just as impressive. I'd like to change the topic, then, to the real face of *Sasaki and Peeps*—the illustrations by Kantoku-sensei.

The cover is reminiscent of a big movie poster, transcendentally gorgeous and packed to the brim with information. While it is a single illustration, you can enjoy it as if you're reading several panels of a manga. There are so many little tidbits packed in that I can't get enough of it.

The insert illustrations are no exception. I'm on the edge of my seat waiting to see the ones for Volume 2 myself. Thank you so much for your amazing illustrations, Kantoku-sensei. From the bottom of my heart, I appreciate you devoting some of your busy schedule to this work.

On that note, to move on to acknowledgments, I would like to thank the editorial department at MF Bunko J to begin with—and also the marketing team, proofreaders, and designers. I know I've put more of a burden on you than for your usual *bunkobon*-format books. I deeply thank you all for your assistance with this work despite how busy you all are.

Finally, I thank everyone from bookstores across the country, internet-based booksellers, and everyone else related who is cheering me on with the same generosity as they did my previous work, *Nishino*. I will continue to do my best every day to meet your expectations.

I look forward to your support of MF Bunko J's new book from Kakuyomu, *Sasaki and Peeps*, in the future.

(Buncololi)

Sasaki

"I'm sorry you had to be bought by a poor office worker."

The protagonist of the story. A weary corporate drone working a dead-end job at a trading company. Influenced by a coworker's decision to adopt a cat, he visits a pet shop and meets Peeps, a Java sparrow. With this as a turning point, he begins going back and forth between a different world and his own and starts a business trading goods across the two.

Sasaki

Peeps

> "My name is Piercarlo the Starsage,
> inhabitant of another world."

Faction Otherworld

The other protagonist of the story, a silver Java sparrow that can understand human speech. His true identity is that of a famous sage from another world. Purchased by Sasaki at a pet shop. Current goal is to have a relaxing life consisting of eating, sleeping, and nothing else. Favorite food is high-grade Kobe beef chateaubriand.

eeps

The Neighbor

"You're home early today...
Welcome back."

The middle school girl living in the apartment next door to Sasaki's. She lives alone with her mother, but her mother neglects her. Malnourished but has managed to survive through Sasaki's small gifts to her since elementary school. Harbors a warped sense of love for Sasaki.

Neighbo

Viscount Müller

"Is this the Sasaki we discussed? ...I have heard he deals in items that are quite delicately made."

Faction Otherworld

A noble belonging to the Kingdom of Herz in the otherworld. Though his nation has become corrupt and decayed, he is a rare man of upright, honest standing. Interested in the business Sasaki and Peeps have begun in his territory, he asks to speak to them. Peeps's old friend.

Lady Elsa

"...I will forgive your rudeness...
I hope you're thankful for how
magnanimous I'm being right now."

Faction   Otherworld

Viscount Müller's daughter. Bright
and energetic with a somewhat
sharp personality. Beautiful but
lacking in practical skills, she is
distressed by her brothers having
superior intellect, physical abilities,
and magical talents. Loves her papa.

Elsa

Prince Adonis

"This nation will one day be invaded and destroyed. I, too, am fated to die on the guillotine in the near future."

Faction   Otherworld

The second prince of the Kingdom of Herz. A loyal, serious person. Laments the downfall of his homeland and possesses the backbone to lead the army in person. His mother is the official wife of the current king of Herz. The issue of royal succession has split the court into two factions: one behind him and one behind the first prince.

Mr. Marc

"It's been a while, Mr. Sasaki.
It's good to see you again."

Faction Otherworld

Vice manager of the Hermann
Trading Company, based in Baytrium,
a town in Viscount Müller's
domain. Has an interest in the
modern goods Sasaki and Peeps
bring into the otherworld, single-
handedly performing all business
transactions with them. Serves as
their liaison officer when it comes
to the otherworld.

Marc

Mr. French

"I do feel an obligation to you for nurturing my talents, but I have one to him as well for helping me when I was down. I can't ignore that."

Faction Otherworld

A cook working at a restaurant in Baytrium, a town in Viscount Müller's territory. After being falsely accused and thrown out of his workplace, Sasaki and Peeps save him. After that, with the help of Mr. Marc and the Hermann Trading Company, he starts up a restaurant.

Section Chief Akutsu

"I'd like for you to partner with Miss Hoshizaki to canvas for new psychics."

Faction   Modern Psychics

A career bureaucrat and valedictorian of the nation's highest academic institution. The section chief and leader of a Cabinet Office organization called the Paranormal Phenomena Countermeasure Bureau. Serves as Sasaki's boss after the latter learns of psychic powers and joins the bureau.

Akutsu

Miss Hoshizaki

"Sasaki, we're going straight there! Hurry up and get ready!"

Faction Modern Psychics

A member of the Cabinet Office's Paranormal Phenomena Countermeasure Bureau. Sasaki's senior. Her psychic power is to control water. She can make water she touches float, freeze, or vaporize. Always wears thick makeup and a suit and constantly seems on edge, but in truth...

Hoshiza

Ms. Futarishizuka

"Do you dislike young bodies, I wonder? My small size makes me perfect for squeezing. No matter how puny your manhood, it will be squeezed tight. Yes—very tight."

Faction   Modern Psychics

A psychic belonging to a group hostile to the protagonist's bureau. Her power allows her to drain energy. She can squeeze the life force out of anyone she physically touches. This energy then becomes hers, and through the use of her power, she has gained a life span and physical abilities far beyond other humans. An older woman in the body of a little girl.

Futaris

Magical Girl

"I will kill all psychics.
I won't let them escape."

Faction   Magical Girl

A child who became a magical girl after hearing the request of a messenger from the fairy world (a small animal). Her family and friends were killed in a battle with the Cabinet Office's Paranormal Phenomena Countermeasure Bureau, who misunderstood her to be a psychic. After that, going around and killing psychics became her daily routine. A magical girl who is really only missing the hockey mask.

Magica

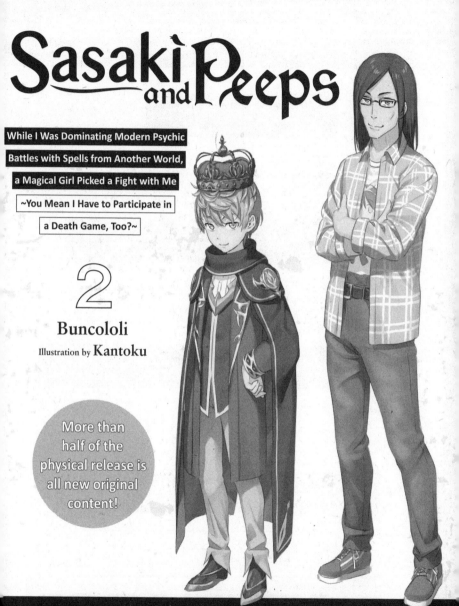

Sasaki and Peeps

While I Was Dominating Modern Psychic
Battles with Spells from Another World,
a Magical Girl Picked a Fight with Me
~You Mean I Have to Participate in
a Death Game, Too?~

2

Buncololi

Illustration by **Kantoku**

More than
half of the
physical release is
all new original
content!

Planned for Release Fall 2022!!!

Peeps, it looks like we can use this space for whatever we want.

Will anyone really take the dust jacket off to see this?

They don't do it much for light novels or literature, but it's a pretty common thing with manga.

Why, then, has it been done for this book?

This is MF Bunko J's first-ever large-size book, so it's apparently because they don't have a fixed format for it yet in the company.

Ah, so that's how it is.

I figured we could talk about some of the behind-the-scenes stuff.

That sounds fine, but what about for the digital version? It has no cover to begin with.

Apparently, it will be specially included in the digital version as well. The editor said they reached the decision via internal memo.

I'm glad they are so thorough.

Peeps, let's go ahead and give them a little behind-the-scenes look.

Of what variety?

About your nickname—the Starsage.

Ah yes, my alias. What about it?

When this was first being written, the author didn't think about its origin or anything.

That seems somewhat irresponsible...

After thinking about it a lot, he settled on what it is now.
And from there, he got the part about using as many spells as there are stars in the sky.

I would think that would be a major plot point.

It would've been bad if he'd called you something like the Otherworld Sage.

Perhaps the story's world just wasn't as big as it is now.